KELLAN: CHILDREN OF ANZULLA, PART TWO

FINDING LOVE IN THE WORLD OF TITANS

CHILDREN OF ANZULLA
BOOK ONE

KASHEL CHAR

Title: Kellan: Children of Anzulla, Part Two. Finding Love in the World of Titans.

Amazon Paperback ISBN: 978-1-998713-59-2

Amazon Hardcover: ISBN: 979-8-242009-93-6

D2D Electronic ISBN: 978-1-998713-39-4

D2D Paperback ISBN: 978-1-998713-40-0

Publisher: Koda Calmz Publishing

Editors: Anita Ford, Teresa Fornoff

WARNING

For Nettie, my only best friend.
When we were young we ran with those unpopular crowds,
Navigating things, like emotions and broken hearts.
You and I, a yin-yang, of storms,
Never conforming to Fochville's norms.
Tempests of hormones, of sin and purity.
Our ion-filled friendship, a cloudburst, lightning, and
supercharged energy.
While distance divides us, my failing memory is what binds us.
Forever unbroken, but old and worn.

And now my readers, get fresh batteries for your flashlights and
charge your headphones. We have worlds to explore and
humans to save.
But, most importantly, let's see if Draxton and Kellan can bring
Ouroboros his tunnel maker.

Themes of oppression and slavery include war, hand-to-hand
combat, bloodshed, intense violence, savagery, deformative
surgeries, and alternate history. The narrative includes death,

grief, burning, perilous mind torture situations, graphic language, and gay sexual activities are shown on the page. One of the main characters has level one autism. Readers sensitive to these elements should take note and prepare to escape reality and face the storm.

Now that that is behind us, let's go!

CHAPTER 1
KELLAN

November 11, 2014.

Dear Kellan.

Son, today I visited the birthplace of our king for nostalgic reasons. I was amazed by the progress made over the last two years. Preparations for the underground laboratory were well underway, and security measures were significantly stricter.

I saw the American Star Connect logo on one of the trucks, and I believe the two other mine shafts will be used for the Russian-American space program. I was overawed by the correlation between what I was told would happen and the actual materialization of the International Space Repopulation Initiative.

The global effort is underway to establish a lunar

presence. It seemed like nothing had changed, so I assumed what had happened in my past did not change the present.

Even more shocking was that I ran into men who knew Ishtar, but they didn't know me. Not yet. They were hiding crates of whiskey as I ran into them. They recognized that I was Igigi, like them, and they offered me blood and more time, but I refused because, selfishly, I couldn't live a day without you or your mother. I don't want to outlive the two people I love most. Please forgive me for leaving you, for choosing to die first. My end is near, and I embrace it.

I'm tired, and my time is running out. I've lived longer than I expected, yet it only meant something the day I discovered what true love is—when I met your mother, and when you were born. My only fear is that if I die, I will never get to tell you for one last time how much I love you.

This is my guarantee that you will remember these words forever when I leave you.

Son, I'm proud of you. I love you and your mother with all my heart.

Even as I write this letter to you, I smile, because I shared a rich life with my wife, and I cherish every second I had with you, my beautiful boy.

Now and always, forever.
Your father.

CHAPTER 2
KELLAN

SNAPPING MY NEW POCKETKNIFE SHUT, I PLACED IT and the small piece of driftwood into my compact leather backpack and got up from the boulder where we had anchored the waiting speedboat.

I was glad I'd followed Draxton's example and worn my high-cut, waterproof hiking boots the day we fell through the portal. They're comfortable in both hot and cold weather. I sighed, loosened the laces, then took off my socks and boots.

"Hey, you better be ready to run if trouble comes!" Simon whispered sharply just as I started rolling up my pants.

"I'll be ready. I'll grab my boots and jump on the boat if needed," I replied. They knew I wasn't interested in guns or shooting. My job was to run, loosen the anchor, and start the getaway if anyone but Draxton emerged from that sewer opening.

I chewed anxiously on my bottom lip, staring at the small waves crashing over my toes in the shallows. Draxton was always on my mind. I worried about him, for him, and over him, even though I shouldn't. Not if I wanted to stay sane. He'd run into that opening with a smile while I imagined him coming out bleeding and dying.

For him, everything's fine as long as we had sex and he could be the hero without anyone stopping him. I found a gray hair in my beard this morning. I'm a cautious worrywart. It's also why I never wanted children.

For years, I carried my father's letter, endlessly pondering his words and his research. It was comforting, yet it also fueled a whirlwind of unanswered questions, leading to countless rereadings and no proper answers. I smiled and scoffed at myself. I'd left the letter inside my wallet, and that was inside my car, parked next to Draxton's caravan at the entrance of the Star Caves in 2025. I wished I had it with me to see if there was some hidden message about what we should do, or if our actions now would have any repercussions in our future.

Father, you articulated the truth, but all I heard were riddles.

I drew in a long, contemplative breath through my nose. The ocean smelled of death, not the rotten roadkill kind, but rather of sterility—the absence of life.

I shook my head, pinching my eyebrows. My senses were registering a feeling that this was not real. A space like an unused surgery room, or rather, an empty conservation laboratory. Yes, that was it. The bright artificial light. The dull hollow sounds, the sharp, highly filtered air, and the absence of moisture were designed to maintain specific environmental conditions perfectly. I'd experienced that at the Ditsong National Museum of Natural History in Pretoria, where my father had worked primarily and where I'd completed my doctoral dissertation in paleontology. It was only eleven years ago, but it felt like eons. My father had passed away just after that, as I was accepting my position as a doctoral professor at the Geoscience faculty at Wits University.

Sniffing another lungful, jogging my senses, I watched the small rolling waves washing over my feet. It was unmistakably the opposite of the Dark Continent, which, although freezing, was dark and chaotic and felt real. The Light Continent was being artificially adjusted, and the temperature and humidity were controlled to protect something delicate, but what?

I would know more once Draxton returned.

All my senses told me this was what my father had described as the void. It felt like emptiness—of nothing—the zero smell of lifelessness, something worse than death.

It looked, felt, and even tasted like ocean water, but it smelled fake. Even plastic had a smell, but not these waves.

A shadow passed by me. I turned, grabbing Snow's attention, who I knew had just walked past me seconds ago. "Hey, Snow, this water doesn't smell like the sea. What's wrong with it? Are there fish or any plant life in these waters?"

Snow, my brother's best friend, stepped closer, shaking his head sadly. "It's full of nanobots and chemicals. All the fish and other marine life are gone. The city's wastewater is polluting it. Further up the coast, and away from Spire City, is less polluted, but mostly it just pushes the pollution further south, towards the Dark Continent. Our waters are plentiful, but if the pollution spreads further, we could have an infertile body of saltwater." Snow rested a hand on my shoulder for a second, meeting my gaze with a serious look in his blue eyes. "That's why we can't let the invaders win," he said.

"That's horrifying." I broke his intense stare and looked out over the lifeless sea.

I could feel his eyes on me. "Kellan, your brother, wasn't doing so well," he said. "Before you, Draxton, and Callisto came into our cave, we were all at our lowest point." Silence filled the deep, contemplative pause, and then he brushed past me.

It felt like my father was speaking to me from his grave. *"Do you see now, my boy?"* I shivered and turned to Snow, but he was already on his way to patrol further up the beach with a homemade shotgun resting on his shoulder.

For the first time, I stared at what my father had described and saw my purpose through his eyes. I stood on the border of human civilization and human extinction, between the life of the flesh and its death, between everything and absolutely nothing, and I finally realized what I was meant to prevent.

"I understand now, Father. I know where I am and where life is. It's everywhere on Anzulla. I see it now. Everything breathing, growing, and feeling is part of life, and without life, there would be fake copies, nothing—only the void—the Zelk."

The Zelk was the result of the lunar experimentation my father had described, which began in an underground laboratory hidden at the bottom of the gold mine near the Rising Star Caves in the Cradle of Mankind. My father told me, once they reached the moon, the experiments involved binding humans and machines on a cellular level and uploading their consciousnesses to a central computer called the Zelk hive. Somehow, Apsu, Ishtar's father, with his hunger to be all-

powerful, a god and creator, had orchestrated it by time jumping. It gets muddled and complicated because the same ship
used to rescue the humans was also what Apsu was using to
time jump and invade Anzulla.

I understood that during a rescue mission of the last
humans from the moon, Ishtar had caused a cross of timelines because he'd thought he'd done good by moving the Zelk
into an alternate timeline, but unfortunately, triggered the
chaos. Since then, the Zelk had been hunting Ishtar and his
offspring, and vice versa, both of whom also originated from
similar experiments.

I'd heard my father say those words, yet never truly
believed them. I hadn't understood because I couldn't visualize the scale of it, so much so that it fell on deaf ears.

Life filled the space wherein every living thing existed.
The Creators weren't enthroned figures or anyone's gods.
They were scientists whose DNA experiments unleashed
chaos from heaven to hell, a chain of errors that ultimately
became their enemy.

Their faulty creations, the Zelk, were consuming everything, killing Anzulla by filling her with artificial copies of
every living organism, just like these waters.

The complexity lay in the fragility of the problem, which
was to protect the original humans—the San people.

One shift, one move, and reality changed. The present
continuously disintegrated while it was reforming simultaneously in the past. That was why my father said that everything
should not have to happen on Anzulla. He meant to say that
the problems and solutions should be dissected and separated,
and that they didn't have to do it in one place and time.

He'd told me once, that history was not forgotten because

it is impossible to remember something that never happened or existed.

That had been the war for Anzulla and the San. That was what he had meant. Only seeing the consumption helped me to understand it—the void. The opposite of life was not death; in death, life continued. Death fed life. Every organism that died gave life to the new, but in the void, nothing new could be sustained.

At the age of twenty-four, my father had taken me to the deepest mine in the world. Western Deep Levels was barely fifty kilometers from the Star Caves System, which was part of the Cradle of Mankind. Within the Star Caves was the Dinaledi Chamber, where he'd claimed the door was and where Draxton and I had entered this time and place on Anzulla. I never understood his obsession with the gold mine. To me, it was all imaginary. I guessed that's why I had chosen my field of study. I was influenced by his works, trying to see and understand what he had meant.

The unpublished work of my father, Gugusan, or Gu, the leader of the San people, titled *The Original People*, described that the Cradle of Mankind, in which the gold mine and the Star Cave system were located, was the source or beginning of everything. He'd described a golden apple, stating it contained the *Tree of Life*. Apparently, the Lord Andrew Whiskey, also widely known as the *Water of Life*, flowed freely from there. It was in that same underground laboratory where the experimentation with human DNA had started and had spread, as far as the whiskey, or *Water of Life*, had flowed, even to the moon.

It sounded like the gibberish of a man who had lived too long and seen too much. I thought his age had caught up with him, that he was senile, or he was getting confused because his brain contained too much information, too much history.

But, he'd taken me there to prove his point. When he'd snuck me into the mine, he'd told me, "Son, this is where the beginning will claw itself out." He'd known and paid the hoist operator a brown bag filled with money to take us down to the deepest level. I thought they were just stories. They never felt real to me. I mean, I saw nothing tangible in 2014. But now, this was unavoidable. It stared back at me, just as I was staring at it.

Simon and his twin brothers, Donali and Kawa, had told us that my father had been right all along, that it was indeed where it all began.

I believed my father, but too late. I never fully understood the true scale of it, even though he had tried his best to explain it to me, a problem he never fully grasped himself. He'd done his best with the knowledge he had. He worked hard, and if I ever returned home, I would not have the courage to tell my mother that his efforts had made no difference.

Simon had lost his husband during the Zelk invasion when their field hospital was bombed by the enemy. Simon was the biological son of Brad McCormick, the leader of Phoenix, from his wife, who had succumbed to the global leak of a neurotoxic biological weapon. She, like thousands of other professionals who were supposed to join them once the scientists and soldiers had secured the laboratory complex in Antarctica, later named Phoenix City, had died and could never join them as planned.

Donali and Kawa were also the biological sons of Brad McCormick, but with his husband, Rick Longarrow.

19

Phoenix City, which happened to be all male survivors, withstood three waves of global catastrophes. The same city coincided with the myth and legend of Atlantis in 2025.

The unwritten history of Phoenix City started when the first cataclysm was the Doomsday of 2046 A.D., marking the conclusion of the Final World War, which gave me second thoughts about returning home.

Simon told us that the World Health Protected Species Society (WHPSS) had been secretly enlisted by the Disciples of the Anunnaki, a clandestine global society, to engineer a genetically superior human race under the guise of environmental projects to launch genetic research initiatives across every continent, and even on the moon. All that was apparently caused by the information hidden in the golden apple, containing the mathematical gene code of the Anunnaki, which my father had told me about.

Experimentation and dabbling with DNA led to the creation of biological weapons engineered within Environment Project Three. This laboratory was in the underground facility in South Africa. The same science project that produced Eryn and his Brawl brothers. The same mine my father was obsessed with.

They were artificially conceived and did not have the same prominent DNA markers. His family was a psychopathic cannibalistic frog-man, and multiple toxic amphibian-like monsters that had escaped the underground complex, and had released neurotoxin spores that spread like the Black Death from Africa to Europe, then across the globe, eradicating all humans within weeks, thus the Final World War.

Yet another research facility called Environment Project One, later named Phoenix City, sequestered two thousand male scientists and soldiers who had escaped the neurotoxic pandemic.

Thanks to the quick thinking of their leader, Brad McCormick, all recorded human history had been downloaded for safekeeping. He'd ordered a lockdown and asked Connor, the second in command, to hastily take control of orbiting satellites. Thus, saving the last of mankind from the deadly and highly contagious neurotoxic leak by being confined for three years inside the glass-domed city of Phoenix.

Having used the downloaded information, they founded Phoenix University to train citizens in essential professions like engineering, architecture, medicine, and food production, all vital for maintaining their advanced city.

Central to their society was Lasitor, a sophisticated AI that not only archived downloaded history but also aided residents with everyday activities.

Meanwhile, Dr. Peter von Leutzendorf, already a product of Anunnaki DNA himself, continued to refine the DNA splicing method initially used in the underground South African lab. This pioneering technique of fertilizing cryogenically frozen human donor eggs with the Romanov sperm and Anunnaki DNA, using artificial wombs, culminated in the birth of the first twins in Phoenix, Cian and Ivan Romanov.

Their birth marked the Year of the Twins (A.T.) when the second wave of natural catastrophes plunged the Earth into a global winter.

For two decades, Peter von Leutzendorf played God. More boys were born, but only with human DNA, and among those boys were Donali and Kawa, Simon's brothers.

The population of Phoenix thrived and continued to prioritize scientific advancement and research. The birth of children necessitated the establishment of a school for their education and development.

Additionally, Dr. Peter von Leutzendorf's life-extension research led to the creation of the Eden Bean, also known as the Peter Pan Cap. This implantable slow-release capsule prevented aging while speeding up healing.

The Phoenician population, although all male, underwent a rapid transformation into a new human race with advanced intelligence and prolonged life spans.

Twenty-one years after Ivan and Cian were born, they were abducted by Eryn's flesh-eating Brawl brother and held captive in the abandoned underground laboratory in South Africa.

Eryn, like Cian and Ivan, was a genetically manipulated specimen with extraordinary abilities. He sided with the humans and killed his amphibious family to free the abducted young men.

Cian and Ivan were enhanced human children, products of human and Anunnaki gene splicing, while Eryn's birth resulted from the splicing of amphibian, human, and Anunnaki genes.

Following the third wave of natural disasters, these three superhumans saved Phoenix by encapsulating it in a protective barrier. As the ice melted and the Earth flooded, Phoenix, cradling the highly sophisticated and advanced human race, was thriving at the bottom of the Earth's ocean.

Despite initially being drawn to each other, these three gifted hybrids broke their throuple after their first mating revealed that Ivan and Eryn were fated mates. This left Cian living a solitary life with a strong, inexplicable pull towards the moon and an obsession with spaceflight and defense.

During their first lunar reconnaissance mission, they had learned about the third group of Disciple scientists called the Zelk, tasked by the WHPSS to study the merging of humans with machines, using body parts harvested from living humans corralled in Grayrak City. Ishtar was waiting for Eryn, Ivan, and Cian on the moon. His time machine's AI, the same AI that controlled Phoenix, told him they would arrive, and that he had to help them.

After rescuing the human prisoners from the moon, some Zelk ships that were not destroyed when they bombed the lunar facility followed them. It was then that Ishtar moved the Zelk to another timeline to keep them from finding and attacking Phoenix City, hidden at the bottom of the global ocean. Unfortunately, that move had kick-started multiple variations of the timeline and history of Anzulla. Then, in their innocent attempt to save Phoenix City, containing the last and advanced humans, they'd time-jumped from 2148 A.D. to this reality, thinking they had escaped Apsu and his Zelk.

However, he'd eventually discovered them. Using the Zelk he'd brought the void, sucking on Anzulla as if it were a *nickerball.*

Simon and his brothers concluded that it was this invasion the AI had predicted and had sent Ishtar to the moon to wait for Eryn, Ivan, and Cian. But Ishtar had crossed timelines again by making another mistake; he'd taken the golden apple to the wrong place and time, which was another long story, because my father had given him the apple long before

Phoenix City had jumped from ocean floor to ocean floor, from one reality to the other.

No wonder my father had struggled to explain it all from his perspective.

Hands in my pockets, I toed the warm beach sand. I was hesitant, but now I agreed that Draxton and I were brought here by Callisto, our size-changing polar bear protector, to ensure that everything living and breathing in our futures depended on that fucking tunnel maker.

If we returned, the world we knew could have changed into something unrecognizable. The future we came from may be directly tied to this war. We must fight for humanity and every living thing. For life.

I've gone a step further than my father. It's time we accepted the supernatural as natural, and the Zelk as unnatural.

Their nanobots infested the oceans. They would relentlessly destroy until nothing remained. But then what? What was their ultimate goal?

This morning, Draxton had said something that stuck with me because my father also mentioned people and things disappearing. Draxton said that if these people start to disintegrate, then we should worry about going home. That meant we could disintegrate alongside them, or the world we know from our time could be completely different. Our future could be like an empty snow globe filled with nanobots pretending to be water, trees, or what Zelk perceived life should be.

This reality was a realm of endless danger and possibilities, and the very unpredictability of it, intensified my emotions. I fell in love with Draxton, and it terrified me. Fear, love, hate, and anxiety—inexplicable depths, all-consuming thoughts—filled every cell of my being. It had seeped into me, bypassed all my defenses, and, like Draxton, now lived in my mind, my heart, and my soul. That's what loving Draxton felt like.

Swoosh! Come to me.

I stepped from the shadows of the pier above us, ankle deep into the water. The hellish heat of the sun beat down on the back of my neck and shoulders. Reminding me of the artificial ozone layer, which caused an unnatural imbalance, I scooped up the sand with my sock-imprinted foot, and it plopped into the small waves. With each backflow into the waiting ocean, heat wrapped around my ankles as I sank deeper and deeper into the sand, like the unavoidable gravitational pull I experienced while in Draxton's orbit. I wanted it.

Swoosh! Come to me, the poisoned waves whispered over and over, as they hypnotized me with each crash.

My waters have always been here.

Swoosh! Come to me. I'm fast and secretive. I'm hungry and dangerous.

Swoosh! Come to me, the ocean said again. *If I don't want it, I'll spit it out. Something. Anything. It's worth giving. If it has rough edges, I'll smooth it.*

Swoosh! Come to me!

My father used to say the sea always returned what it had taken, though when and where were unknown. Waiting for it was futile; disbelief robbed life of meaning. What he put in, it gave back, refined and beautiful, unexpected...just like Draxton.

But the ocean was full of poison. It was dying. The artificial ozone layer blocked the moon's influence on the tides.

Swoosh! Come to me.

The bright rays of light dancing on the surface stung like a brain freeze, making my eyes water. Despite the vapor, the dry wind lashed at my skin, yet inside me, a nervous chill filled the marrow of my bones.

Swoosh! Come to me.

"Screw it," I grumbled to myself. "You're overthinking it." I unbuttoned my jeans. I wanted that chill gone. "I'm depositing life into you," I said cynically and chuckled.

The stench of the day's sweat clung to the fabric of my clothes. I sloshed into the waves until I was knee-deep, and released a thick, dark yellow stream of piss. Sadness and the urge to kill something overtook me as tears dripped down my chin. *Damnit!* I shook my head to clear my mind of the overwhelming emotions. The salty sting inside my nose and eyes exaggerated my emotional pain, and the tears kept flowing.

Swoosh! Come to me.

Draxton had been gone for an hour.

The past two days at Simon's hideout had flown by in a chaotic blur. Simon never stopped talking, and Draxton seemed to be infatuated with the danger and excitement. I felt like a geriatric lovesick teenager.

Simon and his brothers tattooed, trained, and educated Draxton in all things Zelk. All this for a tunnel maker for Ouroboros. Simon and Draxton's beautiful hair was shaved, and their bodies were flushed to resemble Light Continent citizens. He was ecstatic about his '*Entry. Pass. Trusted. Human*' tattoo.

The three brothers were ready to go and rescue Draxton if he got caught. Simon waited here on this side of the tunnel while Donali and Kawa watched the other side, where

Draxton was going to emerge and reenter coming back. That way, we would know if he was followed or captured.

I smiled while sobbing, remembering how I'd made love to him last night. I finished pissing, then swallowed my cries and straightened my spine. My heart raced with violent, nervous anticipation. Any minute now, Draxton should be coming out of that drain opening.

It felt like I was waiting for a runaway train. I was furious about the Zelk. Nervous, but resolved, I steeled myself for the blue wildebeest stampede I felt coming. I wouldn't stop it; I was throwing myself in its path, driven by my love for Draxton and a purpose greater than my own desire to possess him. We were going to help my brother win the war we were born to fight.

I turned back, keeping an eye out on the pier and the four men with guns standing guard, who, like me, occasionally glanced at the human-sized drain opening beneath the dock where Draxton entered and, hopefully, would be exiting soon.

Swoosh! Come to me.

Draxton agreed to find Zaidon Malherbe's office and leave a Morse code receiver for him. He was the son of the informant who was discovered and executed the day Draxton escaped the prison colony. Of course, Draxton knew Morse code. I couldn't figure it out without a decoder chart, but he was wired for things like that. It was what drew me to him in the first place.

It was as if his grandfather knew he would one day find Anzulla and had prepared him just for that.

Simon, Donali, and Kawa had mentioned that Phoenician scientists specializing in neurology had conducted extensive research spanning centuries. It wasn't only the advanced higher education of the citizens that contributed to the intellectual superiority of the general population. Their intensive studies of this diagnosis showed that certain genes remained dormant in those without autism, while those on the spectrum did not, claiming the autistic brain was mid-evolutionary.

However, an interesting finding was that the birth rates of twins and triplets had increased in Phoenix, which increased the autism anomaly.

They figured since the first twins were Anunnaki, and their birth water contained a dominant messenger gene that reduced the breakdown and aging of living cells, the slow-release life-prolonging subdural skin implant could also have contributed to it.

Additional research in the field of DNA anomalies has noted slight structural changes in the DNA of boys born to fathers who are already carriers of the life-prolonging capsules. There was a correlation between autism and high intelligence, though not all individuals with autism fell into the gifted range. However, with additional implantation at the age of twenty-three, the sliding scale of autism, which was initially highly diverse, significantly stabilized and had even improved, while cognitive abilities had increased.

I believed Draxton and I were meant to be here, together, and that falling through the door wasn't a coincidence, and Callisto had alluded the same to Ouroboros.

I'd almost blurted out *I love you* last night—words that would alienate me from Draxton.

Swoosh! Come to me.

I didn't want him to find out I was in love with him. He wouldn't know how to handle that, and he might either push me away or do crazy things like jumping out of an airplane or running into a prison camp to prove his love in the most outrageous, convoluted way.

I had to stay nearby to protect him, but not so close that he thought I was being overprotective or possessive.

My eye caught Snow waving and poking his head inside the drain opening. I waved back. Please let him be safe, I thought, and dove to put my clothes and boots back on, then jumped into a jog to go wait for Draxton with open arms.

"Excuse me." I made my way to stand right in front of the opening to ensure he saw my face first. "Thank you," I said, squinting and straining to see into the darkness. "I hear nothing."

"He's quiet. We noticed ripples in the water—changes in the flow." Snow pointed to the narrow stream at my feet. Sure enough, small swells appeared in rhythm with oncoming footsteps.

"How do we know it's him and not the enemy? Did you do the whistle thing?"

"Of course." Snow poked his head into the tunnel and whistled once. I strained to hear. We waited for a few seconds, and then two confirming whistles floated out of the darkness. Snow turned to me, shot me a look, and nudged me forward. "You go get your man."

I stayed where I was and we watched and waited. "He's not mine. He's not a pet, he doesn't belong to anyone," I whispered as an afterthought.

Snow scoffed from behind me. "Good luck with that approach. You should be honest and tell him how you really feel."

"He knows I need him, but he made it very clear he is not

a dog to be owned and trained. We stick together because we want to survive and go home. That's our main priority," I said over my shoulder and stepped deeper inside the mouth of the opening. Behind me, I felt Snow's disagreeing gaze on my neck.

We waited.

"That man always knows where you are and seeks you out if he doesn't. I think you're scared he will reject you, and you're overthinking something simple—turning it over too many times, which makes it impossible for anyone to understand. You forget about yourself and Draxton, who is actually in the relationship," Snow said from behind me. I sighed. Maybe Snow had a point, but I wasn't planning to make a move unless Draxton gave me a sign that he was interested in more.

In that instant, I saw Draxton's wide eyes and that charming smile he reserved just for me. He froze in front of me, looking both relieved and impressed with himself as his gaze locked onto mine. For a few heart-stopping moments, we stood in mind-blowing silence. He was waiting for me to wrap my arms around him, I realized, then sighed in relief into his neck while embracing him tightly.

CHAPTER 3
DRAXTON

I CAN DO THIS! IF I CAN SKYDIVE, THEN I CAN DO THIS! Do this, do this, do this.

Grinding my teeth, I grunted and pushed upward with all my strength to slide open the heavy, hot lid covering the drainage tunnel. Spittle sprayed through my pursed lips as I muffled my load-bearing grunts. "Fuck, it's burning my palms. Move, dammit." Light trickled in, and relief surged through me as the rusted metal scraped and screeched. "Come on! Move halfway open, big enough for me to climb through," I sputtered. Finally, the sun's blazing heat and ultra-blinding rays hit my face, welcoming me to the center of Spire City on the Light Continent.

My nervous impatience wouldn't work in my favor. *Slow down, and don't be hasty or jittery.*

Carefully, I pulled myself up, poking my head outside. Seeing no one, I leaned back inside to grab my pretend cleaning supplies, reached up, and placed them next to the opening. I forced myself to relax and concentrated on deliberate movements, then rose out of the darkness, using my condensed crash course version of a Navy SEAL's physical, mental, and emotional control.

Simon and his brothers had warned me countless times about moving quietly and slowly if I wanted to enter the building without raising suspicion as a human. Time was running out, so we'd modified the original plan. Simon and Kellan had built a homemade World War II Morse Code handheld receiver using scrap parts. Our plans to spy on the enemy had changed when Zaidon's father was executed. It just so happened to be the day Callisto arrived to free me from the underground prison.

Instead of planting a bug and eavesdropping, we would initiate communication with Malherbe's son. Zaidon Malherbe, who had watched his father die, would hopefully be empathetic to our cause. He was our last and only option for obtaining a laser drill, which would be used to tunnel faster into the mountain so we could get back home to 2025.

Almost crushing my thumbs in the process, I gritted my teeth as I forced the heavy metal back into position, covering the manhole, only leaving enough space for me to open it up again when I returned to our rendezvous point.

Head down, I stealthily slipped into the shadows, trying not to look suspicious. I could feel Donali and Kawa's eyes boring into me, guarding me, or maybe just waiting for the perfect moment to blow this city to smithereens. Honestly, it was hard to tell if they were my protectors or just waiting for an excuse.

Even in the shadow of the tall Malherbe building next to me shooting into the sky, the heat of the near-unbreathable hellish air burned my lips and nostrils dry. Gods, it was so hot and bright; everything shimmered in blue and orange hues.

No one used the walkways. *It's too bloody blisteringly hot.* A dull zipping sound caught my attention as I rounded the corner. I stole a quick glimpse of crisscrossing translucent tubes between the buildings on every third to fourth floor. Looking up, it resembled a complicated network, just like a three-dimensional circuit board—of fucking living computer. My heart slammed around in my ribcage and came to a dead stop as a door slid open, and a short male quickly stepped out. I kept moving, but side-eyed him. My angst lessened when he crossed over to another tube, where, like firing synapses, pods shot like bullets to their next destination. Now I understood what Simon and his brothers meant by the people and hybrids conducting business inside the buildings, and that each building functioned like a city unto itself.

Reaching the entrance, I waited for a small, bald person before me, then followed their lead by holding my forearm underneath the red lights that danced up and down the barcode. I took a deep breath to stay still while concentrating on doing one thing at a time. The revolving door buzzed, signaling for me to move inside. Nervous excitement shot through me. I was honored to wear the tattoo, not that anyone else was qualified. After all, I had more experience with the Zelk and their hoverbots, having been inside the prison before.

I'd promised them, this time with a scannable, trusted human mark, that I would follow their plan. Even Callisto had chuffed at me. I must live, for Kellan's sake. I hadn't realized how much he was emotionally dependent on me.

I'd once thought the depths of his heart were impossible to

reach, but knowing how he felt about me acting recklessly, I didn't want to disappoint him or push him away. He'd told me that he needed me last night. That he would be lost without me. I've never had someone depending on me like that. I wasn't a selfish man, but I was admittedly a selfish lover. I focused on what I wanted and never let others change my mind for me. He knew me better than any other man ever did, and I had to prove to him I wasn't bloody Indiana Jones—a bald one.

Early this morning, before leaving for my mission, Simon had given me the human sterilization procedure they were forced to do to themselves to be able to live on the Light Continent. It was somewhat uncomfortable, but I survived it because Kellan was weirdly turned on seeing me naked and hanging onto the handlebars of a mechanical human waste remover. He liked me stripped and flushed clean. Needless to say, after he'd had his tongue up my ass and had soiled my pristine-shaven body with his ejaculation, I'd had to go through another cleaning session before I was able to dress and pass as a sterile Spire City civilian.

All humans born naturally, without artificial insemination or DNA modifications, were taller, regular-sized humans. Shaven, cleaned, and stamped, I now looked and smelled like a very trusted Zelk-supporting human. That was how Donali and Kawa were able to spy on the enemy and assured us that it would not raise suspicion or be detected by their hovering cameras. After my short but horrific stay in their prison, I had a bit more experience with how to keep my head down than Kellan.

I kept my gaze low, my body rigid, and with my cleaning supplies hiding the Morse code receiver, I entered the building. It felt spookier than those mining tunnels. Bodies moved around soundlessly. Careful not to make a blip on their ever-recording radars, I copied everyone behaving with quiet reverence. Every breath I took in was scented with the fumes of oil and steel. It flowed through the air vents on the floor, the smell of fear and false promises. It sent chills over my skin.

I was scared of the Zelk. We all hated and feared them, but if we wanted a future for humans, we had to use our last chance to establish contact with the one person we'd hoped could help us. I exited the service elevator, trusting my memorized blueprints to guide me to Zaidon Malherbe's office. I pretended to buff the already shiny steel floor as I went. Peeking inside, I saw the brightly lit office was empty. After glancing back to make sure I was alone, I slipped inside.

The whirring of machinery and rushing water startled me. Back against the wall, I carefully peered through the door crack of an ensuite sterilizing room. The ice-cold air stung my eyeball, and a wave of self-preservation forced me not to cluck my tongue. I shook my head at the unbelievable scene. Malherbe stood naked, arms up, legs spread, inside a huge, high-tech sterilizer. So that's why Kellan was so fixated on a clean ass this morning. I could appreciate it, but this was a whole new level of machine savagery.

Malherbe's body was small and pale. Judging by the red lasers running up and down his body, he was being scorched hairless. I saw only his small, tight backside and the tube up his yin-yan hole. Unlike my cleaning session at Simon's earlier, more tubes were connected to the back of his neck, and the tube filled with yellow piss told me he had one up his cock as well. This inhuman ritual was being done three to four times a day, and then again when they slept in their rejuvenation caskets until the next morning.

This was dehumanizing. Especially because these traitors thought it was necessary to be accepted, to be normal. Fuck normal. Who decided what normal was? The Zelk was not normal.

I retreated, turned, and pink-panthered over to the executive desk standing in the middle of the overly bright office. Tipping my head to the side, I listened if he was still busy, then shivered and blinked a few times to wash the horrific scene from my memory. There was a sloshing noise followed by a humming sound. I swallowed down the anxious bile pushing up my esophagus, then refocused on my task. I had but a minute.

Diving onto my hands and knees, I pushed the desk chair aside and flipped over to my back to slide my skinny frame underneath the desk. I scooted deeper on my shoulder blades and stretched my arms to reach behind the last drawer. Hurriedly, I pushed the drawer out to make space for my big hands to work, and then I taped the recorder onto it.

The humming in the sterilization room died down. *He's going to get dressed and come out the door any moment now. I had a second to spare.*

Sweat drops formed on my forehead, and my hands shook nervously. I left the drawer a bit further ajar for Malherbe to discover it. I flipped back to my hands and knees, then reversed out of there, crawled a few steps, jumped to my feet, and returned to the pristine hallway, where I started sweeping the polisher, cleaning the already clean surface.

My quickened breathing slowed as I calmed. Fifty percent of my mission was completed.

The gleaming blue artificial lights cast a glowing reflection on my path. My expression was pinched, and my dark eyes were worried. I let out a soft sigh, hoping the plan worked. We were putting our trust in a traitor solely because Simon knew his father. It could be a trap, because his father was found out and executed for treason. I wondered how he was discovered and whether Zaidon had something to do with it.

Acting mundane in my task, I kept working closer to my exit. The cold air chilled my bald head, and the naked sensation gave me an eerie feeling of wearing foreign skin over my skull. My curly black hair was shaved to blend in with the other Zelk-acceptable humans. Like a blue zebra, I looked stupid in my striped Star Trek suit, and I wondered what the meaning behind the silver stripes around the arms and legs was.

Three more office doors stood between me and the elevator. I moved with slow, seemingly lazy reluctance, careful not to trip any security cameras or arouse suspicion from the everwatchful Zelk. I eluded reluctance as if the task was a burden, while I remained composed, ensuring my heart rate didn't betray the adrenaline coursing through my veins.

There was a movement in his office, then I heard him rummaging and grunting something, and the next second he came storming down the hall. My heart pounded as I shifted my gaze to the floor, preventing him from seeing my face. *Gods, am I under suspicion? Should I tuck and run?*

"Excuse me," he said curtly, with a ten-year-old altar boy tone. I inspected his plastic small-feet shoes and bristled inwardly, before remembering my place and stepping wordlessly to the side. He stepped left as well. We danced for a second, and then I stepped back, melting into the icy wall behind me without making eye contact.

"Excuse me," I blurted. He wasn't moving. He was looking up at me. I blew my breath out slowly and stared down at him. He blinked, and I blinked back at him. His boyish expression of determination and irritation flattened to something I could not decipher.

"No, you excuse me," he apologized, but not one of us made a move. He cocked his head slightly, and I forced one corner of my mouth into a crooked smile to convince him of my innocence, even if I was so tall and looked out of the ordinary. Our gazes were locked, and I hoped he wouldn't sound an alarm.

I wondered if I should talk to him, or just drop to my knees, pressing my forehead to the floor, like I had to do in the mine when the hoverbots had electrocuted me for...shit, the cameras. I was drawing attention.

He stood before me, wearing a veneer of self-confidence, and I thought I saw a blush creeping up his thin neck. He looked like a plastic Ken Doll with no hair, big black eyes, and a smooth, hairless face. His nose was small, and his lips were pale pink. He swallowed, looking nervous as his gaze flicked up and down from my head to my feet. His hand covered his crotch, and he looked like he was hiding something. Was he turned on? *No, that couldn't be.* They suppressed their human urges. Then it struck me, the device. He'd found it.

His back snapped straight. *Fuck, he was going to call security.* "I have an idea. You take your broom out of my way, and I'll move," he said with a sassy tone.

I let my eyes fall to the floor and shook my head as I

stepped back, bringing the broom with me. "My fault, sir. Please forgive me," I stammered.

"No, it's all okay. I'm glad they brought the humans back. My father...um...I mean, I've been stating my case, putting in multiple requisitions for human staff. The place was crawling with bots. We needed this. People. Welcome and carry on," he said, his voice gentle. He was friendly, not at all what I imagined.

I cleared my throat. "Yes, and thank you for the opportunity, sir." With my dark gaze locked on the floor, I hid my face from the prying lenses of the surveillance cameras. Stepping away, turning my back on him, I continued moving with a rhythmic sway, my footsteps soundless against the polished steel floor as I traversed the seemingly endless hallway.

Zaidon wasn't the robotic, emotionless figure I'd imagined. Simon's pictures of his blank face during his father's horrifying, failed Zelk transformation in the auditorium had painted him as cold. But I saw innocent humanity in him.

He was also dangerous, because he was the new controlling CEO of the richest and most powerful mining and mineral research company in Spire City, Zelk Industries.

I refocused. I had to get out of there because if I got caught, he would too. It seemed he wasn't planning on alerting security, and he must have known I had dropped the communication device.

I felt optimistic. Our plan might work. When Zaidon had passed and entered another office, I exhaled a soundless breath I'd been holding, but worked at the same pace down the hall until I reached the service elevator. In the lobby, I continued pretending to clean while moving at a painstakingly slow pace toward the building's exit. Even when multiple black shoes passed by me, I didn't look up to see who wore them. I reminded myself to slow down to evade the watchful eyes of the Zelk cameras and their hoverbots.

I stepped into the open air and took a deep breath, savoring the feeling of freedom. Then, I quickly rounded the corner, away from the street. At the manhole, I tossed my cleaning supplies and broom aside, dropped down, pushed open the heavy steel cover over the drain, and slid into the hole feet first, bringing the supplies with me. Carefully, I dragged the cover back over the opening before disappearing into the dark tunnel.

Ah, thank fuck, darkness, I thought. I was almost safe.

The suppressed excitement made my heart flutter like a captive bird desperate for release. I kept my head low as I ran and smiled. Zaidon Malherbe held the key to our liberation, and by leaving a means of contact, we had taken an audacious risk today.

It seemed I'd executed my mission as planned. His response would determine the fate of our entire operation. His father's sacrifice to make contact and offer help was not for nothing.

Navigating the memorized labyrinth of tunnels beneath the city above, I moved deliberately, every step calculated to avoid unnecessary noise and detection. If I got caught, I would be questioned to death. They would search these tunnels to find out where I came from, and I would destroy years of work done by Simon and his brothers.

Fixating on reaching Kellan and the others, I hunched over, counting my steps to know when to turn either side until I reached the last turn to the end of the drainage tunnel.

Someone whistled once, and I returned two short whistles to confirm to them it was me coming and not the enemy.

Finally, when the light at the end of the tunnel appeared, I lifted my head and saw Kellan's happy face. He lifted his arms wide, and I stepped as fast as I could into his embrace.

Air exploded out of Kellan. "Oomph, oh my goodness, I'm glad to have you in my arms!" He gave me one of his vice-gripping hugs. I stared into his caramel chocolate-brown eyes.

Simon patted me on the back. "Yup, we're all happy to see you. Did it go as planned?" Simon asked.

"It went smoothly. He saw me, but luckily, nothing came of it."

Kellan pushed me away while holding onto my shoulders. "You are safe and whole!" He smiled, and his eyes shimmered with relief as he kept inspecting me up and down.

"Yeah, I was getting anxious to leave. I started to think it had gone too smoothly, worrying it might be a trap, until I saw the light and knew it had worked out. Now for the next hurdle." I leaned into Kellan's warm chest, savoring his scent. Of safety. I closed my eyes and let Kellan kiss me.

"Yeah, one more hurdle. I pray that Zaidon Malherbe won't let us down and will respond to our message," I heard Simon say, with Donali and Kawa agreeing.

CHAPTER 4
ZAIDON

I'D FELT DIZZY AND ICE-COLD AS I CLUNG TO THE handrails above my head. Shutting my eyes, I wiped away the replaying scene of my father being unsuccessfully hybridized a few day-cycles ago. *I was such a weakling.* I sniffled and winced as the catheter vibrated inside my pissing thing. I just couldn't get used to the feeling of being sterilized by the ice-cold titanium rods. The tubes in my rejuvenation casket felt warmer and softer, irritating me less, *maybe because I was lying supine instead of standing.*

I shivered as the flushing of my intestines evoked the telltale feeling of being washed out and vacuumed clean. Sometimes I enjoyed that sensation as I relaxed into it, but not lately because my mind drifted to the scene of my father being drained of his blood, followed by his body's deboning and his consciousness extraction. Usually, the pain-filled screams weren't upsetting. They lasted only a few seconds, but my father's agony had stung far down, hurting me viscerally and simultaneously in my mind, chest, and stomach. I didn't know I could feel things that deeply. It had stirred and nauseated me. They were cringing, squirming, puckering feelings that forced me not to look, and then I'd illegally close my eyes. I'd wanted to cover my ears or run away.

How intense would it have been if I hadn't used suppressors at all? That was why we were forbidden to stop taking them, because even by taking half the dose, I already couldn't stop myself from experiencing bouts of unwanted emotions, so I shed my tears in private. If I were caught, I would be arrested, seen as a sympathizer, and forced to transition without mercy, just like my father.

Interrupting my traitorous thoughts, the tubes were extracted from my body. That was why it was better to be connected to the Zelk cognition grid so we wouldn't be weak, but would be supported. Not being a hybrid Zelk yet, and not taking the full dose of my suppressors, I was feeling and thinking illegal things, and the fine tremors of fear coursing through me constantly reminded me that I was guilty.

Guilt was another foreign, illegal feeling because guilt insinuated a feeling of right and wrong, and that caused upheaval and discord.

"Sterilization complete," the female electronic voice screeched, ringing painfully in my ears. My headache throbbed at my temples as I bent, climbing back into my underwear. "Second sterilization complete for today," the ever-monitoring Zelk program announced. Bending and straightening intensified the headache that usually began at the end of my colon cleansing.

I wasn't in the mood to work, I thought to myself as the door slid open. I cringed and rubbed the back of my neck. The brightly lit office worsened the stabbing pain inside my skull, and a hurtful whine escaped my throat. With my eyes barely open, I slowly made my way to my desk and then collapsed into my office chair. As I twisted my body to fit under the desk, I pressed the call button for my secretary to cancel my appointments.

"What now?" I scowled as my foot got caught on the lower drawer, hurting my ankle. I kicked the thing closed, but it hopped back just as fast. I kicked it harder, but again, it wouldn't budge. It was closed earlier.

Peep-peep, the signal for an incoming call cut through my headache and heightened my frustration.

"Sir?" the AI asked in his usual male monotonous voice.

"Yes, I...have...um." I rubbed my temples and then slid my chair out from the desk to see what was going on with the drawer. "I have another matter to tend to today...and I have a headache. Cancel my appointments for the whole day."

"No problem, I will reschedule them for you...It will be double the work tomorrow, but if you are unwell, you are unwell. Anything else?" he asked, and I rolled my eyes.

"No, thank you." I pushed the end-call button and dove forward. I pulled the stubborn drawer out completely, then slid it back in and out again. It was definitely getting stuck as if something was preventing it from sliding deeper. I poked my hand inside and felt nothing—no obstacles. I slithered to my knees on the cold steel floor and leaned my head closer to ensure nothing was blocking it from sliding deeper. If there were no obstacles, then it must be outside—in the back.

Grimacing, I inspected what was wrong with the drawer. I've never had any trouble with it.

What was that? A faint green light reflected from the back of the drawer. I crawled deeper under the desk. Someone had hidden something there. *Was it a spy or my sister trying to record me?* I stretched further to get the tips of my fingers underneath the tape and tore it free. Blinking and turning it over, I inspected it, then gasped, nearly throwing the thing, then slapped one hand over my mouth.

Hide it! I thought and tucked it down the front of my pants.

What was it? Who would do this? Was it my father? I had to show it to Harrison, he would know.

I caught my breath, scooted out from underneath my desk, and quickly got up, straightening my clothes. The illegal device pressed against my manhood, making it look abnormally large. I sat on the edge of my seat, waiting for my hammering heart to calm down. It was an illegal artifact. *A communicator.* A thrill ran through me. Headache forgotten, I jumped up to make my way to Harrison's office.

A few steps into the hallway, I faltered at the sight of a tall, very skinny cleaner who looked out of place. Uneasy tension swept through me. Tightening my fists, I lifted my chin and strode across the floor. He was sweeping, and I had never seen him before. It had to be him. He was the one who'd planted the illegal device.

He didn't look at me. I knew it was him. He had put it there. I straightened up to make myself taller, took a deep breath, and looked up at him. Towering over me, he tried his best not to see me; on my long, audible exhale, he looked straight at me. Our eyes met as I craned my neck to see his face in the looming light. The air rushed out of me in surprise as both of us gasped, making eye contact. I stared, blinking until his presence made sense to me.

I'd imagined people from the South as savage and unkempt, with terrible teeth. I studied him.

His hair was shaved. He was trying to blend in, but his dark stubble told me it was not lasered like the rest of us. Still, it looked acceptable. He was handsome, and aside from being very skinny, he appeared to take care of himself—his clean nails hinted at that. He didn't look wild like our mine or factory workers, with muddy ropes of hair and torn ears from years of fighting for scraps. I expected to see eyes that were evil and ruthless, but I saw none of that, only persona. His eyes glinted over dark irises, and although they looked shocked, his expression was intelligent. Composed, but very nervous—he was hiding or scared. There was a permanent, superficial line between his eyebrows, probably from constant frowning, showing he was more than just puzzled most of the time, which was illegal in Spire City. The shadows under his cheekbones and around his eyes made him seem precarious. When his mouth twitched and his full lips formed a shy half-smile, he stepped back, still with his lips closed.

Somehow, his big nose made his face look more attractive. I knew this was not an animal, a dirty, dumb beast. There was humanity in his eyes.

A flush of heat exploded in my chest, then spread up my face and to my groin. It was a sensation so rare that I glanced down at my crotch in surprise.

Then, I remembered the communication device. "Excuse me," I said as my eyes flicked down to his bulge to compare sizes. His was bigger than mine. I couldn't decide if that was a good thing or not, so I stood staring. *What was wrong with me?*

He shied away, shrugging his shoulders. "Excuse me," he

said so softly that the rumbling sound of his voice gave me goosebumps.

"No, you, excuse me," I said politely, returning a smile as I finally tore my gaze from his groin. Blood swooshed through my body, and the warm pooling feeling, like a throbbing tingling in my reproductive organ and fluttering insides, told me it was an illegal momentous human-to-human moment— I would probably never feel it again.

The thought brought me back to my senses.

"I have an idea. You take your broom out of my way, and I'll move," I whispered, trying not to frighten him.

He looked surprised but seemed to follow my direction immediately, making way for me. I wanted him to smile at me again—a real smile—because it made me feel things. But he avoided my eyes. I had to say something, do something so that he could look at me.

"My fault, sir; please forgive me," he whispered from behind hunched shoulders.

"No, it's all okay. I'm glad they brought the humans back. My father..." I cleared my throat at the sudden flood of emotions just thinking about him. "I mean, I've been stating my case, putting in multiple requisitions for human staff. The place was crawling with bots. We needed this. People. Welcome and carry on," I said with a friendly tone in my voice, hoping he heard that I was a friend. Please look at me, I thought hopefully. If he looked at me, I would wink at him. Only humans winked, and that would be a clear sign that I was a friendly one.

He relaxed. "Yes, and thank you for the opportunity, sir," he said, not looking back at me.

I straightened my back, adjusting my shirt by pulling the

long sleeves half an inch to expose my golden cufflinks as I passed him. "Carry on, no need to thank me," I said, catching a whiff of his scent as I walked by. It was manly, not recently sterilized. The sweet smell of his male sweat burned my nose, and those foreign tickling sensations ran down my spine, settling in my pants, where they fought for space with the handheld communicator.

Oh yes, the communicator. I shook my head slightly to sober up, then pushed open the door and entered my brother's office.

"Got your message, brother," I lied. Harrison immediately knew something was up. "Go on, I'm listening," I said, rolling my hand and gesturing for my younger brother and my only friend to continue. I slinked over to my chair next to his desk, where I always sat. I was walking as best I could not to reveal what I was hiding down the front of my pants, and it wasn't just the communicator. My balls tingled, and my pissing thing throbbed. I sat down with my legs apart, covering my crotch with my hands. I usually did the flipping one leg over the other thing, but this time I didn't. Harrison followed my every movement with his eyes. Then he locked gazes with me. The corner of his mouth twitched. I gave a slight nod as I closed and opened my eyes, acknowledging something was up.

"Yes, thank you for coming. I was worried you'd never gotten my message. I wanted to show you the numbers for the diamond-crushing factory. They are good; they exceed what we expected," Harrison said as he displayed the latest stats and maps on the holographic screen. He looked up at the projected images and then back at me. Our conversations were recorded in our offices, but we have always been taught to assume someone, or something, was listening.

"Remember the day we got caught slipping out the window to go stargazing on the roof?" Harrison asked, meaning "what happened, Zaidon?" He looked concerned as he assessed me. He knew me well.

"Yes, I remember." I shifted sideways to make space for the device.

"Did something happen?" he asked under his breath.

"No!" It came out a bit too loud. I cleared my throat. "Sorry, I was just in a hurry to get here," I apologized and pinned him with a stare.

"Well, then...I have your attention. What do you think about these areas and numbers? You are now the CEO; what you say matters. How you act matters more."

"I know," I said through my grinding molars. I inspected my manicured nails, then folded my hands on my lap while taking a deep breath through my nose and returned a glowing, sarcastic smile. "And I agree," I remembered to add, then lifting my chin to the side, I showed Harrison that I wanted to talk in private.

He immediately tipped his head up, showing me he caught my meaning.

I got up and ran my hand soundlessly over the wall, feeling for the small button, pushed it, and slipped inside just as the wall slid away.

He pressed play on our pre-recorded conversation and followed me.

We were the same height, just over five feet. "Go on! Quick," I showed him with my eyes. "Hurry!" I waved, eager to show him my discovery from earlier. His eyes bulged when I stuck my hand down the front of my pants. He waited until the door fully sealed us inside our soundproof, closet-sized safe room. He sank to his heels, sitting upright with his back straight and his palms pressed together between his knees. Now that we were alone, the corners of his mouth turned up into a wicked smile.

"You have to play your part. What they did to father, they can do to you. To us. We need to give them a reason to trust us. We are no longer the Malherbe family, the untouchable founders of Spire City," he said with his most sincere and patronizing get-your-act-together stare. "What are you up to today, Zaidon?" he asked.

I gave him a big grin. Since we were children, we'd met inside here, behind a false wall my father installed for private meetings and grown-up conversations. He'd let us play in here. It was our secret. Harrison was my father's first hybrid human, created when Harrison was four years old. My brother got sick, and my father found a way to save him.

He waved to my crotch, where I'd hidden the illegal relic in haste. "Why is your hand in your pants? Did you stop taking your hormone suppressants?"

I fished the big black thing out of my underwear. "What? No, and no, of course not. Not yet."

"I swear I don't want to know. You're insane. You are going to end up snipped and banished or dead. Leave me out of it."

"Shhht." I pulled it out, waving it around. "I think this is what our father died for." Harrison shook his head, frowned, and pushed it back to me. *I doubt I should tell him about the man I saw earlier.* "I need your help."

"Help with what?"

"I don't know. Help me figure this out," I said and handed him the big black receiver.

He lifted his hands in protest. "No, I'm not touching that. It's been down your pants. It's crawling with bacteria."

I scoffed. "I sterilize four times a day. Just did. My crotch is clean."

"Doesn't matter. That is the dirtiest part of your body." Harrison folded his arms, not taking the big communication device thing from me.

"That's why I hid it there—no one searches down there," I said, chuckling nervously. I switched it on, and a loud crackling noise frightened us. I fumbled with it, almost dropping the thing.

"The volume, change the volume to low." Harrison took it from me and quickly turned one of the small black buttons at the top. A high-pitched, barely audible noise repeated.

Peeeep-trrrrrrt, peeeep, long pause. Peeeep-trrrrrrt, peeeep.

"It's a two-way radio, a transceiver. This is an illegal artifact." Harrison threw it back into my hands as if it was going to electrocute him.

"I know. What is it transmitting?"

Peeeep-pep-pep-trrrrrrt, long pause. Pep-pep.

"It transmits and receives messages on radio waves that are not monitored."

"I know that. What is the message?"

"Where did you find it?"

"Behind the lower drawer of my desk. It wouldn't close. I went down on my hands and knees—" Harrison gasped. I sighed, rolled my eyes, and continued. "I saw this taped to the back. Look, this small light, it's red and flashing green. Is this a sign that the message is received?" I pointed to the light flashing as I switched the thing on and off repeatedly. "I should probably stop doing this to preserve the battery so we can intercept the messages." Harrison's eyes stretched wide open.

"You should press the button on the side," Harrison said.

I did just that and whispered, "H-hello?" I released the button and looked at Harrison.

"Say something like this is Zaidon Malherbe, over. That will let them know you found it," Harrison said.

I let go of the button after repeating his words, and the strange clicking and scratching noise went away as intermittent beeping sounds followed.

"How do you know it's not a trick or a trap? Like they tricked our father," Harrison asked.

I should be honest with my brother. I thought for a second, pausing, contemplating whether I should share my encounter with the stranger in the hallway earlier.

"Umm, someone...put it there today. It was not there yesterday because there is no way I could have missed it. That man...um...he was a worker, sweeping and cleaning the floor. He must have hidden this underneath my desk." I sounded unsure, like I was making it up as I went along.

Harrison gave me a skeptical glance. "Worker? Only vetted humans are allowed inside, and especially onto management levels."

"No, he was a vetted employee."

"Maybe this is what the authorities were searching for when they arrested Father. Or maybe...perhaps Zonika...Yes, she was upset about you inheriting the office. She could have planted it to incriminate you," Harrison noted, something I never considered.

"If it was Zonika, what was that cleaner doing in the hallway?"

"A cleaner? Who says Zonika didn't give him access, and you caught him in the act?"

"I see...It could be either a coincidence that HR finally recognized the need to create jobs for humans and had reduced the number of bots doing the work. Or he could be working for Zonika, but our sister wouldn't ask a citizen of the Dark Continent to do this. She would ask someone inconspicuous, someone on her staff, someone close to her, whom she could trust. There are a few possibilities to consider here."

"Dark Continent citizen?"

I nodded enthusiastically. "Yes, absolutely. This was a giant of a man. He couldn't look me in the eye—he wiped the floor. Definitely guilty of something, so I checked his credentials, and I'm sure he passed the review process because he appeared cleansed and wore the mark..." I trailed off. Remembering the handsome smile he gave me. "He showed emotions. They came naturally, and he apologized. Just like our father did when we were little. Zonika's people are all hybrids. When was the last time you saw anyone showing emotions in the hallways?"

"This is serious, Zaidon."

"It is. That's why I came to you directly. You are the only one I can trust with this."

Harrison took the beeping thing from me. "Zonika would never trust such a stupid creature from the Dark Continent to do her bidding. Where would she find such a device, anyway?" He turned the knobs on and off. "You can't keep this in the building."

Hairs rose on my lower arms. This was the first sign of an

internal emotional disturbance. I was a rebel, breaking the law. An idea struck, and I leaned closer. "Maybe it is a secret spy message thing. We could use this to our advantage," I whispered.

"Zaidon, using this object is punishable by death. Breaking the law is easy for you. I'm having a panic attack. Look, I'm perspiring, my armpits are wet. I need emergency sterilization. You are getting all twisted up with illegal things. It's already corrupting you. Are you sure it wasn't there yesterday?" He pointed the relic at me. "Yesterday, you said you thought about stopping taking suppressors. If you weren't my brother, I would have run as far as I could away from you and reported you. You are going to get us killed," he whispered.

"You are not having a panic attack. This is a communication thing. Why is it so illegal?" I pulled more forbidden objects out of the inside pockets of my jacket. I was a real revolutionary today. "It's only a secret until we've investigated it."

"Investigated? What do you know about investigations?" Harrison asked.

"If this is connected to Father's death, then I want to know why. This is maybe the key. Listen, three long ones, two longer wait periods, and then two long, then short, then long —I agree that's...hmm, definitely Morse code. It plays on repeat. Remember? Father taught us this when we were little. He'd said we would need to know this one day."

"I remember!"

Harrison looked like he was about to pass out.

Taking another illegal object, my father's pen, from inside my jacket pocket, I listened intently to the message in Morse code.

"I think you are right." I jotted down the message on the palm of my hand, and together we deciphered it. --..-- / .... He took my pen from me, pushed my sleeve high up, then he wrote in the illegal alphabet on my arm, *Tonight, Midnight, Pier Seventeen.*

"It's tonight!"

I pointed to Harrison. "You are coming with me. I'm not going alone."

"Zaidon, that's risky. What will you do with the information once you meet with whoever is on the other side of the message? It must be a trap. That's how they lure smugglers... what if it's smugglers?"

"I know, isn't it exciting? We can fake working late and use our scramblers."

"Zaidon, excitement is forbidden for a reason. You're breaking the law without blinking. First, you're talking about stopping your suppressants, and now this communication with smugglers thing. If you are caught, you will be severely punished, like our father, and be put to death."

"I know, but isn't this thrilling you just a bit?"

"I have to admit, yes, it is out of the norm for our daily routine, and it's exciting for you because you aren't taking your suppressants as you should. My sense of self-preservation is overriding this excursion." He lifted his hands. "Your enthusiasm is a big warning sign. Danger ahead."

"Nonsense, where is the Harrison that wanted to set sail south, never to return north again? That little boy is still inside you; it's time to let him out."

"That boy has grown up...and that thing is unhygienic and a ticket to death. Your soul won't be committed to the hive; it will drift away forever."

"Like our father always drilled into us, sometimes you have to take risks to get to the truth. There's a reason this was tucked away; they're making contact with me," I said.

Harrison pointed to my arm, and I rubbed at the ink, then pushed my sleeve down, and then cleaned my palm on my pants. Harrison shook his head. "The same reason Father was executed for treason. This will get you into trouble. Let's hand the relic over. Let's alert the authorities and let them take over before we get involved in something we can't explain away. Law-abiding citizens stay alive."

I straightened my spine with a rebellious determination. "No. I'm going, and you're coming with me. Here, use my other scrambler. We're finding out what Father died for, and we're securing our position in the hive forever."

Harrison crossed his arms.

"Come on," I said while looking at my watch. "We don't have much time before it's time to meet them. Plus, we aspire to be close to the Zelk king. Don't you want to visit his palace?" I asked.

Hesitantly, Harrison shook his head but took the illegal scrambler—he would never allow me to leave without him if I leveraged it like that.

CHAPTER 5

ZAIDON

A FEW MINUTES LATER, WE ENTERED THE LOBBY, which was buzzing with hybrids and hoverbots. Some stopped what they were doing to greet us, but, as usual, I ignored them. "This is good, we now have enough eyewitnesses," I whispered to my brother.

He gave me an affirmative glance. "Let's go."

I held the door open to our private elevator. Then, we went back to his office, activated our tracker and tracer scramblers, and snuck outside using another executive elevator, the one my father used to take, which no one but us used, and was almost never monitored.

We stayed quiet until we reached the basement. "If we get caught, this was your idea. You know it's all for show, you're never going to be one of us unless you have the transition surgery," Harrison mumbled, sounding like he was gargling rocks.

"These criminals won't trust a hybrid. I'm going to find

out what our father was doing with these smugglers before I let myself be cut up and pumped full of nanodiamonds. I'm staying human as long as possible, I'm enjoying my research on the reactions of the human body," I told my brother. I stayed quiet about the details, especially about crying and the earlier throbbing in my pissing thing when I'd spoken to the cleaner.

Harrison palmed his chest and held his head high. "I trust you, Zaidon." I widened my smile, showing him my teeth. He shook his head at me.

My brother was sick and dying of cancer when he was four years old. My father had developed the bone marrow diamond nanite technology to save him from leukemia, but the Zelk soon took hold of the technology and made it mandatory for all who wish to be Zelk to have diamond nanites inserted in their bodies, replacing their blood and bone marrow. At first, everyone thought nanodiamond spin-tronics was a way to cure death and disease, but as soon as they received the treatment, it became clear that the hybrids were under the control of the Zelk, like they had logged into a massive network, being monitored and controlled.

Where all the blood went after the procedures, no one knew. I thought maybe it was burned, but there were rumors that the blood was processed and recycled to be food. I didn't want to worry about that, too, so I chose to ignore that rumor. Harrison was the first and only hybrid not connected to the Zelk grid because the Zelk hadn't yet tainted the technology to their own benefit. Therefore, my brother is the only hybrid I trusted.

An hour later, we found ourselves under the seventeenth pier. A cold breeze blew, and I pulled the lapels of my jacket up and stuck my hands in my pockets. In one pocket, I played with my panic button, and in the other pocket, the tracker and tracers' scrambler. And in the front of my pants was the Morse code receiver.

The dockside was eerily quiet. Our building was the tallest in Spire City. It rose up behind us, casting shadows over the harbor that had closed down many years ago. A few seagulls floated on the wind, hoping to spot food, but I knew there was none. "This is a good place to meet," I whispered, "No one ever comes here anymore."

"It's also a great place to get killed and disposed of," Harrison grunted.

"Should we try to get deeper underneath the pier?" I asked, glancing over my shoulder. "Let's look for that opening we used to climb through," I said, checking and making sure no one saw us.

I didn't touch anything; neither did Harrison, as we carefully made our way down the cracked cement stairs. The last time we came here, we were young boys exploring. We waited for about thirty minutes when a seaplane drifted closer, as if it were flying and had switched off its engine.

I turned to Harrison. "Hmmm, I thought they would arrive by boat." We watched as a dilapidated aircraft floated past us and stopped further beneath the walkway above. It was high tide, and they seemed to know where to stop, so they must have used this spot often. No lights were on in the cabin, but there was enough light outside for me to see only two hulking figures preparing to climb out. Rusted doors creaked open. The pilot jumped down to secure the aircraft. I appreciated the passenger's long legs as he stepped out with a practiced one-two-three move, which I could never replicate due

KELLAN: CHILDREN OF ANZULLA, PART TWO

to my short legs. He wiped his hands on the sides of his legs, but as he looked up at us, my stomach dropped in disappointment; he was wearing a mask. I wanted to see his face. I knew they were men—real men. The way they moved exuded strength and masculinity, like that cleaner. I'd hoped I would see him again.

He sized us up as we sized him up. He took a step closer to us. "Wait for me," the other one said, tossing a rope over a peg driven into the ground to anchor their aircraft. He was also wearing a mask.

"Let's get this done so we can figure out what they want. Just keep an eye out and check for weapons. Stay quiet and pay attention," I told Harrison.

We watched as the two met and began a heated, whispered debate about who would speak first.

The pilot, who had caught up with the passenger, who had been meant to wait, said, "Let me speak; I'll handle the talking."

The passenger did a double-take. "What? I have the trusted human mark; I should speak. Your brother said you fly, and I'm leading this. Simon, Donali, and Kawa agreed with him."

The pilot came to a halt about ten steps away from us. "That was just to get into the building. We're not in the building now. The man we wanted to meet is standing right there. Please, for the love of...let me lead. Don't be so stubborn."

"Stubborn. You're the stubborn one. I'm here because you're too black to qualify for this mission," the passenger said, then continued walking toward us.

"You didn't just say that," the pilot muttered, remaining still.

The passenger turned to the pilot. "Yes, I did. You resemble your brother."

The pilot raised his hands above his head. "That's why I'm wearing a mask."

"Now the masks make sense. I thought you were overreacting since he'd already seen my face," the passenger whispered, but we heard every word. That must be the cleaner, I thought. They were whispering, and I wanted to hear that rumble in his voice again.

"Will you let me take the lead, please?" The pilot caught up with his partner, who seemed eager to reach us first.

"I'll assist where I think you are fucking it up," the passenger retorted.

I couldn't recognize them by their eyes; it was too dark. They weren't wearing our city's attire. Instead, they dressed like free humans—brown and cream, animal hides, and hand-made clothing.

"Are you sure these are the people we're supposed to meet? They seem a bit disorganized for professional smugglers," Harrison asked, intently scanning them for weapons.

"Who else would show up at this time and at this rendezvous? Of course it's them," I muttered.

"I hope you know what you're doing," Harrison said, and I regretted not bringing a weapon. "My optical scanner confirms they're human. The guy on the left has a weapon tucked in the back of his pants. They look eager and nervously cautious. Keep your finger on that panic button," Harrison whispered without moving his lips.

Once the men came to a stop, Harrison turned in a circle,

scanning the walkway, the stairs, and the sky to ensure we were alone. We weren't exactly hidden. I've never had military training, and even I could tell that we were being foolish. This could be a trap. They were tall, taller than any man in Spire City, and likely taller than anyone in the entire territory of the invaders. I hoped they weren't planning to snap our necks.

"Are you the ones who received our message?" the man on the left asked the most vague question imaginable. His accent was foreign, clearly different from that of the man I had encountered in the hallway earlier today.

I cleared my throat and stood taller. "Yes, we're the ones who found the illegal relic. What do you want?" I asked tersely.

"To talk. To ask for help," he said through his black face-mask. The skin around his eyes appeared dark, and I scrutinized their hands for skin tone, confirming that the one on the left had a deeper complexion than the one on the right. They seemed threatening, ready to pounce and knock us off our feet.

"Our people knew your father. We thought you could help us now that he has passed away."

A chill swept over me. "So...you know he's dead? That he was killed because he was in contact with you?"

"Yes, we heard. My leader sends his condolences and is sorry to learn about your father's passing. We don't know how your Zelk authorities found out about him, nor are we certain if it was directly because of us or a connection to us. We heard he was a good man—perhaps the last good man in Spire City," said the one on the left.

Come on, cleaner man, when are you going to speak up? I

hoped to hear him say something again. He seemed distracted, though, glancing around at everything except me.

The pilot seemed to be the leader as he spoke again. "Our people have known him for a couple of years. They believe that if the invaders tortured him for information about us, they wouldn't have executed him if they understood precisely what it was. They would have waited to see what he could provide us. You see, we need something of great importance that must be kept secret. We believe you are the only one who can assist us, Zaidon."

"How do you know me?" I asked.

The cleaner suddenly exclaimed, "Aren't you next in line to manage your family's slavery business?"

"Hm-hmmm," the one on the left coughed. "Sorry, my partner is a bit blunt; he meant to say Malherbe Enterprises?" The cleaner man on the right crossed his arms, turning his body half away from the conversation.

The pilot continued. "Your father led us to believe that you can be trusted. He asked our people to watch over you if something happened to him. I'm glad you found the receiver; that makes our job much easier." The man on the left glanced at his partner, who neither agreed nor disagreed; I couldn't interpret their nonverbal exchange. The way he grunted and shrugged confirmed it was definitely the cleaner. It had to be him. I would recognize that low rumble anywhere.

My heart raced, and my nerves were on edge. I started to sweat and ran my hands over my scalp, something I should never do in public for fear of drawing the wrong kind of attention. Harrison mouthed, "No, relax," at me and gave me a reproachful glare. I dried my palms on my hips and composed myself. Was this how humans felt all the time?

"How confident are you about that? For all you know, I might have the authorities waiting around the corner for you," Harrison added.

"You are both your father's sons. You resemble him," the cleaner remarked.

Harrison tapped me on the shoulder and whispered loudly as he read his retinal scanner. "There's a ninety-nine percent chance they aren't lying or being deceptive." I pursed my lips and gave him a slight nod before stepping closer to them.

"So, what is it?" I said hurriedly. My fingers fiddled with the panic button in my pocket.

The pilot on the left glanced at his partner and then back at us. "We can't discuss that here. We need to go deeper." He pointed to an even darker, secluded corner farther underneath the pier. "We trust you simply because we trusted your father. But if we're seen, if anyone sees this—what we want to show you—we're all going to end up dead. Human or hybrid."

"Just get on with it already. Your faces are covered; if any hoverbots spot you, you can't be identified," Harrison barked at them.

The pilot pointed at Harrison. "You see, trust has to be earned. And with a comment like that, I don't think you have much time before you end up like your father."

I didn't like this man who wanted to be in charge. His tone and bossiness would irritate Harrison too. I didn't want to argue; I wanted to listen to what they had to say, so I stepped in front of my brother, palms up. He frowned in confusion, but stepped back since I was blocking him. "Stop it. I agree. I'm curious enough to hear you out," I said cautiously, glancing at Harrison over my shoulder.

Harrison scanned the skies and our surroundings again,

then groaned in agitation. "It seems safer to get out of the open. Their presence screams humans from the Dark Continent. Even if their faces can't be identified, their height alone could cause suspicion," he said, waving us to the side.

"Lead the way," I urged, gesturing with my hand. We walked further into the darkness under the pier. Harrison was right. I was going crazy just following these men to a better spot to kill us. My shoes sank into the sand, and I heard Harrison complaining as we moved deeper under the pier toward the stinky secluded area. It smelled terrible, and the danger lurking in the shadows made me feel sick to my stomach.

"This is getting more intriguing by the minute, they might have answers for us," Harrison said under his breath. *Now he was the reckless, inquisitive one?* We joined them, standing as close as an arm's length, with the cleaner again on the right side as we formed a tight circle—in the dark. My heart was racing, and I was sure Harrison was about to complain about perspiration.

"Our father died because of you," I said shortly. "He was arrested and forced to become Zelk. How do you know he was tortured?" I asked, hoping to hear the reason for my father's arrest.

"We were told the Zelk tortures everyone. He was a contact, in the sense of telling us where to trade, green-lighting certain areas to help feed people, and giving us information about the Zelk."

"Oh, that," I muttered.

"Yeah, we lost contact a few weeks ago. We suspected he knew they were on to him and didn't make contact in fear of revealing our methods of communication," the guy on the left explained.

"What method?" Harrison asked.

"It's a secret," the cleaner man interjected.

I crossed my arms. "If I found the illegal relic this morning, someone else can too. You are putting our whole family in danger by trying to make contact," I said.

The man on the right cleared his throat. "I was impressed by the speed you picked up on it. Good job." Mr. Floor Cleaner praised me, and I perked up with self-pride.

Harrison stepped closer and whispered. "Yeah-yeah, get to it. The lives of my brother and me are at risk for meeting with you. How sure are you that your plane wasn't seen?"

"We fly low, and we do not have any electrical instrumentation, plus some additional preventative measures which I will not divulge," the guy on the left said.

"You never answered my brother's question," Harrison grunted out. "Are you responsible for our father being arrested?"

The man on the left moved from one foot to the other. "Not sure. We don't know who he had spoken to or where he was poking around. We contacted him for equipment. This is a very valuable and high-tech piece of equipment. The authorities can't find out about it."

I glanced at Harrison with a side-eyed expression before asking the men in masks, "What equipment? Is it contraband?"

"Probably. It's illegal to give anything to us on the dark side. It is a laser drill to cut through lava rock. Iron rock no chisel or hammer can break," the man on the right side said.

"Holy shit!" I slapped my hands over my mouth.

My brother shook his head in disappointment. "There you are swearing again." Harrison nudged me with an elbow. The men exploded with laughter, then coughed and excused themselves.

I gave them my best intimidating look. "Why do you need it?"

"To make tunnels, of course. It would take us years to excavate, and we don't have that much time." The man on the right, Mr. Cleaner, reached into his shirt, removed something from around his neck, and held out his fist. Harrison and I stood unblinking, waiting for him to turn his palm up. "One of the children found it while playing in a stream that springs out of the mountain and runs into the ocean. We want to open it up and see what we can find. It would also help tremendously to dig deeper into the mountain for when the winter storms come. We can't do it by hand, with chisels and hammers."

Mr. Cleaner uncurled his fingers to reveal a small glowing stone I'd never seen but had heard about. It was small in his giant-sized palm, but would be much bigger in mine, which said a lot about the size of his hands.

"What is this? Is it a diamond in an iron rock?" I turned the rock, which had sharp edges, revealing what looked like small, bright glass, illuminating the palm of my hand.

The one on the left answered. "No, it's a crystal, a light energy enhancer. When the boy showed it to us, we also thought it might be a precious stone. We noticed it glowed as if it were filled with fire. We think there could be more. Like I said, the rock is impenetrable."

"So you found that energy crystal near your homes?" I asked to confirm. This was what the Zelk had been searching for. It would be an incredible discovery—*maybe enough to prevent me from becoming a hybrid.* If the Zelk discovered it was on the Dark Continent, they would annex it and eliminate every last human and animal living there. If Malherbe Enterprises could secure another contract and establish it as a human mining colony, it might save them—and me.

The man on the left pointed to the shimmering stone. "Yes, we're showing you this because we trust you. We believe this is part of what the Zelk war is all about."

"Our people died defending that place. They are trusting you with a big secret, and if you stab us in the back, if you rat us out, they will bring the war to your shiny Spire City, and I will be the first one to drive a knife into your pretty mouth. I will cut out your tongue, then stick it so far up your pompous, tight ass until you can lick your brother's Zelk cunt with it," the grumpy man on the right threatened.

I froze, my eyes widening. Harrison gasped. "That vulgarity. Really? Finally, you're showing us your true side," I said, with a shocked, condescending tone.

Harrison side-bumped me. "Such unpolished and raw language is beneath us," he whispered. We couldn't see their expressions, but they could see ours.

"Yes!" both answered. They were serious and in agreement.

I swallowed nervously. Harrison shot me a go-on-or-die look. "Where...is...this place exactly?" I asked, knowing that my father and every other prominent family vying for favor with the Zelk had scoured the globe to find it.

Mr. Cleaner looked at Harrison and me, probably assessing whether we could be trusted or not. He settled with a vague answer. "On a peninsula just a few hundred miles from the Dark Continent. Children like to play there when it is low tide."

The man on the left pointed a finger at us. "Listen, this is more valuable than anything we can barter. Could this be used against the Zelk?" He leaned closer. "Do you think this could be weaponized?"

Why did he ask that? Was he testing us, or was he truly so naïve as to think I would tell them how to kill my people?

"So, you came to ask us if this could be used as a weapon?" Harrison asked skeptically. But I knew he understood this was our ticket to gaining full control, to possibly meeting our leader for a golden handshake. Only the best families of Spire City get to meet the Zelk king. This was our way to prove our worth and ensure that Malherbe Enterprises could continue into the future.

"Look," Mr. Cleaner said, starting to walk a few steps to a spot where light streamed through a gap in the boardwalk above. He held the stone up to the moon for a moment. Then, he walked back to us. My nerves were shot. We were breaking so many laws that I lost count of how many times I had sentenced myself to death. It glowed a bit brighter, and a thrill of excitement ran through me, making me shiver.

Harrison crossed his arms. "Put that away, you are going to get all of us killed. If the hoverbots see that—"

I interrupted my brother. "We've been mining for these. They need this for their power plants. Not sure if it can be weaponized." I lied.

Mr. Cleaner quickly hung it around his neck and pushed it

underneath his shirt. The light disappeared, but the yellow hue was still visible through the material. "Can you help us?" he asked.

"Give me two days, and I will return with a laser drill," I said hurriedly.

The man on the left blurted, "We can't pay you."

"I know. You can pay me by taking me with you. I want to see your home and this place."

"Absolutely not," they both replied.

"You will be missed, and your ass can be tracked. You have tracers in your bone marrow," the man next to Mr. Cleaner blurted.

"No, I don't," I told them, clearing my throat. "Um...I don't have tracers, but I do have implanted trackers," I added, so they would know I couldn't be abducted.

"Our trackers are all inactivated," Harrison said, spoiling my forewarning. "I will cover for you, Zaidon. We can say you are needed in a place where no one can reach you. Maybe we could use your yearly inspection as an excuse and say we are going to be visiting the factories and mines?"

Mr. Cleaner stepped closer into our personal space without making eye contact. "You mean the penal colonies where humans scavenge for scraps of food to bring you, your Precious!"

"Um...um," I stuttered.

"Excuse us," the left one muttered something to Mr. Cleaner.

Harrison whispered in my ear. "Zonika won't want to go, and if I make it seem like one of us is urgently needed, she will send you instead." Harrison urged me because he sensed an opportunity to learn more about the crystal's location.

I gave an agreeable nod and turned to find the tall giants waiting for us with crossed arms. "There, like my brother said. I'll come with you, or no laser for drilling tunnels for you." I could hear the men rolling their eyes at me. Even if I didn't find the location, I wanted to see the Dark Continent. Our hoverbots and transportation vehicles, whether by sea or air, can't reach it. But they, with their falling-apart aircraft, could bring me closer to the place. Closer than anyone since forever. The one on the left pulled my cleaner man closer for another private deliberation.

Harrison bumped me with an elbow and winked. "I know, and stop elbowing me." I glowered at my brother, vibrating with excitement.

When the two masked men seemed to conclude, they turned back to us.

"Okay. Two days. We will wait only two days, and if we don't hear from you, we will have to attack a mining operation to steal one."

"No! That would be suicide," I said worriedly.

"Exactly. That's why we need you." Mr. Cleaner retorted.

"Then it's final. I bid you a good night, gentlemen. In two days, this time, this place. No need to make contact with me," I added and then turned, fished the communicator out of my pants, and handed it back to them. "That thing is too risky to keep." Mr. Cleaner Man took it from me. "Next time, write a note and leave it under my office telephone or somewhere I may find it, like my sterilization room." I waited for confirmation. They nodded in agreement. Harrison and I turned and made our way back to the walkway and then circled two more blocks in case we were being tracked. Once underneath the central city bridge, we continued wordlessly as we made our way back home by taking the Tube train. To avoid raising suspicion, we went back to the office via the same executive elevator we had exited earlier. Then we spent ten minutes there before disarming the tracker and tracer signal scramblers and departing our separate ways back to our homes.

CHAPTER 6
ZAIDON

PING!

I opened my eyes, ceased massaging my throbbing temples, and stepped out of the elevator into my silent, sterile home.

"Welcome home, sir. I hope you had a productive day," greeted the robotic female voice of my home management system. Like the hoverbots, she was part of the invader technology—the system that existed wherever humans gathered in Spire City. "How was your day?" she asked as usual.

As always, I emptied my pockets onto the small hallway table; my antique ballpoint pen, a set of remote keys, but no scrambler. I loosened my tie and kicked off my shoes. "Good, thank you."

"I noticed you came home later than usual. What is the reason for this?" she asked.

I sighed. "I have a headache, so I was less productive and worked slower than usual. There were fewer results, but I made sure they were satisfactory before coming home to rest," I answered, knowing exactly what to say without raising suspicion. "Open the blinds, please. I want to see the splendor and appreciate the beauty of Spire City."

"Of course, Zaidon." The soft sound of ratchets clicking and the blinds opening up revealed the bright skyline, only viewable from the Malherbe Spire City tower. Ours. Now mine. "Sorry to hear about the pain in your head. Would you like me to play something relaxing while I prepare your dinner as you sanitize?"

"Yes, please." I stood with my back straight, legs apart, and my hands clasped behind my back in front of the enormous wrap-around window. Soft electronic music started up. Mimicking waterfalls and birdsong, painting a picture of the rising sun behind a tropical forest. I found myself too nervous and afraid to think about tonight's meeting. About the cleaner, with his deep voice and the glint in his dark eyes. His big hands and long, slender fingers I had touched when I inspected the crystal. I had to bend my neck backward to look up at him. The tone in his voice was low, with an alluring promise of danger—of death. I smiled inwardly, thinking about his threat to cut my tongue out. That was so psychotic. I think I liked it for some reason. That was the crudest, sickest thing to say.

Harrison was right; I should be cautious. I was the only one not filled with Zelk nanites. Only I could set foot on the Dark Continent. I needed to find the source of that crystal before another family claimed it. I had no idea how I would manage to sneak a laser drill from the mines and get it delivered to the pier without anyone seeing, but I would figure it out. I could say I was working on it. Maybe I should ask around to find out which mine had a broken one, so I could arrange for it to be picked up and brought to me, and have it fixed.

As I stood there staring at the sunlit sky, and our protective shield shimmered, I remembered. Remembering was like a religion to my father. He told us that remembering was what kept us human.

As children, my father had shared the stories his grandfather had shared with him—tales of a time when the open sky had enveloped our planet, long before the invaders arrived. Thunderous bombs shook the ground, sending gigantic waves flushing the coastlines, while propelling fighters and flying creatures into the sky to battle for our survival. Below, the cries of hundreds of humans pleading for help filled the air. Bombs fell, and the screeches of those injured intensified while the fighters and angels fell to the ground, electrocuted. Artificial lightning currents filled the atmosphere, burning anything they touched. Everything burned and exploded, sizzled to a crisp. Young children cried, parentless. Their faces were dirty with gunpowder and black soot, tear streaks running down their chins, across their bare chests, forming pools of mud on the scorched ground they stepped upon. Thousands of people were marched into labor prisons. Most had been forgotten, but in the spaces between the walls, my father, and his father's father gathered in private to remember. Once we forgot them, we were lost. So many were already lost. Spire City was almost completely cleansed of humans.

My own sister had cleansed status. She had forgotten what my father had died for. She was a traitor to our kind, and now, with my father's execution, to her own family as well. All because she forgot the people who worked for us in the factories and mines. If we didn't remember, they would be forgotten and sacrificed for nothing.

My apartment was on the top, 380th level of the Malherbe Tower in central Spire City. Our head office and homes were conveniently tubed to the building, erected by my grandfather. Our family was among the privileged. But even our luck was running out. We'd managed the diamond and tungsten mines of Spire City and were the sole contractors drilling and constructing towers for our founders, the invaders. The towers stood like waiting rockets, reaching into the clouds, prepared to be shot into the sky. My father received the designs from the invaders and was instructed to build them. Each had multiple elevators running through a central shaft that opened on every floor. One tower housed everything a human needed to work and rest. No one had to leave. They could if they wanted to, but no one did, because why would they? All apartments, offices, recreational areas, and factory floors were round, each occupying an entire floor. Therefore, we referred to a floor as a "cake," as my father called them. Each family owned a cake and was allowed only two male and one female child. Reproduction was regulated and fully controlled by the authorities based on the health statistics of our nation. We were designed and birthed by the will and grace of the invaders.

Contrary to what I was told to remember, everyone believed that the lightning storms and sun would have incinerated us to ash if not for the bioelectrical shield the founders deployed, which ended the war before we were incinerated by our atmosphere. The stories of our ancestors were nearly lost, forgotten, and deemed unnecessary for human survival as we coexisted with the invaders. My father had worked hard to keep us human for as long as possible. But it was up to me, filling his shoes, to ensure that we continued to be the most favored company and family in Spire City. We followed the authorities' directives while honoring the people who worked for us in the mines and factories. It was my duty to sustain the human race as best I could.

I rubbed my eyes, staring out of the panoramic window at the vast orange expanse and the tiny blue binary moon orbiting with us around our shared sun. We live in the light, while the humans on the Dark Continent remain cloaked in its darkness. Our continent sat to the north—the complete opposite of the southern continent, which was darker and colder. It was impossible to access if you were Zelk or hybrid because the magnetic fields surrounding it damaged the nanites. The two men from earlier were from there, and I wanted to see it, even if it was illegal.

The story I liked best, which was probably the most outrageous, was about a dragon that burned the crust, magnetizing the cooling lava rock that covered the Dark Continent and blocked Zelk's access to it.

We'd adapted and believed that the invaders had saved us from ourselves. Most hybrids swore that without the shield, we would have either frozen or burned to death, depending on the continent. The invaders were the heroes rather than oppressors; they were protecting Spire City. It was easier to live day to day, forgetting the past and following the rules.

I was looking ahead and planning. I wanted to know what my father had died for. *I wanted to know why my father had helped those from the Dark Continent.*

My eyes filled with tears, and I turned and sauntered straight to my room to get undressed. I concealed the tracker and tracer scrambler inside my shoes. The automatic clothes dispenser opened, and with a quick, well-practiced move, I bundled up my clothes and dunked the ball as if I were playing basketball. Tomorrow, a fresh set of clothes would wait for me. As a human businessman and ambassador, I have the privilege of wearing black and white instead of the typical blue and silver suits worn by all Spire citizens.

After my fourth hot laser cleansing session of the day, I stepped out of the sterilizing room naked and made my way to the dining room table to have my final drinkable meal. It was a bland concoction of vitamins, and I never liked the taste; I might as well be licking the walls clean. After gagging it down, I sat bare for a moment, gathering myself and thinking about the cleaner. My eyes roamed down to my pale, hairless crotch. My pissing thing lay limp, pink, and ugly.

A robotic arm descended from the ceiling, and the single-eyed camera floated in front of me to capture my attention. "Yes, what do you want?" I asked, feeling irritated.

"I've programmed your rejuvenating regimen to provide pain relief and antidotes for your negativity, which is contributing to your chronic headaches."

I exhaled a long, tired breath, rubbing the back of my neck. "Thank you," I muttered. I was fed up with being micro-managed. On the other hand, maybe I'd think more clearly once my headache subsided. It had been getting worse since my father's death.

In two days, I would ensure that I made a difference, as I'd promised my father.

CHAPTER 7
DRAXTON

FEARING WE WERE BEING FOLLOWED AFTER OUR initial meeting, we didn't return to Simon's but rather reverse-parked in an alcove of a small island where the shadows of the overhanging boulders covered the seaplane. High cliffs flanked us, and noisy seagulls nested nearby. I sat for a whole day looking like the Karate Kid, with a black and white bandana covering my ears to muffle their screeching. Although it had been a good idea yesterday, it wasn't effective today. Instead, it irritated me more, so I untied it and used it as a sweat cloth around my neck.

Time dragged on and on and on while Kellan and I waited until it was time to meet Zaidon again.

"The longest wait for the shortest man," I said with a grunt, and turned sideways. I was itchy and uncomfortable both inside and outside of my body.

Punching, kissing, or better yet, fucking Kellan would alleviate my frustrations.

I was hot, sweaty, and sitting with a hard-on. Waiting, waiting, and waiting. Of all the wonderful things I could do, I'd never been good at waiting. One minute felt like hours to me.

"Fuck, I wish I had a map. Even a pen and toilet paper, anything, something. Doesn't this airplane have an owner's manual?" I rummaged around again, finding nothing interesting or worthy of studying. Sitting and waiting on a wooden crate lined with elk fur made my asscrack itch furiously. I couldn't decide where to sit. Outside on the float, where it was cooler but too far away from Kellan, or inside the tin can, where I could speak to him. In short, this was one hell of a long wait for me.

My grandfather had taught me a few tricks on how to calm myself and adapt to an environment that made me feel that way. I closed my eyes, chasing the welcoming darkness behind my eyelids while slowly inhaling through my nose. Sweat trickled down my brow, and I wiped it away with the back of my hand. I clicked my tongue in irritation. The sticky moisture between my fingers reminded me of sex.

"*Grrr*," I growled instead of blurting my thoughts. I gave Kellan a look, then stared out the window again.

"Ah, fuck! I'm so tired of this shit." My frustration won.

Kellan remained calm, oddly grounding me in his silence, like the stillness of the caves.

"You know what? Your quiet darkness is unique," I noted and waited.

His silence seeped into my being, and I chased it with my eyes closed. Then, after a calm, bloody minute, a seagull screeched. *Damnit.* My eyes flicked open.

"Am I?" Kellan asked.

"Um?" *What was I saying?* I rolled my eyes at myself. "Yeah, like the sun never reached you—ever. Cool and calm."

Maybe he was silent on purpose to pass the time.

He stopped carving the figurine to test the sharpness of his blade with his thumb. "What do you mean? Is it because my complexion is darker than yours, because that doesn't make sense. If you sit in the sun all day, you'd get darker, so I can't be black because I never see the sun." He looked up at me with furrowed brows. There wasn't a drop of sweat on his face.

"I was speaking about the still darkness of the caves. You're like that, and I love it."

"That's the nicest thing you've ever said to me."

"Thank you."

"It's a beautiful compliment, especially since I know how much you enjoy crawling in and exploring the darkness," he said as he returned to work.

I blinked. *Did he just invite me to crawl into him and explore his body?* Thrumming my fingers on the dashboard of the cockpit, I mimicked a trance song I used to like listening to. "I've noticed less sexual interest coming from you. It's been too long. I assume it's because of the heat and sweat and maybe the stress of our mission." I shifted to the side to avoid the sting of the bright, constant light that hurt my eyes. "God, how do these people ever relax and sleep?"

"Uh-hum, two and a half days?" Kellan's voice vibrated low but finished with an uptick as if questioning me beneath the surface. Was he asking me whether I think it's really been that long, or was he asking to fuck me? *He was so vague and confusing sometimes.*

There's more space in the back of the plane. Hunching

forward, I shot up and squeezed between the two front seats to sit in the back, then plopped down with an exasperated moan and waited for him. The reflections of light dancing on the water felt like they were trying to carve my eyeballs out of my skull like razor blades. I huffed. "Ridiculous!"

I crossed and uncrossed my arms. "I prefer the cold and darkness, where I can light a fire to see and put it out when my day is done. At least I can throw something over my shoulders and sit closer to you or the fire when it's chilly. But in this heat...even if I stripped off all my clothes, I'd still be too hot... and judging by the looks of it, I also wouldn't get any action," I said with a dramatic sigh of longing. "I miss the caves. My shorts, my flip-flops."

"Uh-huh, looking and sounding like it," Kellan agreed, not lifting his gaze from the piece of wood in his hands. "At least you have the hat I made you," he said.

"I like it. It's almost the same as the one I wore back home." I tipped it like a cowboy. "Thank you, kindly, dear sir." I removed it dramatically and placed it next to me.

"Made it for you with my hands, to protect your shaved head and your beautiful mind from the deadly sun," he muttered. It seemed that the piece of wood was far more interesting than the log I had in my pants waiting for him.

I stretched lazily, then laced my fingers behind my head. "I suppose I should add the prison tunnels to the list of cool and dark places I crawled through," I said in my best seductive tone to remind him I was eager to crawl over him.

He ignored me...

"I'm not adding Ouro's cave, or maybe I should. At least someone was always trying to pin me down to extract more of my intelligence and bravery loaded inside the sperm you like to drink so much. It's not long before little Draxtons will be running around, conquering the Dark Continent. And if they are like me, that mountain will be open in no time. Perhaps if I weren't gay, I'd feel less aroused all the time. Women would line up eagerly, ready to ride me. But...I'm gay...there is no line. Only you...You'd think I'd be sexually satisfied after draping myself over Ouro's log for my contributions to their population expansion, but I'm abandoned to my own hand." I sounded scornful, I thought as I loosened the bandanna around my neck to wipe between my slippery fingers. *This was neither cheerful nor alluring.*

"Uh-hum, hmmm," Kellan grumbled extra long, then finally looked over his shoulder at me.

I gave him my sexy, irresistible smile. "I suppose I should be direct about my sexual needs instead of hinting that I'm bored and think sex could be a healthier and more enjoyable way to pass the time, maybe even helping both of us relax here in the back of the airplane," I explained while patting the seat beside me to clear up any misunderstandings on the subject. "Please?" I licked my lips dramatically while rubbing my crotch furiously.

Kellan barked a laugh. "No. Go jump in the water. You seem happier when you are swimming. Go on. I'm not stopping you. We're not having sex...not here," he said, disinterested. *Was he disinterested in sex now because of the heat, or was he disinterested in sex with me?*

Gaping at the back of his head, I changed tactics. "I guess my leathers are begging for water, but it's so much work to take them off in this heat." I sounded like an overdramatic, spoiled boyfriend, hoping Kellan might offer to undress me. Did I really think I was his boyfriend? Gods, just a few months before, I would have run away from the idea of answering to a man or being any man's anything, let alone a boyfriend.

Kellan sighed, half shrugging and rolling his shoulders. "Then take your time doing it. It will keep your hands busy." He turned back in his seat, and the *scrape-scrape-blow-blow* started again.

I dropped my head, shaking it. "What I meant was...that when I get out, by the time I get dressed again, I'll be hot and dry within seconds...I don't have to take them off. But this pig leather would shrink to two sizes smaller," I scoffed playfully, giving up waiting for him to join me. Jumping up again, I made my way back to the front, sniffing my armpits as I hurried into the passenger seat.

"If your pants were two times smaller, your basket would look two times bigger," he muttered, chuckling and teasing me.

"No wonder you don't want to join me in the back seat. I wish I'd tucked a bottle of antiperspirant into my jeans' pocket the day we fell through the door in the Dinaledi Chamber. Maybe if I didn't stink, you'd be all over me?"

Kellan *pffft* at me. While pretending that he was ignoring me, I saw his thin laugh lines deepening.

"No, really, why else would that lump of wood in your hands be more important than mine?"

"Draxton, besides the hoverbots, the fact that we are currently behind enemy lines, yeah, my eyes tear up at your revolting smell. Look at me wilting away." He was joking and enjoying my antics. I loved his sharp mind. He got me. As a speleologist, I didn't care if I smelled natural. In fact, his sweat was like an aphrodisiac to me.

"Inviting you to the back of an airplane is useless. At least when it's cold, I can invite you under the furs and lock my legs around your hips and force all your attention on me and my wood." The corner of his mouth twitched slightly. "Maybe I should just jump in. Sitting and waiting makes me itch both inside and out. I'm ready for another wash, especially right between my...do you want to scratch my itchy places or not?"

"Uh-hum."

"You know what, forget it!" I bent down and started loosening my boots again. "I'm jumping in, clothes and all."

"That's the spirit." Kellan chuckled without looking at me. "I'll join you when I'm finished here," he snickered.

Not wanting to seem desperate, I replied, "Okay, take your time," then shifted the subject, only because he'd joined me for swimming already twice today. "I can't believe these people choose to live here."

Kellan grimaced as he concentrated intently on the piece of wood he was carving. "These Spire citizens never leave their air-conditioned buildings. They artificially control their environment, like everything else," he said in a low tone.

I slid off my seat, my feet burning as I quickly and quietly climbed over the sun-exposed section of the float, sat down, and eased into the waveless, lukewarm saltwater, socks and all. It felt refreshing, so I dunked my head to rinse my stubbly head and face. One by one, I removed my shirt, pants, and socks, washed them, and laid them in the sun to dry. I splashed around, soaking my crack and armpits while I waded through the water, watching him. "It's quiet out here..." *My boner's gone, might as well stay longer.* "With my ears...submerged in water...it's peaceful." I closed my eyes.

"Hmmm, it is," Kellan said.

My eyes opened at the sound of his voice. Light shouted at me to return from where I was drifting too far away. "Huh?" I asked and changed direction, gently kicking the water to return to Kellan.

He shook his head as he turned the piece of wood over, examining it from every angle, and began carving the small figurine with his large hands again. I loved watching him. I floated on my back, gazing up at him, gripping a rope that dangled from the side where we had anchored the seaplane, and relaxed. He was good at waiting. He blew away the carved wood chips with a few puffs, then assessed his handiwork again, and then continued, focusing on what I suspected was another four-legged farm animal.

"What's that going to be? Is it a cow or a horse?" I asked, enjoying the hollow sound of my voice as I kept my ears under the water.

"It's a sheep," Kellan said. His voice sounded far away. I lifted my head to compare. "Can't you see? This is a woolly one. It has shorter legs and a fatter body. It's going to be one of a flock of ten, I'm making it for Sopora's niece for her fifth birthday." He showed me the small lump of wood, which was shaped like nothing.

"Nice," I said and dunked my ears back under the water. "She will love it," I said, to compare the sounds.

I frolicked and gargled salt water, then spat fountains. "You should join me. I have a few ideas for how you can entertain me to pass the time faster." I scooped another mouthful, gargled, and spat longer fountains.

"I wouldn't do that if I were you. Snow told me that nasty chemicals are being pumped into the ocean. Tomorrow, your beautiful long cock is going to be shriveled up like a dried earthworm."

I startled and gave him an *are-you-kidding-me* look. "You said to jump in. Come join me...you can suck my earthworm until it's plump and juicy."

Kellan looked up and raised his eyebrows at me. "I didn't say to ingest the water."

Nearly drowning myself, I spat the water out and coughed. "Yeah, you're right. I'm gonna get out. The visual of a shriveled-up cock is not funny anymore."

"You are so gullible." Kellan chuckled. Grabbing the handle on the side of the float, I pulled myself out of the water and rolled onto the narrow platform. I lay sprawled on my back, my arms and legs wide to give my junk and armpits air, and waited for my clothes to dry.

A long, comfortable silence lingered between us. "What do you think of Zaidon?" Kellan asked out of nowhere.

"I don't know. We'll see if he's setting us up or not." I turned onto my stomach. "Hmmm, this feels better." I closed my eyes, waiting for Kellan to respond. Fifteen minutes later, I was dry enough, so I pushed myself to my feet, grabbed my stiff, dried clothes, and rubbed them between my hands to remove the salt and soften them before getting dressed. Just in case we had to leave in a hurry, I climbed back into my seat to put my boots on and waited.

"Gods, I'm bored." I tapped my fingers on the dashboard to the tune stuck in my head while I softly whistled.

Kellan whittled while I whistled and engaged in small talk. Like my grandfather, he understood me. We had all sorts of conversations. Even silent ones. Sometimes, I would let out a grunt, and he would respond with another grunt, and both of us knew exactly what we were grunting about. Inside the winter cave, we spent the whole day saying nothing, and later that night, we would wrap up our conversation by grunting a goodnight.

"Tell me again, how did you know Zaidon's father?"

"While you went to meet the devil, I didn't just build you a shithouse and play hut. I got to know our enemy. Simon and Snow organized a meeting with Zaidon's father. I trust Zaidon solely because I met his father. It's the only reason. Being imprisoned, you know how difficult it is to find a human to trust—on this Light Continent. We took a chance to contact Joseph Malherbe. It was a quick meeting down at the docks. This happened just days after you were taken prisoner. I was upset. I took every chance I got to get to know these bastards."

"Ah, you missed me, and you acted out," I teased. But secretly, I was feeling shittier every time the subject came up.

"I decided if you are reckless, then I should be too." Kellan lifted his head proudly. "After our meeting, Malherbe cut the hoverbot patrols along the coast. Something I suggested, so Simon, Snow, and I were able to do a few extra pickups and drops along this coast. Hence, the flush toilets and other furniture."

"Did they use the boat?"

"Yup, the boat. It's the only way Callisto agreed to travel with us."

"I think that if I'd met him, I'd be more upset about the horror and what was done to him," I said quietly, wiping the white residue of sea salt from my arms and face.

A long pause, perhaps two hours, passed before Kellan said, "I wish I'd asked my father more. I have a fear, a foreboding feeling that my brother's plan is insufficient."

I sighed and shrugged. "That is, if and when they figure out how to breach the magnetic field."

Kellan grunted affirmatively. More time passed.

I picked up and continued our discussion from earlier. "I hope his father's compassion has spilled over to Zaidon."

Kellan let out a huff while shaking his head. "From what I've heard from Simon about Zaidon's brother and sister, I doubt they inherited any. His sister, Zonika, is pro-invaders. You've met Harrison, and he seems untrustworthy. It's like he'd rather save his own skin and betray everyone."

I contemplated. "He's not a hybrid, but not fully human; I had the impression that he's maybe a half-one. I'm not sure."

Kellan turned to me. "After falling ill as a young boy, Joseph Malherbe saved his son with bionic white blood cells. Harrison was the first hybrid prototype. The invader technology cured his son's leukemia."

"Yes, Luci had mentioned that...along with any other human illness."

"Precisely. That's why their sister and every other person, including her Zelk hybrid boyfriend, choose to live here like this. The lure of life everlasting...the ultimate promise to people...who can resist that, while you see everyone around you accepting it as the new normal?"

"Fucking *normal*, I hate that word." Kellan agreed with me by nodding his head once. "I guess it's enough reason to be more machine than human if you are born into it."

"It won't surprise me if it was Zonika who reported her father," Kellan said.

I stared out over the vast ocean beyond our little alcove. "Zaidon and his brother are different."

Kellan smiled at me. "You came up with a good side story

about the children playing in a stream, and that the tunnel maker would help shelter them from the winter storms."

My heart raced at his praise. "Thank you, Professor."

"Anyway, Snow and Simon have been spying on them for many summers. Hopefully, like his father, Zaidon wants to keep humanity alive and has influence over the Zelk because they depend on the Malherbe family for their research and mining."

I bristled at that. "If they are in charge of the mining operations, then they are as guilty as the Zelk in my eyes. There is nothing but slavery down there. The people inside the mine are so broken, they are almost beyond saving. Children are being born down there. They have accepted their way of staying alive as just the way it is. I would love to help them, but it's going to be one massive operation to get them out safely from those tunnels."

"Let's help Ouroboros first, then worry about freeing prisoners later. I mean, if we somehow defeat the Zelk, then we can take our time to liberate the people. It's going to take years before everyone has acclimated to being free," Kellan noted.

I grimaced. "It's either that or we will all be killed."

"At least now we know what's going on down there. We know Luci is there, for example." Kellan looked up at me, and I appreciated that he helped me see the positive side, even if it was the only positive thing after that ordeal.

"Yes, at least we know that. But it still feels like it's not enough. It's just something we say to make us feel better or that we are still figuring it out and don't really have a clue how this is going to go once Atlas is awake." I admitted honestly.

"You know, I followed you inside the Star Caves even if I didn't know what was going to happen to us. Now I know it was my destiny. Sometimes it's better not to know things. I'm not as brave as you. I overthink things," he said.

I smiled and looked lovingly at him while my insides went fluttery. "I'm glad you fell through the door with me and that we are experiencing this together. I can't imagine doing all this without you."

Kellan shrugged. "Just know that I respect you, and I'm not hopelessly dependent on you. We're a team. You're the strong one, with an abundance of perseverance. Never think I want to hold you back." He pointed a finger back and forth between our chests. "I know now why I'm here. I'm here to hold the flame for my brother while you guide us through the unknown." Kellan sounded strangely unlike himself. He knew exactly what to say, what I wanted to hear. It was as if he had read it in a book and was repeating it, even if those weren't his true words.

I don't like this sweet, syrupy version of Kellan—a follower holding a flame. *What the hell?* I prefer the sarcastic, disinterested-in-sex Kellan, the one who teased and challenged me until he decided it was time and let me have my way with him. The Kellan who said he was lost without me.

Maybe he was tired of me but still had a job to do—to get us home. Maybe I was too much for him. Maybe he didn't want me around all the time. Perhaps, while I was gone, he'd realized he preferred having more alone time with his brother and his people.

I was more confused now than ever. Did he want me or not? Were we playing, or was he serious all this time?

Kellan shuffled in his seat and put his lump of wood and

knife away. "You should also rub some of that positivity and perseverance on Zaidon. Maybe we can convince him to tell us how to kill the Zelk."

"Hmmm, I hear you," I said and turned my back on him. I was so done with this chasing game.

He put a hand on my shoulder. "Simon said that here on the Light Continent, lives have become extremely intertwined over the years, and that's what the hybrids want. The few humans left here are like toads in boiling water, not jumping out as the temperature slowly rises. They think they can stay a little longer, but end up boiled alive," Kellan said with bitterness.

That was an interesting analysis. I turned back to him. "When did you boil toads?" I asked jokingly while forcing a smile.

Kellan looked at me with eyes full of wisdom that seemed to have seen many lifetimes. God, his mind made me weak. He was just as beautiful as the day we met, even if he wasn't wearing his crisp gray suit, and even if he appeared all dangerous and rugged. You'd think a man in a suit would complain, but Kellan hadn't fussed about comfort or luxury. I eyed him, wondering if I was truly seeing him for the first time, or if he was concealing something with his words.

Fuck this, he didn't have to say it. I didn't have to say it. In this short time, we've grown to love each other fiercely.

"You never complain about us looking wild and nearly like cavemen," I blurted.

"It doesn't bother me at all." Confirming what I was thinking, he said, "I'm more worried about their lives, their existence. I wonder if we can change history by helping

Ouroboros, if it is even possible. I worry about what the world would look like if we returned."

"Yeah, it's almost unfathomable…all this and your brother still isn't giving up on the war. It's worrisome, much more than our lack of electric shavers."

"Now that is fucking sad," Kellan joked.

"I'm going to do my best to influence Zaidon. Make him see that their technology is not what matters, what matters is how much of their humanity they've lost already," I said.

"Donali and Kawa said some of them were questioning their way of life. There are always some who do, but it's easier to stay quiet."

"Must be, but they are weeded out either by their tracers or their friends and family, believing they are weak links in their pristine society."

"Zaidon's father was apparently different. All this time, he played both sides, and suddenly, he got outed as a traitor. Simon said it was Zonika, his daughter, who reported him. She wasn't happy with Zaidon, the youngest, stepping into their father's shoes. Simon thinks it won't be long before his sister works him out of his seat and finds something to accuse or betray him with."

"I hope he is smart enough not to trust anyone, not even that brother of his," I scoffed.

Kellan gazed out at the water shimmering in the sunlight. "Are you interested in him?"

"Of course not. I can smell his virginity miles away," I said, and I thought I saw Kellan wincing.

"You can teach him; what's wrong with that? You won't be the first man in history, nor would it be wrong for him to want to learn from you," Kellan said.

"No. What we have is sufficient for me," I said sternly. "Even if you didn't want to fuck me earlier," I added, giving him a lopsided smile, hoping he noticed the twinkle in my eyes for him.

"You know what I mean," Kellan said. "I love you more than anything, but I don't own you; that would be selfish. I won't smother you. If the opportunity arises and he is willing, you have my blessing. I'll make myself scarce and visit Ouro for a few days in the mountains."

*Just as I thought of him as my boyfriend...*Obviously, he still wanted to fuck around with others and spend more time with his brother. I never had brothers or sisters, so I shouldn't expect him to choose me above Ouroboros. I stayed quiet because it felt like I was going to say the wrong thing.

"He's talking to his animals. That's why I want to go. I want him to show me how, maybe teach me," Kellan added.

I mentally rolled my eyes at myself. I shouldn't make everything about me. "I'm sure the majestic beasts are breathtaking. Sopora said they are as white as Callisto and taller than two men standing."

"Then I will go once we have you guys sorted," Kellan said with a finality I hated.

"I should go with you. We can share Zaidon if he is interested in men."

"Not one like me. I'm a caveman compared to you."

"He is taking his suppressants to prevent him from feeling, from getting aroused, from being human. A perfect man, just like the Zelk authorities want. Pure cleanliness clings to him like the smell of new garbage bags. Did you see those clean black trousers and crisp white shirt, concealing hands in pockets beneath a tailored coat? He thinks he is better than us," I told Kellan.

"What was he supposed to think of your mask and your Indiana Jones hat?"

"Fuck off, it was your idea to wear the masks. And stop comparing me with Indie. I'm telling you, Zaidon is straight and not interested in sex with men or women, especially not big hairy men like us. Sopora's nieces and nephews are taller than him. How do you think he will react to kissing, and what about butt stuff?"

Kellan burst out laughing. "Ha, hahaha! He gets enemas all the time. Sorry, sterilizations."

I cringed. "Snow said no one is permitted to touch themselves; their genitals are considered impure. The tracers in their blood report all their hormone levels and emotions, which reveal their feelings and thoughts like built-in lie detectors. Gods, I don't want that baggage."

Kellan laughed. "Zaidon says he has a scrambler. That should be reason enough to believe he wants out. He wants to come with us because he wants to know. You should use this time to win him over. Convince him to stay."

"Na-ah-ah! No, he has to ask or stay on his own. No convincing anyone of anything." I said, thinking about what Ouro told us about free will. "Ouro said Callisto and Atlas are the only ones who know how to open the door. They need that drill. As soon as that door opens, we are out of here."

"Draxton, stop changing the subject. Did you hear how Zaidon sucked air between his teeth when he saw us climbing out of the airplane and towering over them? He liked it. Once you spoke and he recognized your voice, his attention was solely on you."

I dug the heels of my boots into the rusted floor. "He wasn't, and although our height is normally between five and six feet tall, he was shocked—not in lust. The Zelk preferred humans to be shorter because smaller humans are less trouble; they eat less and take up less space. Four to five feet was his norm until he saw us. They probably do that with gene manipulation. That's why he was looking and drawing in surprised breaths."

Kellan pointed at me. "All I'm saying is, if Ouro were here, he would tell you to befriend him too. This society is not human—at least, not anymore. You must teach him. We need intel. That's why we are here, after all."

I took the piece of wood he was carving, inspecting the four nubs, which I assumed would be legs once he was done with it. I turned it over. One side was wider than the other, which would probably be the head and backside. "I hear you very well, Professor. I'm just saying I prefer you first. That's all. I'm blind to others' advances. As much as you think you know me, sometimes you read me completely wrong."

Kellan took the sheep, rolling it between his fingers as he inspected it. His head hung low, and he appeared deep in thought. He took a deep breath but kept his chin tucked into his chest. "This is a slow genocide. We must stop them. Ouro said we stand a chance against them with that healing crystal. The warriors should last longer during battle, especially with the extra helping of dragon fire behind them. Unlike before the invasion, Atlas might be the predisposed weapon they need. If the Zelk discover a way past the magnetic field surrounding the mountain, there would be no reason for them not to exterminate all of us." He paused, and I counted, one, two, three, four, five, six...

"We need Zaidon not just to keep our secret, but also because we can use him. I've been thinking, maybe he knows about something that would weaken them, like Zelk kryptonite." He chipped away at a nub, deepening the groove between the future back legs. "We need his laser drill, his intellect, and his position. That drill and that man are important to have on our side. He knows everything about the Zelk, including their weak points. Please try your hardest to make friends with him."

I grunted, flames of fury burning behind my eyes. "So, that's the only reason you want me to befriend and sleep with him?"

"Yes, that's what I said."

"Hmmm." I sat silently with Kellan, staring out over the water. "It's what you don't say and do that matters to me," I whispered.

"I prefer you first, too, but we are here for a reason much greater than ourselves. I'm a big boy. I can wait for you." Kellan took my hand and kissed it. I shivered and inhaled a shuddering breath. "Ouroboros and our futures depend on this."

I'm not sure how long we sat, but when Kellan finally spoke, I realized it was dark. "I'm going to untie us; it's time to go," he said with a sigh.

CHAPTER 8
DRAXTON

"HERE WE GO. THERE'S OUR BACKUP WAITING FOR US where Simon said they would be, see?" Kellan reached down to cut the fuel and switch off the engine. Suddenly, it was deadly quiet, and I watched him align the wings with the fast-approaching black waters below.

I clutched his shirt with one hand and the side of my crate with the other as the small motorboat grew in size just as we touched down. Luckily, Kellan made it seem like the airplane was as light as a feather. We landed just a few feet behind the breaking line of the harbor waves. Darkness and the soft sloshing of water accompanied the faint moonlight glistening on the calm ocean waters. I counted four of Simon's men as we drifted past them and the floating orange bobbing marker.

I knew, as Kellan had explained before our previous visit, that over one hundred miles to the right, up the coastline, was where Simon and the rebels' hideout was. To the left, far down the coast, the old white lighthouse peeked through the mist. I knew from skydiving that the mining prison lay just beyond that, and up that hill was where Luci waited for us to breach the penal colony to free them. The rest of the land glowed like a science fiction city, eerily blue and purple light breaching the night.

"Hello there!" Kellan stuck his head out of the door.

"Yeah, hello. It's low tide, so you won't be able to float all the way in," one man said, clipping a cable into the front of the floats. A motorboat engine was attached to their speed-boat, but they opted to row and then jump into the water to pull us soundlessly underneath the pier. I was nervous; the sudden void of sound felt unnatural and wrong, and no one spoke, keeping as quiet as possible.

Once the four men helped us, they pushed their boat out of sight and then came back to turn our small aircraft around to ensure a fast take-off.

"Thank you," Kellan whispered once we were in position, and the men scattered into the darkness to cover us.

"Operation warm up to the enemy is a go," I said through thin lips as I pushed open the door, swung my feet out, gripped the spreader, found my footing, and jumped as far as I could to land on the dry sand. Just as we'd decided before landing, Kellan joined me, and we quickly moved deeper beneath the pier to hide in the muggy darkness. I wasn't carrying a gun, but Kellan and the others carried weapons to protect me.

We stayed in the shadows, waiting for Zaidon.

Unlike two nights ago, we weren't wearing any ski masks in the hope of appearing more trustworthy, but that didn't mean we trusted Zaidon.

Kellan's warm breath on my ear shot tingles down my

back. "Are you sure about this? Maybe you should make friends and fuck him into putty? Zaidon seems to like and trust you more. You should go for it. Ouro and Snow, even Simon, Donali, and Kawa, will appreciate it. Not to mention every suffering human." He patted my shoulder. "I'll follow your lead. You are in charge of this operation. I support your choices. I trust and believe in you," Kellan whispered, and I agreed with him. This was going to be an easy mission. All I have to do is turn up my charm. Using my looks...yeah, I thought with newfound determination...I could prove myself. I grinned at Kellan, showing him I was ready and in on the plan. We hunched down and waited.

An hour later, scrunching seashells alerted me. I jumped up, nudging Kellan so hard he nearly toppled over. I grabbed his arm, pulling him up with me. "Be quiet. Someone's approaching."

Kellan chuckled. "No shit, Indie," he whispered into my ear, licking the shell of it in the process. I really didn't want Zaidon; I wanted Kellan, but this mission was important. *What I wanted didn't matter.*

I didn't have time to ponder more on the subject when Zaidon stopped and stared directly at us through the mist. "Hello," he called. "Where are you?"

The seaplane was camouflaged with magnets, and we each carried one in our back pockets.

"Here, over here," I called low, hardly raising my voice. We stepped closer. As if suddenly seeing us, Zaidon snapped straight and quickly approached us. "It's us, Kellan and Draxton." The little man was daring. My mouth hung open. The dark, stubborn look in his eyes told me he was serious about coming along.

"Hello, I'm Kellan."

"Here." He handed Kellan a black suitcase, then he removed the one flung over his head and shoulder and gave me a stern nod.

"Hi, I'm Draxton."

"Nice to meet you face to face. Here, this is it. The drill." His cold, emotionless gaze left me short of breath, and like a pebble tossed into a pond, ripples of warnings reached me. I gave Kellan a look, and he smiled, greenlighting me, leaving me dumbfounded by Zaidon's coldness. I wanted to wipe that emotionless expression off his face, make him smile, and even cry, make him feel. Our hands touched. His fingers were cold and soft.

I tipped my head to Zaidon in greeting. "So, you decided you are coming along? We might not be able to bring you back. Heck, the plane might not even make it home."

"That's the deal. Don't worry, I have ways to find my way home. Harrison would find me if I didn't return." He narrowed his eyes, giving both Kellan and me a serious side-eye glance. "Let that be a warning if you decide to take me hostage, to trade for more equipment. Harrison has orders to let the authorities know and then they will come with an army and finally wipe your filthy vermin from the face of the earth. The invaders' words, not mine." He clucked his tongue, gave me a thumbs up, and winked.

He was such a little shit. Maybe he wanted to show us he knew how to be a crude, tough human like me. I let Zaidon take my usual seat in the front next to Kellan. I leaned inside to throw a thick coat over Zaidon's shoulders. He looked surprised at me. "Sit tight, our men will push us deeper into the ocean." I pointed to the rubber boat behind us. I jumped in and took a seat in the back. At least the laser drill was on the seat next to me in the back. And I planned to play with it.

"Do you do this when you come ashore every time?" he asked over his shoulder, all bright-eyed and nervous as he fidgeted with his coat sleeves, then sitting back like a little king on his throne. His shiny shoes and snappish uniform were not appropriate dress for this occasion.

"Yup, so far so good. Kellan is the expert," I answered just as Kellan joined us. He looked so serious and sexy in his homemade animal hide bomber jacket and goggles.

"Your authorities don't think we can fly, and their water mines have all been disabled a long time ago for a landing strip, thanks to your father."

"What do you usually do here, apart from searching for laser drills?"

"We trade meat or vegetables for medicines or whatever we need."

"Meat?"

"Yes, you would be surprised how many of your perfect people eat real meat and vegetables instead of your fake vitamin-infused drinks," Kellan said. I swore I could see a flick of the corners of his eyes, maybe to leave a smart-ass retort, but Zaidon said nothing. Hands folded on his lap, he sat up, as if he remembered not to show an ounce of emotion. Impeccable. He made me think of an iguana, ready to hiss or run into its hole.

"Where is the back door?" Zaidon asked with a look of someone riding a Ferris wheel for the first time.

"Don't worry, you won't fall out," Kellan waved his arm out his window, giving the signal and then we soundlessly drifted out of the bay to the open waters.

"Where are they going? Is that a boat?" Zaidon pointed to Simon's longship, resembling a Viking ship carved from wood.

"Look, they know exactly what to do," Kellan explained. He was impressed by Simon's setup. As soon as we neared the ship, two men ran across a beam overhanging the side. I assumed it's to hoist fishnets from the sea, and they jumped and flew through the air like old pirate sailors. One pulled the nose of the airplane away, so we didn't collide, while the other flipped the propeller. Suddenly, the engine roared to life, and we took off to the Dark Continent. Zaidon was speechless. He sat like that for four hours.

When we lowered altitude into the darkness, Zaidon turned his body slightly to Kellan, who wasn't saying a word, flying the plane without any instrumentation to evade the invaders. Kellan grunted, and I grunted back. *Yes, the little shit is scared of the dark.* I smelled the pretend courage wafting off him. He flicked me a look and turned his chin up.

I had opened the shoulder bag a while ago to put the drill together and was taking it apart again to pack back in the bag, checking if the little shit had actually given us the complete drill. I knew what I was doing because I had experience working with it, and Zaidon didn't know that I was imprisoned for nearly a month. At the end of a shift, we had to take it apart to clean it for the next shift. It was their most valuable tool, their bread and butter. That's also the reason I couldn't take it. "This thing better work. It better not be a dummy drill," I said, playing dumb.

Zaidon clutched the headrest, turning to the back and facing me. "What? Why would I come along, bringing a dummy drill? What is a dummy drill anyway? I've never heard of such a drill. I should know, my father designed and built the machinery."

I blinked at him. *How can he be so know-it-all, but truly not know anything at all at the same time?*

I shrugged at him, and he turned to face forward again. I watched him, and as we descended, he migrated to the edge of his seat, so his feet touched the floor while gripping the dashboard. "Are we falling? I can't see anything." He sounded like a nervous child, as if he had forgotten to play CEO for the first time during our flight.

Kellan shifted from side to side, and when he looked over his shoulder, I realized something was wrong. "We have a few miles to go before landing. The fuel is running out, and we've been flying on fumes. Soon we'll be gliding," he said. I wiped a hand over my face.

"Okay, time to get rid of the weight. I don't want to go down in the icy water. The sea is too rough to land on." I quickly packed the drill back into its bag, pushed it between the two front seats, and then turned to start unlocking the rear seats.

"What are you doing?" Zaidon shouted as I tossed his heavy suitcase out the door. "Those are my food, my steriliz-ing, and rejuvenation equipment. I need those!"

"No! You don't! Our lives are more important than enemas. Whatever you need, you can borrow from me," I shouted as I ripped and tossed the back seats out too.

"Just don't throw the laser drill out, because..." Zaidon began saying stupid shit.

"Shut up, I'm not an idiot!" I barked a retort just as the engine spat and sputtered and died. Silence and the whizzing of the wind filled the space inside the rattling airplane. I sat down on the floor and braced for impact. Zaidon white-knuckled the sides of his seat.

"That helped, Draxton. We'll make it," Kellan said.

Zaidon hyperventilated. "Do you know what you are doing? I see nothing but water!"

"I know where we are, I don't have to see to know it's there. You will see when we are gliding closer to the water, the land will appear. Look for small fires." He pointed to the left. "There's the coast, and in front is the Dark Continent. Look, it looks like little stars."

Zaidon's eyes flicked back and forth. I wanted to tell him to stand so he could see better. But as we glided closer, he exclaimed with an outstretched arm, "There it is! I see it, a line of fires. Draxton, there, do you see?" he shouted. I cringed. He sounded so boyish, so innocent, and was that excitement I heard? *So, he wasn't feelingless.*

"Draxton!" Zaidon called again, looking back and forth over his shoulder. "I see it, Draxton, the Dark Continent, I see it!"

Why did I feel I wanted to gather him into my arms and hug him?

Zaidon shifted in his seat, gazing in awe at the view below. "Finally, I get to see what my father had told us about. It's white as far as I can see! Look at that mountain range, it's higher than the Spire City towers. It looks like an old man looming in the darkness."

"Hahaha!" Kellan laughed. "You sure sound excited. It's the snow, it reflects light. Now sit back and hold on."

Zaidon scooted back in his seat and gave me a quick look,

his eyes wide with wonder and amazement. He gasped as we touched the bay water. Kellan steered the plane, and we drifted the rest of the way into the calm waters of the harbor, where Libre and his friends waited.

"Zaidon, don't forget to breathe, and whatever you do, don't stare. Don't say anything about these people being big, dirty, filthy, or dumb. It's best if you smile and say nothing for now, okay?" I said just as Kellan flattened the flaps and finally locked the yoke.

"Yes, that makes sense," Zaidon eagerly answered. I waved him over. He unbuckled his seat belt, jumped after taking my offered hand, and I helped him disembark.

"I need to piss," Kellan said, giving me the side-eye while disappearing around the tail of the airplane.

"Me too," I replied with a chin lift as an acknowledgment of our silent conversation. *Operation-Win-Over-Zaidon, activated.*

"I need a sterilization," Zaidon added.

Patting the small of his back, I stooped my neck to whisper in his ear, "I will help you with that later." His jaw dropped open as he stared and visibly shivered.

Kellan waved goodbye to me and then shouted, "Libre! Please bring that heavy bag." Libre pointed to the black shoulder bag where I'd tucked it between the pilot and passenger seats. "Yes, that! Please bring it to Snow. Then, go to Rocket and tell him we need fuel and back seats. That the fuel he'd cooked last was not enough." Libre nodded, then sprang up on the deck, bringing a thick rope with him to anchor the floating plane to the dock.

It sounded like Kellan had it all under control as he shouted orders at the boys helping Libre. I turned to give

Zaidon my full attention. Torch fires lit the pathways, casting enough light up the small hill where our new village waited for us. A thin layer of fresh snow covered the clay-domed roofs that stood in rows of five behind the small fish market and up the hill.

"Winter's here. It seems the snow is here to stay," Kellan noted my thoughts loudly to Libre.

"Yes, we are supposed to return to the winter cave, but my mother said to wait for you. My father agreed to wait a little longer because you are bringing the tunnel maker. Each one of us old enough to carry a weapon has been practicing, because most of us have never held a real sword. Spears and bows, yes, but that should not be the only weapon a man should carry in a battle. I can't wait to practice with a real sword, for now it's only wood, because we don't want to kill each other before the war starts. Come to the village square; you'll see us each day." Libre rambled loudly enough so we all could hear him.

"The little one comes with me," I said as I reached for Zaidon to help him up the gangplank. He was featherlight. My hands folded around his waist, my fingers touching as I picked him up and carried him to steady ground. *I must look like a giant to him.*

"Um, thank you," he said, straightening his clothes and hugging himself.

I tipped my new cowboy hat low. "You're welcome. I will get you some local clothes. It will help you blend in until everyone has had time to meet you."

"I need to use the facilities to sterilize, please."

I heard Kellan grunting behind us, and I knew he meant an *I-told-you-so.* I smiled slyly, and before I could say something sarcastic, I whirled around and said, "Come, I will show you where you can wash the dirt and grime off after sitting and doing nothing the whole day." *Okay, maybe less sarcastic than I first intended.* With his brow line deepening, Zaidon hesitantly jumped to follow me up the muddy road.

"Are you coming?" I asked Kellan, to make sure he truly wanted me to go through with our plan to make our guest comfortable—to win him over.

"Go on, I'll join you later. I'm going to see Snow to ask if he wants to go with me to deliver the drill to Ouro." Kellan stepped behind a stone wall, probably to have a piss.

"Okay, see you later." Then, for some stupid, inexplicable reason, it slipped out of my mouth before I knew what I was saying, "Love you, Kellan!" I slapped a hand over my mouth. What did I say? Why the fuck did I say it? *Draxton, you idiot. You just said I love you for the first time, with another man under your arm, while your lover was having a piss. So fucking romantic.*

I stopped walking and waited. There was a very long pause. I had to see how he would react. Either he heard me and was ignoring me, maybe pretending he didn't hear, or he genuinely didn't hear me. Damn, I didn't know what I was doing anymore.

"Love you back, two times more," he replied in a singsong from somewhere behind the wall. My heart, which had stopped for a second, started back up again, fluttering with joy.

"*Brrrr*, I can't believe how different the weather is from Spire City. Wow, you do live in the mud. Look at those huts, all squashed in, looking like a child tried to build them. Awful architecture," Zaidon said, breaking the weird, magical moment between me and Kellan.

Excuse me, I thought. I was proud of our accomplishments. But I kept it to myself. I was supposed to be nice to Zaidon, and that was going to be taxing for me. The more he spoke, the more I wanted to run to Kellan, but I had to listen to Zaidon. Be nice, be nice, I told myself.

I didn't even have headphones anymore.

I took a deep breath. "Yes, it's the polar opposite." I chuckled awkwardly. "Get it, north and south, we are opposites?" He pulled a face. "Here, cover yourself." I threw the fox pelt I'd brought with me from the plane around his neck and over his bald head.

"Thank you, yes, this is much warmer," he sniffed, "though it does smell a bit funny."

I lifted my knees and started a steady march up the muddy road. It did smell of pig and goat shit. I didn't know what to do about that, it is what it is, as my grandfather used to say. Halfway up the road, the little man heaved. It was his fault, he claimed to be a smart architect, so he should be smart enough to exercise. But Kellan asked me to be nice, so I decided to see things from Zaidon's perspective. He couldn't help being short and unfit, so maybe I should be kinder to him. With his short legs, he had to give two, maybe three leaps to one of my own, so I slowed my pace for him to catch up. "Do you want me to carry you?"

"I'm good, thank you, just a little out of practice."

"Out of practice," I said. "Where do you ever walk? I saw only tube trains and flying cars moving people about the past week."

"So, you've been spying?"

"Not spying, waiting."

"We have gyms, but it's not needed because our bodies get the exercise we need while sleeping."

"Now there's a load of shit if you ask me. Who the fuck exercises while sleeping?"

"We do, and it's called electro-muscle stimulation."

"Electro fooling yourselves, I say. Look at you, you can't even catch your breath."

"We've been walking uphill, for me it's like running."

"One more row, then a left, and my hut is the last one on the street. Five more minutes, can you handle that?"

"Yes, of course I can, I never said I can't handle it. You are the one who thinks I'm unfit. I'm merely breathing faster to provide oxygen to my body. It's normal when a person is running."

"Come here!" I scooped him up and threw him over my shoulder. I shouldn't have done that. He gave me one hard kick to my balls. "Fuck, that hurts," I shouted.

Suddenly, the door of Rocket's hut flung open. "Who's there? Draxton, are you back?"

Oh no, now everyone will want to come over.

"It's us, sorry. Go back to bed. Will talk tomorrow!"

"Draxton, is that you?" Rocket hollered, already coming toward us. I put Zaidon down and pushed him away.

"Go-go-go! It's not a time for introductions. Move those short legs," I whispered, but he stood frozen in place. "Go!" I whispered. "Run to the last hut." I pushed Zaidon and, thank the stars, he ran. "Rocket, I will talk to you tomorrow!"

"Shut the fuck up, Rocket! Draxton said he would talk tomorrow," Sopora yelled from inside her hut. I turned and hurriedly followed Zaidon, ignoring Rocket. I was worried more people would wake up and think coming over was a good idea.

Hands on knees, Zaidon waited for me at the door. "Go inside; the door is open."

"I can't just go into a stranger's home."

"It's my hut, and I told you to go in." I opened the door and shoved him inside, hoping no one was following us.

CHAPTER 9
CALLISTO

OLD SMOKE, EMPTY SILENCE, AND HAUNTING memories hung in the air. The hut felt lonely, and I longed for Draxton and Kellan to come back safely. The cold hearth waited for wood and fire, its empty belly as hungry as mine. It reminded me of Atlas—if he were here, he would have lit a fire, and we would have thrown a fat pig or two in there. The faces of my family and life before the invasion flickered in and out of my thoughts, and I must have drifted off because I started to dream.

I hit the ground with a deafening thud in the snow. I was hopping around like a ball when I came to a stop deep inside a snowbank hanging over a ledge.

A few minutes passed as I lay there, taking inventory of myself. After deciding I was alive, I got up. Not moving, I stared down the mountain. In the distance, branchless, dead trees stood like needles in the snow-covered valley, and beyond that, the gray-blue ocean swayed with white waves cresting. I sat down, surveying Anzulla and the frozen devastation.

I panicked, and no matter how hard and fast I tried to breathe, my lungs wouldn't fill. I swayed from side to side, panting until my breathing evened out.

Deciding if I wanted to see what waited for me in the white and charcoal reality, I sat back down, feeling sorry for myself, for agreeing to do this, and for all the devastation I couldn't prevent. I was stuck, and my only way out was to lie down and die or face my solitude until I could find Atlas.

I sat watching the ominous clouds that shrouded the sides of the cliffs. The same clouds I had been tumbling through.

I would have to find food and shelter, I thought, and I got up, just as fresh hard pellets of ice rained down.

I walked faster.

The further I walked, the lower the temperature dropped. It was by no means the comfortable, sweet air of Anzulla I used to know, but I had thick fur, wide paws, and long toenails, ideal for icy terrain.

I thought I heard Atlas's voice; it kept me going.

I trotted, searching, smelling, and waiting for a sign.

I sat down, looking up in hopelessness, searching for answers.

The one thing Atlas had asked of me, no matter how much I wanted to do it, was looking like an impossible thing to do. I wasn't going to find our fathers. I wasn't going to warn or save anyone.

I ventured down, my big paws sturdy. When I reached the ocean, I dove in, searching for fish. I swam, opened my eyes, and found a whole school. I ate until my stomach was full.

I sloshed around in the shallow water, starting to enjoy the feeling of ice and snow. I wasn't cold, and I felt better, as if I was meant to be here. I strolled along the rocky beach and then sat down, asking my brother to show me the way.

Suddenly, I saw two men plummeting from the sky, tumbling downwards before landing hard on the mountainside. Just beyond them, I noticed a cave, and what looked like people inside. I jumped, working myself into a jumping jog, zipping back up the mountain. I knew I had to help those men scurrying around and freezing.

"Thank you, brother," I said as hope filled me. I wasn't alone. Those two men needed me. They were as lost as I was.

I scaled the side of the mountain like a Titan of this ice-covered world, eager to help them. They were important. I was there because of them. They were the sign I was waiting for.

I enlarged my size, shielding them...guiding them, fulfilling my new purpose as I helped them to the cave for shelter—teeth chattering, moaning, and swearing.

A loud noise woke me—their airplane. I sat up, listening intently.

Joy surged through me. It was them, Draxton and Kellan.

Only a few more minutes and they'd be home.

The remnants of my dream lingered as I waited.

The doorknob turned, pulling me fully back to the present. Draxton and Kellan were home!

CHAPTER 10
KELLAN

I STRAINED, ARCHING MY BACK, AND PUSHED A THICK stream of urine out. The release made me shiver, and the sharp smell and steam rising from the rock covered in melting yellow snow was satisfying.

"Are you coming?" Draxton called as I stood cock in hand.

I peeked over the top of the seawall, and a pang of jealousy hit me as I saw the two of them waiting halfway up the small walkway heading home. If I hung around, Draxton wouldn't be able to connect with Zaidon as we'd planned. I ignored the possessiveness puckering my heart. "Go on, I'll join you later. I'm going to see Snow to ask if he wants to go with me to deliver the drill to Ouro." Gods, now I felt like crying. Like I'm losing him. I watched as my piss ran down the crack of the seawall back into the ocean—something I would never have done back home.

"Okay, see you later. Love you, Kellan!" Draxton shouted. I

froze midstream. Did I hear or imagine that? I looked sideways over my shoulders. No, I'd heard that, because those words reverberated into the misty darkness. Quick, say it back, before the moment was lost, I thought.

I cleared my throat and hollered casually into the night, "Love you back, two times more!" My entire body vibrated with joy. I hurriedly tucked my cock away, tied my drawstrings, and skipped around the wall to run to Draxton, to scoop him into my arms and kiss him. I skidded to a halt as Draxton bundled Zaidon up and threw an arm around his shoulder. My mood fizzled as I watched them walk up the hill, back to our hut, where he was most probably going to fuck in our bed. *I'm such an idiot.*

I could follow them. Yes, maybe I should. We could both try to befriend the enemy. Zaidon reminded me of a twinky young boy, which wasn't my type at all. I cringed; the thought was so uncomfortable, I doubted I could even get hard with him around. Now that I'd considered it, it was unfair of me to dump that on Draxton. But he didn't protest. Although he who protests too much...he really didn't protest at all.

Shit, I'd unintentionally forced his hand because of misplaced loyalty to Ouroboros and the fear of showing Draxton I was in love with him. Fuck, what have I done to myself and to the man I love? I'd sent him to sleep with the enemy.

I waited for Libre and the four boys as they came up the stairs from the deck below. I held out my hand. "I'll take that to Snow, thank you, boys."

"Oh, no problem. So, do you still need us to deliver the message to Rocket?" Libre asked as I stared vacantly up the road as Draxton picked Zaidon up and threw him fireman style over his shoulders just as they turned to our row of huts. *What the fuck have I done?*

"Kellan. Do we still have to go to Rocket!" Libre waved his hand in front of me to get my attention.

I winced, realizing I had made the biggest mistake of my life. I've managed to push the man I'd loved and yearned for, for months, right into another man's arms. The sick and twisted enemy's clutches. How did I not see that? He'd said he loved me, and now he'd want to show me how much. Just as he'd jumped out of the airplane to steal the tunnel maker... Gods, I should never have asked that of him.

"Kellan!"

"What?" I shouted with tight fists.

"Do we still have to go to Rocket?" Libre asked.

"Yes, please! I'll walk with you. I'm going to Snow's. I'm hoping to run into your father," I said and sighed, looking at my stupid feet walking up the stupid cobblestone road.

I should have turned toward my home, but my feet halted. Libre was talking, but all I registered were the silhouettes of Draxton and Zaidon disappearing into the fog on their way to the home we'd built for us. An ice-cold rush of regret hit me at a snail's pace, freezing my blood like cherry red Slush Puppy, and I zoned out.

"Happy dreams, Kellan!"

"Hmm." I realized I was being spoken to. Libre and the boys were waving, already at Rocket's door. I returned a wave, whispering, "Good night and thank you," then returned to watching my man. I should go home, I thought, but my feet weren't moving, because suddenly, the whole neighborhood was awake and shouting *hellos* and *welcome homes* at them. I retreated into the shadows to lurk longer like a lame panther in the darkness. Draxton put Zaidon playfully down, then patted his backside, telling him to run to our home at the end of the grove.

"I'll see you tomorrow, thanks. Sweet dreams," Draxton called out, then took off after Zaidon. He was actually enjoying himself, and with another man, all because of me. What was I trying to prove? That I wasn't some jealous, possessive, lovesick stalker who'd been obsessed with him way before we even met?

Loose rocks crushed beneath my feet. I stumbled, flailing my arms. "Gods, the fucking drill!" *I'm such a wussy nerd.*

I snuck further backward and waited until Draxton closed the door behind him.

"Ugh!" I sighed, shaking my head at myself, then reluctantly made my way up the rutted, narrow dirt footpath to Snow's isolated hut right on the far edge of the village, where beyond lay nothing but black and white patches of boulders, ruins, and mountains. He was seldom home, and even if I thought he might be here, I wouldn't knock, knowing the whole village was awake and could show up here if they noticed something exciting happening, like me, carrying their promised tunnel maker.

They knew Draxton and I had left on a mission to retrieve the drill, which Draxton had failed to bring the first time after spending a month in a prison colony. Knowing we were back was reason enough for everyone to come running, asking questions. That would lead to someone starting a fire, and the next thing, the whole village would be here. That's why

Draxton told Zaidon to run, of course. He wasn't playing; he was anxious to hide him. That thought made me feel a little better, but not enough to let it go.

I put the bag with the drill against the far wall out of the way once I snuck inside. Snow's place was simple. He grew up in a cave, so he was using that for reference. It was not like our home. It was a hut with a fireplace. Nothing fancy. In front of the hearth were bedrolls of furs and pillows strewn across the floor. Soft snoring came from under the heap of furs. Thank goodness, he was home. On second thought, it could be anyone, because sharing was second nature to these people. The coals were ashes, meaning whoever was sleeping had been sleeping for more than an hour or two already. I removed my boots, threw two pieces of chopped wood on the dying fire, fanned them a bit, then sagged down to sit cross-legged and stared into the flames for answers.

There was a stirring next to me, and then Snow's voice croaked, "Who's here?"

"It's Kellan. Go back to sleep. We can talk tomorrow," I said shortly, not in the mood to socialize.

Furs and pillows went flying. "Hey, brother, you're back! We received a crow message early yesterday, telling us you'd be arriving home tonight. Are you safe? Where is Draxton?"

I clucked my tongue, shaking my head with the deepest, troubled look on my face. "Not with me," I said sourly.

Snow snapped upright like a vampire emerging from its casket. The growing fire illuminated his messy white hair and wild eyebrows. "Don't tell me he had gotten himself arrested again!"

"No! Not that." I cracked a smile. Everyone was fond of

Draxton. "No, he is fine. Everything is fine." I threw a thumb over my shoulder. "The drill, it's there in the bag."

Snow tilted his head, looked at the bag and read the morbidity in the room. "Why do you look like he was cut up into pieces and fed to you?"

"Jesus, Snow, that's a horrific thing to think and say."

"You look like it." He scooted closer, surprising me by not diving for the bag as I thought he would do. "Tell Snow all about your fight. Did he kick you out of the furs?"

I ran my hand over my thick curly mane. Snow side-eyed me, waiting.

"No!" I scratched my beard. Fuck, I needed a shower, and the only shower in the village was in my home.

Snow chuckled. "You did something seriously wrong. Is Draxton alive and back home, or what?"

"Leave it, Snow."

"Okay. Have it your way." He wildly flung himself over to his side, facing away from me, and covering his head again. Signaling a fuck off.

I swallowed down the queasy knot in my throat and let out a defeated exhale, then continued searching the flames, but got no answers. I fed it again with a wood block, then lay back, lacing my fingers behind my head, staring up at the wonky-looking clay roof. I was so stupidly fucked.

"Whatever it is, Kellan, I think you are inflating it, like you usually do. Go to him, talk to him. It's probably not what you think it is." Snow's muffled whispers were correct. I was overreacting, I thought. Silence fell over us, and the fire crackled to life. Minutes later, soft snores came from underneath the furs.

"Draxton said he loves me…and I love him," I said. "We've

slept with you and Ouro, which didn't break us up. If anything, it brought us together. I wanted Draxton to feel he's not different, while hiding my true feelings. I'm not jealous. It's the fact that he'd said it, and I couldn't hold him and look into his eyes while saying it back. If anything, the little man might freak him out. I'd pushed this on Draxton. He was only doing what I asked, what I had suggested. I'm wondering if I should go to him. If he needs me, or is it me looking for an excuse because I need him? Maybe I should tell him I'm sorry and that I was wrong...." Silence, no snoring, came from the furs, so I assumed Snow was listening. "We have the drill, we don't need a spy or Zaidon or his cooperation."

I reached for my boots, getting up and putting them back on. "I'm going home. Then I'm going to take that little shit back to Spire. I don't want him near Draxton."

"What little shit?" came from under the furs.

"Fucking Zelk supporter. The mining magnate, Malherbe junior, is in my home with my man."

Snow jumped up. "You fucking did what?" In a blink, he had his spear pointing at me. *He looked ready to kill me.*

I lifted my hands. "Hey, I'm your friend, remember."

Snow narrowed his eyes at me. "Ouroboros is going to have a fit. You'd better get that man and remove him. If Ouro hears this, or sees him, he will kill him, and you, for bringing the enemy to our home where the children can get hurt, drill or not," Snow whispered, scowling and pointing his spear straight at me.

"Okay, I'm going! It's been bothering me this whole fucking time. I'd stupidly asked Draxton to befriend him after Zaidon said he'd bring the drill only if he could come with us."

"Kellan, what did you tell him? Why did you say we need the drill?" Snow grunted through clenched teeth, looking like a tokoloshe with white hair. Luckily, he'd stopped poking the spear in my direction but pointed it at the door.

"You should never have sent us alone! You know we are not from here. You know we don't know anything about this, but still you send us on these wild errands."

"Errands? You volunteered! Kellan, what did you tell them?"

I blew out a breath. "Draxton showed them his necklace—"

"No!" The spear was inches from my face again.

My heels and shoulder blades hit the wall behind me. *I had nowhere to go.* "Hey! Calm the fuck down! We didn't say it came from the mountain. We said children were playing out on the peninsula and found it in a stream. We said the tunnel maker is to help us drill caves into the mountain for shelter in the winter." I gulped nervously. *Did we really fuck this up?*

"You confirmed the crystal was here by showing it to them. Why do you think the Zelk mines diamonds and anything resembling them? They want the magic of the crystal. That's why the whole mountain is impenetrable and impossible to find. You went and put all their focus, all their attention, back on us! For over one hundred years, we've managed to keep it a secret. And you went and showed it to them!" He sputtered and pointed to the door again. Thank fuck. "And, then brought a Zelk right here where he can see and confirm it!"

"Umm, yeah, I see your point. That just confirms what I just said, we are not the fucking heroes you think we are. We are modernized, spoiled rotten, comfortable, and non-violent anti-war non-racist history-loving people who don't know anything about living in it or this war and weird Zelk alien things invading Earth while Atlantis is jumping all over the galaxy and meantime you and Ouro fuck your brains out to prevent human extinction!"

Snow's eyes narrowed, pinning me with a deadly look. "You'd better go get that stinking Zelk supporter," he growled, his jaw tight.

"Calm down, you sound like Callisto!"

"Callisto?"

"Zaidon claimed he wasn't Zelk, but a human," I explained, defending Draxton. Then the awful truth hit me, something I hadn't considered. We'd wronged these people, bringing the enemy to them, and he was in my hut, with my lover, in my bed.

"It doesn't matter what he'd said. He'd say anything to get more crystal."

"I will go get them, take Zaidon back, tell him...what should I say? It's dark, I can't say we are taking him sightseeing." I couldn't believe what I was about to propose. "Or do you want me to kill him?" I asked quickly, hoping he would do the job, because I wasn't a murderer. Killing animals for food was already traumatizing enough.

Snow narrowed his icy blue eyes, looking at the sharp point of his lethal weapon, then back at me, patronizingly with a questioning look. "Kill him?" His jaw dropped. "No, Kellan, if we kill him, more will come looking. Don't you know this thing in the sky tracks them?"

"You mean the fake ozone layer?"

"Yes, whatever it is. If Callisto hasn't mauled him yet, take him home. Be nice, thank him, and tell him...tell him the mountain is about to explode...Yes, tell him it's not safe. Tell him and Draxton, I just told you it rumbled and liquid fire is coming." Snow paced to the door and back. "I will find Ouro know, and let him know. We should start drilling right away. When they come looking for the crystal, we must be waiting and ready for war," he said, waving me out of his hut with the spear.

CHAPTER 11
ZAIDON

HORRIFYING GERMS FLOATED AROUND ME IN THE darkness while the stench of rot smothered me. I was afraid to touch anything, so I stood with my arms crossed in the pitch-blackness, smelling like intestines, while foreign emotions shouted at me to run.

With my feet planted, I wondered how I should react. *What should I say to sound friendly and accepting?*

I gulped back the ball of sick that threatened to spew out of my mouth. Draxton lit a candle, and the sweet smell of the melting wax masked the nauseating odoriferousness of the space.

Unsure of what to say, I stood still, shaking with cold and nerves. Every minute that ticked away, the further I traveled, the more I realized this was a much more daunting excursion than I had first anticipated. In the back of my mind, I could hear Harrison telling me that he'd told me so, that once I broke one small law, it would escalate, pushing me to break the next one, until I was forgotten in the darkness with no connection to the Zelk grid. I was already invisible, due to my tracer scramblers.

"*Grrrrr!*"

A low, throaty growl made me jump to the side. I reached for the doorknob, ready to run with my skin crawling and my heart racing, while Draxton laughed happily.

Wide-eyed, body vibrating, ice-cold and fearful, I asked, "What is that?"

Draxton smiled, gazing at the source of whatever made that noise on the floor. "How do you see in this low level of light given off by one dying candle?" I asked. I was used to bright lights, and Draxton seemed to see like an animal in the dark. "Draxton?" I whispered in question, fearing being attacked. "I've heard stories about creatures being born on the Dark Continent," I noted shakily, still eyeing the door and not sure of what to expect.

Draxton ignored me and went down on one knee. "There you are, come say hello to our guest."

A deep growl, a sound I've never heard, vibrated through my core. It promised me dismemberment by teeth and jaw. I blinked, not unaccustomed to the shivers of terror rattling my bones. I felt the same way when my father yelled for me to help him. It groaned, and a dark shadow emerged from the floor. Two bright blue eyes shone like elevator button lights, while the clack-clack-clacking of what I assumed were feet coming toward me sounded.

"Don't be scared," Draxton said, and I couldn't tell if he said that to me or the beast, because the beast didn't seem like he was comfortable with either of us here in his home. "This is my protector...actually, Kellan's too. Come here, boy,"

Draxton reached out to its face. The growling stopped, replaced by what sounded like happy gurgles. My headache was back with a vengeance. This level of stress will kill me. I blinked, trying to see the animal step into Draxton's waiting arms.

It sniffed and sneezed, followed by throaty breaths. More sniffing ensued, and then it emitted a strange chuffing noise. I couldn't quite see what it was. It sounded large and, by the height of its eyes, taller than I was. It was the source of the roasted meat and the smell of wet sand.

"W-wi-will it...eat me?" I stammered, wondering if the door was close enough to open and escape. I side-stepped, taking one, two, three small steps while my eyes flicked about, measuring my escape route.

Stiff-necked, I watched the gigantic animal stepping into the flickering candlelight.

"Ooh, you are soft and warm, aren't you, boy? You smell better. Did Sopora wash you?" Draxton rubbed his face into its pure white mane. I had no clue what it was. The animal puffed its foul, warm breath over us. Draxton obviously didn't have any sense of smell. Maybe not being able to smell is part of being human here in the stinky darkness. How else would they survive in conditions like these? "This is Callisto. Kellan and I adopted him, or no, he adopted us, first." Draxton scratched its head and behind the ears, and it closed its eyes, leaning into the loving administrations.

The beast, Callisto, licked Draxton's face.

Disgust, nausea, and terror knocked my breath out of me, and I clenched my jaw, digging my fingers into my upper arms, while sucking air through my teeth, and hugging myself. Draxton threw his arms around the animal's neck, rolling his face in its fur. I gasped again at the illegal animal, doing illegal things to Draxton, and both seemed to enjoy it. It made me sickly jealous.

I slapped a hand over my gaping mouth and said through shaking, cold fingers, "You let it lick you? The saliva, the teeth, the hair, the filth. I'm going to be sick. Where is your sterilizing room?" I asked, staving off regurgitation.

They broke their embrace, and Draxton got up from the dirty floor. "No, sorry, no sterilizing rooms here. We call them washrooms."

"Wa-wa...washrooms?" I uncrossed my arms, running my hands over my cold bald head, suddenly frightened of the conditions of that. I've heard stories of people defecating, getting up, and walking around as if they haven't dumped a load of germs.

I swallowed my nausea away. That airplane ride was stressful enough. I needed a cleansing, rejuvenation, and a new set of clothes. "Oh, no! My suitcase? You threw my suitcase out of the airplane." I shifted from one foot to the other and crossed my legs, my bladder was about to burst, I already had water in my eyes. The smells, the terror, and the bodily functions nagged at me. It worsened as I watched and waited for Draxton to fill a bowl with water.

"I hope you plan to wash your spit-slobbered hands and face?"

"You are a funny-funny man," Draxton chuckled. He turned to Callisto. "This is our guest, Zaidon, and he is about to learn what it is to be human," Draxton said as he dug into his shirt.

He stood up. "Let me show you how this can help us." He held the crystal he'd shown me the first night we met and led the way down the hallway, now lit by a bright light given off by the light-producing crystal. Draxton stooped his neck, and we entered a smaller dome through a low arch, where he removed the necklace and put the light source on a narrow shelf above a basin, then turned to me with a wide smile.

"Time to show you how the human body is supposed to be emptied."

I looked up wordlessly as the giant squeezed by me with his arms in the air, maneuvering himself around me, careful not to touch me. He cleared his throat, grabbed hold of my shoulder, and gave a gentle squeeze, then dropped his hand as I stared up at him, my full bladder forgotten, while I waited to see what was going to happen next.

I heard him loosen his belt buckle on my right, he elbowed me in the ear, and quickly moved to the side. "It's claustrophobically small in here," I yelped. He made a throaty sound. I wanted to see, but I melted into the wall on my left. He waited, standing stock still. I leaned over to see what he was doing. Slowly, he reached into the front of his pants, fiddled around, and I froze as he suddenly stood with his big, flabby pissing thing in his hand. He was tall, and it made sense that it was almost longer than my forearm, I thought, and swallowed nervously. I couldn't believe what was happening to me.

He was still waiting for me to look more. Dark stubble surrounded his thick reproductive organ. It was the same color as the hair on his face and the shadow of hair I'd seen on his head. This was another huge hygiene issue. I'd better stop counting because I'm going to pass out measuring this level of uncleanliness. The amount of germs in one drop of sweat coming from this man's body wouldn't fit under a microscope.

He gave a small grunt. My mouth was hanging open. I snapped it closed. He appeared uncomfortable but did his best to teach me in their way. The whites of his teeth and eyeballs glowed bright in the artificial light. I tried my best to hide my astonished, disgusted face. "What are you doing?"

He grunted again. "Look, I'm trying to urinate. Learn how to do it because I'm not showing you again. Kellan should be doing this stuff, but now you have me, so concentrate. I'm not a teacher or a professor like him. We don't have your BDSM sterilization machines here in this village. Come to think of it, this is the only fucking toilet on the whole continent. So go vanilla and piss, for fuck's sake."

I looked from his death glare to his hands. They were dirty before he touched his pissing thing. He was aiming at the weirdest, smelliest, receptacle chair thing as he held *his very thick manhood*. Thick, thick, thick…a nervous knot formed in my throat, and I gulped to push it down.

"Now, look and learn," he said, and the sound of water resonated up from below as he leaked like a fountain. The smell of sweet rotten fruit and ammonia made me see double, and I grabbed for the wall to steady myself.

"That's just wrong. So wrong. So backward. No, I can't do this. Are you sure you don't have a sterilizer or rejuvenator?"

"No, here you take a piss, shit, and shower like a human." His tone was crudely aggressive. The sound of the water rushing into the receptacle urged me to take notice of my full bladder. "This is barbaric," I muttered, but the urine stinging inside my pissing thing was already starting to drip.

I reached down and squeezed. Pinching it closed. "This is

why I came with you. I wanted to experience this. I wanted to do this!" I felt brave, like I was about to jump off a cliff. I'd felt like that when I'd stolen the laser drill, and before that, when I'd stopped taking my suppressants. I was growing into a liar, a traitorous thief. I'd waited under the pier for Draxton, and I'd climbed into that ancient airplane. Every step since I met him was so wrong, but so right, and I can't say the feeling is lessening. I was breaking basic rules of hygiene. Laws that could cost me my life. I could be put to the forever death with no connection to the everlasting collective Zelk hive. My mind and soul wouldn't join the others. Each law I broke was a step down into the mud, and I was already going to serve so many life sentences that I should pull myself together and do what I came here to do. I should join Draxton urinating.

"It's not barbaric. It's a normal bodily function. You are human. You piss and shit from the day you are born until you die. Let go and piss like a man," Draxton urged me with an irritated, commanding tone.

A high-pitched noise escaped me. "Hmmm, okay." I didn't hesitate any longer. That commanding voice pressed me to do as he said. With a hint of amusement in his dark eyes, he met mine. That strange pulsating heat rushed up through my tummy. A chuckle bubbled up from inside me, completely catching me off guard, and I enlarged my eyes.

My suppressants. It must be because I'd stopped fully taking them after meeting Draxton. I let go of the tip I'd been pinching, aimed down, took a deep breath, and relaxed. A flash of memory shot through my mind. I was doing something I hadn't done since I was a little boy.

The stream stung, but not as much as the sterilizer titanium rods. The urine burst out of me. The feeling of relief, like an itch being scratched, gave me goosebumps as it ran down my spine. It was freeing. At first, there was stunned silence as Draxton watched me empty my bladder, but once our eyes met, the ridiculousness of what was happening wiped away all seriousness.

"My stream's bigger than yours," he said, smiling. I was sure he was teasing me. It was another quirk I hadn't figured out yet. Harrison was the only one I trusted enough to joke with, but it never came out this funny. I felt light and confident enough to try a comeback.

"Don't make me lose my concentration," I said, and turned my body as if aiming for him.

"Hey, look where you go!" He chuckled, and I quickly aimed back at the receptacle.

"What's the reason your receptacle looks like a chair?" I asked because I suspected what was coming next, but he tucked his thing into his pants and turned to wash his hands. Thank Apsu, I thought. That calmed my nerves a bit about touching ourselves down there. I was a wildling now, so I copied Draxton, returned my pissing thing to my crotch, pulled back up my suit pants, and then commenced the hand-washing routine.

"It's not a chair, it's a toilet. Humans piss and take a dump in a toilet."

So that's what they call emptying their intestines.

"Hmmm, that thing you do when you actually eat real food and the byproducts have to be dumped. That little hole in your butt is for that...and maybe other things..."

"Other things, too?

"I guess you Spire citizens wouldn't know because you plug in at night and let your bodies rejuvenate. You can't get aroused because you are pumped full of hormones. Do you push tubes into your holes yourself, or do the machines take over and suck it out for you when you are unconscious?"

"Something like that. We sleep inside the rejuvenator. As soon as we shut it and get comfortable, the system takes over. We relax as we are put into a deep sleep. Our bodies are sterilized and emptied, our energy levels restored, and yes, I guess all waste products are removed. That's why we don't have body hair. It is all part of removing the outer layer of our skin and cleansing ourselves. However, during the day cycle, we have to repeat the process consciously because we are being productive."

"Sounds to me like you are slowly being made non-human. Alright, let's eat, and then I will show you where you can sleep. I'm starving. I haven't had a decent meal in more than a week."

We returned to the domed area of the home, and Draxton went over to the kitchen area. Callisto lay on his pillow, his blue eyes following me like little hoverbot lights. I sat down at the long table with two low chairs. His hut was different from what I'd imagined. Everything was in shades of brown. The roof and the walls seem to be some natural dried substance.

"Is this dried mud?" I asked.

"Yes, it is. It can withstand thousands of years of harsh weather conditions. Maybe not flooding," he said.

Ten people could sit around this table, and the chairs were simple round disks with three sticks for legs. My eyes drifted inquisitively to see what else was here. More of those low three-legged chairs were moved out of the way and stowed on one side of a big opening in the wall and roof where a small fire burned. Next to that was Callisto's bed.

There wasn't much else except for wooden and clay utensils. Two cups, two plates, two pots, made of silver metal, probably stainless steel, and stolen from the Light Continent, were waiting on the far side of the table. Although packed with germs, the space felt warm and welcoming. Not at all, like my home.

"What's that?" I pointed to a rusted box about my size, excitedly. I wondered if maybe it's an old rejuvenator.

"An old refrigerator," Draxton said. "It doesn't work anymore. We don't have electricity, but it's still good to keep the bugs out and the food fresh for longer." He opened a bottle and poured something into the cups, and pushed one over to me.

I sniffed it, and it didn't smell bad. So, I took a sip as he watched me. It tasted both bitter and sweet at the same time. It was a struggle not to make a puckered face. I didn't want to offend him. "This is…"

"Fermented potatoes. It's an alcoholic drink. Do you like it?" He waited for an answer as I took another small sip. That time, I coughed as it burned my throat.

"Careful," he warned. "Better not drink too much at once. Maybe that's enough for you tonight. Sopora never let Libre or his friends have more than one sip. You are his size, so I assume your liver is their size too. Plus, I have no idea how you will react to it."

"How do *you* react to it?"

"It relaxes me, and if I drink too much of it, well, let's just say, I'm ill-coordinated, loud, and very happy. Until I pass out, sleep, and wake up sick with a hangover."

"Then why do you drink it?"

"You will see, once you get used to it, it can be fun. We use it to celebrate and be merry. Basically, for any occasion, we want to be social with people. Like you and me now."

I pointed to my chest and back at him. "We are social now, aren't we?"

"Yes, that we are." He stared at his hands as if thinking deeply for a few seconds. He did that a lot. I used the time to see if Callisto had stopped watching me. No, he was still drilling holes into my back with those eyes. He shuffled his big body as if getting ready to get up. Quickly, I turned away, showing him no interest.

"*Grrrr*," he rumbled behind me.

Draxton got up. "Hmmm, yes, I'm boiling potatoes and making you a meal to chew and swallow. I'm not feeding you meat or vegetables, not yet. I will have to feed you small amounts. I don't want you to have a tummy ache, although I think that is inevitable. Just mashed potatoes for us tonight, something soft and bland. I will introduce food to you like we do with babies."

I sat up straight and smiled. "Whatever, I trust you."

"So fast?"

"I do, otherwise, I would never have followed you here. The authorities say you live like animals, fighting for food scraps. But my father told me about this place and its history. I always wished I could come and see it; it sounded exciting and mysterious. My father said the smart and brave live here. I want to be brave, like you."

"Hmmm," Draxton grunted. He used a knife to remove the outer shell of what looked like rocks.

"Can I see it?" I held out my hand. I couldn't believe I was going to touch food with my bare hands.

"Sure, feel it, and smell it. It comes from the ground. We

planted them in the grove early this summer, but these come from the winter cave. It's very popular here because it likes to grow in wet soil. We boil it, grind it into powder, mash it…"

I interrupted. "Make drinks from it."

"You learn fast," he said, taking it back from me and peeling it with a long, shiny knife.

"Po-ta-to. Potato," I said repeatedly because it sounded funny to me.

Strangely, it was the best dinner I'd ever enjoyed. His potatoes tasted nothing like rocks. It was salty, and when he added what he called butter to it, it tasted even better. At first, my eyes watered, and my nose flooded as I spat and coughed after my second bite. In my defense, I'd forgotten how it felt to chew my food. Afterwards, he'd shown me a heap of stinky animal pelts and told me that was my bed.

LATER THAT NIGHT, I couldn't sleep. I didn't know how to fall asleep outside my rejuvenator. I even wondered about getting into that 're-fri-ge-rator,' as he'd called it.

I'd gotten up twice, to try to get my pissing thing to work on my own, but I couldn't, so I returned to my bed. The third time, on my way back, I tiptoed to sneak a look at Draxton and Callisto. The animal stirred, while his eyes were still on me.

Draxton muttered something, but he did turn my way. He wasn't covered, so I stole a few glances at his big, muscled body, and swallowed a mouthful of saliva, just as I did seeing and smelling those potatoes.

His one arm was folded underneath his head, like I've

heard of humans sleeping on their sides. The other arm rested on his side.

He stirred again, and I turned to climb back into my bed on the ground. Suddenly, he was scratching his chest and mumbling. He was a sight. My pissing thing twitched in my pants. Feeling warm and pulsating. I rubbed my palm illegally over it.

The thing was standing up straight and hard like my index finger.

I jumped up, threw the blankets aside, and returned to the washroom. I washed my hands, slapped cold water over my face, and stood there, not knowing what to do with this pissing thing and unsure what to do with my problematic feelings.

Should I wake Draxton and ask him?

I don't have a sterilizer, rejuvenator, or suppressant.

I squeezed the hard, offending appendage. "What's wrong with it? Did it want me to piss again? Or...did my body want to make babies? Babies were illegal." I sighed. This pissing thing was becoming a nagging problem. I took it out of my pants, but no matter how much I pushed and squeezed, no leaking happened.

"Come on, piss! Piss you pissing ding-dong thing," I grunted, wiggling the stock hard, angry-looking organ.

"Zaidon, what's going on? Why are you talking to yourself? Do you have stomach cramps? I knew you shouldn't have eaten a second helping," Draxton said, scratching his belly, wearing very small, short pants, watching me in the dark.

I felt like crying. "My ding-dong penis thing is broken. I can't piss, and it's hard. It's blowing up like a balloon because

I don't have a sterilizer, a rejuvenator, or a suppressant. It wants to make babies, I think. This is why it's against the law to do these things. I packed everything, even a mobile sterilizer, and now it's floating somewhere in the ocean. It feels like I want to burst open. It's itching on the inside, I want to scratch it, but I can't. The sterilizer rods can, but I don't have it, and now I can't piss!"

Draxton didn't say anything. He just stood like a statue, while looking at my defective ding-dong pissing thing.

"Draxton, please say something. I want to do something. Like, break it off, or pull on it, or maybe I should stick something inside it? It's painful!" In the dark, I saw Draxton's body twitching as he pressed his lips together. His eyes told me he wanted to laugh.

"Pull on it, and try to break it, let's see what happens," he said after he collected himself.

"What? Here? In front of you?"

"Yeah, sure. Show me," he said, and now his voice was more profound and serious.

I wrapped my fingers around it, strangling it. "Draxton, I think I'm dying, and not my ding-dong!" I cried, feeling weird with an urgency I didn't know a man like me could handle. "I think I'm about to pop or should pop. I'm dying, and I never saw your continent or spoke to anyone. I don't know where you got that crystal. What a sad and terrible way to die of ding-dong penis pain."

"Please stop saying ding-dong. It's a cock!" Draxton blurted, holding his tummy as he exploded, laughing at me.

I'd never seen or heard anything more beautiful than him being amused. I wanted to hear and see more of it. I started laughing with him. After I'd collected myself, the thing in my hand softened.

Suddenly, it wasn't as funny as I thought. My lips curled down. My ears swooshed, and another type of pressure built up inside me. My tear ducts stung, my vision blurred...oh no, now my eyes were leaking and not my pissing thing. I looked up at him.

"I'm pathetic at being human," I cried.

Draxton stopped laughing and hesitantly scratched his head. "Damnit! Why is Kellan not here?" He whispered into the darkness. "Callisto, go get Kellan, tell him..."

I cried louder. "I'm a defective human!" I put my deflated reproductive organ away.

Draxton was looking away, talking to himself.

I cleared my throat. "Draxton!"

He flung himself around. "Oh, I'm so fucking sorry. Zaidon, please come here." He opened his arms, and I let my head fall against his broad chest. My eyes sprayed water all over him. I cried more. *His nipples were pink.* I ran my flat hand over his rippling abdominal muscles, and I felt the cold drops of tears splashing over my naked feet.

Overwhelming feelings and questions overflowed and flooded my being, swooshing, crushing, and cutting a path through my chest, confusing my mind. *Shame.*

Blazing heat followed by an ugly guttural wail exploded out of the depths of my heart. I tilted my head, trying to contain the waterworks of snot and tears.

"Shhh," Draxton cooed, and before I could protest, my face was pressed deeper into his stubbled, hairy chest. I scratched my nose clean as I smeared viscous tracks from one nipple to the other. It was warm, and he was smothering me between his two pink nipples.

Nipples, nipples, nipples!

All I saw were perfectly round nipples. But the tighter he hugged, the louder the excruciating sounds bellowed from inside me.

"Let it all out. Cry. I got you." I pushed him back to refill my empty lungs.

"Bleh-he-he-he?" The horrible sounds blurted out of me. I wiped my nose. "Bleh-he-he! I don't cry. I don't know how to cry-y-y-y!" I sniffled.

"Really, then I must not know what crying looks like. Because to me..."

"Bleh-he-he-he," I interrupted, falling into him and throwing my arms around his hips. He patted my head and dragged me with him to the huge hump of fur, where he'd been sleeping in front of a fireplace. He folded my legs and picked me up. *Holding me and smothering me again between his pink nipples.*

"What is this? What is wrong with me? Something is wrong with me. I'm broken. I think I'm dying of depression. Yes, that's it. I picked up a virus. Is my nose bleeding? Is blood coming from my eyes?" I rambled.

For some inexplicable reason, I found relief as I melted into Draxton, letting him envelop me with his long arms and big warm hands. I didn't mind as he stroked me and petted me. It felt so good—between his perfectly pink nipples.

I felt so conflicted—relief and fear—all at once.

As if hearing my thoughts, Draxton said, "Everything will be alright. You are safe. This is being human. This is how it should be." He cooed, and I liked it...*my penis pissing cock thing too!*

"Bleh-eh-he!" I shook my head, crying.

"It's okay. Cry, and once you feel better, we can talk, but for now, cry, and I will hold you until you say you are done," he told me.

"Callisto, go get Kellan. I'm not asking you again," Draxton said with urgency, his voice rumbled in his chest cavity, and I snuggled my ear against his chest.

I cried and cried and cried. Until my eyelids shut and I fell asleep in Draxton's strong arms.

CHAPTER 12
KELLAN

LIKE A THIEF IN THE NIGHT, I WANDERED AROUND THE village, going back and forth, up and down, around and around the hut, all over the village, except into our home.

I hunkered down, waiting for Draxton to wake up. With my back against the wall and my legs pulled up, I hugged my knees while resting my forehead on my kneecaps. I'd finished five rounds of patrolling the well-trodden path Callisto had trampled around the house. That must have been what he was doing while waiting for us to finish fucking? Sadly, I understood how he felt.

It was depressingly cold and quiet in the village. Everyone was peacefully asleep, but not me. No insects buzzed, stung, fluttered, or crawled; it was deadly silent, unlike the stuffy nights in Soweto, back home in South Africa. The ground was cold, and after an hour of sitting on it, I remembered my mom always saying sitting on the cold ground would give you hemorrhoids. So I got up again and decided to do a couple of additional security checks, thinking, if Draxton was still not up, then I should go and wait for daybreak in the airplane.

The first two rounds were slow and lengthy, so I decided to check on Draxton, just to be sure. If he was still asleep, I'd wait for him at the docks. I really needed to rest; I was exhausted, and if we were heading back to the Light Continent to drop Zaidon off, I should be well-rested.

With my back against the wall, I inched closer to the door opening, like I did earlier, but this time I was going to crack it open, just wide enough for one eye to peek inside.

Our door, like everyone else's, wasn't on hinges. It was a piece of wood resting against the doorway. It scraped the ground, making a sound like sawing glass. I cursed wordlessly, shoulders shrugging an *oopsy*, and then the smell of Callisto's warm breath greeted me as he nudged the door open wider. I ignored him, poking my head around his big face.

My eyes immediately went to our furs on the other end of our modest kitchen table, near the hearth. Dizziness struck as the tension I'd been carrying around eased away at the realization that Draxton and Zaidon were sleeping apart.

Callisto's head snapped from me to Draxton, then back again, as if saying, *See, he is alright, now go or come in. It's cold, close the door.*

He sniffed me lightly, a long, quiet, indrawn breath, as if he could smell the angst and panic I'd be wearing like cologne lately. His crystal blue eyes shone angry bright, daggers, and he looked ready to scoop me up and toss my sad ass over his head.

"Yes-yes. I know," I whispered, placating with my hands. "I'm going to wait on the airplane; my ass is freezing out here."

He gave me a bear whisper, answering with a soft sneeze and a chuff.

"I'm not coming inside. I will return with daybreak, okay?"

He shook his head once, agreeing with me.

I gasped and sank to my knees as Zaidon suddenly jumped up, flying from his furs like a man possessed by an incubus. I melted into the shadows, evaluating his intentions with my man. *My* Draxton.

I was set to confront him, ready to unleash a possessive, "what the fuck do you think you're doing?" when a sharp, high-pitched sound pierced my head, simultaneously deafening and blinding me. The pain was so intense I went blind for a moment, an ice-pick stabbing upwards, straight through my brain, a clean slash from my medulla oblongata to my frontal cortex. *Bloody hell!* I pressed my palms against my eyelids. Gods, it felt like a brain freeze.

Everything went quiet, and then I heard a voice, like Libre's, but not exactly.

"*Get down, Kellan, stay where you are,*" the boyish voice said as Zaidon ran straight into the washroom. *Who had just spoken to me?*

I searched over my shoulders outside. Seeing no one, my jaw dropped as I made eye contact with Callisto. He puffed out his chest and sighed at me, his black nostrils flaring. It was just him and me here. "*It was me,*" said the sweet voice.

Tears started to stream from my eyes. What a beautiful moment, and Draxton was sleeping. I should wake him and tell him. Pointing a finger at my forehead, I mouthed to Callisto, "*Was that really you?*"

"*Yes, it's me, how many times should I confirm that for*

you?" His voice vibrated like a chorister singing Ave Maria in my skull. "*Leave him. He's tired. You can tell him later,*" his boyish voice reprimanded me. Callisto gave me another icy look, then tilted his head to the opposite side as if listening for Zaidon returning. From his angle, he could see into the smaller dome I'd attached to the side of our original hut to serve as an addendum washroom.

"*What's he doing in the washroom?*" I asked the obvious, as if people did anything else in there. Callisto closed his eyes, like he was rolling them at me. "*Is Draxton safe?*" I asked. Callisto gave an exasperated chuff, then jerked his head to the side as Zaidon returned, and stopped dead with a small gasp and covered his mouth.

Oops! I slid back down to my knees, nearly biting my bottom lip in half. Callisto growled softly. I waited, wondering if I should take a peek, but another soft *grrr* answered that question.

I just had to look, what if Zaidon decided to cut Draxton's throat while he was asleep?

Carefully, I lifted my head. Callisto stepped forward, hiding me behind his big, jiggling bear butt. He growled at Zaidon. I fell to my tummy, hiding and checking around Callisto's paws. I saw no weapon, and I doubted Zaidon could throttle Draxton; his hands were too tiny. He stood unmoving, not seeing me but staring at Draxton sleeping, like a fucking creep. *I will wring his thin chicken neck, I swear I will if he does something to Draxton in his sleep. If he touches him...*

Callisto puffed a loud, explosive breath—a warning as he mimicked getting ready to pounce—Zaidon snapped out of his trance. He knew he was having unholy...no, illegal thoughts. Guiltily, he climbed back into bed, scooting down and taking loud, short breaths.

Callisto settled and gave me an exasperated look.

"*I got this, Kellan. Either come in or go, but don't wake Draxton, or I will wring your neck with my teeth*," Callisto whispered the warning in my head.

I shrugged and gave him an eyebrow whip, then narrowed my eyes. "*Now, you talk to me?*"

He gave me a shrug, then continued keeping an eye on Draxton. I closed my eyes and attempted my first mind-to-mind conversation. Concentrating on thinking the words, I said, "*We'll talk about this later.*" But he ignored me. "*I'm going to the docks. I'll be back in a few,*" I told him, pushing myself up on my feet and reversing out of there like a duck, ass up, head down.

I should have gone to bed with Draxton, but I wanted to give him space. Now that I knew he wasn't sleeping with the man-child, my nerves eased a bit. Callisto had reached out to me mentally and spoken. I smiled; it was amazing. He sounded young, which made sense since he'd jumped forward in time. He was young when Anzulla was invaded. His size had thrown me off. If I'd known Callisto was that young, I would have treated him differently when he feared getting on the seaplane, or when Draxton had jumped out of it to skydive down to the prison. I had spoken down to Callisto, but he was just a boy. He was correct about Draxton and me; we'd been awake for over two days. The little we'd managed to sleep while waiting for Zaidon was not enough. I should shut my eyes and sleep.

When I passed Rocket's hut, I heard movement and saw light under his door. I'd knocked but smelled the fuel wafting out and thought, I'm not going to bother him; he was already busy. Libre and the others must have given him the message. I wasn't in the mood to dawdle or have small talk; I wanted to hold onto my fluttery, happy feelings. It'd been one hell of an eventful night. A bear communicated with me telepathically, and the man I've longed for said he loved me. I never thought I'd hear those words from him. I felt like jumping and clicking my heels as I skipped to the docks with the broadest smile and my hands in my pockets.

Come daylight, when everyone was awake, I planned to talk to Draxton and get Zaidon out of there before Ouroboros found him and started yelling at us. I didn't think he'd kill us, and I didn't care if he killed Zaidon, but I didn't want him to make Draxton feel like he'd failed, no matter how he phrased it. I knew Draxton felt he had something to prove. He liked to show off and be independent, and I wouldn't take that away from him. Besides, Draxton and Zaidon were just sleeping, not having sex, and after Callisto rescued him from the mines, I trusted him with Draxton's life.

When I reached the docks, the wind and snow had calmed down, just like me. The wooden platform creaked, and the water sloshed against the sides of the small fishing boat, *knock, knock, knocking* against the side of the airplane. I sighed, grabbed onto the rail, and slipped into my seat to get comfortable, and although it was cold, my fur coat was toasty. The salty tang of the sea air, mixed with the faint scent of fish, filled me as I took a deep, calming breath through my nose. The rhythmic creaking of the boat and airplane, along with the lapping of waves, lulled me into a calm state, just like I used to fall asleep when my father was driving. The tune of the song my father used to play in the car when we went on one of our many excursions popped into my mind.

The chorus of the song by Bad Company, "Feel Like Making Love."

Baby, if I think about you, I think about love.
Darling, if I live without you, I live without love.
And if I had the sun and moon, and they were shining,
I would give you both night and day...

THE COLD BIT at my exposed cheeks, but the fur's warmth cocooned me, and a quiet anticipation settled over me.

THE WAILING of a child pulled me from sleep, and I sat up, wide awake, listening. That was not a child, but a man wailing. I knew that irritating voice; I would recognize it anywhere. It had ground my nerves all the way from the Light Continent.

I jumped out of the plane. Shot halfway up the gangplank, stopped, and wondered what Draxton would think if I came running like that.

Damnit! Fuck this! I might as well go and wait at the house, in case Draxton needed me.

By the time I reached home, panting, all was quiet again, and I was a mess.

I started pacing again.

After I rounded the hut twice, I decided it was time; I would sit down, hemorrhoids or not.

I waited. Listening. Soft sniffles drifted from inside. Draxton's voice murmured low and soothing. For a man with autism, he was very capable of expressing empathy. He was comforting Zaidon. Despite my craziness earlier, I knew I'd made the right choice by hearing him. He would make a wonderful father one day, and I imagined how he would get all excited, telling his child how he'd wanted to meet the advanced race and how he did it.

But...as soon as daybreak came, I would tell him I was sorry and *kiss* him.

I rested my forehead on my knees, relaxing. Sleep finally claimed me.

A cough, "huh...um," and guttural throat clearing woke me. My eyes fluttered open. Seeing shuffling boots, I shot awake, but fell to the side as I tried to jump up, flailing. My legs were numb and not cooperating. Panic surged, and a harsh growl told me Callisto was close. I craned my neck, looking up into Draxton's perplexed, scowling face.

"Callisto, go watch Zaidon." Draxton pointed the way. The bear barked softly and then turned to leave me alone with my man while I twitched like a stranded jellyfish—all tentacles but no movement.

"Morning," I said as I pushed myself up, dusted off my frozen ass, and smiled.

"Why in the ever...You know what...I don't even want to fucking know..." Draxton said, waving at me from my head to my feet, repeatedly, his eyebrows knitting into a glower. "For someone with a professorship at the most prestigious university in South Africa...Kellan, what the fuck are you doing?"

"Um...It's a long story," I muttered. "But I didn't want to impose...I know it was my idea, and I'm sorry. You said you *loved* me, and I wanted to be here. I wanted to say it's not really what I want...Umm...for you to be here and doing this for me...for us...um...for Ouroboros. What I mean is I can help you...Anyway, Snow said to get Zaidon home before Ouro found out about us bringing the enemy here...um..." I rambled, scratching my head and rubbing my face. This was not coming out of my mouth in the correct sequence. "Actually, it's dangerous here in the village; the mountain spewed lava yesterday, and we have to get Zaidon away from the Dark Continent...take him back...to safety. That's what we are going with...yes."

Draxton looked at me bemused.

Without asking for permission, I fell into him, threw my arms around his neck, and started kissing him. He stiffened but caught me on my hips. He would know I *loved* him. If I kissed him and showed him I wanted him, he would know, I thought as I kissed him aggressively. Not asking or waiting, I forced my tongue between his lips. At first, I could tell I'd caught him by surprise, but he spun me around and pushed me up against the hut, kissing me back. When we broke the kiss, Draxton smiled. "Thank the heavens, you are smiling. I was so worried and waited the whole night for you," I said breathlessly.

"For this?" His eyes crinkled at the corners, and he ground his hips against mine.

"Yes, that, but, but, but...I came to tell you, we have to bring him back to the Light Continent," I said before I forgot.

"Kellan, I got this. Stop worrying about me."

"I'm not worried. I'm...honestly...a bit jealous, but not in a way that you won't like. I promise. I don't want you to think I own or order you, or expect you to do these things for me. I want you to do them because I know you can."

Draxton gave me a look. "Kellan, I know."

"Really?"

He gave me a crooked smile. "Yes. I know...and I know, you love me. Come with me; I need to get Zaidon some clean, local clothes from Sopora. I also want to ask her about teenagers—Zaidon's moods, his hormones. I can't talk to him about that, and judging from his tears and confusion, he needs the gentle touch of an experienced mother today. He may be an adult, but his development is so stunted, he's got the emotional intelligence of a ten-year-old."

"But, he has to go!"

"I know...but, I'm telling you so we could do that together, are you coming with me?" he asked. "If we're nice to him, he will think twice about hurting us. Don't you agree? So, let's go."

"Um..." I said hesitantly. Draxton actually had it all sorted, and I was overreacting. I jumped and kissed him again. He laughed. I felt high. Happily high. So I said, "I will wait for you at the docks. I'll get the plane ready and fueled up. I trust you."

We kissed again, melting into each other. His mouth tasted of potato ale. "Tell him about the lava, or say we are going sightseeing," I said heatedly into his open mouth. His eyes were dark, and rubbing together had both of us hard. "Time to go, otherwise I might not leave. Snow said if Ouro found him here, he would kill him. It was dangerous to bring him here. We shouldn't have shown him the crystal. I'm serious. We are putting all these people in danger by having him here."

Draxton shook his head. "He told me no one can find him.

His tracer scramblers are hiding his location from the Zelk. But yeah, I don't trust him either. We got the laser drill, and he saw the Dark Continent. I'll play along and steer him home."

"Doesn't matter if he says he can't be traced. You are right not to trust him. Snow wants him gone. They want to start drilling. Zaidon is not welcome; he must leave, or they will kill him. Having him here is dangerous." I reluctantly let go of Draxton and backtracked down the path.

He waved. "Don't worry. See you later, Professor!"

I jumped back into his arms, suddenly remembering why I was really there. "Love you, see you soon?" I asked, kissing him again.

He pulled me close, his arms tightening around me. "I love you more," he chuckled softly.

"Okay, I'm really going now. Don't make me wait too long, please."

"Give me a couple of hours. You get the plane ready, and I'll bring him!"

I spun out of his embrace, feeling as light as air.

CHAPTER 13
ZAIDON

WAKING UP, I FOUND MYSELF UNDER A HEAVY, handwoven blanket. It reeked of Draxton's scent—a mix of airplane fuel and a sweet, pungent smell of sweat, smoke, and fish.

The empty silence pushed down on my chest. I sat up, breathing hard. I wasn't alone—the stirring sound of Callisto's toenails scarping told me so.

I yawned, stretching my arms above my head. "How long was I sleeping?" I groaned, knuckling the corners of my stinging eyes, convinced my fingertips were crawling with bacteria. Sandy residue of dried tears stuck to my eyelids. The feeling was strange, yet a pleasurable sensation like scratching an itch, so I kept it up. Floaters danced before me when I stopped rubbing my eyes, and seconds later, my vision adjusted, and my eyesight was better.

When I looked up, Callisto sat before me, pinning me with his laser blue eyes. I swear it looked like the animal was looking right through me and my intentions. A fleeting feeling of guilt shot through me, but was quickly replaced by angst when I realized I was alone with the bear.

"Where is Draxton?" I asked. He got up, his body swaying as he went to sit next to the door, which prevented me from leaving; he'd trapped me inside.

We sat facing each other, sizing each other up.

I fiddled with the blanket. Wondering where Draxton was and what this bear thought he was doing.

Minutes later, hunger and the urge to urinate *again* motivated me to get moving. I sighed heavily. "You win, I have better things to do than look at you the whole day," I muttered, pushing myself up into a standing position.

It was cold, so I wrapped the blanket around my waist and proceeded to that horrible byproduct purging room to remove the contents of my ever-filling bladder. This time, urinating came easier, and the rush of satisfaction forged through me and into the receptacle, turning a dark yellow brown.

I quickly finished up, shaking the small, shriveled appendage until no urine dripped from the tip, tucked it away, washed my hands, and then rushed to throw the blanket back around my shoulders. Just as I turned, the dull light emitted from the red crystal Draxton had left for us to see better caught my eye. I grabbed it before Callisto saw me. If Draxton asked me where it was, I would say I took it so we could recharge it together outside, where it was brighter than last night, but still not as bright as the light back home in Spire City. I fisted the crystal when I heard Draxton speaking to Callisto. He was back. Hastily, I slipped the necklace into my pants' pocket.

"Draxton!" I called, rushing out to meet him.

He gave me a worrisome look as he sat down at the table. With one hand, he rubbed Callisto behind the ear as he inserted himself between us. The other, picking up the cup from last night, looked at its contents, not saying a word. He tipped the cup to his mouth, looked at it again, seemingly upset that it was empty in his hand, and put it down with a loud thud. *Deeply contemplating something.* He was dressed in brown leather pants and handmade animal hide boots...and he was shirtless. *Did he go outside in this frigid cold, bare-chested?*

Silence passed as I stood staring at what he was doing. As if realizing we were still greeting each other, he said, "Morning." I got a lopsided grin as he smiled at me, and my insides made little whirly scratchy feelings. The blanket trailed after me, and I tucked it more under my arms.

I pulled a chair out. "Morning, hello. May I sit?"

"Yes, of course."

"How long have I been sleeping?"

"The sun is rising."

"No!"

"Yes, we live in perpetual twilight. I promise you it's daytime. But we have a couple of hours to kill. I don't mind spending them talking to you," he said, giving me a half smile. "I had time to think and went to talk to my neighbors."

"What will your boss say if you don't go to work today?"

"Boss?"

"Your leader. Your manager. Kellan, with the darker skin? Do you need to be somewhere?" I asked, hoping he would take me to where they are mining the crystal.

Draxton's face lit up. "Oh, he's going to like that. No, Kellan is not my boss. Remember last night, he'd said he wanted to take the drill to our leader. It's not Kellan, but his brother who is our leader. And no, we don't have work hours like you have in Spire City."

"Hm, that sounds interesting. Do you not have hours for work? How do you get things done?"

"We work, but mostly when we want to, and when the weather permits. We built huts this summer. We do get things done. The people stayed in tents and temporary homes during the summer, but we started laying clay bricks as soon as the snow stopped."

"Then why do you need the drill?" I asked, feeling he was lying to me. If they live in huts, why would you cut shelters for them?

His eyes widened, and he waved at me. "Oh, the manmade caves? Yeah, the drill will help them move deeper to set up something more permanent. We'll see, but at least they have a choice now."

He had the weirdest mannerisms. Was he lying, avoiding me, or listening for something? I cleared my throat after a few silent minutes. *Where did his mind go?* He appeared to be switching off or on; he was more absentminded today, even more so when he thought I wasn't assessing him. But not fully so, he was tapping his fingers rhythmically on the table. Was he listening to something with a beat? Maybe my hearing wasn't as developed as his. Perhaps by living in the darkness, they had adapted by hearing better? These people were a strange human breed indeed.

"Today, you are *my* assigned task. To do my job well, I needed some free time, so while you were sleeping, I went to visit my neighbors, whom I had promised to see last night, remember. I also had to thank them for taking care of Callisto while we were gone, and to tell them, maybe warn them about you. I figured they would see you later today, and I thought it would be better to prepare them for what to expect. They've never seen a small man like you, except for one or two men who trade illegally in Spire City. So, seeing you would be like seeing the evil Zelk's little helper," he said with an uncomfortable chuckle.

I pulled my lip up and frowned. "They can trust me. I have no intention of hurting them," I said, wondering if that was the truth. If the Zelk had known about the crystal and found a way onto this patch of magnetized rock, these people would absolutely have been herded off to choose between being a Spire City civilian or imprisonment.

"I'm not worried about them. I'm worried about you." Draxton put his mug down and gazed into my eyes with his dark, secretive orbs. *This must be a hoax. No one can be this caring.*

His eyes were beautiful. They carried a rare friendliness. A good soul, my father would have said. "My father said you can tell a lot by a man's eyes."

"Yeah?" he asked, perking up. "What do you see?"

That your goodness is going to cause your death, a permanent, lonely death.

"I see strength and honesty. I see friendliness and I see...I see depth," I told the half-truth while Draxton never broke eye contact, nor did I. He stayed still for a second. I do not think he objected to my blatant, concocted honesty.

He wordlessly reached down, lifted his backside from the chair, and removed a book from where he had been sitting. *Did he hide the book by sitting on it, by covering it with the part of him that excretes smelly stuff from the body?*

Pushing it reluctantly to me on the table's surface, he licked his lips nervously and gave a slight cough. "Earlier this morning, I was coached and told how to talk to you. Sopora, my neighbor, sent this book about the changing body of a teenager."

What's he talking about?

"I don't have the experience to talk about your haywire emotions and tears, so the book was an excellent idea. As we spoke, more neighbors with teenagers came to greet me. They talked a bit about being an understanding parent, what you are going through, and what youngsters in puberty go through. So many changes are happening to you that it would make not only me but also you feel anxious, confused, or stressed. I'm supposed to talk to you, listen, and guide you. I have to explain to you the physical changes and your emerging sexuality. Going off your suppressors, you are going to experience pain and a flood of emotions, which are normal, but will feel like a living hell. I wanted to help you, do something kind for you, because it's a momentous moment in your life, and may help you make more empathetic choices down the line. I've asked for volunteers to help me, but I was told that you are my chicken, and it's my responsibility to collect the eggs."

Oh, it's about last night. I frowned. "Alright, I'm listening," I said carefully.

Draxton was pale-faced, with twitchy fingers playing with the book's pages. "Zaidon, I'm going to have the birds and the bees talk with you," he said.

I rolled my lips inward, not sure what to say here. This seemed serious. "Birds and bees talk?"

"Huh...um, we call it that when the kids are reaching

puberty and become aware of their bodies preparing to procreate. I don't think anyone ever spoke to you about feelings and hormones, and I think you are going to go through a massive transformation, and I want you to know, you should know, it's part of being human. There is nothing wrong with you."

I broke our stare, looking down. "My father tried."

Draxton got up and poured something from a pot into a cup. "It's tea." He offered the cup to me.

I took it and curled my fingers around it, loving the warmth in my palms. "Thank you," I said shyly.

"None of that. I want to see the stubborn, self-assured Zaidon."

"I will try," I replied, returning a false, uneasy smile.

"What has happened may confuse you because everything about you that makes you human has been robbed. I'm glad you are here; now you will see what has been stolen, and it may give you a reason to share the secret of the invaders' weak points, as you might start to hate them as much as we do."

I pulled a face. "Secrets?"

"Yeah, something that would harm and kill them instantly."

I shook my head slowly. I didn't like that. But I had to play along.

"*Grrrr!*" Callisto sat up. I swung my gaze to him. *Did he growl at me, at my thought?*

Draxton glanced at Callisto. "Yeah, a weak spot. You will come to see we hate them, not because we have to live and hide in the cold. No, because they are systematically killing all of us, stealing our planet, and it's time we fight back," Draxton said with a look of determination.

I liked his appearance when he became excited. He was a vigorous man. My father would have liked him. But I couldn't ignore the budding fear in the pit of my stomach. I didn't know how to respond to such words of rebellion. I remembered the conversation with my brother. This information could help Malherbe Enterprises advance above the other families. Maybe even meet the Zelk king. But I liked Draxton, even this big white animal, Callisto. Maybe there is truth in his words. My father used to say the same things. I should be brave so my father didn't die for nothing.

I tried a different tactic. "Maybe showing me where you found the crystal can jog a memory while I breathe fresh air. I think that is more important than my changing hormones."

"I agree that is an important subject, but one we will deal with later. But now I want to talk about your body," Draxton said, waving his hand from my head to my toes, then gently tapping his finger against his temple. "About what is happening to you." Draxton shifted in his seat. "This book is old; see, the pages are yellowed and torn. It's from a time when humans lived free and were allowed to be human. There was no Zelk at that time," he said, but I wanted to talk about the crystal.

"This is a forbidden relic," I told him, handling it carefully as if it could burn me. I opened it and read the inscription written in the human language on the first page.

For Jessy, from Granny. I hope this helps you understand what's happening to your maturing body. Once you've read it and have questions, Granny will listen. Love you always.

My brows pulled together as I looked up questioningly at

Draxton's nervous-looking face, but his eyes blinked as he stared at something above me. I shrugged, following his gaze and looking up, seeing nothing.

I returned to inspecting the book. "Okay, thank you, I guess," I said, fingering the curled, dirty, torn pages.

He rolled his tongue inside his cheek. "The book—it's old, very old. I don't know who it originally belonged to, but Sopora, my neighbor, gave it to me, and I agree—you should read it. If you have questions, well...ask." He let out a long sigh, as if relieved, then relaxed.

I bit my lower lip. "Thank you," I said awkwardly, turning to the next page. Thick black round letters of the illegal alphabet accompanied a picture of a young man sitting in a bay window, looking sorrowful. "Puberty?" I asked, looking up at Draxton.

CHAPTER 14
DRAXTON

With my arms and legs crossed, I sat deep in thought, waiting and scowling at the fire, staring into the dancing flames. After counting to sixty ten times, roughly estimating ten minutes, Zaidon sauntered over, searching the fire for whatever he thought I saw or didn't see.

"And, what do you think?" I asked, turning and noticing Callisto had positioned himself between Zaidon and me, again.

Zaidon crossed his arms, tapped his one foot and drummed his fingers on his upper arm. I smirked at him, looked him up and down with eyebrows raised, waiting.

With a look of disgust, he straightened his arms, wiping his palms against his hip. "Draxton, I believe I've wasted your time. I must return home and speak to Harrison. These strange things that are happening...I'm changing too much. Maybe it's better if I talk to someone I know. That book is for children. We don't know each other on that level, and I think it is better that I speak to someone I trust and on my level of... um...intellect. I want to talk to my brother about how I feel. I thought it wouldn't be a waste...you have your laser drill. If you show me around today, then I can be back home before the sleep cycle starts. I promise that once I tell him about this place and how I feel now, and what I've experienced since landing here, he will agree that we should take action to help you. In the meantime, I have work...um...to find...your... um...secrets."

He pointed at me with his short index finger. "Also," he continued, after stepping away from Callisto, giving him lip, "I could approach the authorities to write a clause into the Zelk hybrid protocol to halt all suppressors before any hybridization procedures. I feel uncomfortable, but I *really* need to get home," he said with a firm tone.

Fuming with intense anger about his disinterest, I reeled that back in. My usual reaction to people who thought I was stupid or something flared up. I hadn't felt like that in a very long time, and not once since Kellan and I met or came to this reality.

Sopora had told me to listen and calmly explain the facts of life and puberty to Zaidon. She also agreed that Ouroboros would not be happy to have the enemy so close and that, although Zaidon gave us the laser drill, we should have devised an alternative plan or fabricated a reason to avoid bringing him here. If it weren't for Callisto watching him, she would have recommended skipping the talk, but taking him straight to the docks, where he could wait on the airplane.

I aimed to be as friendly and open as possible, at least by doing my best to pretend. Given Zaidon's reaction last night, I wanted to use that to persuade him to help us. If he truly understood what it meant to be human, he might fully support us. I suspected he had ulterior motives, but my grand-father always said being nice would get me further. Still, being nice and pretending was unfortunately my weakest trait. I hoped he would understand what his father did and why, and I wanted to remind him why his father helped us and would continue to give us access to their building, to understand and weaken the Zelk by finding their vulnerable spots. His sympathy and understanding would only be a benefit, and that's why I wanted to turn him into an informant in his father's place. His father had done so much to help Simon, and if I could figure out how to disable or disarm the enemy, we might avoid Ouroboros's ridiculous approach to fighting the Zelk—doing it the same way but with fewer troops than during the invasion. We needed a miracle, and I wanted to help make it happen.

Kellan had asked me to make friends quickly and get him off this continent. I blinked, smiled, and softened my expres-sion, making sure I kept friendly eye contact with Zaidon. He did say he wanted to bring change, which was a good thing. However, there's a difference between saying it and truly meaning it. Callisto didn't like him, and although I sided with the bear, I had to play along. "Alright. I understand. You need time to figure things out. Will you want to come back, or would you like to stay in Spire?" I asked in the friendliest tone I could summon. This was hard for me. I wanted to tell him to fuck off and die, but I couldn't.

So, I took a look at Callisto. *"Yeah, buddy, I see this fucker for what he is. Don't worry,"* I said silently.

Zaidon grabbed his elbows, curling in on himself as his shoulders drooped. Callisto made a small, throaty crying sound, looking at me with his puppy eyes. *"Please don't fall for this,"* he whispered into my mind, and this time I was sure it wasn't my imagination. I'd heard his voice countless times when I was a prisoner in the mine. I'd started to wonder if it was just my mind playing tricks on me, something I conjured up to keep my hopes up and stay alive. I smiled, shaking my head while giving him a thumbs-up. *"I got this. It's all fake, politics."*

Zaidon flapped his wrists to get my attention. "I'm not sure...um...of anything anymore. I appreciate your understanding. I feel confused and lost. I think I had this fantasy, and now it's all becoming too real, too fast. We can stay in contact," Zaidon said, and I got up, dusting myself off. I was ready to perform.

Why did I even give him the book? He's using it now as an excuse.

"Because, Draxton...you have a good heart," Callisto said sweetly, making me feel good all over.

"Ugh! Listen, whatever you are feeling. We should talk about it. Look, even Callisto cares about you," I said, and the bear tilted his head to one side.

"Are you fucking serious?" Callisto asked. I ignored him.

I pointed to the table and chairs. "Let's sit down and talk. I can ask Kellan to stand in if I'm not your first choice to speak to. He is a smart man. He's a professor...I mean, he was until..." I waved that off. "You can talk to him if you'd prefer." Callisto sneezed.

Zaidon curled his lip back and wrinkled his nose as if he'd caught a whiff of something foul. "That is exactly it. This whole place—that weird animal, the gross bathroom, every-thing—it's just making me uncomfortable. I can't stay. But maybe Kellan could give me an aerial tour of your continent and that island, show me where you found the crystal, and where you're planning to make tunnels. You trust me, right?"

"*The little shit! Trust him? Not at fucking all,*" I told Callisto.

"*Yes, that's the spirit. Tell me when it's time to eat him. I will eat him up in one gulp.*" Callisto sounded funny, so I chuckled.

But Zaidon didn't know about my second conversation with Callisto. "Of course I do trust you," I lied. "Kellan is already getting the seaplane ready for your tour. I understand how you feel, Zaidon. Sometimes being around others can be overwhelming, especially when you're going through so many changes at once." I waved my hand above my head. "Just remember, it's okay to feel uncomfortable. Take your time to process everything; we are here for you. Stay in contact, and ask as many questions as you like," I said and tried my best to sound like my grandfather.

"*How was that?*" I asked Callisto.

"*Just keep saying you trust him,*" Callisto said. "*He will open up to you. He wants to think that you are gullible. Let him.*"

I put on my most earnest expression. "I *really* do trust you. After all, you're the one who brought us the drill, right?"

He sighed and laid his small, extra pale, cold hand on my arm. I wanted to slap his hand away.

"*Grrrr,*" Callisto growled.

As if touching a hot stove plate, Zaidon pulled his hand back. This was the most challenging thing I've ever done, but I would see it through. Zaidon's cooperation comes first. We needed him, I thought as an uncontrolled shiver shook me.

"I'm sorry, I just need a relaxing day or so to recharge. I'm sure things will get easier as I adjust. This is all so new to me, and it feels like what I thought I knew doesn't quite translate to your world. It's taxing to be human. I feel overwhelmed, but I trust you, too, Draxton. Maybe you should explain everything as the day progresses. I don't think I can handle more raw emotions right now. I need a breather, and I'm not ready to empty my bowels in that...um...washroom," Zaidon whispered and snuggled against me. "Please understand."

"*Does Zaidon really think I'm this fucking stupid?*" I asked Callisto.

"*He does.*" Callisto chuffed at me.

"Are you saying you want to stay one more day or not, because now you are confusing me?" *Just give me the secret weapon, already!*

"Don't worry," he said, chuckling. "I'll be coming back." His breath smelled, and his eyes looked like beady rat eyes. I was going to throttle him, and it would be Kellan's fault. How could I have thought it was going to be easy? The book obviously hadn't worked. I should roll it up and hit him over the head with it, but I said, "We could show you around and introduce you to everyone, before leaving."

Actually, he was playing right into my hand. We needed him gone, and at least I didn't have to lie about the mountain spewing lava and that we wanted to evacuate him. I knew from experience that getting the seaplane ready took hours. I didn't know how much fuel was cooked up already, and sometimes during safety checks, Kellan and Snow had to get a fire going to melt and bend the iron to patch it up.

"I think my body is awakening, and it's a shock to me. Now that the information is sinking in, I think it is better to spend the day showing me around, like a tourist," he said in a weird, predatory tone fit for a molester, as he batted his hairless eyelids at me.

Kellan didn't like or trust him. He'd been waiting outside all night. At first, I wondered who the hell gets up that early to visit me, until I saw him and realized he wasn't an inquisitive neighbor but that he'd never slept. I had the fleeting thought that he monitored my progress with Zaidon. After all, he was the boss, as Zaidon had pointed out.

But after Zaidon woke me up with hysterical crying, I stayed awake and couldn't fall back asleep, so I waited for an acceptable time to wake up Sopora for advice and clean clothes for Zaidon.

Last night, I was uncomfortable sleeping without Kellan and with a stranger so close. I'd made an extra bed for him near the fire where Callisto could keep an eye on us.

Kellan's behavior both infuriated me and gave me the mental strength to see our plan through.

Luckily for us and Zaidon, Ouro lived a day's walk away, so we had some time. I realized that, like me, Kellan never slept well either. The professor could have slept in the hut with me—warm and cozy. It would have been good to show Zaidon what it looked like for two humans in love. Kellan was trying his best to pretend he wasn't interested in sex. I think he wants me to want him even more. How much more does he want me to want him?

"*Maybe Kellan hurt his head when you fell through the portal,*" Callisto said snarkily.

"*Could be. I hope he's okay. He looked so lost and upset earlier.*"

"*I told him to go wait on the airplane. But with Zaidon*

whaling, I guess he couldn't stay away. He's constantly worried about you. He loves you, Draxton."

CHAPTER 15

DRAXTON

THE THEATRICS AND BULLSHITTING STARTED AGAIN after breakfast, which was mostly mashed potatoes—two helpings, no less—and three cups of tea, which Zaidon seemed to genuinely enjoy. That, and his open disgust with our living conditions, were the only honest things he'd shared so far.

Libre's borrowed clothes fit him perfectly. At first, he'd refused to put them on, and once they were on, he'd wanted to take the *animal skins* off, until I said that if he didn't wear them, Sopora would take offense, which would spread like wildfire, and by the time we reached the airplane, Kellan wouldn't want to take him sightseeing.

"*Yeah, that trick was the finest manipulation tactic I've ever seen, Draxton. You are very good at it,*" Callisto said from far inside the house.

"*Yeah, but it confirmed what Kellan said—that he's a man in a boy's body, and that kind of man wasn't his thing. It's not my thing either,"* I replied, enjoying how easily we communicated. It was effortless. I just thought it, and he heard me. It was amazing, and yet another thing I would have loved to tell my grandfather.

Zaidon stumbled and swore all kinds of creative swear words containing shit as he fell over the shitting drain, awful shit rock floor, and the shitting unevenness in the road. I was used to the shadowy world, and I felt at home in the dark—also, another thing I didn't like about Zaidon.

"Just play along and get him off this continent. Don't say anything about magic or crystals, or anything they can use against us," Callisto reminded me.

"Don't worry," I replied. *"This kind of 007 work comes naturally to me. My grandfather always said so. I kept secrets all my life, and I know how to avoid spilling them. My grandfather always advised me to act like the others if I was unsure of what to say or do. I was becoming an excellent actor. I'm just mirroring what he thinks of us."*

I took Zaidon's small hand to steady him and told Callisto that he had insisted on wearing those damn Light Continent rubber shoes, refusing to wear another man's shoes.

"You know, I understand that," I said to Callisto. *"I hated going ten-pin bowling and wearing shoes that many other men wore before me. I shivered just thinking of unclipped yellow toenails scraping away the inside. Unwashed feet, sweating, and shedding fungi and plantar warts."*

"Yuk!" Callisto exclaimed. *"I'm so glad I don't have to wear those things. Ha-ha-ha!"* He laughed as if it were the funniest thing ever said.

"Why is it so cold? It's supposed to be a day cycle," Zaidon interrupted us.

I sniffed the cool morning air. "It's clean, fresh air, and it doesn't make me cough or sweat. It's perfect. You will get used to it."

He clucked his tongue, then almost swallowed it as we rounded our hut, and the village appeared down the hill. From our home, we can see over the red-grey roofs, the smoking chimneys, all the way down to the harbor, where Kellan and the others were scurrying around the airplane and the fishing boats. Beyond that, the horseshoe coastline stretched for miles, until the dull sunlight filtered over the hills, tracing lines through the blue-black curtains of clouds and dividing them into yellow and orange streaks that whipped upward like feather tails as the wind rearranged them into pure white cirrus clouds, and beyond that, a gloomy storm filled the horizon, waiting to strike.

"Come," I urged. "We should hurry, a storm is coming." I tugged on his hand, eager to move things along. Kellan was waiting, and if I didn't hurry, we could be trapped on the Dark Continent for days.

"*Better hurry, Draxton. That's why I'm staying home today,*" Callisto said.

"*You're staying home because you're afraid of flying, and you're using the storm as an excuse,*" I replied, picking up our pace.

"*Maybe,*" he said, sounding amused.

We approached Sopora's igloo-shaped clay house, hoping to slip by unnoticed. I was close with Sopora, and while Kellan, Ouro, and Snow stuck around, the others drifted in and out, never staying as long or talking as much as she did.

"Slow down. Tell me about your home." Zaidon huffed behind me.

I rolled my eyes, then added tour guide to my resume. "We started building a couple of months ago, at the start of summer, and now, with winter approaching fast"—I grunted worriedly, side-eyeing the surging accumulations—"I guess we will see what survives the blizzards. If it doesn't work out, we always have the caves we'll be digging deeper. Each block of five huts has a communal strip garden and livestock, which we call groves. Groves produce everything from eggs, milk, mint leaves, berries, and vegetables. Most are hardy and survive in darker, colder, and wet soil, like pigs and chickens." I pointed like a weatherman as I spoke, noticing him sniffing the air and scrunching his face like he was sniffing a donkey's arse.

He caught a glimpse of me scrutinizing his facial expressions, then jumped. "Oh, really, that is so interesting. Tell me more." I could hear the calculating gears spin behind his glassy black eyes. If he had a camera, I imagined him spying and clicking nonstop as he inspected every detail from the footpath and beyond the horizon.

"Yes, like humans, the vegetation and animals have adapted and thrived in a perpetual state of dusk. Most keep chickens, goats, and small pigs. The village is divided into five rows of huts," I said proudly, then pointed in the direction of the small fish market located in the harbor. He frowned in question. "Umm, there." I pointed. "Where we landed the airplane last night, fish and other seafood, like crabs, are traded daily. People only catch what they think they will eat that day."

"How much do they ask for a fish?" Zaidon asked.

"What do you mean?" I asked.

"How much do you pay for a fish, a crab, or whatever is on

the menu? I've been smelling the fish all night. It must always be on the menu, fish and potatoes," he said with a chuckle, and I didn't like his sarcastic tone.

"*He's asking because he thinks we trade with crystals,*" Callisto added.

"*I know,*" I told the bear mind-to-mind.

"We don't use money, like you on the Light Continent. There aren't shops or a monetary system. Everything is provided or traded as needed."

Then, remembering what Simon had explained, that the mark on my arm was one way of being rewarded, I said, "If what you are asking is whether or not, like you, on the Light Continent, we get awarded for dictated complacency, the answer is no, not at all, not with money, tattoos, or privileges."

He started jumping like a three-year-old. "Money, no, not money. How many points, or if you don't have points, maybe you pay with something else?"

"*Hmmm, and there it is,*" Callisto injected.

Growing irritated, I let his hand go. "No, we don't have that kind of system. We trade freely or ask, and that seems to be enough for us to get by. If I'm hungry, I pick, hunt, catch, or trade. It's that easy. No one fights or competes to have more than the other. We are a community."

He noticed my agitation, then changed tactics. "That's amazing. We were told you were living in the mud, fighting for food with animals. We are reminded constantly how horrible life is without the Zelk, that you are diseased, suffering, and have poor nutritional status, and if not dying, or killing, they say you gouged your eyes because you couldn't handle living in the dark."

I scoffed. "No, nothing like that, but we prefer they think

that about us. We don't have crime or bullies. Our village relies on simple human decency rather than laws, and no one is interested in running anyone else's life. We don't believe in anything but community, love, and acceptance. Lots of love and we believe in..." I halted mid-sentence. I was speaking of us, and we, as if this were my village and my people. My home. *"How did that happen?"*

"Yes, you are, and that's okay. You belong here with us," Callisto said.

"If Kellan hears that, he will have an existential crisis," I told Callisto. *"He is committed to finding the door and going home. He has his mother and siblings waiting, maybe even searching for him."*

"Why do you believe you can beat the Zelk?" Zaidon interrupted. "If you can't even manage a small town? Soldiers need structure and rules. Otherwise, they run around shooting each other instead of the enemy."

"Then you have stupid soldiers," Callisto snarked, echoing my thoughts.

"It seems like you live in ignorance, thinking you can use a secret weapon and make the Zelk fall, defeated," Zaidon added. "Do you honestly believe you can make them disappear? How do you plan to attack without infrastructure? Without a leader? If Kellan isn't your boss, then who is?"

"Zaidon is fishing."

"And he's being deceitful," added Callisto.

I ran my hand over the stubble growing in on my head. *"I'll do the same. I'll give him half-truths."*

"Hmmm, some say it's the magic...um...of the Dark Continent..." I trailed off, not knowing what the fuck I'm going to say about Callisto, and decided against mentioning the mind-to-mind communication, the time portal, the shrinking, his brother Atlas...the tunnels...

Callisto called out to me. *"Draxton, don't tell him that Ouroboros is obsessed with winning the war with one dragon, a bear, and a pack of giant wild animals!"*

"I know!"

"No need to shout, I hear you clearly," Callisto said scornfully.

Ugh! I was having two conversations, and it was messing with my head. I had to be very careful about what I said and to whom. I replied to Callisto, *"My grandfather trusted me with secrets. I searched for this place, I know it's somewhere special, and something sacred. I know I should keep it to myself, for us, as a people. I also know I can't share too much, in case this backfires, and Zaidon betrays us. But I want to share enough so he can learn about us. Maybe something would ping inside his tiny brain."*

Then I told Zaidon, "Our way of life is simple and peaceful. If we had a secret weapon, it would be something we should share with you, to help all of us." Then, to drip some extra honey on the bitter pill, I said, "Your father would be proud that you are helping us. It is what he would have wanted."

"That's it!" Callisto enthused.

"Thank you," I smugly replied. *"I thought that sounded impressive."*

But Zaidon turned his back on me as if he had lost interest. "Where is Callisto now?"

He was good, and I had to give him credit for that. If Kellan hadn't come to speak to me this morning, I wouldn't have been so motivated to play this game.

"He hates flying, he's hiding," I said.

"That's funny, but I totally understand that." Zaidon laughed, looking like he was really enjoying our walk.

"*Maybe I was winning him over.*"

"*No, not happening,*" the bear chimed in.

This morning, Kellan mentioned that Ouro would be upset because Zaidon was considered the enemy. He apologized, thinking we had made a mistake. I reassured him that I had everything under control. He looked at me with a strange, fearful expression, and then he kissed me. It was incredible! When we waited for Zaidon on the beach under the pier, I realized the butterflies that man stirred inside me were more than just the need to get off. It took me a while, but when I felt them in my belly, it hit me—my grandfather used to tell me about butterflies and how they only flutter for the one who was meant for you. Kellan wanted and needed me. He truly loved me, was practically obsessed with me, and tried hard to hide it, like when he was ignoring me on the seaplane. Now that I knew, I was going to show him every day how much I wanted him too. Sometimes, for such a brilliant professor, he was so clueless.

"I think this place is protected by magic. It's as if someone took a massive bucket of liquid iron rock and tipped it over," Zaidon said, and waited. The sparkle in his eyes could be because he was hoping for it to be true.

"Could be," I answered vaguely.

"We heard stories as children. About a dragon." His head turned up with a hopeful look.

"A dragon?" I pulled a face. "I'm not sure," I lied. "I thought you weren't allowed to know those stories, that they are illegal. Like books."

"My father made us remember, we spoke of these things in secret places where the Zelk can't record or monitor us. It's becoming increasingly difficult to find private places in Spire City. I was surprised that they don't monitor the pier."

"I can imagine how horrible it would be to be monitored and managed every minute of your existence," I ground the truth out.

Zaidon frowned and jerked his gaze away. "Returning to the dragon, we were taught to remember but never to speak of it. There is *much* you don't know about us," Zaidon said, patting his chest with his flat hand. He looked proud of himself. His bald head must be cold. *I should have given him a scarf.*

"Yes, a scarf, to hang him with. He forgets that he runs a slavery factory."

I agreed with Callisto and couldn't stop myself from bursting into laughter. I recovered quickly and reined that in as fast as it exploded out of my mouth. "Yes, I heard stories about a dragon too." I chuckled and added, "But it's been over a century since someone saw one. They say the dragon died during the Zelk invasion."

Uncomfortable silence hung between us. "Did you say the crystal was in the sea or on land?" he asked, and I ignored him by looking the other way.

Just when I thought we were past Sopora's dome, she came around the back of her hut and headed right for us, feigning surprise. She'd changed her clothes, and her hair was combed straight, like straw. I didn't even know her curls could do that. Was that berry juice smeared on her lips? It wouldn't surprise me if she had been waiting there, and this was all an act. "Good morning," she said, smiling broadly. She had a basket in her arms—collecting eggs, using that as her excuse, no doubt. Overly friendly, she continued, "Morning, Draxton, and morning, Zaidon. Welcome to our brand new, but very humble, village."

Zaidon stepped back, frightened by Sopora's sudden appearance. "Mo-mo-morning, and thank you," he stammered. I didn't know where to look while they stared at each other. It was growing uncomfortable. "Zaidon, this is Sopora. She shouted at us last night, and you're wearing her son, Libre's clothes."

"Don't make me look like the bad guy here before our guest. You were making noise, first with that airplane and then shouting on your way home. We weren't aware you were bringing guests." She batted her eyelashes. "Thank you for the tunnel maker. Hopefully, you won't get into trouble for bringing it to us. Did Draxton give you a proper breakfast?" she asked, leaning in to whisper to me. "Did you feed your guest?"

"Not now, Sopora," I muttered through pursed lips.

She covered her mouth with her hand and began frightening Zaidon. The more she talked, the wider his eyes grew. "Draxton said you needed help with your changing body. You are turning into a man overnight. Did the book I sent help, or do you need more support to talk about masturbation? It's normal, you know. Your hands won't fall off, and you won't grow hair on your palms. That's stuff parents tell their kids if they're doing nothing but pleasuring themselves all day. Some don't even stop for lunch. That's not healthy, so I think it's just how kids interpret it and then keep telling their children the same thing, and so on. I'm here all day, and I have nothing to do but be the mom and discuss these things with you."

I rolled my eyes.

Zaidon flushed pink. "Thank you."

"Oh, good. That's good," Sopora said. "Well, come in and have a cup of tea with me. I think my Libre will be in shortly. He went to help Kaikus get seats for your airplane, and then it's time for deworming."

"No, thank you. We are in a hurry," I said, widening my eyes at her.

She flapped her lips, giving me an exasperated look.

"Deworming?" Zaidon asked, astonished.

Her smile returned. "Absolutely! We can't eat the pigs without deworming them. Sooner or later, all of us would die from worms in the brain." She giggled.

"*Gods, help me,*" I groaned.

"Sopora, you will give Zaidon nightmares!" I said jokingly, pushing him behind me.

"Agh, no. The sooner he learns, the sooner he will get over it." She laughed, brushing it off while giving me a don't-be-rude side-eye.

"Okay, time to go. Kellan is waiting for us."

"Then, go ahead. Kellan doesn't enjoy waiting for you. He was so freaked out when you were...oopsy...boring information." She caught herself revealing too much, then chuckled and shooed us away.

"I thought you said he's not your boss?" Zaidon asked me.

"She meant something else. He had to wait for me for a month until I returned...um..." I gave Sopora a pleading look. I had almost run my mouth, just like her.

"Kellan loves Draxton and misses him if they aren't tied at the hip," Sopora said, waving her hand dismissively. "Nothing that serious. If anyone is the boss around here, it's Callisto."

She changed the subject. "Oh, Draxton, if you see Libre, tell him to hurry; I'm waiting for him." She walked away, saying over her shoulder, "I will go put the eggs in your refrigerator." She waved to Zaidon, who waved awkwardly back.

"Thank you, Sopora. Please chase Callisto outside and tell him he is getting fat. He needs exercise." I steered Zaidon by his shoulder.

Just as we turned, Rocket came hopping out of his door. "Morning-morning!" he greeted, as always, with an extra skip in his step. His hair was disheveled, as if he had run his fuel-laden fingers through it too many times. As always, his dark chocolate eyes sparkled with exuberant optimism.

"Morning, Rocket. How are you?" I asked, nudging Zaidon to go faster. I knew how this walk would go. One by one, people would show up, seemingly headed somewhere.

"Good, good as always and high on fumes, busy cooking, and just on my way to help Kellan fill up the airplane. I hear you're on your way again."

"Yes, we are. Rocket." I grabbed Zaidon by the sleeve and pulled him in front of me. "This is Zaidon."

"It's good to finally meet you, Zaidon. And listen, we really appreciate the laser drill. It'll let us work so much faster. That mountain is solid rock; a hammer and chisel just wouldn't cut it. We don't have time to waste; it won't be long before the Zelk wipe us out. So, thank you for giving us the tools to carve a path inside."

I sighed, grinding my molars numb. Rocket was a talker. He sniffed too many fumes, and once he started talking, well, he took off like a rocket, and there's no stopping him. I craned my neck, shaking my head, hoping Rocket saw it.

"Glad to help." Zaidon pointed at the rusted, ancient

jerrycans in Rocket's hands. "So, are you helping Kellan fuel up?"

"Yes, I'd just cooked it up for him. He is in a foul mood this morning, though," Rocket said to me, and now I really wondered what had happened to him during the night. Kellan's never moody. Rocket looked at my hand on Zaidon's shoulder and raised his eyebrows at me.

"Time to go, we're late."

CHAPTER 16

DRAXTON

"READY?" I HELPED ZAIDON DOWN THE GANGPLANK TO where Kellan was hanging belly-deep from the nose of the airplane, working on the engine.

The ratchet *krrr-krrred*.

"Morning, Professor," I greeted cheerfully. Hoping Kellan would look better than earlier. His body stiffened, and a second passed before he reversed out of the engine.

With one hell of a dull thud, he bumped the back of his head and swore a slew of native South African swear words. "Jou ma se fokken poes! Fokken kont se naaihare se fokken vervalle fokken engine!"

Wide-eyed, Zaidon and I waited for him to calm down and greet us. I wanted to see Kellan's beautiful face. But, as he turned in slow motion, rubbing the back of his neck, I suddenly felt guilty for steadying Zaidon on the jetty by having my arm around his shoulders, because when Kellan lifted his head, the face looking back at me was not the same as the one of my professor from earlier, after our kiss. He looked sleep-deprived, his usually dark complexion was pale, and his hair was rusty with dirt and engine grease. His normally friendly eyes appeared puffy and hollow, giving him a wild, rough look.

"Morning, I'm glad you made it...fi-nal-ly," he said through clenched teeth. Those tiny muscles in his jaw twitched like rubber bands about to snap. He had reached a point far beyond furious.

"So far gone, not even you could bring him back from that dimension. I'd never seen Kellan like this. Was this jealousy or exhaustion?" I asked Callisto.

"Both," the bear chipped in.

"He was the one telling me to win Zaidon over," I practically yelled at Callisto. *"Now, he's acting like a possessive...I don't know who the most fucking murderous possessive entity in this universe is, but this in front of me is not okay."*

I pointed a finger at Kellan. "You and I should talk. What the fuck, Kellan? Are you okay? When was the last time you slept for more than an hour? Did you even sleep last night? I thought we were on the same page after I found you skulking around the hut like a lame beggar, and now this," I said, then pushed Zaidon to get into the plane. He wanted to protest, but I ignored him, focusing on Kellan. "We need to talk now."

"That was nasty, Draxton. His nerves are shot. He's worried about his brother catching you guys here with Zaidon. He doesn't want to get you guys in trouble. Actually, you. He's protective of you," Callisto said.

"But this is not my Kellan," I said weakly, feeling like shit.

Kellan spoke over me. "We are almost ready. Rocket,

please make sure she's filled up and leave a full jerrycan of fuel for us in the back."

I had forgotten about Rocket, who was waiting behind us.

"Will do!" Rocket unscrewed the gas top.

"*What in the ever-loving fuck?*" I watched Zaidon move into the airplane and sit in the front passenger seat. When I looked back up at Kellan, he grunted at me, clucked his tongue, and flung himself around, disappearing into the engine again. I stood, hands on my hips, watching his ass. Minutes later, Kellan closed the engine. I was still waiting, wanting to discuss this, so I stood my ground.

"Not now, Draxton. Later, please. We must go. Zaidon has to leave now. The enemy could be tracking him." He gave me a half grin, then pushed by me and jumped inside.

"Okay, Rocket! Ready!" Kellan shouted, putting his fly goggles on. Rocket looked at me, raising his hands.

"Yeah, start her up!" I said and quickly climbed into the back seat, which was nothing fancy, just someone's two-seater wooden bench.

The airplane sputtered to life with a loud noise and a gust of wind, making it impossible to talk to Kellan without shouting. Zaidon stared at me over his shoulder, eyeing my back seat. I bet he wished he were the one sitting in the back today. I flicked my head to the side, looking out the window as Kellan prepared for takeoff.

Dark storm clouds loomed ahead, obscuring our path across the ocean to the Light Continent.

Leaning forward, I tapped Kellan on the shoulder. "Kellan, should we fly into that?" I pointed north in the direction we were going. Kellan nodded once as he flipped more buttons and then increased speed.

"We must take Zaidon home!"

"Okay, Professor, you know best!" I returned to my seat. I wasn't going to try to talk to him any further. I crossed my arms and pouted; I didn't like fighting with him. Something felt wrong—unbalanced and out of sync. It felt like I was heading in a direction not meant for me. Maybe I should jump out the door and swim back, I thought, but we were already drifting into open waters.

"This is exciting, but I expected a lazy show and tell, not this," Zaidon called loudly over his shoulder before pinning Kellan with a death stare. "It's not more important than our lives! I can wait another day," he said, and, as if he had a death wish, touched Kellan's arm and leaned closer to him. "Before any procedure, I've decided to suggest that people go off the suppressants for two weeks, then after that, they should decide if they still want the surgery to become a hybrid Zelk. Somehow, I have to try to give the power back to the people. What's happening is wrong, and I'm sure this is what my father meant when he said it would feel horrible, but horrible is better than feeling nothing. I didn't understand what he meant, but now I know. Because I feel shitting horrible!"

"I'm happy you feel horrible," Kellan snapped at Zaidon, then swatted Zaidon's hand from his arm as if it were a spider. I was starting to enjoy this side of Kellan.

"We're taking you back; you can go sort your people out. Write a note, a book, or a fucking song. See if that would change a century's oppressive genocide, and may I add wrongful imprisonment and slavery," Kellan roared sarcastically, then rolled his hips from side to side to get comfortable for the long flight.

Zaidon sat back in his seat with his nose up. From this angle, his pale skin flushed a bright pink. Perhaps it was fury, possibly shame, or embarrassment.

Out of nowhere, he swung himself around, aggressively asking me authoritatively, "You said you'll circle the island where you found the glowing crystal!"

Okay, that was weird. Why does he think he can talk to me that way? Especially if it sounded like Kellan was about to chuck him on the nearest beach and forget about him. *Doesn't he see how upset Kellan is?*

"No!" Kellan said with finality. He was off his rocker. Zaidon's going home, no doubt about that.

I shrugged at Zaidon. "I'm not in charge, and I'm not flying the airplane."

"But I gave you the tunnel maker. You owe it to me to show me around!"

Kellan exploded. "Ha! I'm not going sightseeing. Look at the storm looming in front of us!"

"Then turn back. Aren't you worried about the lightning?" Zaidon asked, looking at me with question marks in his eyes.

"No!"

We flew most of the way without speaking a word.

"You aren't scared of anything, are you?" Zaidon muttered later.

Suddenly, Kellan perked up. "Nah, I'm never scared of lightning, especially not with Draxton around. We've been traveling together for what feels like ages. He's my good-luck charm," Kellan chuckled, rubbing Zaidon's nose in it. "Draxton and I are in love, and no one will ever hurt him or come between us. I'd kill for him," Kellan said with an edge that made him sound like a psychotic Zelk-slayer. *Gods, what's wrong with him?*

My backside was getting sore on the wooden slats, which was a good thing because I knew I had been sitting too long, and that was a sign the flight to hell was nearly over.

The airplane spat and farted. Kellan tipped his head up to the roof and yelled, "Draxton, now is a good time to fill my baby up. Rocket left a can for us behind you!"

"Okay, got it!" I was glad Rocket had brought us the extra fuel, but I immediately worried about our return trip; it seemed we would be out of fuel again. Hopefully, Simon can help us. "I would think by now you would know how much fuel you needed for a round trip!"

"The tank is small, and fuel is leaking somewhere when the pressure increases."

Once I wiggled myself into the tight space, I unscrewed the canister's top, inserted the funnel into the tank's mouth, lifted the jerrycan, and started pouring the homemade kerosene concoction into the plane's empty belly. Zaidon was standing with his knees on the passenger seat, watching me anxiously, gripping the headrest wordlessly as he rolled his lips between his teeth.

"Done!" I shouted, closing the lids before maneuvering my tall, lean body back to my seat again.

"Thank you!" Kellan sing-songed. I smiled watching him kiss his fingers, then rub the dashboard like it's his girlfriend when she purred happily.

I was scarcely back in my chair when the sunlight broke through the clouds and the Light Continent appeared on the horizon.

Zaidon turned back in his seat, facing the front. "There is

my city of everlasting light!" Zaidon said, clapping his hands like a child.

"More like the city of everlasting fright for me," Kellan remarked.

"Agreed!" I shouted.

I jolted to the side, grabbing futilely for handles as the airplane suddenly took a terrifying turn. "The left wing!" Kellan roared.

I snapped my head left. "Where the hell is the left wing?" I shouted in disbelief as we spun out of Kellan's control. Violent turbulence flung us around, and all I could think was that we sounded like a kamikaze airplane going down.

Zaidon screamed. I held onto Kellan's seat and yelled, "We must jump now!" The airplane zinged, and everything trembled. The engine's thunderous roar drowned out Zaidon's screaming. The wind whipped, gravity pulled, and the blue ocean blurred in and out as we nosedived from the sky. A deafening boom told me we had to jump. Smoke billowed from the engine. We were hurtling toward the vast expanse of the waters below.

Kellan grabbed the handheld device, holding it near his mouth, and shouted, "This is the Snowbird, we are going down, south of Simon's landing, I repeat, this is Snowbird, we are going down, south of Simon's landing!"

"Jump! Jump now!" Kellan shouted, leaning over, pulling Zaidon out of his seat belt, then dragging him out the door with him. I followed, diving headfirst out of the door. In a heart-stopping moment, I thought none of them could skydive or have a parachute, but before I could finish that thought, I smashed my head on a piece of debris as we crashed into the warm turquoise waters.

Somehow, we all got tangled together. I shoved Kellan up, trying to get him to safety, but I was sinking fast as Zaidon yanked me down by the ankle. I kicked and flailed, but it wasn't enough. Zaidon used me as leverage, like climbing a tree, then kicked me in the head to launch himself upward.

My lungs hurt. My mind whirled. I held my breath. Checking to see if I was upside down, I followed the directions of the bubbles. A hand—Kellan's hand—clasped mine. Shadows of Kellan's boots floated past me. *My boots!* I kicked them off. We torpedoed through the surface, hungry for air. With mouths open, the waves crashed into us. Water filled my lungs. I coughed and struggled to breathe, inhaling more salt water. I was a chaotic mess, trying to breathe, to swim, to survive. Flailing and coughing, I registered the blinding sunlight. Kellan wrapped his arm around my neck, forcing me to lie back.

"Calm down and breathe. Just breathe, I got you!" I saw black spots, bright light, and was frantically overwhelmed by the saltwater burning my eyes, nose, and lungs. For a second, I saw Kellan's desperate face, and then I was tumbling, rolling ass over head. I kicked, paddled, and flailed.

A wave. Another wave, and then Kellan lost his grip on me.

I wanted to cough. I couldn't—the noise of my voice disappearing into bubbles made it worse. I struggled against the water. I needed air. Just one breath, but which way was up? I was terrified, and it was deafening.

Fear. So much fear.

I'm dying.

My heart slowed. I surrendered and breathed, inhaling

water. I kept my eyes open. Where's Kellan? I wondered, petrified, that I'd lost him.

"Kellan!" I shouted with my last pocket of air.

The quiet came like a thief; it crept upon me. Silence surrounded me.

I waited, listening to the last beat of my heart until all thought vanished.

Nothing, nothing, nothing as I drifted away.

CHAPTER 17
ZAIDON

BEFORE THE LOUD RUSHING NOISE OF WAVES WOKE ME completely, I knew I wasn't going to wake up in my rejuvenator. Cold wetness washed over my lower body, and I winced slowly, blinking my unfocused eyes. I reached for my itchy, burning face, realizing I was lying on sand because I was rubbing it into my eyes, nose, and mouth. My sunburned skin told me I had been baking in the sun for a while. The sound of waves crashing and water surging up my legs again kickstarted my primal survival instinct.

We'd crashed. I'd almost drowned! I was on a beach. I'm alive, I thought, relieved. If I'd died, that would have been it—eternal death—no mind uploaded to any hive.

The waves kept lapping at my lower limbs, trying to get a hold of me, trying to swallow me back into its depths, to drown me.

I sat up, orienting myself. Light sparkled off the water before me as the waves rolled over my half-buried feet. "No, no, no." I dug my heels in deep, reached back, and crab-walked backward up the steep dune until I found myself among pebbles, broken seashells, rotting seaweed, and long-dead fish carcasses.

"Yuck." I hurried past that mess until I found a safer spot to rest, taking stock. My head dropped, my arms and legs spread out as I gasped for air with a vacant stare at the netted gunmetal blue sky. I floated in my delirious mind, struggling to find ideas to call for help. Since seeing the low level of light on the Dark Continent, I was sure it was night-cycle time on the Light Continent, in Spire City.

Patrolling hoverbots! Flashing blue sparks and beams of light halted my state of confusion and hyperventilation. The sight of the two spheres was a promise of help to come. The invader drones glowed, then flashed and disappeared.

"Come here! Help me," I croaked and hoped my biometrics were recorded. "It's me! Here, see me!" I waved weakly and coughed. I closed my eyes and licked my cracked, salty lips.

Paralyzed with thirst, nausea, and exhaustion, I wrestled with myself to stay awake and keep my eyes open. I could have been here for seconds or hours, I thought. Another shadow passed over me, and I cracked open my eyes.

"Hey, over here!" A voice, cracking against the roar of the waves, cut through the air. It was coming from my right, somewhere down the beach. I raised my head. "Scan me, you hoverbot bastards!" he rasped, then went silent.

Pushing myself up onto my hands and knees, I called out, "Hello?" But he didn't respond. I had to know, so I started crawling across the hot sand toward the dark figure on the beach—it had to be Draxton, or maybe Kellan.

More hoverbots arrived and zipped through the misty ocean spray, heading north—homeward bound. Shit, they'd spotted us. Double shit! My trackers were in my shoes, but I was barefoot. No! Oh no, my strange clothes? I was shoeless and dressed like a foreigner—in animal skin! I'm going to be misidentified. I patted my pockets and found the crystal tied to a leather string, hidden inside my trousers. I was so glad I'd tightened the drawstring, thinking I could have lost it. Luckily for me, Draxton never missed the crystal I'd taken.

My throat was dry. I was thirsty, and the heat was getting to me. "Harrison, please hurry and find us!" I sobbed, but I kept crawling until I reached the still figure. Looking at him, I felt a strange wave of concern as I checked him for any sign of life. I put my head down, listening for a heartbeat, pressing my ear between his pink nipples. "Draxton, hey, it's me," I croaked, and I heard his heart beating faintly. His breathing was shallow. "Hey, wake up!" I coughed, but he didn't respond. He was unconscious.

I collapsed beside him, hoping to be rescued before it was too late for either of us. Please don't die, Draxton. I kept my hand on his chest, checking for movement, then closed my eyes and curled into him, holding him. Aside from my father, the first person I've ever held in all my life.

"I KNOW that his current situation casts doubt on the authenticity of my statement. Sadly, most people lack the mental capacity or the vision to consider this as an isolated phenomenon. We, with a broader intellect, should understand that the blurred lines between reality and unreality do exist.

Our awareness is shaped by the experiences of those before us, uploaded to the hive. Their physical and mental experiences are now ours. Regrettably, those with organic brain matter consider those perceptions as madness. They say it is a psychological and mental illness of the mind, it is due to ancient human beliefs. Those who can't let go of the notion that the king is here to stay will suffer." The voice of my father resonated in my head, but Harrison's voice cut into it, dividing my wakefulness from my dreams, as I awoke to an inexplicable unease, a looming sense of dread.

"What happened to me?" I grumbled as I rolled my head from side to side. I realized I was in a medical unit and not in my rejuvenator at home. My sister looked at me in surprise. Sunlight streamed through the slits in the blinds, casting golden-brown stripes across the walls, but failing to warm the chill in my bones.

I rose by my elbows from the emergency treatment table, stretching to ease the stiffness in my neck—a stiffness due to bobbing in the ocean trying to catch a slipstream ashore.

As usual, my sister stepped back. With a cold, calculating look and a turned-up nose, she didn't touch anything. "Hello, and welcome back," she said, pretending to help me dangle my feet over the side.

"No need for that," I said, irritated by her fake gesture of sibling affection.

I rubbed the back of my neck. "Why am I in medical? Where is Draxton?"

Harrison jumped to answer, but my sister was first. "You are lucky our father implanted additional trackers when we were born. We found you lying near death and washed up on a beach next to that filth from the Dark Continent. If the authorities had found you, you would have been judged and..." She rummaged for a tissue in her purse, wiping away pretend tears, feigning emotion. "I could have lost you," she said between fake sniffles.

I rolled my eyes at her performance. We both knew she didn't care; it was probably Harrison who found and saved me. She would have been all too happy if I had died so she could take Malherbe Enterprises.

"Zaidon," Zonika murmured and started another round. I wasn't in the mood for her pretenses.

"Where is Draxton? Did you leave him alone with the authorities?" I asked, pointing to the door. She gasped, clutching her empty purse and hugging it to her chest.

"Zaidon, I want to know where you were and what you were doing with that...that...animal. Did you see how beastly tall he was? Forget about him; they will cut him up and make an example of him—as it should be."

"Please just go, Zonika." I fell back onto my pillow, clutching my temples. My head was killing me. "Leave, or Harrison will throw you out of my room." I gave my brother a desperate look.

She looked at me tenaciously as if she'd smelled blood; she leaned closer than ever, her eyes narrowing, dead and one hundred percent Zelk. *She must have undergone the preparation procedure.*

She pointed her finger at me. "Where did you come from? Why were you found with that filthy human? You are hiding something, and I will find out exactly what." My brow puckered as I pulled a confused face. "Where have you been, Zaidon?"

She wanted me to see her new eyes as they blinked

proudly with irritated robotic flicks. "Father left the company to all of us. You must tell me where you went and what you were doing. Was this an abduction, an attempt at ending your life, or were you doing something illegal, like maybe fraternizing with the vermin? I can't think of any other reason for you to have washed up on a beach."

She was referring to the Dark Continent, the only place where the invaders didn't go, couldn't go, or track my tracers. She knew I was there, but not the exact location. "You are the loyalist traitor. You married a Zelk," I spewed at her, then snapped my mouth closed, before I told her that her children were scary little psychopaths.

"I will give you time to recuperate. I would like to see you in the office in two days. I will personally see to the interrogation of that animal you had with you." She whirled around to look at my niece and nephew. Their faces blank, they rose in unison, turned, and slowly twisted one corner of their mouths into a creepy, scarecrow-like smile. I shivered. Those two would strip the meat from a human bone without a second thought.

"No!" I yelled when it dawned on me what she was saying.

Zonika left, with her children falling in line behind her. I waited until the door swooshed shut, leaving me and Harrison alone in the room. He looked awkward as he glanced over his shoulder and back at me. "Thank you for saving me." I smiled, hoping he would share information about Draxton's location. "Where are they holding him? We must go get him now." I pushed myself up. My body ached in places I didn't know could ache and groaned in pain. Harrison pushed me back down.

"No. Rest. I will go; let's give Zonika a minute to leave the building."

I felt dizzy and exhausted. Perhaps it would have been better if I had built my strength before trying to help Draxton. Harrison happily leaned closer into my personal space after pulling something from his pocket. "I found this clutched in your hand. I didn't want Zonika to know, so I kept it," he whispered. Ah, so that's why he looked like he was hiding something. He opened his hand, revealing a leather string and a glowing red crystal resting in his palm.

"Like I said, it was clutched in your hand. Did you find the source of it on the Dark Continent, brother?" His voice was cold and monotonous. Was he nervous, or was something else going on here? I opened my hands to inspect them.

"In my hand?" I asked, wondering where I'd found it. Oh yes, it was in that washroom, at Draxton's house. He'd left it there so I could see in the dark. Guilt pinched my heart, making me feel like crying again. I was worried about Draxton, all alone somewhere, probably already being processed into the system. If he didn't convert, he would be tortured until he either died or agreed. Otherwise, he would be sent to prison to work for them for the rest of his life.

I gasped, my eyes widening in surprise, and my heart raced. "Give it to me, it's mine," I whispered, checking the door.

"Do you remember if there was more. Do you know where they found this?" Harrison asked.

I shook my head.

"Are you sure you don't remember anything?" He sounded expectant, as if he was waiting for me to give him a specific answer.

I stared vacantly at my hands, then inspected the gashes and bruises again. I opened and closed my fingers as memories of Draxton's handsome smile nibbled at me.

My head snapped up. "Yes. There was a storm. They were taking me to see the island where...wait, no, I was coming to see you, to bring an important message to you. What was it again?" I inspected my longer-than-usual fingernails.

"Really?"

"How long was I gone?" Another flash of memory, me looking out of the airplane. The brewing storm. Kellan was upset. *I remembered!*

I sucked in a long gasp, filling every corner of my chest with air, while touching my lips. My body tensed up at the memory of Draxton's enormous arms enveloping me. His hands, his mouth...oh, yes, now I remembered everything. His pink nipples. *Why were his nipples so impressive?* Heat flushed through me as my insides sizzled with excitement. He made me feel things. The sweaty scent of him. The smell of clay and mold. That book. His weird, wonderful, and inviting personality. Kellan's impressive anger issues. The constant drama. Their village. Being introduced to the friendly people. The smell of the ocean and the sight of the mountains reaching impossibly high beyond the clouds.

"I was coming home to tell you we should change the procedure and the rules. We need to convince the people who want to become Zelk hybrids to go off their suppressants for at least two weeks to decide. They must be completely alert and aware of themselves to understand what will be done to them. Otherwise, it is not free will. They must feel what I felt —being human. Harrison, we have work to do."

My brother's voice cut through the jumble of words and

unforgettable memories. "What happened to you? You look different. It's because of the suppressants, isn't it?"

"Give me that!" I reached for Draxton's necklace in Harrison's hand. He was too quick for me. He turned and slid open the door.

"What's going on, Harrison? Bring that to me, it's Draxton's. He saved me." I spoke to Harrison's back while he was looking at Zonika. He held up his hand. The necklace dangled from it.

"Thank you, brother, dearest. I'll take that," Zonika said. Harrison stepped aside. She was listening to our conversation, and he knew that. Behind her, five hybrid guards waited.

"Zaidon Malherbe, you are under arrest. You are charged with treason. You conspired with our enemy, just like our father." At the sound of my name, my heart smashed to pieces. The ghost of my father flickered to the side of them. Realization and disappointment flashed and flooded the cold truth in front of me. Harrison and Zonika? *Father, I didn't know.*

"I'm not a traitor," I whispered uselessly. I was going to provide information about the crystal's location.

"Yes, but you said just now, you wanted people to stop their suppressants. That is the number one law to stay on the Light Continent. You want to stir rebellion." My sister smirked coldly. "Come, arrest him!" The guards made way for two hybrid nurses pushing a narrow mobile bed into my room. I scooted back up onto my bed, sitting on my pillow, holding my knees tightly. My brother and sister had planned this. How did I never see this coming? They were waiting for me to tell them where the crystal came from. They'd planned this!

"Harrison, you waited for them to make contact, didn't you? You knew they would, didn't you?" His stern, cold refusal to answer told me I was correct. "Since Father's death, it was all a pretense to lure them out. To expose them. And you used me."

Waves of distress pummeled the inside of my tightening chest. They are arresting me. Torture awaited me.

"You should never have stopped taking your suppressants. I told you that you would be caught and you would regret it," my brother said. He was not raising his voice and not defending me.

"Wait, before you take him, remove his tooth immediately. Download the location," Zonika said with a vindictive glare. Two hybrid guards picked me up like I weighed nothing.

Kicking and struggling didn't loosen their Zelk grip on my arms and legs. They forced me onto a steel gurney. More hands than I could count strapped me down and pried my mouth open. I gagged as they held my head and poked their fat fingers into my mouth. I bit down, but a bite block was inserted behind my molars, preventing me from closing my jaw.

"We'd forgotten to check Father's tooth," Harrison said. The icy confirmation and frantic realization made me momentarily dazed. A volcano of emotions erupted from within me, and I wailed like a giant baby. How did I *not* see that?

With my mouth wide open, and tears spilling down my temples, and with no suppressors in my bloodstream, I felt the horrifying human emotions as they pinned and strapped me down. I felt powerless, and then someone jabbed something into my upper leg. Tears clouded my vision as I fought futilely, kicking and screaming. My brother's deceit hurt more than the fear. My only brother deceived me. Both Zonika and Harrison had our father killed, and now they were getting rid of me too.

"I won't let you break that arsenic tooth. I won't let you ruin yourself and bite down on that poison. You will not ruin yourself as our father did. You will stay alive. You will fulfill your purpose. We want what is on the Dark Continent," Zonika spat at me, her eyes flickering with disconnected madness.

I knew exactly what was happening, but my body was out of reach. They'd injected me with something that kept me lucid. I was fully aware of all my senses, but paralyzed from head to toe.

The nurse stuck a laser scalpel and a pair of pliers in my mouth. I drowned in my spit and snot as searing pain, and the smell of my burned flesh choked me. Finally, the excruciating pain vanished as I lost consciousness.

CHAPTER 18
KELLAN

I WAS ON THE BRINK OF SHOUTING AND CHASING SNOW and Sopora out of the bloody hut. My hands were cramping, and my neck and shoulder muscles were like a sack of golf balls. I got up from the table where I'd been working, snapping my head this way and that to loosen my stiff muscles. "It took me one full day grinding one ounce of magnetic dust from that damn lava rock, no wonder Ouro said it's near impossible to chisel your way through the mountain," I said, exasperated.

"Ouro never lies, you see," Snow said.

I gave them a tight-lipped smile. "I never said he lied."

"You don't believe him. You don't trust him. You might as well have told him he was lying to you," Snow said, narrowing his eyes at me.

After Ouroboros had announced he needed everyone's help to open the mountain, Snow had sent out crows with a message saying that Ouroboros required assistance and everyone should pack up and return home.

It was pure luck they had found me after I had been drifting for hours, eyeing the coastline. I was caught in a slip of warm water, pulling me further from the coast. Instead of swimming and struggling against it, I relaxed, bobbing and talking to myself, knowing the sea would eventually spit me out somewhere.

I was recovering from dehydration during the village evacuation, which was progressing slowly. Everyone was expected to meet with Ouroboros to discuss individual contributions and participation. New teams were formed, dedicated either to opening the mountain or to preparing for combat. My brother displayed impressive management skills, making it clear why he was respected as their king and leader.

I was relieved when, after returning from their meeting with Ouro, Donali, Kawa, and Simon had offered their help, and now we were on our way to save Draxton.

At first, they wanted me to stay behind while they went to get him, but he was *my* lover, and I wasn't going to wait while building another washroom, *damn it.*

I was determined to finish packing and head to Spire City.

Not knowing where Draxton was held or what they were doing to him was driving me insane. There was a hidden innocence about Draxton, and I feared he would lose his will to live. The thought of him being hurt made me furious, and listening to everyone telling me that he would not be alive or himself was nerve-wracking.

The plan was that once we were inside, Simon would let us know exactly where they were holding them. Simon had maintained a deep cover working at the hybridization amphitheater over the years. He'd gotten word that a public ceremony was being prepared, and there was a possibility that it was Draxton and Zaidon's. He'd heard that two higher-ups were being detained, which is why we suspected it was them.

It had been just over a week, and since Ouro needed everyone here to prepare for war, Simon had convinced him to let us go, so this was our only shot at getting inside. We couldn't use Callisto's help, since we're sneaking in right under their noses.

Donali, Kawa, and I would partake as spectators, while Simon would be on the surgical floor. I had no idea what that place would look like, but if Draxton and Zaidon were being prepared for hybridization, Simon would be able to get to him, and...

I'd rather not dwell on it, but the reason I was sanding the magnets and lava rock was...Simon would euthanize them before they became hybrid Zelk.

Once we arrived on the Light Continent, we had to climb an elevator shaft and slide through service tunnels. They're also planning some explosions, so things were going to get chaotic, and fortunately, Callisto agreed to wait for us on the boat.

One by one, the people returning to the mountain to help with drilling and hauling had stopped by our hut to say goodbye and wished us luck, but not before telling me I was making a mistake. Instead of deterring me, it just made me more determined to get the hell off this continent, because each second wasted was a second he could die.

Donali and Kawa were quietly packing, getting their

equipment and explosives ready. Simon and Callisto were loading the ship, while I sanded the rock for iron dust. Over time, they'd collected all sorts of relics and useful wires, earpieces, radio transmitters, and other stuff that looked like computer innards, either from the invaders or from before they arrived, from when Anzulla's skies were filled with flying antigravity vehicles that carried people all over, even down to the hidden city of Phoenix on the ocean floor. Yeah, exactly the same weird shit my father told me about, and that just gave me headaches, thinking about that.

I had always assumed it was because time had passed, and that it was like playing the telephone game, where one person whispered something to the person next to them, and that person whispered something to another, who then attempted to repeat what they had heard or thought they heard to the next person. And when the last person said what was said to him, it was nothing like what was first whispered.

However, as someone who chased after ancient treasures, I also knew that there was always some truth to a story passed down from generation to generation. Thus, I believed this was connected to the legendary Atlantis. The issue with my explanation was that Ouroboros claimed he saw it with his own eyes. So yes, it was a maddening headache that worried me about whether we'd ever make it home.

Sopora pointed her cup at me. They had been drinking tea steeped from the leaves of a plant native to this area. They said it was like cannabis, but it has healing properties; they called it Loursveto. "Draxton may not be right in the head after this," she said crudely, rubbing me even more the wrong way. "It doesn't help to try to save a brainless person. If I were you and were able to do so, you or Simon, or whoever, would have to give him the poison. You would be doing him a favor. Do not bring him here; it will be bad luck for our people," Sopora warned. "Callisto will not permit it. Ouroboros had given him clear instructions. He will not be your Draxton. By now, the machines are aware of the stolen drill. There's no chance that he or we would accept a Zelk living among us. He would be a shell. Not human. You promised all of us. Remember that."

I shook my head, refusing the cup in her hand that she offered me. I wanted a clear head for my rescue mission.

I crossed my arms, scowling. "I know I'd promised that, but this is different."

Donali agreed. "Even if I put my personal feelings for Draxton aside, we all have an obligation to help him. Each human life is the most precious thing of all nowadays."

"Donali and Kawa," she said, making air quotes, "will do anything, say anything, to keep you happy and save Draxton. They're just looking for an excuse to blow the place to smithereens. If that happens, it won't even be a day before every Zelk and hoverbot is at the coastline. I don't know who's dragging whom along on this useless expedition. He's already dead, Kellan. It's been a week," Sopora said.

A frustrated sound escaped my throat. "No! I refuse to believe that!"

"Please be careful. Keep in mind my warning that you might have been tricked, and they are using Draxton to lure more of us there," she said softly, touching the necklace she had made for me around my neck. If my mother were here, they would have been friends; they were so alike.

"Kellan, time to shower and get ready. Don't listen to

them. Simon and Rocket had refueled the speedboat. The ship's sails are being raised; the last run to Spire is underway. Hurry," Kawa called, saving me from the unending barrage.

We were taking the speedboat for the rescue mission, which was faster and large enough for eight men and a miniature Callisto on the top deck, and a small medical bay below. Everyone was on high alert, this was the last evacuation of their hideout on the enemy soil to gear up for war. It was better to have two vessels in one place at a time, in case one was destroyed, or if something else happened, we had a backup to return home.

Sopora placed her hands on my cheeks, gazing into my eyes with her beautiful and caring hazel ones. "Be careful, Kellan. Donali, the poison, take my advice, please, boy."

"We will," I said and leaned in closer for an extra-long hug. She was only giving her opinion. So I won't stay mad at her. She was saying those things to prepare us for the worst. "Okay, here, I packed food and drink for you and the others." She rubbed Callisto's head. "Bring them back safely. If Draxton is Zelk, do not bring him here," she told Callisto while giving me a side-eye.

Callisto gave a soft growl in answer. *"Draxton is not dead, not yet. I would know. And he isn't. I agree with Kellan. You are being negative, Sopora."*

"Kellan will thank me for my words. Anything better than that would be the best outcome for Draxton. I was only giving you the worst-case scenario. But when I say nothing, he will hate and blame me for it. He would say, Sopora, you should have known and you should have told me. So, tell me if that isn't wise foresight," she told us.

I sighed and jumped to get ready. "Okay, thank you, and

thank you for the piglet. Now, please go, and take Snow with you."

"Good luck! I pray he's alright, for all of us," she called back, linking arms with Snow. "May the wind be at your back!" she added.

CHAPTER 19
DRAXTON

For a moment, I thought my eyes were being scooped like rum and raisin ice cream, but then bright lights blasted me, reminding me I could still see. Thoughts and fears buzzed and scrambled, and I didn't know which strand to tug, test, or pull to escape the chaotic abyss. Everything I thought, felt, saw, heard, and even tasted was real one second, and the next it was some other terrible sense warning me of my impending death.

The onslaught stopped. A mixture of the stench of *my* fear, of *my* breath, of *my* sweat filled the grave silence. The faint whizzing of air, and my rapid breathing, sniffing, and grunting were all that remained. "Hello?" I croaked weakly after I'd been screaming in terror for what felt like forever.

In a sober fraction of a minute, I knew where I really was. I called to Kellan, to anyone, for help, but my voice echoed in the emptiness of my strange prison. I found the source of the ice-cold air whistling. It was blowing in from above my head.

It chilled the tip of my nose and my dry, cracked lips. I gasped for a breath to anchor myself in the here and now, searching for something, anything to focus on. But I couldn't.

My entire body felt horribly wrong. My head, my hands, my arms, my legs, my feet, I couldn't move them. From my chin to my toes, I was numb to the cold. The air on my face was frigid, but otherwise I felt nothing. Desperately, I tried to lift my head, but it felt leaden. I was utterly immobilized. I was paralyzed.

"No!" I shouted. My voice reverberating in the stillness worsened my throbbing eardrums. I was trapped inside a chest, a casket, or maybe it was a pod. I squeezed my eyes shut, then reopened them. All that greeted me was blinding light. "Hello? Where am I?" My words tumbled out, slurred and awkward. My tongue and lips felt like cork—so dry. My hands...I felt my fingers! But my arms? I couldn't move them. My legs? They were definitely there, but they wouldn't respond. "What the hell is going on? Get me out of here!" I yelled, the shout ringing painfully in my ears. Each breath came louder, more panicked as I gasped for air. My heart raced, adrenaline surged through me, while the dead stillness pressed down on me from all sides. I was encased and trapped.

Not even a slight shake of my head was possible.

Light glared, and I felt relieved as I realized I could feel the throbbing pain in my head. I calmed down a bit as I closed my eyes, pretending I was underground. When I opened them, a reflection of my terrified face stared back at me. The stubble I had been growing was gone, but it was clearly me. I was sealed inside a glass container. A ghostly glow pulsed rhythmically below, reminiscent of distant police lights on a highway at midnight—not bright, but unmistakably there. It pulsed with a faint beeping sound. My heart rate?

"He's awake!" a male robotic voice from outside announced, muffled. Two crimson eyes, cold and metallic, glared at me from a cold, menacing face that hovered just beyond the glass.

"No, no, no! Get me out of here!" I screamed, terrified at the Zelk showing no emotion, no hint of empathy, of any emotion—only the sinister gaze of those eyes, assessing me.

"You have been found guilty of trespassing, espionage, and treason. You are sentenced to eternal wakeful death," the Zelk said monotonously. "You will be kept alive, awakened only to realize you are trapped over and over for eternity. You will come to wish you were Zelk, but it will never happen. You are not worthy."

My forearms and ankles warmed and movement returned to them. They were spread wide to the sides, I realized. Suddenly, my head snapped up. I could lift and move my head slightly. Ice-cold metallic clamps held me in place, around my ankles, knees, hips, torso, elbows, and wrists.

Slithers of fear, unlike any I had ever known, crawled over me like maggots about to devour my flesh. My body warmed as I watched tubes protrude from my chest, right at the solar plexus of my stomach, my cock, and my wrists. I was inside one of Zaidon's rejuvenation caskets, I thought, as a fight-or-flight urge overtook me. The age-old survival instinct of a living creature was used as a tormenting method, and I couldn't escape it.

"You would feel that for the rest of your existence until you passed out from the overwhelming emotions no human could bear consciously. Your escape would only come when you were so scared that you would wish you were dead. You would realize passing out was your only reprieve, but you would be awakened, only to realize you were still in the same situation, repeatedly forever," the Zelk said and vanished from my sight.

"Noooo!" I screamed, my chest rising and falling. My fingers extended and my toes splayed open as my body went painfully rigid and numb again. My head lowered involuntarily. Once more, I lay unmoving, shouting for help.

"Kellan!" I called, as the rush of being drugged with stimulants overwhelmed me with drowning, blinding terror. Horrible sounds screeched out of my throat. Muscles spasmed. Teeth crunched. Spittle dripped from the corners of my mouth as tall, dark figures encroached with saws to cut me in half.

Stay in the bright white light, I reminded myself. They can't find you in the light.

My body and mind locked up in a searing agony, as if a trillion needles were piercing me. Wasps? Ants? Lightning? It felt like fire! Flames consumed me. My skin blistered and melted from my bones. I was being boiled alive, my brain was melting.

"Please!" I begged, praying someone would take pity. "Stop, please!" I croaked, my voice raw. "Just let me die!" I cried, pleading.

My thoughts spiraled back into a chaotic mix of fear and despair.

The Zelk was right, I realized; death would be a kindness. Then, darkness consumed me.

CHAPTER 20
KELLAN

THE WIND SOPORA HAD WISHED FOR US HAD BLOWN from behind and in our favor.

The voyage north, back to the Light Continent, was fast because we took the speedboat, and we carried no cargo, except our gear and medical supplies. Ten hours ago, we'd landed. Most of Simon's men were already on the Dark Continent and helping Ouroboros on the mountain. The last handful of men that stayed behind were cleaning out and evacuating their century-old, patched-together headquarters here on the Light Continent, to make the Dark Continent the new permanent base. They were also on standby, having the big sailboat ready in case something went wrong, but we hoped to make a fast escape once Draxton was safely extracted.

Simon had given us a brief overview of the building and dropped us off at the same drainage opening where Draxton had entered to go into the Malherbe building to make contact with Zaidon less than two weeks ago.

We've found out it was Zaidon's torturous day, and that Draxton was held for interrogation. The plan was to create a distraction at Zaidon's hybridization ceremony. Simon wanted to stop the process, mainly to prevent Zaidon from switching sides and betraying us, but also to show him mercy. Afterward, Simon would detonate the bombs and wait for us at the pier. Kawa would come with us, but serve as our lookout while Donali and I went to get Draxton and leave the same way we came. The rendezvous was set under the pier, at the opening of the drainage tunnel, where Simon would have the speedboat ready to go.

Strapped down, fully immobilized as if he were already dead, Zaidon lay unmoving on the enormous platform bed in the center of the surgical amphitheater below. Big mechanical arms waited, ready to start cutting, slicing, and chopping with crooked claws.

"Hear me!" Zaidon's voice bellowed up over the crowd. "Never forget. Remember! Stand proud, stand together. Free yourselves from this delusion!" Startled, the hybrid scientist walked abruptly around the table. His eyes were black and emotionless, but at the speed he was moving, I deduced that he was pissed off at himself for forgetting to shut up Zaidon sooner.

I shifted in my seat, bumping against Donali on my left and Kawa on my right.

"Those words will both annoy and scare the Zelk because they stir rebellion inside those waiting to be freed," Kawa whispered, not moving his lips. "Sit still, this mission depends on us not being discovered."

Right. My mannerisms should match my dress code, which was formal. My behavior must be exceptionally calculated.

The artificial cold air prickled the exposed hairless skin on my arms, neck, head, and face, and I shivered as the machines started up. Zaidon's message of hope was about to be cut short, but he shouted, evoking a fear I imagine my father lived with all these years. Now I truly knew what he was trying to prevent.

"To break you, they are killing the ones you love.

To disparage you, they strip you to expose your nakedness.

To warn you, they cut me up.

To enslave you, they dehumanize you.

To exalt you, they make you one of them.

Do not become the slave of the machine or be seduced into becoming its master, for doing so would wipe away each of your footprints on this planet.

Avoid them. Burn them if you can. Kill them because it's either them or you!"

They will not do this to you, Draxton, I thought, and hoped somehow he had heard me and was hanging on.

The throaty screams made me want to cover my ears. Clouds of smoke and the smell of lasered flesh, burning grease, and bone plummeted like steam being sucked into the ventilation hoods. I wanted to run and hide, but I sat still. I watched until a nauseous silence followed.

The silver-polished surgical arms flew over his body.

"They want to take his vocal cords," Kawa whispered. I struggled to hide a gagging sound.

"This is disturbing," I said, hoping it would all be over.

"I'm glad his ceremony was before Draxton's; they're

saving the best for last. Don't worry, you will see him soon. They will not do this to Draxton." Donali cracked a half smile. "Sopora's piglet is going to have this whole place in chaos once they discover it, and by then, we'll already be home. I'd choose Draxton's life over Zaidon's," Donali said. I nodded, knowing his voice may be gone, but Zaidon's pain had only just begun.

My eyes rolled to the corners of my eye sockets while I kept my head stock still. The Zelk Medical Auditorium was both breathtaking and terrifying. It was a vast space, with thousands of filled seats lining the interior of the cone-shaped building, which stretched into the clouds.

My bald head was sweaty, and I couldn't wipe at it for fear of revealing my discomfort with the heat and nervousness about the execution of Zaidon. Sitting up straight, with my knees pressed together, I sat with my feet flat and my arms hanging unnaturally at my sides. My perspiration could give me away even though I pretended to be cold and emotionally numb. I sat stock-still, rolling only my eyeballs slowly from side to side. Silent spectators sat just like me, watching. No hybrid or human was reacting to the demonstration of machine barbarism and dominance far below. My eyes roamed up and up the circling pavilion seats lining the upward slope. Specs of heads where their faces should be were growing recognizable as my gaze traveled from above to below. Each spectator focused on Zaidon in the center of the floor, awaiting his death as a human, and, if lucky, his *rebirth* as a hybrid.

This was a ceremonial declaration of supremacy.

Despite the colossal number of attending witnesses, it was quiet. Not a shuffle, a cough, or any indication that someone with emotion was watching another human about to experience the most horrible and prolonged pain anyone with living flesh and pain receptors can endure.

I blew out a shaky breath, hiding my disquiet.

"Look and don't shy away. His pain will subside. Simon has done this before. He will infuse the magnetized solution, and the diamond nanites will die immediately upon transfusion. Most of his screams are from fear and horror, not pain," Donali explained almost silently.

Some of the traitors were close enough for me to see their faces lit up. They practically clapped their hands when the sounds of the surgical machines started vibrating, breaking the sick silence in the crowd. I shook my head. I wanted to help him. I was seconds away from getting up and running to him. But I didn't. I forced myself to sit, to watch. My lips tingled from my silent hyperventilation. In, out, breathe, breathe. I closed my eyes. I prayed that Draxton would be alive by the time we got to him, that his soul would not be sucked into the hive. I prayed and prayed.

The blood-draining and sucking noises, as loud as a pit of snakes, suddenly halted. The machines retracted and switched off.

Two hybrid scientists inspected Zaidon's untouched body and said something to Simon as he pretended to assess him.

"The brain and nanites are spoiled," they announced. "He is unworthy."

"That's unfair. If he's not Zelk, Malherbe Enterprises is doomed." Zonika exploded in anger two rows below us. I smiled inwardly while I wore a mask of aloofness.

The insult, "Belligerent revolutionist!" turned heads. Zonika gasped, her hand flying to her mouth. Zaidon's sister was alien ugly, bald, with big black eyes, and as short as Zaidon. Her indignation quickly dissolved into a display of all-too-human fear.

"Get up, it's time to go, but do not make any abrupt moves," Kawa cautioned me from the corner of his mouth as he activated the small bomb under his seat.

Zonika, face flushed with anger, hissed, "Come on, let's go." She linked her arm with her spineless, hybrid husband's and pulled him up the stairs, brushing past us.

I lifted robotically from my seat and followed Kawa, with Donali heading to the tiny door next to the elevator.

"Here!" Kawa shoved me to the side. "There!" We slipped inside. "Fucking monsters," he muttered as he held the door open to the air duct. I jumped into the ventilation shaft with Kawa on my heels, just as we'd planned. I didn't have time to take stock of myself as I was free-falling at a ninety-degree angle straight into the drainage tunnel.

The air cushions Simon had placed *poofed-poofed-poofed* with dull thuds, and I bit my lip as Kawa fell right on me. "You okay?" he asked, dragging me upright.

"Yeah, go!" I said, and he jumped, heading for the other service door. I followed Donali, who was already inside the elevator shaft. The elevators were amazingly fast, zooming up and down, creating a whirlwind of sucking and pushing drafts.

"Here, hurry!" Donali called, and we dove to grab hold of the stairwell rails and climbed.

"Draxton, please be alive. You bloody damn well better be," I said, keeping my eye on the next bar, careful not to fall to my death.

"He's alive, it's his mind that I'm worried about," Donali said from below me.

Excitement to see Draxton pushed me to go faster. Soon, I would have him safe in my arms again. "Callisto will heal him. He told me that with the magic of that crystal and his powers, Draxton shall recover. The only thing Callisto said he couldn't do was bring Draxton back from the dead or turn him human, if he was Zelk. He'd said something about the Ferryman not allowing that."

I skipped three stairs at a time. They were easy to scale since they were built for smaller people. A safety rail wrapped around us, which calmed my nerves, and the repetitive grab-step-grab-step was my sole focus. If I slid, I would fall onto Donali, probably making him lose his footing too.

"So, Callisto finally decided to speak with you," Donali whispered.

We stopped for a break and rested, catching our breath and chalking our gloves one by one on the bags we'd tied to our sides to improve grip and prevent slippage on the bars. "Yeah, I think he waited to see if we were worthy. The tunnel maker was probably the deal breaker." We chuckled, then refocused and continued the climb.

When I reached the level marked by the red intertwined triangles, I knew this was it. I tapped the talk button on my earpiece three times before it beeped. For a moment, I thought it had died on me. "Donali and I are here; we're going in," I whispered, then pulled the mask over my head and hunkered down.

Donali looked up at me, giving me the go-ahead. "I'm opening the door...um...hatch," I reported to Kawa to let him know where we were. No one had ever set foot in this building, and we were working from our memory of Simon's century-old schematics drawn up before the building was erected. Donali and I had repeatedly gone over the steps of our plan with Simon and Kawa. Rescuing Draxton drove me, that and the super-healing power of the crystal around my neck. If we determined Draxton wasn't Zelk, we would take him home to the Dark Continent. If he were Zelk, I would set him free by injecting the magnetic poison into him, but I chose not to dwell long on that possibility.

We waited for the elevator Kawa would send up from below, specifically to this floor, because the elevator's steel door had to be in direct contact with the building's door-frame before the door could open without sounding an alarm. It stopped soundlessly, and the door to the floor pinged open.

Donali opened the small box of fuses and wires and cut the white wire to keep the hallway door open for us once the elevator had taken off again. That was my sign to swing inside, and Donali followed. I was grateful for my rock climbing skills as I turned to pull Donali up with me. My heart nearly fell out of my mouth as I gasped at the height of the steps we'd had to climb to reach this level, over a hundred floors high.

Donali checked the corridor. "Go!" He offered me a hand and pulled me upright. "Fuck," I whispered. "We still have to come back this way."

"I know, now go!" he said as we followed the strange triangles on the floor, pointing toward the battery of closed-casket detention cells. This building was designed with one massive floor connected centrally only by the shaft of eleva-tors to the floor above and below. That's why we had just scaled the steel rod stairs to where Simon's middleman had informed us Draxton was being tortured.

Boom!

The sound blasted and vibrated through the floor, but held steady. I was worried he had blown the entire city up, but it seemed he had contained the explosion, which was good.

"That's the first bomb. We are right on schedule," Donali said and nodded. By now, Kawa was busy planting the bomb set to detonate when we reached the exit at the bottom of the elevator shaft, and one last bomb for when we climbed into the escaping speedboat. The ship was being loaded with its final cargo and would be making its last trip ahead of us, and we would follow by motorboat.

The cold sadness of the place chilled me. Before us, the massive security gate stood locked and unmanned. Behind it, as I stooped carefully looking through the tiny glass windows in the solid titanium door, I recognized the two arches flanking it on the left and right. Draxton's cell was down the right hallway. "I don't see anything or anyone," I whispered and hunkered down on one knee. "It's as Simon said, the place looks and feels unattended," I said, and removed the battery-operated screwdriver Snow had gifted each of us. I then started to unscrew the security door hinges, as once the door was open, the bots would be mobilized, and an alarm would go off. Every camera in this place would turn our way. So we were taking the whole frame and door out of the wall.

"Yes, all the guards, every bot, and camera must attend and record the compulsory hybridizations."

Sweat trickled in streams from the inside of my mask down my neckline. "This thing is too hot. I don't care if they record my face. I'm taking the damn thing off."

"I'm not going to tell you to hurry, nor am I going to tell you we have fifteen minutes left," Donali whispered. I took the ski mask off, threw the thing aside, and continued unscrewing one screw at a time. Donali was working from the top, and I was working from the bottom.

In five minutes, the door was removed and lying on the floor. I waited until Donali tapped me on the shoulder, showing me he had finished disarming the continuous live recording system. The hallways were shiny, polished titanium. My reflection looked better than I felt. My limbs shook like stale Jello as we moved through the right arch and down the labyrinth of halls as stealthily and technologically loaded as Russian submarines.

Draxton's cell was located in the circular observation room, where visitors could sit and watch the entertainment. Donali and I weren't trained to be covert or tactical, but we marched alongside each other while he checked left and shook his head, and I checked right until we found the area where Draxton was. It reminded me of an intensive care unit, where nurses monitored patients.

Donali took off his mask, explaining, "I didn't want Draxton to get scared or think he was in danger if he saw us."

"Good thinking," I replied.

The room was brightly lit. The only piece of furniture was the glass casket plugged into the wall, with tubes pumping air and fluids like those used during open-heart surgery.

I blew out a relieved breath. It was a good sign. If he were a Zelk hybrid, he wouldn't produce any byproducts or need oxygen to breathe, I thought, and checked in with Donali, who was watching the monstrosity with a distant expression.

"What the hell are you waiting for, Kellan?" Donali whispered while I stared at the pale body I'd kissed and loved.

"Motherfucker!" I spat through clenched jaws, feeling like smashing the pod open with my fists. "They're going to pay for this. By the gods, I'm going to burn all of them." Fury turned my vision red. "How could they?"

"Kellan," Donali called me down from the precipice of hellfire. "Focus!"

I gritted my teeth and narrowed my gaze, looking at my Draxton through tear-filled eyes. "I'm going to fuck shit up, Donali. I feel like throwing this pod over."

Donali conceded. "I hate these machines, for fuck's sake. Why do they do this?" He winced. "Kellan," he whispered. I flexed my hands, closing them into fists.

I sniffed, shook my head, staving off an outburst. Tears blurred my vision. I was about to roar, letting out crazy, fucking mad crying. "These machines make me sick, Donali." I stared down at Draxton. "Help me, Donali. I'm going to do something wrong, and I do not want to hurt him. "Look at him," I cried. "He looks peaceful." I stood undecided and shaking. Silver bands held Draxton in place, and lights flickered while a swooshing noise accompanied the movement of Draxton's chest. "I don't want him to wake up, but what if I break the thing and then suffocate him?" I wiped the tears from my face and crossed my arms.

"I agree," Donali whispered. "Hand me that syringe in your backpack. I'll inject it into that tube." He pointed to the thin tube running into Draxton's femoral artery in his groin next to the tube inside his penis. I wanted to rip it out of him.

"No!" I placed my hands on the cold glass, the vapor of my breath clinging to it.

Donali's head flipped up. "What?"

I lowered my voice to a gravely low tone. "I said no. That's not what I meant."

"Please don't do anything drastic, Kellan." I pointed to the piglet in his backpack. Donali jutted his chin. "We give him the solution. That was the deal."

"No!" I grunted defiantly. "He is still connected to the tubes. He's not fully hybrid. Not yet."

"Then the injection won't hurt him."

I snapped my head up. "Why do you think he deserves the injection? Of course it would hurt him."

Donali pointed to the glass container hanging on a hook above the pod. "That solution hanging there, it's nanobots. It's glistening like diamonds."

I forced my words through pursed lips. "It's not yet connected to him."

Donali's expression softened. "That's true, Kellan, but what if that is the refill waiting?"

I shook my head. "Or they are waiting to start the process until after today's ceremony." I removed the syringe from my backpack, threw it on the ground, and smashed it under my boot. "We override the mechanism, making it think Draxton is still inside. Like we planned. Give me the fucking pig," I said, not taking my eyes from Draxton. "Hurry."

Donali stared at the black-brown fluid mingled with crushed glass on the floor. With his nostrils flared, hissing and sputtering, he said, "Ouro will not be happy about this. If Callisto sniffs him and he says Draxton is a Zelk hybrid, no one will allow you near the Dark Continent. What then? Are you prepared to die with him at sea, or be torn apart by Callisto? Because that is what Ouro ordered him to do."

"Then I die with him." I cried and reached for the piglet Sopora gave me. "Just give me the fucking tranquilized piglet." I held out my hands.

I was still waiting, opening and closing my fingers, telling him with my dark gaze that I wanted the damn piglet. I checked my watch. The Speedmaster had stopped ticking since we fell through the portal. Still, I checked it out of habit.

"Fuck!" Donali flung the backpack from his shoulder with a wide, exaggerated swing to the floor. "Do you always follow your heart and not your head?"

"Yup, are you ready?" I asked sarcastically, not waiting for his answer, and placed the AI scrambler on the electronic pin pad.

Donali held up the sleeping pink piglet. "Yes!"

I heaved the door open. Donali placed the piglet beside Draxton. I desperately wanted to rip out the tubes, but I took a deep breath, focused, and got to work.

"Hmmm," I grunted.

"Hmmm," Donali grunted back. "It's okay. We knew this was what we would find. Keep your emotions under control," he whispered as we worked by removing the first tube from Draxton's urinary tract, then pushing the catheter up the piglet's little penis. I unplugged Draxton's asshole with one hand, and with the other lifted the piglet's little tail and shoved it into his rectum. The femoral artery line, I carefully removed, applied pressure while Donali inserted it into the anterior aorta located next to the pig's trachea. Lastly, we removed the feeding tube from Draxton's stomach, rolled the pig over, and forced it down its throat.

"Sopora's suggestion was actually genius," I muttered and started to unscrew the clamps holding him down.

I scooped Draxton's rag doll body into my arms. Fear coursed through me. He barely breathed. With his nearly translucent skin and his limp, unconscious state, he looked dead. His head hung to the side. I stroked his delicate earlobes, checking his blood flow. His lips appeared just as inhuman. They were supposed to be pink, but like his fingernails, the return of blood when I pressed on them was nonexistent.

"He needs blood, lots of it, or he will die," Donali said hurriedly, stating the obvious. "I will let Kawa know to get the transfusion set ready, for when Callisto has determined he isn't Zelk yet. Will you be okay carrying him out of here and climbing the stairs down the shaft?"

"Yes, here." I held Draxton up so Donali could take him from me, and I dove around to put on our homemade baby carrier. Donali draped Draxton over my back, then quickly placed Draxton's feet through the holes and strapped him tightly to me, so his legs rested on my hips. "He lost so much weight during his imprisonment in the mine," I said. "Now he's as light as a sack of potatoes."

Donali helped wrap his legs around my hips and tie them so they would not dangle or get in my way as I climbed back down the elevator shaft. "Put socks on his feet, please," I asked, and Donali smiled at me and then did so. "Thanks. I think we are ready."

Draxton's breath felt cold on my neck, and his body was like ice between my shoulder blades. Gods, I was nervous to get out of here and furious about what they'd done to him. The Zelk were monsters.

Donali closed the pod and led the way outside. I checked our reflections as Draxton's body stiffened. His eyes flicked open and locked onto mine. I couldn't hold back my grin. Draxton's expression was nondescript.

Donali saw us and pulled me by the arm, helping me over the security gate we had removed earlier. "Wake up, princess, we're saving you."

Draxton sat unmoving and quiet as we approached the open door to the elevator shaft. He gasped weakly.

"We should go." I didn't wait for a reply as I passed Donali holding the door.

"Go, go, go!" Donali carefully held onto the side to slip my foot down to the first step.

Draxton, realizing what was going on, grabbed me around my neck, constricting my windpipe. "What the fuck!" I coughed. "Hold on, but ease up on strangling me."

He loosened his grip. "I'm dying. Help me, Kellan!" he croaked.

"We're saving you! Draxton, please stop swinging around. Don't look down. We have hundreds of steps to go."

"I'm naked!"

"Yes, you are," I said, climbing as carefully and fast as possible.

He was shaking. "Oh, no! Oh no, oh no," Draxton cried, and I knew he realized where we were. "You came to help me die!" He was clearly out of it.

"Draxton, please sit still, I'm going to lose my footing." I felt his head falling against the back of my neck. I climbed frantically to get out of that sick place. Draxton was quiet for a few minutes, and then I felt the wetness against my back. *He's crying.* It was a good sign, which meant he still had feelings, I thought. "I know, I know. Once we are outside, I will let you cry and hold you. Okay?" His head moved up and down, rubbing against my upper back and neck.

"You okay down there?" Donali called.

"Yes," Draxton answered in a whisper. "Oh, Kellan. My Kellan. I thought you'd forgotten about me. I thought you went home, leaving me here to suffer for eternity."

My heart broke for him, but I focused on climbing down. Left hand, right foot, right hand, left foot. My shirt warmed as the wetness of Draxton's tears continued to soak into it.

"I will never leave you behind."

CHAPTER 21
DRAXTON

My eyes flicked open, and I realized I was alone. Utterly alone. Alone, alone, alone in the dark. Darkness was good, silence was good. Tears welled up, then dripped down my cheeks, dampening the pillow. The dim candlelight on the floor reflected off the dark walls, and it struck me that I wasn't in the glass pod or a cave, but in a bed. Warm fur covered me, and the familiar scent of the clay hut, candle wax, and food told me I was back in the village. I slowly, soundlessly, released the breath I'd been holding.

I lay unmoving, immediately conscious of my body as my bladder prickled and called to be emptied.

Dark-dark-darkness. So happy to see you. My friend, silent darkness. I hoped it would listen and stay.

"Kellan!" my voice boomed worriedly, and I cringed at the noise I was making. I wasn't sure if I was truly safe, and if this was just another false construct my mind had conjured up, only to be yanked away again.

The torturous visions of doom tugged at my reality as I followed the shadows dancing on the wall. They grew long black fingers, reaching for me to drag me back into that hellish prison I couldn't escape. Horrible memories of disfigurement, dismemberment, and the worst kinds of mutilation resurfaced. Terrorizing me with doubt. Was I being haunted in my dreams, or were they bleeding into my waking life? Was I about to be burned alive or electrocuted to death?

My jaws quivered with fear. "Kellan, help me!" I called, just like I did from my glass prison.

"Give him some time, Kellan. Here, put another bigger crystal near his pillow for him." Sopora's gentle voice cut through the chaos inside me. Realizing I wasn't strapped down and was *not* forced to look up while lying on my back, I took the opportunity to move. I flipped onto my side, pulling my knees up into a fetal position, holding my head, covering my ears, rocking back and forth, squeezing my eyes shut, trying to find the darkness where I felt safe.

"Thank you, I don't know where he lost his necklace. I think the Zelk took it."

"All the more reason to get ready and prepare for their coming to wipe us out and steal our crystal. That crystal would have been the proof they needed. Take care of him. I will send you dinner with Libre," Sopora whispered, and I heard the squeaking of a door. A warm, gentle hand touched my shoulder, and Kellan's soothing voice calmed the storm raging like rolling thunder in my head. The bed dipped behind me as he pressed against my back, his arms wrapping tightly around my chest. "Draxton, you're awake. You're home. I'm here. You are safe. It's going to be all right. You are home, in our hut. I have you. They won't hurt you again. I will protect you. Listen to my voice." He kissed the back of my head, then trailed kisses down my neck, finally resting his chin in the curve of my neck and shoulder. Over and over, he repeated those words. He never let go. I cried until I believed him. I was home. I was safe. He was here with me. He would never let me go.

I stopped rocking and slowly let go of my head. The room was still dark, but those inky hands reaching for me were gone. The faint red hue of the crystal around my neck pulsed, and the realization helped me to uncurl my body and roll onto my back.

Kellan placed his palm flat on my chest, looking at me with caring concern.

"Hi," he whispered, smiling.

Seeing him made my heart leap. His scent and warmth eased me even more. "Hi," I croaked.

"Do you want to get up?"

"Yeah. I think so. I want to pee." Sitting up, Kellan rolled over and stood up next to our bed on the floor.

He offered a hand to pull me to my feet. "Hey." Kellan hooked his arm underneath my arm, and I leaned into him as I got up. Too scared to open my eyes.

My lips vibrated. "Please help me. I can't...I can't..."

"It's okay. You are doing great. Remember, you said once I'm your darkness and your quiet. I'm here, and I'm not leaving you for a second," he said as he led me to the wash-room. My legs were numb, and my feet weren't lifting high enough. I stumbled, but Kellan kept me upright by holding onto my hips.

I fiddled with the drawstring of my sleeping pants.

"Empty. Pee. Let me sit. Empty my bladder." I spoke, but my voice sounded far away, like it wasn't my own.

Kellan carefully spun me around. "I've got you. Relax. I have you." He held me still while I kept my eyes and ears closed. My heart raced, my ears swooshed, my eyes stung, and I burst into sobbing. "I'm peeing. I'm peeing. I'm peeing." The urgent feeling was replaced by relief, and the strong smell of urine wafted to my nose, anchoring me in the here and now and stopping my tears from flowing. I breathed in deeply, filling my lungs with the surrounding scents, and the feel of Kellan's warm, steady hands holding me. The faint red glow of the necklace around my neck tempted me to unclasp my fingers behind my head. Slowly, slowly, slowly, I lowered my arms. The noises vanished, replaced by Kellan's breathing. We breathed the same air—air that floated freely in our wash-room. In our home.

"I'm home," I whispered shakily.

"Yes, you are, my love." Kellan kissed the back of my neck. His lips were soft, warm, and tender. "I love you," he whispered between kisses. I reached for him, grabbing hold of his pants. He was here, and I was touching him. "I'm here. Home," I whispered.

Kellan kissed my naked shoulder. "Yes, I have you. I will never let anything like that ever happen to you again. You are safe. You are home."

I don't know how long I sat there or how long he spoke softly, and so very kindly, encouraging words to me while I hung my head.

Breathing. Listening. Smelling. Feeling.

He filled the bare crevices of my broken mind, patching,

cementing, and restoring me, orienting me back to the present, to what is real and safe as he helped me stand and pull up my pajama pants and wash my hands before leading me back to our bed.

Kellan moved my bedding to one side and gently pulled me toward it, and my feet shuffled over. "Come. I will hold you." He steered me, helping me bend my knees. I recognized the color and the smell of newly changed bedding. "That's it." He tucked me in on the right side, walked around, and came to lie next to me, on my left. "Okay, you will be okay. I promise you," he said, kissing the side of my head, and snuggled closer to me. I closed my eyes. Feeling warm and protected.

Much later, I was awakened by Kellan's voice. He wasn't beside me, but outside. "Draxton got up once. He is trauma- tized, and I'm not going to let you inside until I know he wants to see any of you. He needs time. He's been hurt. Mentally. He says the most disturbing things in his sleep."

I sat up, rubbing my eyes, feeling groggy. "He's been through horrific things. He needs time." Kellan whispered, but I heard him. I wobbled closer and started eavesdropping at the door.

"What things?" It was Simon's voice.

"It sounds to me like he had been tortured, burned, stabbed, and cut. But I can't find any wounds or scars. The list goes on and on."

"They gave him stimulants. It hijacks the brain's fight-or- flight center, and you constantly dream up scenarios where the worst possible thing is happening to you and you can't escape. The fear either makes you lose consciousness or kills you. They decide, and you experience it repeatedly. They can keep you alive for as long as they want or until your visions bore them," Simon told Kellan.

"Can they see what you dream?"

"Yes, and no. They read the pattern of your brain activity. The more your brain lights up, the better the show."

"Sick fucking things." Kellan's voice grew louder, and I jumped, unsure of where to go. Before I could decide, the door swung open, light pouring in, and Kellan's silhouette filled the frame. He stood tall with a spear in his hand, like a black marble statue of a war god, but a surprised expression crossed his face.

I crossed my arms, hugging myself, unsure if I was allowed to be out of bed. "You are up and on your feet," he said, moving slowly as he closed the door to keep anyone from seeing inside. He placed his spear next to the far wall, moving slowly and deliberately as he spoke gently while holding his hands in a placating manner, as if he were worried I might flee. I stood wide-eyed, my breathing quickening.

"Do you want to try to eat something?" He pulled out a chair for me and then took the one opposite. "No need to talk." He smiled, and I sat down, daring to meet his friendly golden-brown eyes. He was bald again, which meant he must have shaved his head when he came to save me.

With a small, uncertain shake of my head, I said, "No, thank you, I'm not hungry." But I didn't hear the words leaving my mouth.

"Okay, no pressure. Let me know when you are peckish. I have all your favorites here," he said.

"Thanks." I cracked a smile at one corner of my mouth.

"If you are up for it, I will make us some tea." Kellan stood. His beautiful face saddened me.

"I am sorry," I whispered, not truly sure why I was apologizing. I felt guilty about things that didn't really happen. They were dreams. Illusions. They were not real. This was real.

Kellan took my hands in his, kissing my knuckles as he kneeled next to me. "No, none of that. You didn't do anything. You are innocent of anything you think you could have done to me. To anyone." He wiped away the tears from my cheek while his eyes brimmed with his own tears.

I nodded, and my eyes fell closed. I cleared my throat. "Thank you for coming to get me," I croaked, not opening my eyes.

"We fell into this place together, and I'm not leaving without you."

"Thank you," I said shakily, staring into his sympathetic eyes. His gaze up at me was unwavering.

"Simon and his brothers helped me. They detonated a couple of bombs. Euthanized Zaidon too. He was not Zelk."

"He wasn't?"

"No, it was his brother and sister. They got away, and Simon's men are hunting them. They are trying to get to their leader and free the prisoners. But don't worry about that now. The most important thing is that you are safe, and we are not leaving, and no one is visiting until you say you are ready," Kellan said.

"I'll thank them eventually, just not today. I'm just exhausted, Kellan."

"That's perfectly fine. We're going to relax, and you can heal at your own pace. I already told them...no visitors, no questions."

My breath hitched, and I swallowed the lump of fear stuck

in my throat. "I love you," I whispered while visions still swam with the memory of the blinding, screeching noises. "I don't think I would have made it if you hadn't come for me. I was so scared. I begged them to let me die in there. You're always my rock, a steady presence in my shitstorm. You saved me. You're my hero."

CHAPTER 22
CALLISTO

SNOW WAS STARTING TO FALL, AND OURO HAD ordered everyone back up to the cave where they were drilling into the mountain. The village wasn't safe, and Kellan and Draxton couldn't stay there unprotected any longer. Once inside the mountain, we would only leave to fight the war.

"*You sound like you are certifiably insane,*" I told Kellan.

"Oh my god, what do you know about someone being certifiable?"

"*That's something my father used to say; it sounds exactly like you look now,*" I said accusingly. "*Now, try to shut your mouth for a second, because the whole mountain can hear you.*"

Kellan nearly burst his seams. He closed his mouth with a pop, looking like a blowfish with constipation.

"*Just talk mind to mind to me. Days passed, and instead of joining Ouro and helping him, I'm here daily, checking up on Draxton and you. It's time we find common ground about Drax-*"

ton. *The man is bitter. To make matters worse, you feel sorry for him. Plus, it's all your fault."*

"*I know, I should never have told him to befriend Zaidon. I should never have taken off flying through the storm with that bloody fucking airplane. Its fucking wing just fell off. Like one second it was there and the next it was ripped off, like a fucking Band-Aid.*" The expression on Kellan's face turned sour with guilt. He looked like that blowfish again, struggling to take a shit.

I widened my eyes, biting back a retort.

"*I know Draxton must leave the house,*" he screamed into my mind.

I shook my head to the side. "*Not so loud.*"

"*Like this?*" he asked.

"*Yeah. Now, let's get your man; he doesn't have a choice anymore. It's been a month,*" I said, hoping it sounded convincing. "*The time of staring into the darkness has passed. Draxton has healed physically, and mentally, he will only fully heal if he comes outside and sees people. You can't hide him or tuck him away. You are enabling him. I think you are a bit overprotective.*"

I wanted to say, "*I'm helping you,*" but the bear noise I uttered made Kellan madder at me.

He pointed a finger at me. "*I'm so sick of you growling and snarling when you don't get your way! He is mine to protect.*"

"*That's why I say you are insane. We are all here to protect him. There isn't a single person on this continent who would hurt him.*"

He locked his fingers behind his head in exasperation. "*We want to go home. We didn't ask for this!*"

"*I know, and I'm sorry. It's not that I chose to bring you. You were in the wrong place at the wrong time. We've told you Atlas can help us send you guys back,*" I cried. Then lay down, hiding my face beneath my paws.

Kellan fell to his knees, wrapping his arms around my neck. "*Callisto, do you hear yourself? You were sent by Atlas back in time, but you fell here, one hundred years later. How do you think we will get back home with those odds? We are scared, my boy. So very scared. We are not used to this level of violence, and we realize, chances are, we may never go home,*" he said in despair.

I whimpered. "*Oh, Kellan...I'm really sorry. I didn't mean to. That's the only way I know how to get you back home, and I'm so sorry, Kellan. Please forgive me.*"

"It's not your fault," he mumbled into the thick fur on my cheek. "*I want you to understand what we are going through. What we are dealing with. There is so much that Draxton and I have to work through, and it's not that we can't go anywhere. We just needed this time to come to terms with our situation. Draxton has his own way of processing things, and I have to support and protect him as best as I can. It's just that once we go up the mountain, we will never have this chance to be quiet and experience the stillness Draxton needs to get back to himself. He has flashbacks, and they are going to bring up questions. They are going to scratch his wounds open!*" he said telepathically.

"*What wounds, Kellan? You've done everything possible. Can't you see how unhealthy this is?*"

Kellan got up from the mushy frozen ground. "*You don't understand. He could have died or been made Zelk. He could have been a machine.*"

"*You both need to get out of this hut. You are feeding each other's fears. You have me, and you have this whole village waiting to help you both. Everyone is waiting and sends get-well messages to you each time I come down to check on you. I know this is hard, but he's alive!"*

Kellan puffed a breath and looked at me with narrowing eyes. I growled, showing him I was determined today.

He sighed, lowered his gaze, and, thank goodness, reached for the door and fidgeted with the doorknob.

My short, stubby tail wiggled happily as I stood up, ready to run inside.

He threw the door open, and I shrank my size to fit through it and not mess up their home. *"Okay, I will let you inside. We will start packing when you leave; we will come up the mountain to join the village the day after tomorrow."*

"Good boy," I said teasingly, the way they always praised me as if I were a puppy, and waltzed inside their home, ready to say hello to Draxton. I'd missed him. Kellan had only let me inside to heal him, then decided to keep Draxton all to himself for an entire month.

CHAPTER 23
KELLAN

I FELT RELIEVED WHEN I SAW DRAXTON'S TEETH peeking from behind a wider smile.

Callisto's words echoed true. It's been four weeks since we'd rescued Draxton. His body had healed, but his mind was another issue. He seemed more chipper after seeing Callisto.

"*Alright, I'm heading out. We'll see you in two days, right? If not,*" Callisto said, cutting me off and glaring at Draxton, "*I'm coming to get you. And I'll carry you both back in my mouth— something you germaphobes definitely won't enjoy.*" I hurried to open the door for him so he could leave.

"Yeah, we won't like your fish breath."

"Kellan!" Draxton called me.

"*Now shoo!*" I pushed Callisto out the door.

I sat on our bed as Draxton scooted over to make space for me. "How will I share about myself with them, if I don't know how I feel? I'm disconnected. I know my whole life has revolved around searching and crawling inside caves. My family was obsessed with finding exactly these things. I should be more eager, but all I'm thinking is that we are hidden and lost, just like these people who'd died thousands of years before we even started searching. Your mother is alone and waiting. That's why we needed the drill. We wanted to open the mountain to go home. But as soon as I settle into the memory of Atlas and the mountain, of going home, those fears flare up, and suddenly I'm back in that dark place. But it's becoming less daunting to remember. Maybe it's time, as Callisto said."

"I promised him we'd be there in two days," I told Draxton. "We have time to pack. While we do it, you talk to me. Tell me everything, practice as if you were back with everyone waiting for us inside the cave." I took his hand and kissed it.

Draxton's brows flicked up and down. "I used to like to crawl around in caves, into cracks and holes?" The sound of his amusement and joy was fulfilling; it confirmed that my efforts were worth it. I placed my hand on his thigh and squeezed, then slowly slid my hand up his leg. He stopped laughing. Our eyes locked, and the smoldering flames of interest flickered in his eyes. Since we'd returned, I had cared for him only out of concern. But now I wanted him to know he had someone who loved him; I wanted to show him with my body, not words and deeds.

"Let's see how much I love you." My voice was low and steady. Stoking the flames between our minds. I wanted him to feel. "If I make you uncomfortable. Suppose you want me to stop. Just say stop. Okay?"

He tipped his head to the side, shyly. "Yes, show me. Please."

I got up. It was warm in the hut because I kept stoking the

fire to keep Draxton comfortable and warm. I tossed another log on the orange coals and watched him, waiting for cues to show me he was serious. Sometimes it took him a while to act on his words, as if his mind and body needed to catch up and agree on what to do next, so I didn't want to rush him. All I wanted was for him to feel safe. When he opened the furs for me, he was wearing only thin sleeping pants.

He awkwardly loosened the drawstrings with shaky fingers, and then shoved his pants down to his ankles and kicked them aside. This was a first since his return. So far, he'd only undressed, showered, and changed clothes, then returned to bed, ignoring me. Slowly, his legs parted, and he sagged down on the bed so that he lay before me like a feast. His flesh was pale and smooth—the opposite of mine.

His chest flared bright red blotches, while his ribcage moved up and down, much faster than usual, as he waited for me.

I was nervous. My cock was plump, not filled as hard as I knew it could get for him. Draxton looked at it with lust-filled eyes, but when he licked his lips, I knew he was ready for me.

My heart pounded as I pushed my pants down. I lifted my leg to straddle his narrow hips, but I didn't lower my pelvis or touch him with my lower body. I rested my hands on my thighs. With our gazes still locked, I said, "Stop me any time you feel uncomfortable, when it doesn't feel good, or it becomes too much for you. Tell me exactly what you want."

He nodded, biting his lip, and I waited patiently for him to take me in as his eyes roamed down my chest, pausing at each of my ivory pierced nipples before trailing further down my manhood, which stood erect and thumping and hot, begging for a hand, for any tight relief. But I still waited. I observed his face—his wide eyes. Then took in his trembling hands as his breath hitched, coming out in short, panting gasps.

"May I ask you a question?" he whispered.

"Of course you may. Ask me anything."

"Is it normal to feel this lightheaded and short of breath?" He seemed worried, with a deep frown between his brows. "I feel different, very peculiar." The perplexed expression on his face tightened as he told me he battled many voices in his head.

Draxton's chin quivered as he held back the tears. I wanted to wrap my arms around him, but I waited calmly with a supportive smile. He could ask or say anything to me, and I would understand. Even if I didn't, I would try to. His mind needed healing, and it would take a long time. He turned his head away, his bottom lip peeling down. "No, leave it."

"Hey, none of that. Ask me. If you don't want to ask me, that's also fine. Just know that I will always be here and ready to answer. Talk to me. To anyone, please promise me you won't hide inside your mind. It worries me," I said tenderly.

"I'm sorry, I don't know why it happens, or why I'm even crying anymore."

"It is all right. It is how it should be. My mother used to say that we must cry now and then to wash away the things that clog our minds. You can't think and make plans with a clogged-up mind."

Draxton seemed to forget his tears as he smiled at me. "I'd love to meet your mother one day."

"That's a positive approach. We should both be looking forward to seeing her again," I said.

Draxton surprised me by changing the subject back to other things. "When are we going to pack?"

"We can pack tomorrow, or now; you decide. It looks as though the weather will hold. Callisto said we have two days, or else he will carry us back," I said jokingly, still waiting for him to touch me.

"Callisto told me just now he has a surprise for us, for me, actually, but I know he meant you, too. He said there is a hidden city below the mountain."

"Oh?" He scowled. I looked away, thinking I should climb off him.

But Draxton wrapped a gentle grip around my doubting penis and squeezed. I met his smoldering gaze. The silence stretched for eons as our eyes spoke volumes, and then he pushed back. Stretching my foreskin so far, the pink head turned pale in his hand as it hardened again. He did that a few times. He watched and felt it as it grew in his hand.

I hissed softly and closed my eyes. Showing him I was enjoying it. "You make it difficult to control myself. I won't touch or do anything you don't want me to."

Draxton flushed red up his neck. "You may explore me as I explore you." Finally, he smiled that sexy, seductive smile he only gave me. The last time I saw it was on the airplane before we went to get Zaidon and that damn laser drill. He ran his thumb back and forth over the head of my leaky cock.

"I'm ready to explore the fuck out of you, if you need me to." My voice rumbled out of my chest.

"Come lie yourself down beside me. Touch me. Show me you want me." He removed his hand from my cock. *I was surely going to have cement balls tomorrow.* This was about Draxton and his comfort. I promised him to take it slow, and I would. Putting my hands next to his shoulders, I kissed his soft lips. Just a peck. Then, two long kisses before I gently fell to his side with my head spinning and my leg thrown over his hips, covering my erection. I was dumb with arousal. *Gods, help me be patient with this man.*

I smiled. "You have the gentlest soul and the most beautiful mind." I ran my pointer finger from his temple down to his cheek, to below his jaw, feeling his carotid artery beating under his pale skin like water rippling. He lay still, his fingers gliding down my throat, over my chest, twirling his finger around the few short black chest hairs, lastly around and around each hoop in my nipples. His explorations felt like he was taking me in for the first time again. The look of awe brought a smile to my face. With his eyes closed, I could tell he was relaxing under my touch.

"Feel me touching you," I said, slowly stroking over his chest, enjoying the feel of his bumpy flesh caused by popping goosebumps and tiny hairs rising, and swaying with static electricity. I licked my finger and ran it over his rosy, flat nipples, lazily teasing them until they hardened under my touch, then teasing them with my tongue. I sighed into his chest, listening to his heartbeat. Slow and steady. The feeling of love and trust was exchanged just by touching, stroking, and caressing him until he fell asleep. I rolled onto my back, hooking an arm behind my head, while Draxton lay curled up, resting his head on my other arm. We were sharing breaths and our hearts again, and the peacefulness I'd missed and thought I would never have again.

"*Thank you, Callisto,*" I thought as I drifted into slumber with Draxton in my arms.

CHAPTER 24
DRAXTON

"HELLO, ARE YOU BOYS UP AND READY?" SOPORA called, knocking nonstop. The irritating sound made me want to hide or run outside and break off a finger or two.

"She came to wake us up, come on." Kellan took my hand to drag me after him. I might as well be wearing a collar attached to a damn leash.

I got up, flying after him. "It's too fucking early!" I groaned as if I had a choice in this matter of going up the bloody fucking mountain today.

Before we reached the door, Sopora opened it, peeking inside. "Oh, there you are," she said with pretend surprise. "I'm just dropping off something to eat and drink for when you start your trek back up the mountain."

It was her way of reminding us to hurry, but also to ensure we were fed. She handed us two parcels of cloth tied at the corners, smelling like fresh bread. "Here, and don't forget to throw out the food that could spoil. Pack everything you can carry, and don't forget your tent in case you have to stop for the night. Please don't run around in the dark and make us search for you. Pack smart, because we won't be coming back, not before next summer, and not before the war. Do you need me to take something up for you?"

We shook our heads, rubbing the sleep out of our eyes. "Hmmm, no, thank you. We'll manage," Kellan said, scratching his stomach.

"I'll start with breakfast," I said, ignoring Sopora. She was too loud and far too energetic.

"Okay then, no rush. I'll see you later today or early tomorrow."

"Thank you," we called after her as she closed the door.

Kellan yawned, stretching his arms. "She means well," he muttered and went to use the washroom.

"I know."

After breakfast, we tidied the hut, cleaned out the box fridge, fed the crows the food we weren't taking with us, then showered one last time together before we returned to living like cavemen.

"I could have easily stayed for another month," I growled while packing and then again when rolling our bedrolls and tying them with leather straps. I was as reluctant as an innocent at the gallows. However, as we got to work, I grew more excited about searching for the hidden city, and Kellan seemed happier when I appeared upbeat and talkative.

At least we had something new to talk about other than my mental torture at the hands of the Zelk. Callisto should've mentioned the hidden city earlier, though I suppose it just never came up since we were always sailing or flying between the continents.

Things had settled into a comfortable rhythm between Kellan and me, but it's been weeks since we had sex. For some strange, inexplicable reason, every time I touched him, fear bubbled up inside me. It felt as if I was standing on the tallest building in the world, about to jump off without a parachute. Kellan thought it was because my mind associated our falling together through the time portal with my fear of losing him. I suppose that could be true, since we fell in love and our story began after arriving here. Now my mind believed it was protecting itself by not allowing me to fully give myself to him. Perhaps my brain had associated falling with Kellan, falling in love, and the fear of face-planting after jumping out of an airplane. Regardless, Kellan wasn't rushing me into anything I wasn't comfortable with.

Once we'd loaded ourselves like beasts of burden, we shut the door to the hut, not knowing if we would ever see it again.

"The sooner we get this behind us, the sooner we can find out where the crack in the sky is," Kellan said, skipping like a three-year-old imitating Tigger.

I raised my brows and puckered my lips. "That is, if Atlas is even asleep—I'm hesitant to believe he's waiting like Cinderella to be woken up before midnight. That is, if they can get inside, drilling through solid magnetized rock without burning out the drill, or before the Zelk wipe us all out first."

Kellan proclaimed, "I'm going to take it step by step. Day by day. As long as I have you by my side, whether we make it home or die together, it will be an adventure!"

I rolled my eyes. "Callisto seems to be correct about the weather," I told Kellan as we ventured up the well-trodden path from our hut to the edge of the now eerily empty village.

Kellan sighed. "I guess he has a sixth sense about things like that."

"Or he reads the clouds and wind and makes a calculated assumption according to the atmospheric conditions," I noted.

Kellan turned and walked backward. He gave me that cheeky look; I just knew he was about to come up with something really stupidly creative. "Or..."— he chuckled—"he has a built-in atmospheric barometer inside his head," he joked and turned back to walk like a normal person, preparing to scale a mountain. By foot. Through muddy snow. In subzero temperatures.

When we passed the rubble of the destroyed amphitheater, I stopped to take one last look at the damaged obelisk. In silence, for one final time, we paused to say goodbye to the village we built with our hands. "It feels like a year ago and not a couple of months since we arrived here," Kellan said softly.

My eyes stung like someone had poured red pepper in them. "I understand now why Ouroboros didn't care for it. It was a waste of time." A thick swelling of sadness was stuck in my throat. I coughed, shaking my head at my stupidity. "We were so excited to do something other than fighting in a war. Now look where we are. On our way to kill Zelk, and rightfully so."

"No, it wasn't for nothing. People had a safe place to sleep with their children. They appreciated it. Even if we don't come back here, I'm sure they will spend next summer back here," Kellan said as he patted my shoulder.

I pursed my lips, nodding, then straightened up, met Kellan's determined gaze, and a feeling of calm optimism filled me. It finally felt like I was leaving the octagon of my mind. We sniffed the air and looked at the town. It was really empty, like a ghost town. All the chickens, goats, and pigs were moved back to the livestock cave. There was no smoke coming from the chimneys and fireplaces, no children laughing and playing, no noise or movement, except for the crows feasting on the scraps we'd thrown out.

"If they win the war, things will be different," I said, and turned my gaze away from what had become our home. We thudded our spears into the icy ground and started the long upward climb. It will take us twice as long, especially going upward.

WE STARTED our climb on a cloudless day with streaks of sunlight forging a path for us through the boulders, but the further we climbed, the darker it grew as storm clouds started to gather around the crest of the mountain. I was fit. Just like Kellan, our bodies were in the best shape we had ever been in. We walked and climbed for hours without even breaking a drop of sweat. We had grown accustomed to the vigorous battering of our bodies, and we tested our endurance by climbing, discussing how superhuman we were becoming. The thought made us halt so we could laugh at the idea, and the further we climbed, the more we found out we had almost no limitations. Our bodies were changed, and so were our minds and hearts. We were not the men who went into the Dinaledi Chamber months ago.

The moonlight had disappeared, and clouds hovered around us. The trail was becoming dangerous, and we were sliding backward more than moving forward on the slick, icy path.

"We should make camp for tonight," I said, catching my breath.

Kellan was two feet behind me, and he stuck his spear into the ground to steady himself to prevent slipping backward down the steep, slippery slope. He smiled, nodding and catching his breath too. "I agree. Right here is a good spot. I'm happy for the tent, blankets, and provisions Sopora insisted we bring with us. They expect us tomorrow, not tonight, so we don't have to rush."

I slipped the homemade backpack off my shoulders. "I told Callisto we wouldn't go out in the dark and get lost," I explained, glancing back. Truthfully, I was more concerned about the people we were going to see. "I just don't feel ready to meet them yet, Kellan. If we can postpone it another day, shouldn't we?"

"Stop worrying, we will be fine. Let's enjoy this. Once we are home, we can tell my mother about the night we spent camping on the mountain," Kellan said from behind me. He changed direction, climbing over a boulder and pushing himself up with his spear.

Small iron lava pebbles rolled beneath our boots like marbles.

"Let's find a flat enough area to set up camp," I said with an oomph as more rocks tumbled back and Kellan struggled to find purchase on the wet rocks.

"Good idea." Kellan huffed, then leaned against the side of the cliff. "Not sure about a flat surface, though."

"Okay, this looks like a decent spot to pitch the tent. Kellan, get away from there! You're going to fall." That familiar fear of death by falling returned, but this time it was Kellan's potential demise flashing through my mind. "Be careful!" He just looked at me, smiling like a lovesick fool, but he was watching his step. "I think we must have taken a wrong turn somewhere. This doesn't seem like an area where the children would be allowed, or would even come."

"That's okay. Callisto will find us." Kellan unloaded himself, stacking our bedrolls and backpacks against the farthest wall of the overhang. He gathered wood by breaking branches from a dead tree and collected a handful of tall grass, then kicked the largest movable boulders aside, rolling them to create a circular barrier for a fire later, and came to help me set up the tent.

Minutes later, we relaxed as I built a small fire right by the tent door. We'd set it to avoid suffocating while I heated soup for us to eat, but also close enough to provide heat. After we ate, Kellan unrolled our bed furs, and then we took off our boots, pants, and shirts. I hung them to dry over a makeshift clothesline I'd strung diagonally from the tent, past the fire, and secured with a tent peg I had hammered into the rock-face.

"Just imagine, Kellan, the city Callisto described could be right beneath us," I said with suppressed excitement. He held the top blanket of soft fur open for me.

"I know, but don't expect too much. They also said a dragon was sleeping there, and I don't think dragons worry about preserving the architecture." He held out his arm, and I snuggled closer, throwing an arm and leg over his warm body, and sighed. Together we enjoyed the silence, listening to the wind softly whistling around the corner and the fire crackling behind us.

I swallowed down the knot of anticipation stuck in my throat. "I can feel it. The things I imagined all my life. The things my grandfather had told me about. The way Ouro described it. I can imagine the blue sky filled with men with wings. His tribe, the jungle. The light, the colors, and the smells of grass, trees, and flowers. The breeze wafting in from the ocean," I whispered as confused feelings made tears brim. Secretly, I was mad at myself and furious at Kellan for letting us crash. I knew it wasn't his fault. We both should have decided not to fly into an electric storm, but still, I blamed him because I had no one else to blame.

"I can see and smell exactly what Ouro described too. My father spoke of Anzulla fondly, though only seldom." He kissed me on the head. "We will see what happens tomorrow. I prefer not to get excited, so anything I find is a surprise and not a disappointment."

I mulled that over. "That won't work for me. How will I keep searching if I can't imagine what I'm searching for? I will be like a bulldozer, not enjoying my work."

Kellan poked a finger into my ribs. I yipped. "Hey, that tickled." He poked me twice more. "Hey!" My heart swelled with playfulness and love. "Okay, Professor. Tomorrow then." I chuckled.

"Sounds like a plan." Kellan kissed me. He checked on the fire, scooted down, then turned on his side, and I moved down to spoon him. The heat between our bodies built to a toasty, comfortable level.

"Hmmm," Kellan groaned sleepily. "Love you...night."

"Hmmm," I grunted. My hand around his hips roamed down over the stretchy fabric of his underwear. "Can I touch you? It's been so long since I touched you."

"Yes, you may. I'm quite bloated in the balls." Kellan

turned onto his back. "I've missed you." His voice was thick with arousal.

"I know, and I'm sorry. I've missed you, too. But..."

"Hey, I told you. I love you, and when you feel you are ready, I will still love you and be here."

"I see now it was a useless endeavor to try to blame you," I admitted.

"Please...stop...blaming either of us. We should blame the Zelk. Not even Zaidon...he paid with his life...for coming here and bringing us the laser drill. Everything has its place in the big scheme of things. When we see Ouroboros tomorrow, I'm sure his happiness with the progress they've made will make both of us forget the bad. We have each other."

"And we have a hidden subterranean city to find," I interjected.

"Yeah, and that." Kellan sighed as my hands softly traced over his tight pecks.

"Still, I'm sorry. I blamed both of us for what happened," I whispered as I rolled his hardened nipples between my fingers.

Kellan lay with one hand behind his head, the sweat in his armpits not bothering me. I loved it. I loved him. He stroked the side of my face, playing with my new short black hair, then slowly slid his hand over my shoulders and rubbed my back in slow circles. "I'm sorry about what happened," he whispered.

I found his dry, cracked, but still very plump lips and kissed him. "It's not your fault, I know that. I'm sorry for blaming you." I rolled onto my lover, my friend, my every-thing in this foreign place, and slowly, thoroughly, and completely showed him how much I'd missed him by making love with my lips. I nibbled, licked, and sucked, exploring all the hidden places inside his mouth with my tongue.

His hand roamed lower, and I pressed my backside against his palm, indicating that I wanted him to cup, squeeze, and knead my butt cheek. He did just that, and I purred into his mouth. I rolled my cock against his hip bone, hinting at where I wanted his fingers to go. We kissed slowly while the warmth between our bare bodies filled me with a sense of safety. I needed this. We needed this.

"Ahh, it feels so good to have you in my arms. Stop me if it becomes too much," he said into my mouth.

I was short of breath. "I will...and this feels good to me too. I missed you." We retook possession of each other's mouths. His other hand joined in working my tight glutes until they were warm and soft in his palms. We shared breaths as the tips of our noses touched. Anticipation built between us. I let the want between us settle, forcing the neediness to subside and encouraging my soul to open up. "I love you, Kellan. This is something I could never have with another person. You demand nothing, yet I know you need it. Do you understand what I'm saying?"

His forehead rubbed against mine as he nodded and rolled his cheek against mine. "I do. I fell in love with you almost instantly. I didn't want to push my feelings for you down your throat. You are a complex, solitary soul. I wanted to give you space to recognize what special bond we had."

I rolled my hips, rubbing my hardness against his. I opened his thighs with my knees, making room for me between his legs. We were nearly the same height, so our bodies fit flush against each other. He growled into my mouth. I flicked my tongue out to lick a trail around his bottom lip and then the top. He gripped my hips and bit into my bottom lip.

"Why did you partake in orgies with Ouro and Snow, if you loved me already?"

"Because, if I didn't and if I'd told you I wanted you for myself, you would have thought of a reason, consciously or subconsciously, to run off without me. By showing you I could enjoy myself, you didn't see me as a threat. As someone who wanted too much from you. I wanted to give you the space to get to know me and realize there was room for me."

"But...?" I forgot what I wanted to say and panted into his mouth, enjoying the way I was dragging out the tension and heat building between us. Having this conversation was a long time coming, and in a way, I felt our minds were already making love. Our bodies could wait because this was important to Kellan. To us.

He poked and played around my hole, not quite entering it, teasing it. "I discovered myself in the meantime. I got to know my brother very intimately," Kellan said jokingly. "I even thought I'd never known myself at one stage, maybe stuck the wrong label on my box. But, I think because we are in such close proximity to Ouro and Snow, I felt I knew them as I saw them as great men with strong morals and purpose. They are beautiful specimens, but I also knew that you were watching, always observing my every move, it was a turn-on for me in itself because I knew you had been attracted to me since we met, but you wanted me to fuck you, and go away, disappear back to my office, so you can be alone to explore the Star Caves on your own," he said with a smile and groaned into my mouth. Our cocks were leaking, and we pumped our hips into the warm, slippery mess between us, and it became slipperier. Gods, it was erotic as fuck.

"You are way too smart, Professor. You should have told me this a long time ago because you drove me insane with your never-tiring, calculating mind." I nibbled on his right earlobe and worked my way over his pronounced Adam's apple, buried between the sinewy muscles of his neck. He arched his head back, giving me better access as he moaned his pleasure at me, exploring his neck by slowly licking and biting him on his left earlobe.

"I was attracted to you, yes. I even hated you at one stage, and later, I decided to stop trying to understand you and just enjoy you. Whatever you gave me, I cherished in secret, because I didn't want you to know that I was secretly admiring your ability to adapt much better than myself. You may not know this, but I leaned on your strength without telling you I needed you to hold me up." I breathed out, and my eyes rolled back.

Our breathing accelerated. Our bodies started the slow dance of writhing. "And that's why you jumped out of the airplane to protect me and to prove something." Kellan's voice was deep, almost unrecognizable.

"Probably, because I think I would do anything for you."

"That is why I was so upset with myself for suggesting you seduce him. I wanted you to know that I won't suffocate you. You are free to choose whomever you want, but I inadvertently told you it's what would impress Ouro. I was wrong. I was wrong to make you feel like you have to prove something and not give you an option to change your mind. I'm not as smart as you think I am. I'm a fool."

"No...I think that you think yourself into tight circles...

and...hmm...You have no way out because your mind is in a... hmmm...never-ending...struggle...hmmm...to move all the rationalizations to their right places. But...people aren't always rational...hmm...And that's something you just have to accept...And you can't," I said between low grunts.

"I think you are the smart one between us, Draxton Dubois. Now that we've determined that, can you please fuck me?" Kellan's knees were quivering as he opened them to make more space for me. I slid lower to line my cock up with the crack of his ass as I lowered my full weight and settled down on top of him. I pushed myself up to my knees to spit a wad on my cock. His magnificent sculpted body was difficult to make out in the dark. He lay quietly waiting. His breath hitched when my cockhead pressed against his crack.

"Open up for this, it's going to be a dry fuck." I panted as my cock pushed against his resisting hole.

"Spit, lots of it," he said as he lifted his knees higher, so he lay ass up and his ankles nearly next to his head, almost folded himself double for me.

"We need oil. You need prep."

"We don't have any. Spit on it, I need this."

"You sure?"

"Yes, totally, absolutely, without any fucking doubt. I need you to fuck me like you've never fucked anyone before!"

"Okay, Professor." I sat on my heels, spitting a handful onto my palm, rubbing it into his tight sphincter. Slowly, I tried to plow into him. He gasped, but I wasn't moving further than an inch. The resistance, the heat...I waited for a second.

"I'm thinking of airplanes and hoverbots so I won't orgasm too soon," Kellan blurted. His unforgettable dark eyes closed, and he hissed like a woman delivering a baby. *I'm going to hurt him.*

The idea popped like a Christmas cracker. "Butter! We can use butter!" I reversed and rummaged for the butter Sopora had made from goat's milk.

"What?" Kellan asked, pushing himself up on his elbows.

"Now I'm going to bore into that tight hole." I quickly lathered my cock and moved back into position, and grinned down at him. "Ready?" I asked.

"Yes, three, two, one." He chuckled, the sound a warm rumble inside the cold tent. The urge to be as near to him as possible thrummed through me. His lightheartedness, understanding, and patience simmered, and my need to be inside him, to have him all around me, snapped that final thread of false fear that constantly pulled us away from each other. I doubted I could have matched his quiet, supportive endurance through those long days of deprivation. He allowed me to return to myself at my own pace.

I found his gaze in the dark and nodded, mentally preparing myself to make love to him fully. To pour all of myself into him, here on the mountain in a tent, while only the wind listened to us. Mentally, I was cleaning the house and redecorating with all things Kellan.

"I'm taking it slow," I whispered.

"And I'm savoring this moment with you," he said lovingly into my ear. The meaning behind his words hit much deeper than I ever thought possible. I closed my eyes, resting my head on his shoulder, cherishing this moment of truth between us. I heard nothing else, nor did I envision any back flashes. It was just his warmth, his scent, his breathing, his gentle touches. Being as close together as two humans could be while I rocked into him.

Gripping my shoulders, Kellan lay silent. Not moving and barely breathing.

"Is something wrong?" I asked, lifting my head.

Silence.

"Kellan, please say something." In the darkness, I thought I saw him shaking his head. *Was I hurting him?* I pushed myself up, ready to remove my cock from him. He clutched my shoulders, pulling me down while hooking his ankles around the back of my legs.

I fell with an oomph onto him.

"Nothing is wrong. It's perfect. You are perfect. I love you so much, Draxton." He was sobbing silently. This strong, intelligent man was crying. "Ignore me, just make love to me, please. I need you." I found his mouth, drinking in his tears and his words.

My body moved, building into a sensual glide. "My perfect man. My perfect match," he whispered. The words pushed me to plant myself as deep as I could inside him, then halted, holding still, kissing him, to bring myself back from an early climax. I wanted this to last longer, needed to calm my emotions in one direction—toward him.

We devoured each other. I soaked up all the good, replacing all the bat-shit crazy. All the irrationality, the anger, the fear—that *guano* had to go.

His hand reached between us, and I lifted myself. "No, Professor, let me," I said, rolling to the side to free up my left hand. I'd scarcely touched him when his hole clenched around me. "I'm not going to let you come, not yet." I pushed my right arm underneath his armpit and took hold of his shoulder.

"Ah, fuck, yes!" He arched backward.

"Now, let me show you on this mountain how much I love you." He wasn't making a sound as he waited. Without warning, I slammed into him, held him tight with my legs pinning him up. I ferociously pumped his cock until I felt it swell to the maximum in my hand and stopped, clamped his throbbing dick at its base, then let loose on his ass, to fucking love him, as hard as I could, so he would never forget this night. My passion was so intense that I'd reached the apex of my orgasm so hard I saw the birth of a galaxy behind my eyelids. I released my hand from around his cock while blasting my cum as hard and deep as I could. My voice boomed over the cliffs and into the night. Kellan howled as I loosened my chokehold, coming warm spurt after warm spurt over my pumping fist.

"Ahhh, ho-ly shit!" he exclaimed, heaving air while clutching my forearm. He was hanging on while I pumped my hand until he was sensitive and laughing. "Stop, stop," he begged. "What, the, fuck, was, that?"

"That was me fucking the life back into us, Professor."

"Best sex ever. Hardest I ever came." After our heartbeats settled, he said, "I will remember that for the next week. I don't think I can walk after that."

"You will walk, only very carefully." I slapped his hip and slowly let my cock slip out of him. "Stay still. I will grab a rag to clean us."

"Please, I'm not seeing straight."

. . .

THE NEXT MORNING, the fire was dead and covered with snow.

"Don't get up." I removed the last tea and sandwiches Sopora had packed for us from my backpack, handed Kellan's to him, and joined him under the furs. "I love it here. We can easily stay another night."

Kellan gave me a look.

I shoved the last of my sandwich into my mouth and chased it down with the cold, bitter tea. "Yes, I know," I said with a full mouth. "I was just saying."

We got dressed and packed in silence. I chose to remain quiet. Honest silence felt better than insincere words that didn't reflect my feelings. We took our time, without any forced levity. There wasn't much else to say, anyway, we'd said it all night. Over and over.

I led the way to the winter cave. The higher we climbed, the colder and windier it became. Soon, there was nothing but white as far as three feet in front of me. The feeling of uncertainty grew as I climbed, and I wished to see the black outline of the mouth of the cave. As a sense of doom carried the unrelenting snowfall, the terrain grew more rugged. "This is why we should trust Callisto's forecast," I shouted over my shoulder to Kellan.

We came to a dead halt about three thousand feet above the village, catching our breaths. "Going down went so much faster," I shouted, wiping the snow from my frozen face and joining Kellan by re-wrapping our faces with our scarves.

"The cave is probably just around that boulder, but we won't make it if we have to climb another hour," he said. "Maybe we should wait for the storm to pass? At least warm up before continuing. I'm afraid of frostbite."

"Agreed!"

The wind blasted us around. The search for a hiding hole did not go any easier as we stepped one step forward and rolled on the loose lava rocks two steps back. At one stage, Kellan disappeared, which worried me. I thought maybe he fell down into a crevice or was sliding down the mountain, but seconds later, he reappeared, waving me over. We unloaded the heavy baggage and hastily hunkered down, wrapping and covering ourselves with the furs and using the tent sail to cocoon ourselves between two massive, jagged rocks peeking from the side of the mountain.

The wind howled and inspired dark thoughts. "Do you ever think of death, Draxton?" Kellan asked, shivering.

I shook my head, clutching the fur, and snuggled closer to him for warmth. I guessed we had to talk about something to pass the time. I pursed my lips, unable to smile. "It's exactly the thing I was just thinking about," I said as my eyes roamed over his distraught face. Inside me, fear stirred with the same veracity as the tumultuous storm around us. "Being dead, who doesn't, but if you meant Death itself as an entity, I admit, I'm so scared of it. For me, it's easier if I ignore its existence, then I have much less to worry about. Why do you ask?" My teeth chattered.

"Hmmm, I know what you mean. My father often spoke of life, saying it's a matter of light and darkness coexisting within the void. Death itself is not worse than the void. The ultimate end of everything is not death, but nothing. Everything alive has a soul, and it passes from one reality to another; even dying doesn't kill the soul, but rather pushes it forward, like a ticket or free pass to the next plane. But those without a soul, whom he described, I assume, as the Zelk, represent the void."

I closed my eyes, listening to Kellan speak, and I realized he was talking to keep both of our minds occupied. I was getting warmer and was glad we had decided to find shelter. We would have to dig ourselves out from the snow that was packing us in, but for now, this was as safe as we could get. Kellan continued speaking. I imagined him talking in front of a class of students, going on and on about history, artifacts, and his thoughts on the cultures. I listened to him because his words were like pictures in my mind.

"And beyond death and dying, one would think it would be an escape, but it's not. We can't win or escape because beyond that is another life. He described life as a river, constantly flowing; whether it's transformed into vapor or snow, it eventually accumulates and is recycled. But the void splits and divides, consuming. Unlike trees and plants that breathe water back into the atmosphere, the Zelk does not photosynthesize but does the exact opposite. I guess that's why it's a desert over there. To try to compensate, Anzulla has this weather to balance the water, attempting to coexist, but the void is growing, and soon Anzulla will be as dead as all the other planets in our solar system."

"This is why I love you, because only you can ground me by talking about Death and shit like that," I said just before falling asleep.

CALLISTO WAS YIPPING. "*WAKEY-WAKEY.*" His voice cut into my dream about flowers and forests. My startled eyes flicked open, looking into Kellan's.

"Let's go see!" We burst from the snow.

"*Surprise!*" Callisto yelled.

"Bloody hell!" Kellan exclaimed. We had an audience.

"We missed the cave by mere inches! Why didn't you come get us? We were like ten feet away from a bloody fucking fire!" I asked, perplexed.

"And that's why you two should never be left alone." Sopora laughed from further inside the cave. The children giggled.

"Didn't you hear us as we were falling around, struggling to find shelter?" Kellan asked.

Now, everyone was laughing at us.

"We thought you were still an hour away." We lifted our knees hip-high, forging a path through the snowbank right in front of the cave's entrance.

Callisto barked. "*We wanted to see your surprised faces in the morning.*"

"Ha, fucking ha! We could have died," I said.

We brushed the powdered snow from us and stiffly ran to the nearest fire, removed our cold, wet clothes and grabbed a warm blanket, covering ourselves.

Callisto joined us as we were offered warm, sweetened milk, just like the night we first arrived here. His bemused blue eyes pierced into my frozen being, and I felt like singing "Let it Go" as I defrosted like Olaf the snowman. Never had I been so happy to see him. "Now you care enough to help us."

Callisto snorted like a warhorse. "*I kept you alive, didn't I?*"

"Only for the joke of it," Kellan muttered. "This is a new, different cave, isn't it?" he said questioningly. He was correct; this wasn't the winter or agricultural cave.

"I'm starving," I grunted, and Sopora and her friends jumped to start feeding us.

"Gods, yes!" Kellan thanked them and dove into his plate of warm rabbit stew. My eyes caught the two jagged rocks poking from the snow outside, standing like perpendicular pillars, weathered and broken by the elements.

"Bloody hell! My grandfather was right!"

"What?" Kellan murmured.

"Look!" I pointed. "It's a bloody fucking golden door!"

"It was a door?" He tilted his head. "Now it's...it's a...Oh my God, Draxton, this is the place!" Kellan said with sauce dripping from the corners of his hungry mouth.

Warm bear breath *huff-huffed* on the back of my neck. Still not taking my eyes off the door, slowly, I got back up, reached for my pants hanging on a wire, put my boots back on, and went to touch it. Callisto walked next to me, and I steadied myself by grabbing a handful of fur.

Callisto puffed, snorted, and flicked his head up and down. "*See, I told you the city was here. We just had to find the door.*"

I palmed my cheeks. "Who-ha-ha-ha!" I laughed into my cupped hands and then jumped with pure joy. Kellan joined me, and we bent backward, howling like wolves calling to the moon. Then, the whole caboodle of us were yipping and hollering.

When I calmed down, I surveyed the cave. "This wasn't a cave after all!"

"*See, best surprise ever!*" Callisto said, and everyone agreed, so we all started celebrating with food and drink.

"Oh, my...is that my brother?" Kellan asked.

"Yeah!" everyone answered.

"It's Ouroboros!" Kellan exclaimed.

I stared at the partially visible face of Ouroboros under his white fur hoodie. Gusts of wind blew strands of hair, dancing across Ouro's pleased face. Standing majestically at least ten feet tall, a pure white elk commanded attention as he carried the mighty Ouroboros on his back. Like deadly branches of ice, its antlers glistened as it lowered its head at Callisto. I locked eyes with the creature, its red gaze unlike Callisto's piercing blue eyes.

"Thank you for my tunnel maker?" Ouro said and pony-kicked the gigantic elk. The animal kneeled right in front of the entrance with the big, melted golden doors. Ouro jumped off its back and landed in a crouch, spear in his hand. For the second time today, Kellan and I stood in awe.

"Thank you," he said to the elk. "I will make my way now." The elk stared at Ouro, then at Callisto. Moving its hooves, finding purchase, it took one last look at Kellan and me before leaping left, right, left, and over the boulders, disappearing from our sight.

"Best wake-up ever!" Ouro shouted with arms wide open, "When I heard your voices and Callisto calling, I thought, those are my kin." He gave a slight bow to Callisto. "Thank you." Callisto puffed a few loud breaths in answer. The magic was piling up. We smiled, blown over by the abundance of it.

"Did you see it?"

"Yes, we did," I said and pointed to the tall doors. "What the fuck happened here? It looks like you melted the gold with the laser drill." I ran my hands over the wobbly, malformed golden door supposed to fit inside a three-story high door frame.

Sopora coughed. The others inspected their feet. Tears

brimmed in Ouro's eyes. "Um, that's a story for another fire," Ouro said.

Kellan laughed. "Brother, that says it all."

"It must have been indescribably beautiful."

"It's even more magnificent inside," Ouro said, taking a seat by the fire.

Before we could sit, Callisto let out a deep growl.

"He's warning us! Hide!" Ouro said, falling to the ground. We followed suit. I had become familiar with that sound. I knew before we saw them.

"Kellan, it's hoverbots!" I flattened Kellan with my body against the rock, hiding in the shadows. "Stay still, Ouro, no one moves! I will distract them. We can't let them know about this place." As soon as they passed by, I ran and skidded left, right, left, right as I zig-zagged down the path we came up from. The loose, pebbled rocks helped me to go faster. I went twenty times faster down than coming up. A streak of white fur shot past me. "Fuck, no!"

Callisto's large body blurred down the mountain. "Bloody animal never listens to me." When I reached the place where we had camped the night before, I paused to catch my breath for a moment, hearing Ouro and Kellan approaching.

"Fucking nobody ever listens to me." Callisto was roaring way below, telling us to hurry the fuck up and bring a gun. If there was one thing that attracted hoverbots, it was noisy humans moving fast and making noise.

Two shots reverberated from the direction of the village, echoing up the side of the mountain. The bots sparked, ignited in flames, and fell into the shallow waters beyond the rocky beach. Ouro and Kellan skidded to a halt where I stood with my hands on my knees, as the cold air slashed my throat and lungs.

Turning to Ouro, I said in between wheezy breaths, "I thought they couldn't reach us...the magnetic field."

"I don't understand it either," Ouro said, spear in hand.

Kellan walked in circles, hands clasped behind his neck, like an Olympic athlete catching his breath after a hundred-meter sprint. "You said they could never come so close to the mountain."

Callisto stomped his forelegs once, twice. Then he stood on his hind legs, front paws up with all his nails extended. Rage exploded out of his wide mouth, his yellow teeth bare and dripping angry saliva. His war cry rolled in waves through me and over the land, into the ocean.

"We have to hurry. We cannot wait for them to realize their scouts aren't coming back. Come. We have to go back. Callisto!" Ouro waved his spear, calling us. Callisto and Ouro turned as one, ready to go back to the top.

"Wait!" I heard someone call from a distance. It was Snow and Rocket running toward us from beyond the village walls, with rifles in hand.

"Wait, Ouro!" I called.

"Good, they can keep watch and shoot more of those things spying on us," Ouro said. The pace of crap flying was too fast for Kellan and me to grasp. We were still coming to terms with the golden doors. We exchanged what-the-fuck looks with shrugged shoulders while simultaneously measuring the distance back up the mountain.

"Ouro, it had taken us almost two days to climb up. Can we at least have a cup of water before we go back?" I asked, just as Snow and Rocket joined us.

Rocket pointed in the direction the hoverbots had crashed into the water. "Did you see? Snow shot those spying cameras right out of the sky!"

Ouro looked pissed off. "Yes, we saw. Come with us. We need you to watch for more of those things," he ordered like a leader on a mission to start a war.

"Yeah, sure, Ouro." Rocket and Snow's excitement turned cumbersome. "It's time, isn't it? The Zelk is coming." Rocket sounded worried.

Snow gave Rocket a stern nod.

Crossing my arms, I protested. "I will not go back up that fucking mountain right this minute. I want to rest!"

"Draxton, this is going to end up in a catastrophe. We don't have time!" Ouro shouted, pointing his spear at us. "Callisto, bring them back up!" He stuck his spear deep into the snow like a gavel of finality.

CHAPTER 25

DRAXTON

DRILLING AND HAULING ROCK CONTINUED FOR TWO more weeks. "He'll collapse from exhaustion, and that'll be the end of him," Sarinka said with conviction, and the fifteen men in her crew behind her agreed. I figured she was a woman, given Donali's reference to her pronouns. The first time I saw her, I wasn't sure of her gender. I wouldn't want to cross her; she flung boulders like tennis balls. "It's been over six hours. It's time for him to take a break, and let us go in."

"Yeah," her crew murmured.

Seconds later, an abrupt halt was followed by Ouroboros yelling and swearing loudly. Then, his crew spat from the rubble-strewn opening in all directions, their faces a mix of fear and relief.

The unpredictable mountain weather kept everyone on edge, especially Ouroboros. We all wished, second by second, for the bloated dark clouds to hold off just a little bit longer. Our crew had been waiting for our turn to hitch Callisto to a wagon for hauling debris. He managed most of the heavy lifting, moving rocks from the tunnel and dumping them down the mountain.

One moment, two moments, three moments...I counted to four moments when Ouro emerged from the dust cloud shrouding the tunnel entrance, annoyance clear in his stomping feet, drill clutched in hand, and face screwed up like a toddler's. He shoved the drill into Kellan's lap. "It just stopped zapping, buzzed a couple of times, then died. Can you fix it?"

Kellan looked at Ouro, then pensively at the offending tool. "I can open it, see what's wrong. Hopefully it's something small, something I can fix." Kellan put the drill on the table, grabbed a cloth, and started to clean the thick layer of dust.

Ouroboros stepped back and crossed his arms. "Thank you, I will wait over there, hauling crystals." His eyes flashed with exasperation at Sarinka and Donali's crew. They received the wordless order to get moving and skedaddled to collect crystals. I wondered when Ouro had last taken a nap. Sopora's face rippled with concern, but she kept quiet and moved to help collect the crystals.

Kellan lifted a brow. "Does anyone have a knife or a small flat screwdriver so I can open it up?" Kellan's words still hung in the air when, suddenly, twelve knives pointed his way.

He chuckled. "Hmmm, thank you. So many to choose from!" He bit his plump bottom lip. "Show me the sharpest, flattest one." Leaning closer, he examined the weapons intently. "This one," he decided, pointing at Snow's blade. Snow flipped it expertly, and Kellan caught the handle of the short, curved skinning knife. "Thank you."

Snow smiled and said, "No problem."

At the table, I ate lunch while watching them dismantle the drill across from me. We'd found bags of crystals, but no city or dragon yet.

Imprisoned, we mined diamonds and anything glittering. I wondered if those diamonds were merely replacements for these crystals. Zaidon's explanations were vague, mentioning diamond nanites as the foundation of Zelk's grid and their use of diamonds and crystals in power generation. Discussing the Light Continent and Zelk was agonizing; my face would become vacant, lost in those terrible memories. So, I stopped answering questions about the invaders.

"Kellan, could you perhaps re-engineer weapons from the scraps we bring you?" Ouro asked him after shoving an entire chicken drumstick into one cheek, downing a cup of bitter berry wine, and pointing to the heaps of innards of salvaged technology Simon's men had been collecting and carrying up the mountain.

Kellan said emphatically, "Yes, we are repurposing that; we will find something useful for it."

Kellan snapped shut the small cover and gave Ouro his drill. "It should work now. It overheated and activated the automatic shutdown. I refocused the laser and reattached the electrical current. You only have a day or so left before the battery dies." He handed the knife back to Snow.

"Snow, let Simon know to bring more of those old scrap-yard things."

Snow acknowledged. "Will do, Ouro."

Kellan sucked his cheek, a habit I'd noticed when he was deep in thought. "Your tinkering skills are amazing," I said, prompting thanks. "We've accomplished so much and much faster with your help!" A chorus of gratitude followed, making Kellan wave it off modestly.

Later, Kellan came over, carrying something behind his back and winking at me. I offered him a drink. He placed the thing he was carrying on the table, resting his palms on the surface of the makeshift outdoor breakroom, or meeting place, or bar, depending on the time of the day. He leaned slightly forward toward me. He was stunning with that sly smile. I continued to desire him more than any man, every day. His hair was growing back to conserve heat; he never shaved it, except for when he had to save me in Spire City. "I have a gift for you," he said, and he pushed the cloth tied with a leather string over.

The warm feeling rushing up my neck and cheeks probably hadn't hidden the fact that I thought he looked like a sexy, dark ice-age warrior. A seeker of answers, an emotionally rich and wise one. He hadn't just accepted things for what they were. He watched and dug for the truth. Back home in the Dinaledi Chamber, he wanted to get to know me better. Now, our circumstances were worse, but our knowledge of each other was as intimate as ever. We were facing another winter, and inevitable attack, and were all on edge because of the slowdown.

I fingered the cloth. "What is this?"

"Open it," Kellan said with a playful twinkle in his eyes. I pulled on one of the loose strings, slowly undoing the bow he had tied. I looked up, scowling. "It's not going to bite you, don't frown like that. I made it for you myself. Especially for you."

I untied the package. He had used the shirt he wore the day we fell through the time portal to wrap my gift. It was surprisingly still in good condition. I wouldn't even know where mine was. Oh, yes, I'd torn it into shreds to make bandages for my feet while I was imprisoned to find a laser drill for Ouro.

My eyes widened when I realized I was holding a leather cowboy hat. "You made me another hat?" I laughed, wondering why he thought I needed another hat.

"You look so sexy in one, and it reminds me of the day we met in my office. You seemed to like wearing them, but you lose them faster than I can make them, so I thought to surprise you with a new one." He took the brown leather hat and put it on my head, then tied the string below my chin. "There, Draxton Dubois, the world's best cartographer," he said, as if he were proud of both his handiwork and me.

I cracked a shy smile. "Thank you, I love it."

"Cartographer?" Libre asked, cleaning his plate and getting ready to haul rocks again.

"Yes, I'm a cave explorer, always drawing up maps of tunnels in my mind, wondering what lies hidden beneath us. Always somewhere else, searching, wondering, and daydreaming, wondering what I will find next. My grandfather had said I'm the only one who does what I do."

"Yes, you are," Kellan said and gave me a peck on my cheek.

I sat up. "We should go and help Libre," I announced because I had a secret imaginary timer pinging in my head, telling me it was time to return. However, Kellan was still eating, so I switched it off and said to him, "Isn't it amazing that on one side of the globe, technology has taken over, but here I am scraping potatoes from a wooden bowl. We sit on tree stumps for chairs, while you look so sexy in your leathers, regrowing a wild mane, and demanding presence, while I'm wearing a handmade cowboy hat."

Kellan threw his head back and laughed. "What's amazing to me is that everyone is stressed and working hard, but you always find time for sarcasm and jokes. Wear the hat, don't wear the hat. I just wanted to thank you, and that's all I know you need. When we arrived, I thought living in the village was safe. I thought jumping out of an airplane for a tunnel maker was a risky endeavor. It's all because of you that I feel accomplished today. My fear has grown into this constant thing I want to overcome, especially when I look at you and wonder, if we succeed, will this history be widely known when we return? Will our names be written in history books? Who knows, when we return, they might take a picture of you with that same hat on."

I had no clue how to respond to that, so I shrugged and scooped my last heap of mashed potatoes into my mouth. "We'll see if we get home in one piece."

My eyes followed Kellan as he got up and walked away. I finished my cup of potato ale, and my heart galloped looking at his tight ass. This was our chance to be alone. "I'm coming with you. You can show me where you water those rocks."

"I'll show you that and more. How does that sound?"

"I was hoping to see more," I said and took Kellan's waiting hand. He led me out of sight, far away from the well-trodden footpath. The ocean looked calm, almost peaceful today. We squeezed past the arching boulders and slipped to our private spot, where we usually disappeared to. Right next to a small frozen waterfall.

We fished out our cocks to take a leak. Small, icy droplets from the rushing waters cooled my face as I flicked off my hat and let it hang from the leather string around my neck. My heart thump-thumped. The silence between us was ever comfortable. Pure and honest. This man was strong and honorable. Smart and classy, even without the crisp suit. Now he was rugged and sexy. I turned to him, taking him in while he emptied his bladder. I realized that together, our compass needles pointed to what was right and just. He cleared his throat and stepped closer. He reached behind me, bringing my hat over my head, removing it, and throwing it to the side. "You're so good. You see only the best in people and ignore all the bad," he said.

"I do?"

"Yes, like it doesn't exist. That's what makes me extremely attracted to you. Since the first day we met, you have made me hard with your determination, your jean shorts, and your flip-flops."

"Ha, shorts and flip-flops. You won't see me in those anytime soon."

"Doesn't matter. I know what you have underneath all these layers of fur. My recklessly beautiful, kind man."

"Yours?"

"Yes, no matter what happens, I know you and we share something unbreakable. We fell through a hole in the sky together."

"I was just thinking the same." I took his hand and kissed it. "Yes, that was certainly a turbulent first kiss."

"Exactly," he said, pulling me closer. "When your 'savior' button's pushed, when the Bat-signal goes up, you become a runaway train, dragging me along." Our bare stomachs and chests pressed together, and I melted into him. "If it weren't for this crystal, I swear I'd be gray already. Do you know how much I love your brave ass?" His brown eyes, flecked with orange, searched my face before locking with mine. Such a romantic sap. "All this," he continued, smiling to reveal a dazzlingly white grin. "All of you. Your eyes, your smile, your intensity. The way you just say what you believe in, even when we disagree. You never back down."

I chuckled. His complete focus made me as hard as the lava rocks around us. "You are amazing, and sometimes I feel inadequate," I admitted.

His eyes softened as he said, "You know what?"

Heat rushed to my belly, warming it. "I know you love me."

He stared right into my soul. "I do." He pulled me closer. I reached for his hips, pulling him tighter against me. Our exposed, hardened cocks rubbed against each other.

"Me too," I whispered, my words lost in the heat of our kiss. He pulled me closer, deepening the embrace. We tumbled to the frozen ground, our kiss unbroken. Tongues entwined, my hand tangled in his short hair, as his found my aching length. He nipped my lip as we surrendered to the moment.

"I should have brought a bedroll," I gasped. I squeezed and pumped my hand. Our beards were tangled as he kissed my neck, then bit the shell of my ear as his body went rigid.

"Gods, I'm gonna come!" he roared as he was already climaxing. His warm seed spilled onto my hand around his cock. He slowed down, leaving me on the brink of my orgasm.

"You're incredible," I breathed, then rocked my hips, pumping into his fist. His rough palm, slick with my pre-cum, teased my sensitive head as he played with my foreskin. A shiver ran through me as he sucked my earlobe. My heels dug into the ground as I savored the intense pleasure surging through me.

His warm breath felt exquisite. "Come for me, you brave, beautiful man," he grunted into my ear. The low rumble caused a climactic explosion that I couldn't stave off any longer.

"I'm coming...um...just for you." My eyes rolled back, and my hips bucked as ecstasy shot through me.

CHAPTER 26
CALLISTO

"Draxton, Kellan!" I've never been so excited, but I had to find them first before I could go inside. *"Draxton, Kellan!"* I called louder as I hopped through the snow, my snout up, sniffing the icy air. Crows squawked and took flight. *"Shut up, you noisy birds,"* I huffed. *"Draxton, Kellan!"*

Lately, they wanted to do nothing but be in each other's arms. Ever since I had carried them back up the mountain, they had been on a go-slow.

Ouroboros was working himself to death, while his brother's hands were permanently down Draxton's pants.

"Draxton, Kellan!" I paused, listening. Jumped and spun midair. Tilted my head, hearing only the wind and those damn birds.

Trod-trod-trod. I followed their scent to a gorge that ended in a number of brown to black-colored rocks, which gradually thinned out to create an irregular ring. Beyond them, the ground descended gently into a grassy, undulating mountain pasture surrounded by a narrow stream of rushing water.

"*There! Laughter!*" I hurried down the trail between two massive boulders, my heart pounding, eager to tell them the good news. They approached. *Shit!* I was too big to hide; I had to shrink and backpedal. Stay, hide, stay, hide, yell surprise, I thought at the same time as I remembered they don't like that.

Dry twigs snapped underfoot. "*Oh, crap!*" I jumped, trying to make myself smaller mid-air. But my paws slipped on landing, and I tumbled, slowly and dramatically, onto my back at their feet.

They stood rooted to the spot. I blinked. "*Surprise,*" I croaked lamely, much too late.

They blinked.

Hastily, I scrambled onto the slippery ice. Oh shit, down I went again.

"Ha-ha, you are half-shrunken. Your hind legs are taller than your front ones." They laughed, and I joined them, laughing myself silly while I sagged forward.

Seconds later, I was proportionally transformed.

"Were you spying?" Draxton asked.

I puffed warm air through my nostrils. "*No!*" I said, but it sounded like I was. "*Why would I? If I wanted to watch, I'd watch openly. I'm not a creep,*" I stammered, my voice cracking uncomfortably. Ever since they'd heard my voice, they treated me like I was a baby.

"Relax, I'm just teasing," Draxton said, waving and slinging an arm around Kellan's shoulders.

"You were spying, weren't you?" Kellan chuckled.

"*No, I wasn't!*"

"Yeah, right, we believe you," Kellan said sarcastically.

I whipped up my head, looking down my nose at them. *"Ouroboros sent me. They broke through...come...It was supposed to be a surprise, but you spoiled it."*

Their eyes bulged. But before Draxton could say a word, Kellan kicked dirt in my face and darted past me, propelling through the narrow arch of mossy stone and zooming up the path. "First dibs to see the hidden city!" he shouted, laughing. We jostled and shoved, racing to be first inside.

CHAPTER 27

DRAXTON

THE SUDDEN STILLNESS BROUGHT ME TO A DEAD HALT. Everything was haphazardly scattered in disarray, as if the reaping had just occurred, and I missed the show of "Beam me up, Scotty." Half-eaten meals sat untouched, and two chairs lay overturned. I hesitated, unsure whether to leave the scene as it was. After all, I had just eaten lunch here; was this our mess?

"Here!" Kellan called.

Oh, yeah, we were racing, I remembered.

I lunged as Kellan grabbed my hand and dragged me after him. "You're too fast for me." I laughed.

Kellan slowed down, and Callisto blundered like a circus bear breaking out of its prison through the blown-up hole in the side of the mountain. As designated rock-haulers, our team typically entered after Sarinka's team had finished harvesting the crystals. We climbed over the debris, and the usual fumes of smoke, ash, and dust had vanished, replaced by sweet, fresh, clean air. I assumed that's why Callisto was sent to call us instead of starting to lug the cut pieces outside.

"I didn't realize how far they'd already managed drilling these last few hours," Kellan said.

"This part is wider and higher, it looks older, see there's moss and over there is foliage," I exclaimed excitedly.

We sped up our pace, and the ecstatic shouting of joy reached us. The tunnel ceiling rose higher and higher, while the light grew brighter, calling us to see what was waiting. Suddenly, we stumbled into a breathtakingly enormous cavern, and wow, it was truly overwhelming! Who knew nature could be so...*grand*?

"Oh, my goodness!" Kellan exclaimed and tightened his hand around mine. "Is this what you had imagined, because I didn't?"

We turned backward, hand in hand in a circle, gazing up and around. "Uh, no, not at this scale." My mouth hung open.

The sounds were what I cataloged first after I realized this was not just tunnels and a cave. It felt as if we had just stepped into a butterfly botanical garden, but on an incomparable scale. All sorts of greenery and colors burst forth almost fluorescently under the red light filtering from above. The cave's roof is so high that the tallest skyscraper would fit inside—thousands of them.

"Oh, my god! This isn't just carved caves hidden underground, away from predators, Draxton," Kellan whispered to me.

I was astonished, as if I were having an out-of-body experience. "No," I whispered back. "It's a whole subterranean world. I would never have known. Honestly, I thought they were made-up exaggerated stories."

"Me too," Kellan said in disbelieving awe.

"It's so green, I can hear the plants grow, Kellan."

"Yeah, very rainforesty, look at all the vibrant colors," he answered, his eyes tracing the emerald ferns and the ruby red crystal canopy. A symphony of unseen creatures chirped and buzzed, punctuated by the occasional squawk of a parrot. Warm mist clung to his skin, making it glow under the strange red hue given off by the crystals.

"Right?" I laughed as I stared up. "It's not just a cave, it's a whole paradise below the crust, an underworld, and it's lit by sunlight reflected by those," I said and pointed to clusters of ruby red crystals.

"Look." Kellan let go of my hand. "Draxton, that must be thousands of feet high!"

"Waterfalls!" I said in awe.

"And there's the city." Kellan jumped, jubilantly wrapping his arms around my neck, and kissed me all over my face. I laughed, the joy bubbling out of me as he wrapped his legs around my hips, nearly toppling me over. I stepped left and right like a juggler, getting balanced, then closed my eyes as the magic of the moment swept us up with him in my arms. We kissed while turning in a circle. I've never felt so happy.

When we had both calmed, he said, "We have to go inspect that closer. Look, it's black marble and gold, fine architectural etchings," and I let him slip from my hips.

I picked up my fallen hat, ran my fingers through my ruffled short hair, and placed it back on my head. "Imagine thousands of bodies moving around down here, while we were not aware of this place below us."

"It's mind-blowing. When my father spoke of Anzulla, I

never thought he meant this. Sure, I imagined something like the Incas in the Amazon, but not this," Kellan said.

The sound of someone wailing caught my attention, and I frowned, narrowing my eyes as if it would make me hear better while I searched for the direction it was coming from. Kellan called my name repeatedly as I tilted my head to the side, listening. It sounded horrific. It was urgent, and someone needed help. "Draxton, over there!"

About three hundred yards away, Ouro was wailing near a gray-white manmade structure at the edge of a line of gigantic, fat trees with bulging trunks that bordered a prehistoric forest. We ran along an overgrown stone footpath snaking through green grass speckled with white and purple flowers towards the monstrosity-like jungle. I paused to jog my memory, tipping my head from side to side, trying to remember. "What are they called again?"

"Baobabs or Adansonias!" Kellan said.

"Yeah, that's it," I muttered, stopping and taking in the sight of them, reaching up almost as if they wanted to touch the light streaming from above. "Draxton!" Kellan called. There were so many wondrous things to catalogue. He called again, and I reluctantly joined him.

We waved as we approached hurriedly. Everyone was there, circling a large square structure, their faces marked by bewilderment as they watched a devastated Ouroboros who sat on Callisto's neck while Callisto was pushing, trying to open a stone door.

Once closer, I saw it was a polished stone building. The thing was as big as a double-door garage. I could've easily parked two of my caravans inside it. Ouroboros nearly slipped off as he hung to reach inside it, through a narrow opening.

Snow and four other men were busy pushing from the bottom. The ten-by-four-foot stone door moaned and groaned. Resisting and complaining by grinding raw stone on stone. I'd never seen Ouro like this. He lay draped over Callisto's neck, reaching inside and talking to whatever was being revealed.

"What's happening?" I asked Simon, who stood at the back with his thumbs hooked into his belt loops.

"Oh, hello. Yeah, Ouro's beyond himself to get inside. Look, the end of Atlas's tail is sticking out." I caught a glimpse of a black thing. "It seems the door closed on him and he's been stuck like that all this time." Simon pointed to what looked like a thick black ten-by-ten PVC pipe.

"Looks like driftwood to me," Kellan said.

"No wonder Ouroboros is freaking out. Cruel, that's a bloody damn cruel way to spend a century waiting to be freed," I said, and Kellan wrapped his arms around me. Too many people were trying to see what was happening, so we waited on the side, holding our breaths. The stone scraped further, the sound screeching, making me cringe, reminding me of my time inside the mining prison.

As many hands as possible helped Snow, while others had stuck their staffs in the opening, using them as leverage. They grunted and moaned until finally, a gap big enough allowed Callisto to push his snout inside. "*He's here,*" Callisto announced excitedly. "*Brother!*" he called, and Ouro started to maneuver himself over Callisto's head, pulling himself up by one ear, and then he slid inside.

"Is he awake, Pa?" Libre asked his father, standing on his toes.

"Is he alone in there?" Simon muttered.

"Is he alive?" Sopora shouted.

"Kellan, look!" I showed him the stone wheel beside the building.

"Yes, that's most probably what you think it is. Come, let's go see." Simon saw what we were up to and followed us to the human-sized stone wheel with wooden spokes for handles.

"I forgot about that." Simon chuckled, looking from the wheel to where the others were forcing the door open.

We removed our thick furs. "Help us," Kellan called, and Simon jumped, found a spot, and we pushed. At first, the wheel didn't budge. "Come on, you fucking fucker," Kellan urged through gnashing teeth.

The wheel protested, but started to turn seconds later, as if following Kellan's command, and gave way. Shouts and hollers followed, and we ran to see Snow and the men getting up from being toppled over, and I laughed, because I thought something like that would happen.

Silence followed. My eyes tooted and blared warnings to my brain; this wasn't what I was seeing. It couldn't be. Ouro's wailing stamped the moment with reality. Realization flooded my veins like a sudden mainline shot, and then I understood that what I saw was indeed what I was seeing. It was right there. Undeniably...in the darkness, Ouro was wrapping his arms around its blue neck.

Like a duet, Kellan and I sang the song of joyful exhumation. The find of all finds. "Gods, Kellan, that is a dragon!"

"Yes, I think it is," Kellan whispered.

Now we were on our toes, peeking around Snow and the others. The sight was unnerving. I expected the dragon to jump up, but it lay still with its eyes closed like a carving from stone. I wanted to knock on it, to see if it was hollow. He couldn't have been sleeping, so he was definitely dead and well-preserved.

Ouro made a keening sound that made the hair on my arms rise.

"So dramatic," I said, holding my hat respectfully in front of my chest while shaking my head.

"Hmmm," Kellan agreed.

As if hearing our comments, Ouro stood, craning his neck. He composed himself, found us in the crowd, and gestured for us to come closer. Kellan took my hand, and the people parted for us. "Brother, bring Draxton and meet Atlas." We were blinking curiously. My heart raced as we entered the stone box, cautiously joining Ouro's not-so-mythical exhibition.

"Is this *your* Atlas, Ouro?" Kellan asked as I shuffled closer to knock on it secretly. I had to know, I had to feel what I saw. I needed to hear the truth. So, I closed my eyes, and I knocked. Once. Twice. Not hollow. Then I opened my eyes, and I ran my hand lightly over the wing. Back and forth. It was soft and silky like bird feathers.

The dragon lay awkwardly on the right side, its neck arched in an uncomfortable curve. His narrow head was turned to one side while its domed chest and clawed feet extended to the front. It seemed as though he had tried to pull himself loose from the door, fallen, and died.

Ouro murmured, tears streaming again, while rubbing the dragon's head. Callisto sat, sniffing his ears and probably speaking to him. There was something inexpressibly graceful and sad about them in the presence of the dead creature. It reminded me of when I last said goodbye to my grandfather, lying dead and waiting to be put into the ground. The way the dragon lay with his left wing flared open to the side like a bird with a broken wing. It was clearly reptilian in origin, covered in distinctly black, outlined blue scales that absorbed the light streaming from outside, giving it a glaring dark blue and black appearance.

I curled my fingers and knocked on its side again. It was definitely solid, and not hollow, and absolutely lifeless. It wasn't breathing. I examined it from the tips of its talons to the end of its long but bluntly amputated tail.

"He's the reason we are here. Alive! Feel this," Ouro said, his lip trembling. Kellan touched the blue, scaly forehead while I touched the bumpy cheek. I grimaced. I wasn't a fan of snakes or reptiles.

"Naturally mummified, due to the lack of oxygen, maybe?" I brushed my finger along the dragon's cold, dark blue lips, traced the long gray tooth protruding over the bottom lip, down his chin and his muscled chest, where I inspected the front claws so much like a bird's.

Ouro tapped the rock with the spear's tip, sneering. The sudden noise scared me half to death. I stumbled back, throwing my hands over my head as I sensed my cowboy hat flying off again. The hat was too big for me.

"What the fuck, brother?" Kellan exclaimed, holding his chest from the fright.

"No, not mummification. It's hibernation. But I can't wake my brother, he is sleeping too deeply. His mind is too far. Help us, Draxton. You are so smart with puzzles and things like this." Callisto whined, plopping down beside the dragon, his brother. How are these two even related? I wondered.

"I'm sorry, and to be honest with you, Atlas looks and feels like he's well-preserved. Like solid rock." I couldn't resist knocking three times on the forehead. Also not hollow.

"What are you doing? He's not a watermelon!" Simon exclaimed.

"Sorry, I had to make sure," I said, scurrying to the side, ready to go because I was really getting tired of the shit piling up.

"Hey!" Kellan pointed a warning finger at Simon. "Leave him be."

"Fuck you," Simon snarled.

That's it. I had had enough of these dumb people. "Yeah, I get it. You are sad because of what you think happened here. A hundred years ago. I was only investigating." I waved a hand to the empty steepled apartments with long balconies protruding like landings carved from rock behind us. "Where are all the people? We found the city and a dead dragon. No gods, no people, and I don't see dead skeletons strewn around as if they were attacked. It's like a bloody ghost town. It's beautiful, but very empty."

Ouro fell to his knees, hugging Callisto, burying his face into the white fur, muffling his voice. "You don't understand," Ouro muttered. "You stupid-stupid dragon. Why? Why did you leave me here alone?"

His cries pulled and tugged at something profoundly deep inside me, making me wonder if Ouro had a deeper connection to the dragon than he let us believe. I walked from one dustless corner to the other, inspecting the precision-cut walls and seams, waiting until he had collected himself.

"Atlas is not dead. He is not a statue. He is sleeping. We told you, my people once inhabited the city. Our people." Ouro pointed at Kellan. "This is where our father walked with his people."

"I know!" Kellan shouted back. "Was the place evacuated? Where did everyone go?"

"This was the home of dragons, bears, birdmen, and San," Callisto said quietly. *"And those fucking Phoenicians,"* he added with an aggressive grunt.

"Hey!" Simon, Donali, and Kawa warned, because they were Phoenician.

We stood in silence, listening. They sounded as if they were done crying and ready to talk.

"Dragons and bears? Were there more of you?"

"No, he was just saying those were our homes, in the Heart of Anzulla." Ouro pointed beyond the onlookers to the facade of hundreds of empty, lifeless dwellings.

"We told you. Some disappeared. Others left through the door, while most of the Phoenicians returned to their city underwater, which left as it arrived." He pointed to Simon, Donali, and Kawa. "Some stayed because they were either taken prisoner or tried saving what could be saved."

"Atlas spewed fires until molten rock buried him." Ouro's voice grated with anger, regret, and sadness. I was skeptical. There was no way anyone could be alive and sleeping for a hundred years looking like that, I thought, and gave Kellan a disbelieving look.

Callisto huffed, shaking his head. "No?"

"Then what?" I asked, but the bear grunted, got up, and went to lie down between his brothers' front and hind legs.

I grabbed the back of my neck, rubbing it. "Yeah, we know there was fire and burning rock. But clearly, he didn't die in a fire or lava rock. Suppose that the door amputated his tail. Maybe he bled to death or died from infection."

"Doesn't matter. He would have healed under the...crystal..." Ouro trailed off. "Oh no!" he exclaimed with wide eyes. He'd better not start crying again; it was unnerving.

"I'm sorry, it looks like Atlas was trapped and not sleeping under the red light," Kellan said gently, touching his brother's shoulder for support.

Callisto sniffled. *"Ye-yes, but he doesn't appear to be drowned in lava."*

"We all can see that," Ouro shouted, and Callisto growled back at him. Clearly, neither of them expected this.

Kellan coughed. "It could have looked like it from the outside. Callisto, you were the last to see him, weren't you? You said he hibernated. There are many myths about dragons guarding their horde and sleeping for thousands of years. But look, he was closed inside, this...casket...what is this thing, anyway?"

"I don't see a horde," I said.

"This is the time box, through that wall is a door. If you go in there, the floor opens up, and you land on the outside. Like I did, on this mountain, only it was a hundred years in the future. I promise you, my brother is sleeping. I know he is. He is dreaming. Ouro and I can hear him talking in his sleep," Callisto said, a bit more calmly than before.

"But how do we wake him up?" Ouro shouted into our minds.

Kellan and I jumped and yelped in surprise at hearing Ouro's voice in our minds. Gods, what was happening that we could now mind talk with Ouro? How was Ouro connected to Callisto and Atlas the dragon?

"These crystals give artificial light. Maybe the light bothered him; that's why he chose to sleep inside," Rocket added. Yup, he snuffed a little too much fuel, I thought.

Ouro gnashed his teeth. "The crystal was here from the beginning. Not the time box. The crystal never bothered anyone. This time box is manmade." He narrowed his eyes at me. "That crystal around your neck comes from this magical place. This was their home. Atlas, Callisto, and the birdmen lived here. Their children played and ran there; it was just another city, like all other cities. They didn't hide from the light, and it wasn't too bloody bright for anyone," he told Rocket.

I wiped my hands on my thighs. "Kellan, I'm getting a bad feeling. We shouldn't touch Atlas; we don't know what's happened here. This place feels...plagued with bad luck. We need to be cautious." I gestured towards the waterfall. "Let's go wash your hands," I said, trying to pull Kellan away. I needed to talk to him. We were sinking deeper into their world, their problems. If Atlas is dead, I need to talk to Kellan about going home. Maybe we could use the door Callisto just showed us. I was being realistic. I would stay if he wanted to, but if we could leave and avoid this war, we should go now.

"No! It's not a sickness." Ouro pointed at me with his spear. "I don't want you here or under my feet, or your negativity. Get out."

"Did you just say what I think you said?" I blurted. "This was much more than just an adventure to find crystals or a sleeping dragon. We came here because you promised us that Atlas could take us home. We helped you, and came here for that! For a dead lover!" Ouro leaped, looking like he was going to run me through. Snow stopped him by jumping between us.

Kellan waved a placating calm-down gesture at us. "Draxton, give them time to absorb it all."

"Yeah, what he said. Shut the fuck up!" Snow said, narrowing his eyes at me.

"What do I know? Oh, absolutely nothing," I retorted, rolling my eyes. They ignored my brilliant insight as if it held no importance whatsoever.

Ouro pointed to Atlas. "He is a dragon, not mummified, not dead, and if you say that again, I will sink my spear into that hole in your face spewing disrespect, accusing all of us of being liars."

I gulped, lowered my gaze, shook my head, and turned away, lacing my fingers behind my head.

"Listen, Atlas and Callisto are our protectors. They have hidden powers deep inside them. It's magic. Atlas is alive. But I don't know how to wake him up." Ouro's voice broke as he sagged against the stony dragon. I felt sorry for him. Maybe he was under some illusion.

"This is real life, Ouro. Atlas feels as cold as stone. If something is alive, it breathes and moves. Put your head on his chest and try to hear a heartbeat," Kellan told him.

"This is different. Like Callisto, they are the children of Anzulla. It's magic," he whispered.

I shook my head at Callisto, but noticed next to the door, on the ground, something out of the ordinary. I toed the thing. It was a metallic sign of some kind, covered with a thick layer of dust. I pushed it with the tip of my boot. It sounds like tinfoil, just as thin and the size of an A4 notebook. "What's this? Is this some new-age paper or what?"

Kellan kneeled for closer inspection. "It's not in English and not in Zelk either. It appears to be a hieroglyphic."

I blew the dust softly away. "It's a story about a flower, the sun, drops of water, and a fountain. Maybe the meaning of life."

That piqued Ouro's interest. He stormed over, reading it. "Ah, yes. It's an ancient language of the San. It's talking about the sap of the holy flower!"

"Holy flower?" Kellan and I asked simultaneously.

"The Loursveto!" everyone else shouted, except Kellan and me.

"The ganja?" Kellan asked, his brows furrowed.

"Libre, bring me as many flowers as you can carry!" Ouro yelled, his voice booming like a drum.

I stood watching as the humid air vibrated with excited anticipation when the children scattered, spatting in all directions, their voices shrill like cicadas, "I'll get one!"

"No, I will get one!"

"I will bring the biggest one!"

"I will!"

"No, I will!"

CHAPTER 28

DRAXTON

WHETHER IT WAS POSSIBLE OR NOT, WAKING A
sleeping dragon made me nervous. Cringing shivers ran from
the crown of my head through my spine, reminding me of one
of my dreams in the torture casket—the thought of
catastrophic consequences and blinding pain from flesh and
bone melted by spewed molten fire made me want to run. "At
least Atlas has wings," I muttered. "If the crack was in the sky,
and if he actually does wake up, he should be able to carry
two men. He is larger than my caravan, so carrying us won't
be impossible. That is, if that broken wing had healed, if the
Zelk doesn't zap us, and if their grid blanketing the globe tears
open to let us through."

Kellan's eyes darted around. "Hush, keep it down," he
murmured urgently.

I wondered if he too, was feeling immense disappointment. Ouro's words snapped me out of my thoughts. "Draxton," he growled, "we don't know what happened once he was

inside, locked away from us. Callisto says this isn't the state Atlas was in when he'd sent him through the door. He was in much worse shape before, but now he seems to have healed. For some reason, he's been trapped in the time box. Maybe he fled from something. Maybe he was too weak to escape; we can only be certain once he wakes up. That's our best guess about what happened."

"When?"

Ouro clenched his fists, probably trying to contain his reaction to me and my questions. "If I knew, I would have shouted it out!" He turned to face everyone with a determined look. "Once Atlas opens his eyes, we will know. Stay close, everyone! Don't wander off. Once he wakes up, we'll have answers—and I believe they'll be good ones!"

"I agree with Ouro. Staying close is a good idea," Simon said to his men. Most seemed happy with that conclusion and sauntered inside, taking turns to touch and talk to the sleeping dragon.

"Draxton, let's go take that walk you wanted," Kellan said, and we left to make space for more to come inside to be with Atlas. My fears were spiking almost to the same level as just before leaving the hut, and I knew Kellan saw it in my bewildered eyes.

We made our way outside, with Kellan steering me as my gaze fell on the ground. I was confused and irritated, but I trusted Kellan to take me somewhere to calm my mind.

"White noise should help—the waterfall. Let's go closer," he said as the cool mist accumulated on my skin. He was correct; it was helping me feel better. We waited until I was able to lift my gaze again, and the noise of people arguing, laughing, and talking disappeared.

"What does this all mean?" I asked under my breath.

With knitted eyebrows, Kellan looked at me. "Do you truly think we've fallen twenty thousand years back in time?" he asked me, fixing his dark eyes on my darker ones.

I shrugged. "It's only a wild guess." He seemed to be putting things together. I was pretty sure Kellan had seen or heard something like that before, either in his textbooks or from his father. The whites of his eyes shone brightly in the red hues produced by the clusters of crystal protruding from above, contrasting with his dark complexion and making him look like a paleontologist about to unveil the answer to all mysteries. I moved closer because I loved that look on him; it was magnetic.

He whispered, tugging my sleeve. I leaned in, enjoying his warm breath tickling the shell of my ear.

Water rushed behind me as I closed my eyes, listening to the cadence of his rumbling voice. It soothed me, and my breathing evened out while my mind refocused.

"This is my precise field of study, Draxton. My father's stories and his private research...I never truly believed him, because I wanted concrete proof of it." He quivered in my arms. "He was a strangely deep and metaphysical person. So what he sometimes said sounded like make-believe. My arrival here cemented the truth, but it only meant that what he was trying to prevent his whole life never had any impact, because here we are." I looked up, seeing him smile, revealing he was feeling the opposite of what I was feeling. His boyish excitement told me he believed his brother and that the dragon was only sleeping, or he thought this was a historic find.

He placed a palm on each of my cheeks. "Draxton, I

completed my professorship in paleoanthropology, focusing on the fossils of prehistoric humans and pre-human hominoids—specifically, the homo naledi. The fossils were tangible and offered valuable insights into the diversity of hominin lineages that existed in Africa during the Middle Pleistocene. My dissertation challenged previous assumptions about human evolution, and this substantiates my theory. This is why National Geographic took an interest. We are so far back in time that dragons existed even before this. This city was populated by species whose only remnants are myths and bones that have never been found, as it is the only place not destroyed by fire or ice. The fact that, right here in front of our eyes, the preserved carcass of Atlas lies waiting"—he locked his arms around me—"Atlas? I never thought of this. Do you know what this means?"

I had no idea, but I liked him whispering into my ear. Goosebumps rose as my attention traveled south. At least we agreed that Atlas was dead.

"No, tell me," I whispered, shaking my head, while discreetly repositioning my cock with a quick rub against his hip. I was hoping he hadn't noticed, but he saw me. "Are you saying there might still be a chance of going home?"

"That will have to wait." His voice rasped at a lower octave. *Gods give this man a fossilized dragon, and he is sexy as fuck.* I gripped Kellan by the seams of his pants to pull him closer. He leaned into me, his hardness rubbing my hip. We were humping each other standing upright.

Now it was my turn to speak into his ear. "You know...in Greek mythology..." I said on a breath. "Atlas was a Titan who was sentenced to hold up the heavens for eternity after he had lost the hundred-year Titanomachy." The sparkles in his eyes made me wonder if he had fireworks going off in his skull. He pursed his lips, barely containing himself.

I whispered again, "I know, hmmm." His hands drifted to my hips, and I clutched his shoulders. "Tell me, Professor. Am I on the right track or not?"

The whites of his eyes turned blazing red with lust, confirming my suspicion that he was addicted to shit like this, like I was to him. "North Africa. Everyone knows the myths about the ancients, about Atlas, but he was carrying the world, not holding the heavens up. That could have happened twenty thousand years ago, or *much-much* longer ago. We know the Atlas Mountains are at the far western edges of their world. Over time, it became closely associated with the Atlas Mountains in northwest Africa. But this is where the stories of Atlas, the first King of Mauretania, the keeper of the knowledge..."

"Oh my God, the apple! King Solomon's tomb..."

"Yes, we found dozens of tribal references, myths, and word-of-mouth tales in Algeria."

I enlarged my eyes, panting. "But we came through the Cradle of Mankind in South Africa."

"Everything makes sense and at the same time confuses me."

"What lay beyond the Atlas Mountains?"

He puffed into my neck. I was trembling, rutting like Marmaduke. We were ridiculous for each other. Our brains were fucking. For the first time in my life, I connected with someone on a level that was indescribable and unattainable with anyone else. We hopped and danced, pulled and shoved, balancing on the balls of our feet. It became a challenge not to fall down and rip each other's clothes off. But we stayed standing. It made it much hotter and a lot of fun.

"Draxton, we've discovered Titans in this time and location—"

"It can't be. Atlas wasn't a dragon."

"Who would know, it's only a myth," Kellan said, sounding like he was steering me in another direction. *What was going on in his mind?*

"True, but what if..."

"Yeah?" There was an uptick in his voice. He was fucking waiting for me to catch up. But to what?

"Hmmm, the Atlas Mountains separate the Sahara Desert from the Mediterranean Sea and the Atlantic Ocean. Spire City is in Spain. Depending on the weather, by boat, it takes twelve to twenty-four hours to travel from Algeria to Spain, and by airplane, four to six hours!"

"Yes! Only the water level is higher. Do you know what this means?"

"We've not only traveled back in time but also traveled from one end of the continent to the other. That's where Ouroboros goes when he says he goes behind the mountain. He is fucking traveling down in Africa."

Kellan chuckled. "But there is more."

"More?"

"Yes." He smiled provocatively.

"Tell me, my brain is mush, and my body can't think a second further. I have to fuck you right now!" I grunted through clenched teeth. I wanted to kiss him. But the more we spoke, the better it got. *What are we doing? I fucking love this man.*

Kellan let out an explosive laugh. He slapped his cupped

hands over the back of my head, his mouth so close to mine that our beards and lips were touching. This was beyond erotic.

"Yes, my father said…"

"Oh my god, Kellan…tell me!" I urged.

"The moment I tell you, your cock will soften in shock."

"Nothing can soften him now, not even a sledgehammer."

"My love, my man, my wonderful, one-of-a-kind man. No one is like you, not even in one of the other four galaxies will I find someone…"

"No fucking way!"

"That's what I think."

"That there are four galaxies. Four of everything."

"Not four but five."

I understood why Kellan was excited. "So you are saying there is a very good chance that this subterranean world stretches from Algeria to the southern tip of Africa, but not only is this another time, but a reality, actually one of five? Do you mean that when we came through the star door, we could have landed in any of the five places, but also forward or backward in time?" I asked to be sure. It was not that I thought Kellan would make things up or tell me lies. I'd learned to trust him and his word, but I struggled to visualize it, because what would the chance be to return home at all?

"Something as crazy as that, yes. Maybe. We should ask Ouro." He snickered like a villain.

"Do you think we can try to get to South Africa? We now know where one of the doors is. Or at least the entrance. I wonder if Atlas doesn't miraculously wake up, we could try going through it." I kissed Kellan's forehead because I didn't want him to stop talking.

"I love that amazing mind you have in there," he said, and then our lips collided, halting the talking as an unstoppable heat rushed through me. Our connection was as rock-solid as the magnetic iron rock of this mountain. It transcended time and space.

We broke apart from the heated kiss. Gazing into his deep brown eyes, I knew he felt it too when he said, breathless from our kiss, "I love you truthfully, intensely, and profoundly, with every cell in my body."

"Me too, Professor. I was thinking the same thing." We rested our foreheads together.

"How'd you know?"

"Know what?" he asked.

"About the five galaxies?"

"My father left me a strange letter before he died. Like he knew he wouldn't wake up. I'll show you; it's in my car. If it's still there, that is."

"Oh, okay. I came in my pants."

He laughed. "Me too. We're going to suffer if we don't do something about it soon."

CHAPTER 29

DRAXTON

IT TURNED OUT THE WATER IN THE WATERFALL WAS lukewarm. We found a secluded spot, which I assumed the early residents had used for the same purpose as we now were. Old jars with various soaps and oils were stacked in hollowed-out areas of the rock shelter, which protected us from view. The pebbled floor beneath our feet sloped away, allowing water to seep somewhere underneath, making these shower areas both fauna and flora friendly and practical.

"Must be all natural, environment-friendly," I said as water sloshed over my face, and I scooped a glob of the soapy stuff smelling like honey and lavender from between the moss-covered soap containers onto Kellan's back.

"Must be and probably is. This place is the perfect example of a balanced footprint. They've integrated their activities into the natural environment in a way that minimizes disruption and maintains ecological health," Kellan said, standing with his arms up like a scarecrow while I washed him. I tapped his right ankle, and he lifted it so I could wash it. I did the same with the left, returning the favor he had done me earlier, so thoroughly.

"All done!" I announced, stepping out of the best shower I'd had since we got here. "Our clean clothes are still in the winter cave, though. I almost don't want to put our sweaty, dirty ones back on, especially since it's too warm for furs anyway."

"Agreed, let's just put on our boots and pants."

A long, high-pitched whistle drifted from the direction of the time box.

"We've dawdled too long, let's go! They're calling us." I gathered our things under my arm. "Ready?" I asked, watching Kellan tie his boots.

"Yes, always," he said, straightening up and running his hands vigorously through his short black curls, sending drops of water flying. Another whistle sounded, disrupting the calm Kellan and I had created.

"The plan is simple," Kellan said, waving to Snow in the distance as we rounded the secluded shower area. "See if the dragon wakes up. If he does, we will say our goodbyes and ask him to take us home as soon as he can fly. If he doesn't wake up, or he can't take us home, then we ask about traveling through the time door in their time box." Kellan halted mid-step. "Or...we could say our goodbyes and check if our subterranean world theory holds up. If we keep heading south through this cave system, we might discover more exits and see if it stretches all the way to the southern tip."

He was giving me a lot of options to mull over. I really wanted him to go home; his mother was probably sick with worry, and I wondered what Tobias was doing. Were there

police and search and rescue teams looking for us? "Agreed!"
I plastered a smile on my face, walking briskly and following
Kellan's lead.

A-A-A-A-AND...ATLAS truly was a sleeping dragon. Among
the sweet, rosy smells, the white petals of flowers were
discarded at Atlas's stirring, awakening body. His nostrils
narrowed as he took a long, indrawn breath, filling his lungs
and exhaling a sigh that echoed in the stone box, so loudly I
had to cover my ears while keeping my gaze on the flickering,
long, thick eyelashes fluttering like willow branches in the
wind. Blue-black scales rippled, and his eyelids flickered
heavily as Ouroboros removed the petals from another flower
and broke open the very coconut-like receptacle at the thick-
ened end of the stalk. Thick oily drops of Loursveto oil, mixed
with the blood from Ouroboros's pricked finger, fell onto his
bottom lip.

"Why the blood?" I asked.

"Shhhht!" everyone answered.

I remained silent. The drop was tiny against the dragon's
massive lips, but as it was absorbed, the seconds stretched into
what felt like minutes. Slowly his iridescent color returned,
making him the only dragon I had ever seen, and the most
gorgeous. I was about to turn around and say something
sarcastic with my arms in the air when the floor trembled,
crystals flickered, and the primordial giant awoke from his
slumber. With a groan that sounded like a volcano erupting,
he pushed himself onto his front legs, tipped sideways, found
his footing, and slowly rose from where he had been sleeping
for a hundred years. His four claws scraped against the

polished marble, and I hoped he knew we were friends. I wasn't afraid of darkness or heights, but waiting until I was trampled or burned by dragon fire was not something I wanted to test to see if I liked it or survived. Yeah, the best move was to go now before it was too late. But Sopora and her friends behind us blocked my only escape route.

I tilted my head slightly, attuning to the dragon's breathing while observing the crystals set in the rock and around our necks, dimming oddly, as if the otherworldly light pulsed in rhythm with Atlas's breaths.

"The crystals are pulsating!" I told Kellan, who stood beside me, nodding as he noticed the same magical connection between the dragon, the crystals, and the Heart of Anzulla.

Suddenly, Atlas lifted his head and spotted Callisto standing at the entrance, his silhouette framed by the faces of happy people, parting to make way for them. People reversed out of the box, and I didn't hesitate to get out of their way either. Once Atlas was outside, he lifted his head, opened his wings, stretched, and puffed a warm, stinky morning breath laced with the smell of Loursveto over our heads. Callisto shook his head and began to gallop toward his brother, his paws and body growing larger with each trot. We enlarged the human circle as the air changed around Atlas, and in that instant, a significant shift in the atmosphere swept over us. His body lifted off the ground, and his scales expanded and contracted over his muscles and bones. It was the same sound as when I scratched my beard. Just much louder.

His nostrils opened and closed, and his wings clinked together like stainless steel plates as he moved, shaking the ground beneath my feet. Hundreds of tons of dragon erupted into happy growls as polar bear and dragon collided, nipping and nuzzling each other while hopping in sync. Immense joyous shouts erupted at the reunion of the two brothers. As fascinating as that seemed, safety had to come first, so I grasped Kellan's arm and pulled him away from the danger.

"Wait, I want to watch this!" Kellan exclaimed in awe.

"Watch from a distance; that dragon will flatten us, and there's no recovering from that. Your bones would be crushed," I said, moving far back so we could still see and hear them, but have a chance to run if the dragon came for us —at least, that was my hope. Kellan didn't resist; he took my hand, and we walked backward until I stopped.

"He's a magnificent dragon, Draxton! Can you believe this?"

"I see it, and I believe it. I understand now why some people wanted to kill them. The size—"

Atlas lifted his head, and a tooting noise escaped his throat.

"Oh my God, I understand him!" Kellan shouted, and I agreed. I understood every damn word as well.

"*I smell Zelk!*" His roaring voice boomed in my skull like cannonballs.

I covered my ears, swearing.

Kellan looked around frantically, the question "Should we run?" written all over his face.

"*Kill the Zelk!*" Atlas roared again. The smell of sulphur, volcanic ash, and sediment wafted by me as the big dragon thumped around, just as Callisto wrapped his front legs around his brother's neck. The two were now the same size.

"Oh, bloody hell no!" I cried out, covering my head. My

hat went flying again, and this time I was scared, so I left the thing on the ground and searched for a safe spot to run to.

No wonder this place is so big. Dragons needed space to fly.

"No, brother, it's not Zelk. The Zelk is far away! There is no Zelk here!" Callisto loudly coaxed.

Everyone was talking inside my head. Kellan covered me with a jacket, and we ran.

"Calm down, Atlas! It can't hurt you!" Ouroboros shouted, just as we dove behind two thick trees and hoped it would be safe here because we were too curious to leave the scene. Ouroboros jumped, dancing through their legs, leaped, and got scooped up by Callisto. Ouro ducked and dove, waving his spear, trying to get Atlas's attention.

"Please, brother, listen to us," Callisto cooed. The fear and anger flashing in the dragon's blue eyes dulled.

In the scuffle, Ouro slid from Callisto's neck, then stood with his arms in the air like an ant trying to stop two berserker elephants. *"That's it! No more Zelk is here, you will burn us to a crisp if you don't calm him down now!"* I assumed Ouro was talking to Callisto, but everyone was answering him by shouting at Atlas to calm down.

"We are friends! No Zelk here!" they yelled, waving their arms above their heads.

Hiding behind the trees, we gasped in awe as Atlas spread his wings. Noticing the left wing drooping awkwardly, he let out a whine and settled down, panting heavily.

"His wing is sore," I whispered.

Then, he looked at me with curious blue eyes—the same color as his brother's. I pretended to ignore him, but I secretly watched everything unfold in slow motion. The dragon's gaze remained fixed on me. His scales rippled, appearing both soft and hard at once. They shone like a snake's pearly skin.

We froze as Atlas's body fully pivoted toward us. His one reptilian appendage—his powerful claws—were coming my way. I hurled myself around, squeezing my eyes shut. My heart raced, and I clutched Kellan's arm while Atlas's warm breath puffed over the side of my face. Slowly, I opened one eye; his nostrils flared as he sniffed me. He turned his gaze to where Snow and the others were waving, shouting, "No!"

I closed my eyes and ears, then hummed.

WHEN I OPENED MY EYES, I realized time must have passed because Ouro and Snow were next to me, speaking to Kellan. They stood between the dragon and me.

"He smells like them because they held him prisoner!" Kellan yelled.

"*Then I will kill them for that!*" The dragon's voice boomed so loud, I saw flashes of light behind my eyelids.

"Loud, too fucking loud!"

"*Yeah, brother, no need to shout. You will give the humans migraines!*" Callisto shouted just as loudly.

"Softer, everyone, calm down," Kellan urged them. I heard people murmuring, and then the volume was lowered.

"Is that better?" Kellan asked.

"Yes, thank you," I said with teary eyes.

"The time of fun and games is over. Atlas, it is time for us to fight," Ouroboros said to the now much smaller and much less intimidating dragon and bear. It helped a lot to see the less frightening size, and I relaxed, remembering the first time

I saw Callisto. I was terrified, but I grew accustomed to him when I realized he was intelligent and kind-hearted.

Atlas shook his head, lowered it, and looked Ouroboros in the eyes. "*My wing...I'm not ready.*"

"Are you okay?" Kellan whispered.

I stuttered, getting up. "I-I'm not going to utter a word...I have no words."

Kellan smiled. Dusting me off and fixing my hair, he put a hand on each of my shoulders. "Tell me, what are you thinking?"

I looked down. "It saddens me that my grandfather cannot witness this. Being far beneath Africa's surface is a marvel beyond my imagination," I said, my mind ignited with sketches and maps as I visualized our location. "I have so much to learn about this place. But Ouro is in a rush to have his war with the Zelk. That leaves the time box portal thing, or..."

"*Only Atlas can use his magic to make it work. My father made it safe for him and for the person using the portal,*" Callisto answered, as if he was listening in on our conversation.

I narrowed my eyes at him. "I was whispering to Kellan for a reason!" I rolled my eyes, turning to Kellan. "But that is not a crack in the sky. We arrived by falling, but what if this is where we should enter?"

"I see what you mean," Kellan said.

"Imagine we stepped through that door; would we step out in the Dinaledi Chamber?" My eyes flicked around, searching for a spot to turn my gaze. I decided Kellan was the best and safest option.

He took my hands, squeezing them, and I breathed deep. "I'll ask Atlas, okay?"

"Okay," I whispered.

Ouroboros called out to get everyone's attention. "Now that Atlas is awake, I want us to split into teams. I need help to bring everything in from the winter cave. Weapons and anything else you might need for a fight. Keep it all close to the entrance so you can grab it and go. Atlas and Callisto are staying put for now; Atlas is still healing his wing."

"So, you're grounding the dragon?" I asked.

Ouro tipped his head, answering me, "Yes. Atlas needs all his strength; he can't use his magic to open portals now. He should heal; that is the most important and first thing he has to do. Our lives depend on him and his ability to fly."

"Kellan is my brother. Listen to him," he said to Atlas. "Stay here with him." He turned to Kellan. "Please watch them closely. Keep Callisto and Atlas out of trouble. They must remain in the cave beneath the crystal. We'll need them at full strength."

Atlas and Callisto huffed. "None of that," Ouro said. "Kellan is Gugusan's boy from a very faraway time. You watch him and keep him safe. He will be happy to hear all about your stories." Ouro gestured to the woman and children. "Don't stray; stay near. We have a lot to do. Boil water, prepare a large stew. I'll need scouts outside while I gather the animals in the valley. Everyone knows their responsibilities."

I jumped. "I want to see! Let me come with you!" My voice was loud as I demanded to be heard.

Callisto and Atlas looked at each other, then, as if agreeing and teaming up, the brothers started whimpering together.

I blinked in disbelief. "Now we have to deal with two of them."

"That's how they are together! I missed seeing you together so much! But our enemy could be coming any minute," Ouro said while smiling.

"*What are we supposed to do?*" Callisto asked sulkily.

"Catch up. Play cards or something, keep yourselves busy!" Simon shouted over his shoulder, then made a U-turn.

Kellan pulled a face, looking at his hands. "Cards?" He inspected Callisto's paws. "How? Do they? Hold cards?" he asked Simon.

"They play cards, and they cheat too!" Simon smiled slyly, pulling a pack of cards from his pants' back pocket, and handed them to Kellan.

Callisto and Atlas sat up straight as if they were human. Eager and ready. "*I will shuffle. Give it to me,*" Atlas said.

"*No, I will. You are still waking up,*" Callisto said.

Kellan scoffed. "No, I will," he said, taking the cards out of the tin can holder. "Draxton, are you joining us?" Kellan asked.

I waved at him. "No, I want to go with Ouro. I need to clear my head. I want fresh air and quiet. I can't handle all the talking inside my head."

Kellan put the cards back in the box, snapped it shut, and threw it to Callisto. "You shuffle, Atlas can shuffle the next round. I quickly want to talk to Draxton."

Callisto caught the cards between his front paws. "*Atlas will share his coins with us,*" he said.

"*Yeah, hold on, I will go get some,*" Atlas said.

"No, you won't. You stay right where you are. Ouro said

the two of you are not allowed to move from this spot," Kellan said.

Atlas rose anyway, tucking his wings. "*I'm fine*," he said. "*I'm a big boy.*" In my mind, his voice was at a lower volume, but he sounded energetic and positive. Kellan was going to have a hard time keeping them still. "*We need money. I'll get it*," he said, all chipper, ignoring Kellan.

I rubbed my temples. "Kellan, stay. I'm okay. Don't worry about me," I barked at him and turned to leave. "You watch the kids!"

"Hey!" Kellan's hand wrapped around my wrist. "Give me a kiss, please."

I sighed in frustration. Noticing beyond Kellan, Atlas was busy sauntering off, looking like a waggling duck as he walked with Callisto on his heels on their way to a road running toward the carved city. "You'd better go. They are going to get into trouble." I gave Kellan a peck on the cheek, knowing he needed to know I'd be okay.

"Don't wander off. Come get me at the first sign of trouble, please."

"I will, I promise. I want to go recharge," I said, closing my eyes as he pulled me into a hug. Blowing out a steam locomotive's breath, I melted into him. His warmth and closeness, a gentle touch to my restless mind.

"I love you," he whispered.

Cracking a smile, I said, "And I love you, but I really need to go now...I want to map this fictitious place...um...in my mind. The more we discover, the more detailed the picture becomes, and the more it proves that what I've learned is irrelevant, which makes me anxious. What I thought I knew never came close to what the maps and symbols actually represented. My grandfather's maps and ideas, which I drew my knowledge from, only existed in my imagination. This puts me right back to when we arrived here, and you never told me about your father, the Star Caves, and that you knew about Anzulla." I pointed to the darkness, further into the cave beyond the city, beyond what I could see.

Kellan followed my gaze. "I know, and I'm nervous too. We are being swept up by their war. You want to go there. Where no one is bothering you, and no one is telling you what to do. You want the silence that is calling you. Don't you?"

"We haven't even started to explore...this place. This is the real world, and I need time...um...to process it. It's messing with my mind. It's as if I knew nothing at all. Zero!" I rambled. I really didn't know what else to say, because Kellan looked like he was fitting in, and I felt like a broken compass running out of time. I had nothing to return home to. If Kellan told me he had changed his mind about returning, I'd vote to stay. But if I stayed, I wanted to know what else might come up, where I fit into everything, and what my role was. The mystery of the darkness was calling me, and I wanted to explore with or without Kellan. I couldn't tell him that the thought of returning home to nothing was the true reason why I was getting nervous—I guessed. That was the true reason I needed time to think and breathe.

"I understand." He let go of me. His warm brown eyes shone with sincerity. "Okay, go. I miss you already."

I gave him one last kiss on the lips, then ran to catch up with Ouro.

CHAPTER 30
KELLAN

I WAS PLAYING POKER WITH A DRAGON AND A POLAR bear. This was my new normal. Draxton had gone south with Ouro and his men to the hidden valley to gather the animals, like that giant elk we saw Ouro ride upon.

It was midnight. Deep in the Heart of Anzulla, a dozen men and women prepared provisions for war. Everyone had spread out up and down the main road in the subterranean city, which I'd learned was where the birdmen and other first people lived.

When I stood with my back to the carved buildings behind me, up the road, to the right, were the waterfalls, the field of grass, with the beautiful Loursveto flowers, and the Baobab trees with the time box just beyond that.

To my left, at the end of the kilometer-wide apartment buildings that stretched up to the cave's ceiling, lived Atlas and Callisto. They each had their own cave, and beyond them lay unexplored territory. Apparently, the other side of the mountain overlooks an ancient city carved into terraces down to its base. I assumed that was the home of the San tribe, since my father had described it that way many times. It was destroyed and buried under lava rock and later ice since the invasion, after Atlas had melted the rock around the mountain's peak.

Some had moved into the abandoned homes, where they'd made the children comfortable for bedtime. We were playing cards near Atlas's cave, where he kept his horde, and where Sopora could help me keep an eye on Atlas and Callisto.

Pots of water boiled, and water pouches were filled. Arrows were cut, and spears were sharpened. After the children had rolled baskets full of bandages, they were told to wash up and go to bed.

The aroma of more pots of stew lingered and wafted constantly as they cooked and prepared to feed the soldiers. Once the battle started, no one would have time to make warm meals.

Sopora took charge while we waited for Ouro and the others to return with the pack of beasts. She told us to stay busy and out of trouble while Callisto and Atlas basked under the healing red crystal rays.

I kept them occupied. They were their most important weapons, so everyone was working except us. Callisto and Atlas's job was to become as strong as possible. My job was to make sure they didn't do anything stupid.

"May I?" I asked Atlas, getting up when he announced that his wings weren't painful anymore.

"*You may, and while you are back there, please scratch that area at the top of my wing.*" Atlas lowered his head, allowing me to run my hands over him. The crackling firelight reflected off his bumpy, scaly head.

"Hmmm, that's the spot," he purred with a low rumble. He turned his head, looking at me approvingly, his blue slitted dragon eyes shining with intelligence. His wing had healed, feeling warm and soft as I scratched it.

"When you are done there, you can give me scratches too." Callisto was trying his luck. Atlas tucked his wings and thanked me, and I sat down feeling more energized and alive as time went on. I saw the change come over Atlas as he recharged like a lithium battery.

"Sorry, Callisto, you don't have healing limbs." I chuckled.

Callisto rubbed his feet together. *"It's the magic light. It's making us itch."*

"Yeah, I don't feel tired. Let's play another round," I told Callisto.

Atlas pushed himself up into a sitting position. *"It's the magic of the Heart; it pulsates through the underground realm."*

"Yes, and you stupidly locked yourself inside the time chamber," Callisto grunted, and I started shuffling the cards.

In the back of my mind, I was hatching my plan on how to approach Draxton once he returned after helping Ouro with the wild animals to help us fight the Zelk. Hopefully, Draxton had had time to clear his mind and be ready to talk to me.

My reality, where my mother, Tobias, and the home I'd always known were waiting, felt distant, like a faded dream after a restless night. Like, I just needed a good cup of coffee to forget it.

We still would have been locked in our hut while I was sheltering Draxton to the point of death for both of us, because I didn't know how to bridge the gaping canyon between us. Therefore, I appreciated that Callisto had insisted on seeing Draxton and had created a way for us to connect through his mind link. Since then, Draxton had given me just enough access to his mind and body to keep us connected by a very thin but strong thread.

In my defense, I was reducing unnecessary stimuli, such as noise and visitors asking questions or offering sympathy, because Draxton has a heightened sensitivity to sound, known as hyperacusis, which I feared was worsening his distress and sensory overload. He disliked certain loud or repetitive sounds that cause him discomfort and anxiety.

My love for him ran deeper than infatuation. I admired his strength and versatility. Anyone who experienced what he did would likely suffer from non-functional post-traumatic stress and need years of therapy. I didn't think Draxton would be able to talk, let alone climb a mountain, camp out in the snow, make love, or smile. But despite all that resilience, I gave him space by creating pauses in time for him to heal mentally because I knew he needed to process it in his own way. He'd had only a month and a half to recover, and I had been cautiously supporting him by protecting him without smothering or shattering his mind in the process. It had been a complex, delicate task, allowing him to come to terms with the savagery inflicted on his beautiful mind.

Just thinking about what had been done to him stirred a monstrous desire to destroy the machines. I wanted to inflict the same brutality on the Zelk with such viciousness as they have inflicted on my Draxton, my father, and every living thing. But the more I thought about it, the more I understood that their hell would be to be erased as if they had never existed—the way to do that has not yet come to me.

In the meantime, I was grateful to Callisto. Without his insistence on helping Draxton, the trapdoor that had been set around his mind would never have been unlocked. I'd witnessed a healing that no therapist or medication in our reality back home could have achieved.

Draxton perceived, saw, and felt our situation on a level so deeply internal that it felt like an intrusion when I offered him comfort by holding him against my chest. I was allowed to hug him because he knew I needed it. He followed practical, calculated steps as a lover, while I sometimes felt like I was hugging myself. I'm not his psychiatrist, and I'm not an expert on autism, but as long as both of us gained something from our exchange, it was fair. I always considered how to give him what he needed without giving it to him before he had figured it out for himself. I've learned my lesson not to push him away, but to communicate honestly while not forcing him in one direction or the other.

Draxton accepted and showed emotional empathy, but compassion was a complicated effort. He expressed it through actions. I watched for cues from him to measure his exhaustion and meaning, but I'd learned that Draxton was abrasive and short-tempered naturally; he mimicked us, for our comfort, but I enjoyed him more when he wasn't acting according to the socially acceptable script. He was intelligent and unpredictable. Breakable and unbendable. Yet, if I took any of that away, he wouldn't be my Draxton.

His emotions were genuine and profound. Hiding them compounded his anxiety. So he just blurted them out, and I preferred it that way. He told me he loved me, and I wanted a life that would satisfy both of us, even if it meant throwing us headlong into a war. His default was to solve problems, and I realized I was using stupid Hollywood social rules to handle our relationship by pushing him into another's arms.

I wanted him to be happy, but not at the cost of myself or, most importantly, at the cost of him.

Draxton doesn't deserve to be tamed by the same rules humanity drilled into their children, becoming dull, stream-lined, rule-followers.

I wanted Draxton to be himself. I wanted him to shine in his uniqueness and not dull his brilliance. He was born to solve problems. He was an adventurer.

Deep down, I knew if we returned home, our relationship wouldn't work. It would crack, my work, my home, my whole life, would kill what we have here. My way of life would be a prison to him.

As long as he searched and mapped caves, he would reach fulfillment. I was convinced his mind was wired not to be hindered. I firmly believed we were here because he wanted to find this place so badly that Callisto sensed us, bringing us with him to this reality. I wouldn't be happy either, living in a caravan, searching for clues. It made no sense to go home and search for what we've already found, what we were looking for. I couldn't do that to him. To us.

However, Draxton was growing increasingly irritated. He had said he didn't want to stay.

Atlas, a dragon, was too much on top of everything else. He had certain expectations. Yes, my secrets upset him, but I believe it was the fact that everything wasn't what he had imagined. He'd fleetingly accepted Callisto because he'd thought once he discovered the advanced civilization, it wouldn't matter. But it did matter. The Zelk wasn't a dream come true, but a nightmare.

He was at a crossroads. He didn't want to get excited about Atlas because he was our taxi home.

Too many things were happening. I wondered if Draxton didn't want to go home because if he did, what would he have there? And yet he doesn't want Ouro's war. So he's stuck— either go home to nothing to avoid the war or stay and face the Zelk, who had mentally tortured and disappointed him so traumatically that he had almost lost the will to live. The advanced race was his beacon, the reason he grew up spelunking. He'd accepted himself as being different, because he was born to be a cartographer—to find the pieces of the puzzle he thought he was building for his grandfather. His whole identity was wrapped up in that, and I couldn't take that away from him.

All I could do was give him space so he could find out what he truly needed without my influence. That was the biggest challenge he had to solve on his own. When he realized and said it aloud, I knew that he would be happy with us staying. Then, I would feel fulfilled in giving him the chance to explore with me. *Here.*

He thought he was doing me a favor by not admitting that he doesn't want to go home, because he empathized by recalling his feelings of not having a mother. In his way, he demonstrated compassion by not voicing his own needs, as he wanted to return me to my mother.

The closer we got to going home, the more anxious he became. Understandably, he didn't want to fight either. Neither of us did. So we'd reached a point where he has to figure all that out for himself, and then we can discuss staying. However, if we were to stay, we would have to fight. Fight the Zelk.

My father's stories wove a world of scintillating colors so vivid that I now understood what he meant when he said they didn't exist on the color wheel from my time.

I shuffled the deck of cards in my hand and placed three cards face up on the left for Callisto and three cards to the right for Atlas, and then three for me, because I was the house. The cards were too small to hold in their claws, so we played like we were in a casino. A grimace twisted my face, and a low, befuddled groan rumbled in my chest. The house held three hearts, unfortunately not in order. I needed a two, three, seven, or an eight of hearts for a straight flush.

My opponents were cheating. We are all mind-linked, and the two brothers thought I was stupid.

Callisto's fluffy white fur shimmered with a bright, luminous blue just before daylight, while Atlas's scales shimmered in the same shade of blue right before midnight.

I smiled, turning my eyes back to the cards. They thought the longer they stayed silent, the more they ramped up the anticipation. So, I waited. The warm, humid air shifted as Atlas repositioned his wings. Callisto's long black toenails retracted and extended as he flexed his toes up and down.

They grunted and made noises, glancing at their cards, seemingly trying to give me the impression that they were thinking hard about their tricky hands. I shook my head at my new reality. Unbelievably preposterous. But so cute. Atlas wasn't nearly as freakishly terrifying as I'd pictured the dragons from stories during childhood.

"We can be deadly if we want to be. We are mighty Titan warriors," Atlas rumbled, sitting up, his tail swooshing lazily, spikes like steak knives protruding from the dorsal ridge.

I suppressed my amusement. He had just confirmed my

suspicion that they were, in fact, reading my mind. "Really?" I teased.

"*Yeah, we like you, and that's why you are still alive,*" Callisto said, giving Atlas a side-eyed look, urging his brother on. Atlas pulled his lip up into a skewed line, revealing his sharklike upper front teeth.

I pointed, laughing at him. "Is that supposed to be a smile, or are you threatening me?"

Atlas lowered his thick, bumpy brows, squinting at me. "*Neither; it's supposed to distract you,*" Atlas purred.

I huffed. "Don't read my mind and don't count the cards. How will the house win fairly if you do that?" I narrowed my eyes at them, and as one, they lifted their eyes to the ferns growing out of the cave roof. They were secretly mouthing something to each other, but I couldn't make it out. Their childlike behavior was adorable, and Callisto had never shown this side of himself to me. They really were just children, as Draxton had told me.

Never have I ever missed my phone more. A selfie with these two would have been amazing. Or, even better, I could go back and show it to my mom.

Sadness tightened in my throat at the thought that she might already be gone. Then again, perhaps it is a blessing so she doesn't have to face the Doomsday of 2046. But that's another twenty years in her future. Draxton and I left her in January 2025. Perhaps that's why my father chose not to extend his life, refusing the blood of the men, the friends of Ishtar, he had run into at the mine.

"*It's your turn,*" grunted Callisto, interrupting my thoughts.

"Yes, it's my turn," I said, smiling. Both brothers sat with their front legs straight, appearing comfortable and waiting like puppies to be thrown a ball.

Sitting on the ground, my butt was cold and numb. I needed to get up and use the bathroom. We were camping out on the city square, but no one would object if I chose a room for Draxton and me to sleep. The place was dusty, but useful things like furniture, furs, beds, and kitchen utensils were left as is when they'd vacated to fight the Zelk a century ago.

"No, he missed his turn. It's mine now. I check-raise." Atlas grunted loudly, staring at his cards, then at the deck in my hand. He shot five coins my way, scraping the tips of his black claw on the rock floor, showing me to hit him five times before he was satisfied with his choice. I played along with their strange version of poker and shoved the unwanted cards back to the bottom of the deck. He didn't have a bad hand. The thought of being burned to a crisp by the big dragon had crossed my mind at first, but they were good sports, so I doubted he would be a sore loser if I won for a change.

Callisto let out a loud bear bark. *"Hey, that's cheating!"* he said to Atlas. *"Careful, Kellan. Are you saying we can't be trusted?"* He chuckled in my mind. Obviously, reading the burned-to-crisp thought.

"Me? Not at all," I said sarcastically. "We should make a larger deck of cards for the two of you since you like to play alone. In secret."

"Nah, we would never play just the two of us, and human hands are too small to hold huge cards," Callisto said, sniffing the air. *"I'm getting hungry again."* Then, his words like an outlaw cowboy's, he drawled, *"Shitty move, brother. You have to know when to fold and know when to hold. You're clearly forgetting how to read the cards."*

I shook my head, bemused. "That was an excellent Texan accent. Where did you hear that?" I threw two cards down and picked up another. Phishing for a heart, but all I got were spades. I was playing out of turn, joining in the cheating, playing our own version of the game.

Callisto swiped his heap of gold coins into the middle with a paw. "*My father used to do that. I'm all in! Hit me!*"

I thought I was teaching a bear and a dragon how to play poker, but they were obviously duping me. They knew all the lingo and had almost all my coins. I threw two cards face up for Callisto. "Hmmm," I said, continuing to search for a heart. Finally, I had a winning hand, a straight flush of hearts, which I knew would win me all those gold coins back. "Okay, I call," I announced, smiling and revealing my fifth card that was face down. Atlas snorted at my hand. "Now your turn." Tendrils of smoke vaporized into the air with each puff over his cards as I flipped the last card face up.

"*A full house!*"

"Not bad, Atlas," I exclaimed. "Two fives and three queens."

"*But I'm not a winner,*" he trailed off.

Callisto chuckled as I flipped his card over. "*But not good enough!*" His big belly jiggled as he snorted. "*Straight flush!*" He leaned forward, dragging the mountain of gold coins to his side.

Jealous flames danced in the dragon's eyes. "*You were just lucky,*" Atlas grumbled. The coins were his anyway. He'd loaned us the gold to play with. Saying he missed it and wanted to play with the gold from his hoard that had been found inside his cave, which was further down from where we had found him.

I maintained a straight face while watching the dragon chew his bottom lip anxiously. Callisto collected every last gold coin, counting them one by one with a satisfied murmur and glinting blue eyes, and pushed them into a small golden coin pyramid, frustrating his brother.

Atlas's dark scales went ashen as color drained from his reptilian face. He sputtered for a moment before demanding, *"How'd you do that? You're cheating. You told me Kellan didn't have those cards, yet there they are."*

"Brother, I lied, just as you had lied to me. Where will I put all my gold?" Callisto teased, asking no one and freaking Atlas out even more.

It was time for me to say something. "Callisto knows it's a game, Atlas. It's just for us to play with. They're still yours."

"I know, but look at him, counting and stacking them, with his spit running all over my coins," Atlas whined.

"It's so funny to see him squirm. He's so pale!" Callisto rolled over to stand on all fours. *"Brother, I would never take your gold, even if I won it fair and square."*

"I'll load the wheelbarrow," I said, getting up and dusting off my backside. "But first I need to relieve myself."

As graceful as a house with four legs, Atlas stood. One misstep and his toenail would slice me like Swiss cheese.

"No, I'll do it. Keep your paws off my gold. Thank you." His dragon breath brushed my face like a bonfire out of control. I jumped backward, skipping as fast as possible in reverse mode. Atlas bounced with an earthshaking plop, then fell into the pyramid of coins as if they were a heap of crunchy fall leaves.

"For someone who loves his gold, you're sending them flying all over the place," Callisto told him, nuzzling his brother's

coins and picking one up in his mouth and spitting it into the wheelbarrow. I stood with my hands on my hips, enjoying the banter.

I sighed. "That was fun."

Atlas scooped more coins into the wheelbarrow with his front claws. "*I'll wait for you. Hurry up, human,*" he said jokingly. His hoard wasn't big by the standards I'd seen in children's books. His cave was just down the road, at the city border. The rock he pushed in front of the opening was too heavy and big for anyone to move. Preening, he trusted me to look around while he bragged about his play money. Apparently, his father loved to craft items out of gold, and Atlas had an array of creations, including chests, coins, and even a gold wheelbarrow.

"Wait for me, don't go anywhere without me," I told them, running into the first apartment with an open door. The ghostly, empty city surprised me with its amenities. The toilet bowls flushed through clay pipes when the chain was pulled.

When I'd emptied my bladder, I followed them back to Atlas's den, where Atlas helped me tip the wheelbarrow and lay it upside down on his mountain of coins.

"*That's better. Everything is as it should be,*" he said proudly. "*What now?*"

"*Don't care. I'm hungry. Let's each grab a piglet before Sopora cooks them,*" Callisto said.

The three of us split up. "I want to go help sharpen the weapons. I saw a nice battle axe I can use to chop up the Zelk. When you're done consuming half of our livestock, come join me." They ignored me. Already planning how to corral two pigs and a couple of chickens. I'd keep an eye on them and the entrance to make sure they didn't leave.

I waved, heading over to the rows of weapons stacked in the armory, where Sopora, Rocket, and a couple of men and women were getting ready and counting the supplies.

"I held onto your axe," Rocket said, clearly knowing which weapon I meant to collect. The copper axe head with its intricate markings had caught my eye immediately, and I'd claimed it then and there. "Thanks."

"It needs polishing and sharpening," Sopora said, hunched over, loading the quivers with the newly made arrows.

"That's why I'm here." The thing had a long handle, and I swung it over my head, like a hammer thrower, to get a feel for its weight. "Yeah, gonna smash the Zelk good with it. I'm not sure about human brains and blood, though. But I guess if they attack and I have to defend myself, this will do."

"Draxton said he has a hunting knife and spear," Rocket told me, and handed me a knife to sheath on my belt.

Sopora gave me a cloth and a sharpening stone, and I settled down to watch my two charges. Atlas was circling the chicken coop as Callisto chased after their food, sending feathers and shit everywhere.

We chuckled while watching them.

"This stone is ceramic. You can use it dry, but usually, we use a little bit of water. Look at what Vera and Joe are doing over there." She pointed to them, three fires over. I was watching them earlier, so I knew I'd be okay. She handed me a bucket of water and threw more axes and spears down next to me. "See if you can do these as well."

"Sure, no problem," I said and got to work.

I finished sharpening my new axe, and just as I leaned over to grab the next one, Ouroboros and Draxton, followed by Simon, Kawa, Donali, and Sarinka, came running and shouting.

"They're coming!"

"They're here!"

"Arm yourselves!"

"Get ready!"

I jumped up, dizzy with shock. Draxton and his entourage split up. Ouro ran to meet up with Sopora. Draxton stopped dead in front of me. Simon, Donali, and Kawa ran for their stash of weapons. His men armed themselves to the teeth with guns and hand grenades.

"Kellan, things are about to get really bad. We need to get out of here now!" Draxton said breathlessly as he pointed towards Atlas.

But the dragon shook his head. *"No time for transportation flights. We fight. Come!"* He flattened his head on the ground. *"Get on, I have a better plan."*

Draxton shot me an exasperated look. Sweat dripped from his temples, and he wiped at it with the back of his forearm. His head and shoulders were still covered in snow. "No, fuck no!" he spat, glancing at the others, who shrugged and rushed to grab weapons. "Bloody fucking hell!" he shouted, pulling at his hair.

"Kellan, Draxton, grab your gear and get on!" The Dragon's icy blue eyes bore into me.

"To do what exactly?" Draxton asked. "Callisto told us that you will take us home. Heck, everyone said so. Kellan must go back to be with his mom. I'm not going to fight in your war. If we die, we will never get back home. Ever!"

Callisto stuck his nose under Snow's arm, nudging him.

Surprised, Snow stumbled. "Hey, careful, I'll drop the tunnel maker!" he yelped indignantly.

"*Give Draxton the laser drill. Atlas is taking them drilling!*" Callisto said, and Snow threw the laser drill into Draxton's arms.

"*Admit it. You don't want to go home. Both of you. You are pussyfooting, and we have Zelk to kill,*" Callisto told us.

"But—"

"No, buts! Do what you came here to do. Help Callisto and Atlas!" Ouro ordered, jogging over with leathers and goggles. "Put these on and get on! Now! There's no time," he said, handing the steampunk goggles to Draxton and draping my winter coat over my shoulders. "No, first the harness, then the coat, and your belt."

I lifted a hand asking for a second. This was not the plan, I thought. I had to check in with Draxton first. I bit my lip, turning to my lover. "What do you want to do?"

He blinked, looking from me to Atlas, the exit, and the two pairs of black leather goggles in his hands. "If you're okay with dying and never seeing your mother again, then I'll stay with you. But if you want to go home…" He pointed to the time box where Atlas had pushed Callisto through the time door and trapped himself inside and hibernated for a hundred years. "Then we take our chances and see if we make it home."

Taking Draxton's hand, I took a deep breath and waited until his eyes met mine, then told him truthfully in a calm, steady tone, "For me, I'm just happy to spend every minute I have with you. If we return, there's no guarantee my mom or anything else will be there."

His eyes flicked, roaming my face for signs that I wasn't

honest with him. "If we stay and actually get to win this war, then we—"

"Would you two please stop fussing? I can sense what you're thinking, and you both want to remain here. There's no need to debate about it. Let's get moving, please get on, now! My brother has explained your involvement...tirelessly. You came here to help, in your father's place. Haven't you?" Atlas asked.

Draxton looked at me with a glint in his dark, determined eyes. I wasn't surprised by the excitement he was trying to hide. The corner of his mouth quirked up in a smile. The one he saved just for me, and my heart fluttered in my chest as warmth spread through me like melting butter. "I thought about it, and I think I'd like to stay. I'm not fond of fighting, but if we go home...Simon and his brothers said it's only a few more years before the American war breaks out and earthquakes start, anyway."

I pulled Draxton closer, kissing him. For a second, the world around us fell away like that day in the cave when the wall gave way before we fell through it. I clutched the back of his head as he tightened his hold around my lower back. His cold mouth tasted like frozen bitter berry wine when I swept my tongue into his laughing mouth.

"Okay, okay, okay! Here you go!" Ouroboros interrupted, breaking us apart like two blue-blooded bulldogs not allowed to breed. Disoriented, I took the fur jacket Ouro handed me, put on my harness, belt, and goggles.

Draxton was all seriousness. He'd had time to mentally prepare, I guessed, because he was ready to go as he placed one foot on Snow's waiting hands with fingers laced to give him a flip up onto Atlas's neck. "Thanks," he said, making himself comfortable. He leaned forward, hugging the dragon's neck. "Hello, Atlas. Nice to meet you. Yeah, I do love him. Yeah, thank you. I do. I am. Yes, I know. Oh, I didn't know you knew that. So Callisto told you? Yes, I am the best. No, I've never been afraid of the dark. Sure, I can do that. I'm horrible with a knife or a sword." Atlas was speaking into his mind, so we heard only Draxton speaking.

Snow patted my shoulder. "You're next once you are ready."

"So it's like a maze?" Draxton asked, drawing my attention to him.

Suddenly, I went flying and landed on my knees, scurrying into position in front of Draxton. Ouro tossed the laser drill and my axe up to us. The area between the sharp spikes on the ridge of Atlas's back and his head, was flattened and resembled a big saddle in which Draxton and I sat comfortably, as there was enough space for our weapons and backpacks.

"If we fall, that's it for us," Draxton said, wrapping his arms around my waist as the drill jabbed into my back. I stuck my axe through my belt loop and grabbed onto Atlas's small neck horns protruding from his neckline.

"*I won't drop you,*" Atlas huffed. "*Let's go!*" he growled. "*Hold tight! Dig your feet into my scales, and don't let go of my horns.*" He leaped, shooting into the air after Callisto.

We howled as we shot through the tunnel, up into the cold early morning sky. The icy wind burned my face, and I struggled to keep my eyes open. The goggles around my neck flapped up and down on my back. "We're going to freeze!" Draxton yelled into my ear.

"*No, you're not,*" Atlas said, making a U-turn around the tip of the mountain. "*I'm transferring you to my claws,*" he said, landing gracefully and lowering his head. "*Slide off, so I can scoop you up.*"

Draxton threw his leg over, lay down, and slid to the ground. Landing like a professional dragon rider in the snow. He was dressed warmer than I was because he'd come running from outside and never took anything off. I followed, copying him, and hastily put my goggles on before I lost my eyesight. "What's the plan?" I asked Atlas loudly to hear myself over the howling wind.

"Look!" Draxton shouted, also fighting the noise. The three of us leaned forward, squinting. I followed his gaze north. Fear, ice-cold fear, solidified in my core as my eyes fell on three enormous warships approaching the coast, like three ghostly nightmares emerging from the fog covering the ocean.

Movement caught my eye, and my gaze tracked back up the mountain where Ouro and his army were exiting the opening we'd drilled into it. "Callisto's leading them to the clearing where Ouro told the elk and wolves to wait for him."

My heart shattered when I saw the masses of black dots splattered across the horizon. "Is that…"

"Yes, it is…We're utterly screwed, and there's absolutely no escape now," Draxton stated.

"*Yes, that's our enemy. They are about three hours away. Let's go. I'm taking you to the shield. You are going to blast it with the laser,*" Atlas said.

"Was that what you were talking about earlier? You said something about a maze?" I asked.

"*The outer defense shield is a maze. That's where Apsu resides. There is one entrance, through the force field, and only a few Zelk have been allowed to enter, and it is only to bring him*" *his offerings. The Birdmen tried to blow it up, but they were all killed."*

"Not Luci," Draxton noted.

"Callisto told me, yes. Not Luci," Atlas replied. Callisto and I had told Atlas about Draxton running into Luci while he was in the penal colony, trying to steal a laser drill.

"Then how are we going to succeed if the Birdmen couldn't?" I asked.

Atlas replied, *"I know where the one entrance for Apsu's spaceship is, but I don't know how to get through the force fields without ending up in the void. Callisto told me that Draxton can move around in pitch-black tunnels and sketch maps from memory."*

"Yes, I can. But how are we going to do it without being zapped into the void, because I use my hands and my other senses to map cave tunnels?"

"We are going to work together. You are going to close your eyes, and I'm going to read your mind. I can sense the force fields and relay them back to Draxton. He will tell me which direction to fly, especially when we make our way back. All eyes are now on the Dark Continent. We have a small window to launch a surprise attack, but once they go on full alert, security locks down, and the force field charges increase. The maze changes, so we have seconds to get out."

Fury flamed inside me. "Holy fuck, that's a suicide mission! No wonder the Birdmen are all dead, because it's a stupid fucking plan!"

"Not stupid," Atlas almost screeched. *"Because we have that laser, once inside, we should activate it and aim it at a vulnerable spot to cut an opening to space, then leave as quickly as possible. That laser will cut its way through the whole struc-*

ture. Once it's been gutted, Apsu will know, and then we have to get to the ground, ready for his attack. They would have two options after going on high alert. Retreat and repair, or catch us and fight. Apsu will fight and worry about the repair later." The dragon described a mission not suited for an archeologist or speleologist with little to no weapons training.

"But they can't access the Dark Continent because of the magnetic field," Draxton and I said simultaneously.

"Oh, Apsu, their maker and leader, will find a way, now that he knows about the crystal. He absorbs life. The life of anything living. That's how he gains his power. That's why he wants the crystals. He doesn't need anything else if he has the crystals."

"But diamonds and gold aren't alive?"

"Everything is alive and can grow on Anzulla. Diamonds grow by adding carbon atoms, and even if gold can't grow in the same way a plant grows, it can be extracted from plants and accumulate in the ground through certain natural processes. Phoenician scientists have discovered that some plants, such as eucalyptus trees or the Loursveto, can absorb trace amounts of gold from the soil and deposit it in their leaves. Additionally, microbes in the soil can help concentrate tiny gold particles, causing them to clump together into larger nuggets over very long periods. That's why the Loursveto is holy to the Anunnaki, it strengthens them, and replaces the need for blood." Atlas's storyteller voice rumbled a soft, low baritone that I can listen to for hours.

"So why not take someone who is good at killing with us, then kill Apsu once inside?" Draxton asked.

"Because I want to help my brother fight, and it's going to be the first place Apsu will go to once we rip a hole through his palace."

"So it's his palace? This thing is covering the Earth—"

"*Anzulla*," Atlas corrected me.

"Anzulla," I whispered into the wind with my hands on my hips.

We stared at the approaching danger, which looked like a swarm of locusts on their way to harvest. After a long pause, Draxton exclaimed, "It's the largest fucking palace! Ever! The surface area of the Earth, I mean Anzulla, is approximately 197 million square miles! One small hole is only going to aggravate him." Draxton was doing the math, I thought admiringly.

"*Exactly*," Atlas purred vapor clouds into the sky as he looked up at the mesh-like reflection far above us, obscuring the stars. "*My father foretold me what to do when today arrived.*"

"Huh?"

"*I'd sent Callisto to go warn our fathers*," Atlas said. He was making no fucking sense because as far as we knew, the bear never made it, I thought, mirroring Draxton's perplexed expression.

But he must have read our confused minds. "*I know what you know, but my father and Ishtar once told me that they'd travelled to a reality where the sun and moon don't shine. Actually, many people were aware of it. They knew about the time they brought Apsu to their time and decapitated him.*"

"Okayyyy?" Draxton drawled.

"*My father told me that I have a bigger purpose. You have to understand that there was a time when the Phoenicians hated my brother and me, and we wanted to leave. We begged our father to take us away from this place. But they told us we deserve this place because we were going to save it...one day...by blasting a hole into Apsu's palace. Um, the night of the blood moon."*

"So that's why the Birdmen killed themselves, they died trying to fulfill a prophecy?" Draxton yelled.

"Yes," Atlas said calmly. *"But the difference is that one hundred years have passed, and there is another blood moon tonight. And on the night of the blood moon, fantastic things tend to happen on Anzulla."*

We stared up. "But we can't even see the moon!"

"I can sense it. There is a blood moon. Its pull is only as strong as we need it to be tonight. I know for certain, beyond that shield is a blood moon waiting to show my father and Ishtar the way inside."

I rolled my eyes. Draxton was pulling his hair and pacing in a circle.

Atlas lay down, corralling us between his claws. *"I know it's a lot to come to terms with. That's why I brought you here, because telling you this in front of the others would just cause an uproar of questions and distract them. Plus, Apsu can read minds on the battlefield. He would know my father is coming, and he mustn't know or suspect anything."*

"So why send your brother to warn them. You thought it was going to happen?" I said.

Atlas sniffed as if smelling us. *"Because the last time I thought their prophecy failed, because—"*

"Because of the Birdmen dying. Because you tried to burn the shield with your fire, and failed. Because Ouro and the others had heard this story before, and you were wrong," Draxton finished his sentence, exasperatedly.

"Yes. But Callisto told me about the tunnel maker. He told

me how you can navigate the darkness. You have a superpower, Draxton. You were born—"

"Na-ah-na!" I waved an index finger. "You will not guilt Draxton into this."

Draxton narrowed his eyes at me. Gods, now I was in trouble for speaking for him. "Sorry, love, I was just—"

Draxton sliced through the air. "Okay, okay, okay! So that's the plan, then? The *only* plan?"

Silence.

Atlas nodded, closing his shiny blue eyes. *"Um, yes,"* he answered. *"There's no better plan than this one."*

"Does this change anything? I don't think so," Draxton mused rhetorically. I shook my head, shrugging in agreement. Atlas watched Draxton, unblinking, as he added, almost casually, "We've jumped on your back to fight, so let's go."

"Yes, we did say we were going to fight," I admitted, a bit sheepish.

"How far is it, and how long will it take us? Are we talking hours or minutes?" Draxton asked a valid question, indeed.

Atlas narrowed his eyes to slits—a dragon smile, I guessed. *"More than minutes, but less than an hour."*

"Alright then, let's get going. We have a hole to drill and places to be." Draxton held up his arms, like a child waiting to be picked up.

"No, sit down, please." We did as Atlas asked. He curled his phalanges around us, creating a safe space for us to sit comfortably. Draxton leaned back in my arms. With us caged safely within his claws, Atlas flapped his wings, and we climbed higher and higher into the denim-blue, chilly sky. We swayed from side to side with each flap of his gigantic wings while Anzulla shrank below.

The height didn't make me nervous, and I could see Draxton wasn't scared either. The wind fluttered across my face; we should've been freezing, but the warmth of Atlas's claws radiated like a toasty electric blanket.

"On a lighter note, to relieve the suspense, I'll tell you something funny," Atlas chortled. *"This reminds me of the time I once stole an airplane, for my hoard."*

"What? No way!" Draxton and I exclaimed together.

"Yeah, I snatched it right out of the air."

"So that's where Snow got his airplane!" Draxton cried out.

"He stole it from me."

"What about the pilot?" I asked.

"What pilot?"

"The pilot of the airplane," Draxton clarified for me.

"I don't know! I was sleeping—the long dragon sleep."

"If you snatched a plane from the sky, someone was flying it," Draxton said.

"I'm just kidding," Atlas snorted.

"I think you're lying, because we are calling you on your bullshit."

"I'm not!" Atlas retorted, craning his neck to gaze up at the sky. *"I caught it. It was burning, falling straight down. It would've crashed. And I swear, there wasn't a pilot inside. How could you even think that? You're hurting my feelings. I may be big, but I do have feelings, you know."*

"Yeah-yeah. So you caught only airplanes shot down, burning, and pilotless," I said, giving Draxton a disbelieving side-eye over his shoulder. "At least we know how Snow's World War II airplane ended up here," I told Draxton. He smiled, shaking his head, and pulled me tighter behind him.

We continued in silence, the Dark Continent and ocean falling away beneath the clouds.

"*Ready?*" Atlas asked. We climbed higher and higher through the thick padding of clouds, and suddenly, terror like I've never known struck me silent.

Fine blue sparks crackled across the force field. It emitted a low hum, like the sound of an electrical substation. The air felt charged with static electricity, the energy, a promise of death for anyone who dared to touch it.

"*Ready yourself, Draxton. Close your eyes, and I'll let you see with my eyes,*" Atlas said.

CHAPTER 31
DRAXTON

Settled cross-legged and secure within Kellan's embrace, I breathed deeply, finding my center. His strong arms held me firmly from behind, anchoring me to him. He whispered against my shoulder, promising that he'd never let go. We sat poised, like right before a rollercoaster plunge. "I trust you," I told him.

I took a deep breath and pursed my lips, then concentrated to pull up that part of my mind where I can lose myself for hours, sketching maps from memory. The moment I shut my eyes, a grid of incredible lights I'd never witnessed burst into my mind.

Beams of energy formed the maze of the security layer protecting Apsu's palace in the sky. It pulsed in various shades from bright green to indigo. I felt the wind swirling and stroking my face.

I bucked my back, but Kellan held me tightly and then

slammed me back down. "I feel and see what you see!" I exclaimed. "Is this what it looks like through your eyes?"

I didn't open my eyelids, but tightened my grip on Kellan's arms as if they were my safety bar over my legs.

"*Yes, you see with dragon eyes now. We share a collective consciousness or psychic energy.*"

"Can you show Kellan what I see?"

"Sure, but only for a second. I need him to monitor and keep you safe, because you can get lost and react physically. Close your eyes, Kellan!"

"Oh, my goodness!" Kellan cried out as his body went rigid and his arms tightened like vice grips around me.

I opened my eyes, but before I could say anything, it stopped.

"Shit, that was intense. It felt like my world dissolved, like being inside a video game! Is that what it looks like when you map the caves?" Kellan asked, elatedly.

"I guess, but Atlas was enhancing it. Did you feel the wind?"

"I did."

"I experience the same when I close my eyes and work on drawing maps."

"Gods, Draxton, that's amazing. Thank you for showing me!"

"That's my mind for only one second," I told him.

"You are incredible. Walking around, seeing the world like that. My vision of the world is bleak when compared to yours."

"*Time to work, Draxton,*" Atlas muttered. I smiled as Kellan kissed my back.

"Let's do this, I got you!" Kellan said, leaving me feeling so loved and adored.

I closed my eyes, and the lights began to dance. They shifted and swirled, forming neon stripes in what felt like every direction, embedding their mesmerizing pattern in my mind—much like when I'd rack my brain to draw maps of the underworld's cave systems.

The same vibrant hues and geometries flooded back, guiding me and Atlas. No machine can do that. No algorithm can capture the raw, visceral essence of what we saw. Blended with Atlas's vision, I analyzed it, committed it to memory for when we had to escape.

"*Yes, that's it. I'm going twenty times slower,*" Atlas said. My chest heaved as adrenaline flooded my system. Kellan's chest was like a wall of steel behind me. It felt like I was about to smash my head in, but it was only in my mind. I dug my fingers deeper into Kellan's forearms.

Through Atlas's eyes, the wind moved, shimmering like threads of spiderwebs in the sun. The usually invisible forces were now made visible, a breathtaking spectacle of nature's hidden artistry through dragon eyes.

Slowly, we approached, gliding down into a gap. Atlas twisted, turned, and then flapped his wings once, soaring upward at a dead end. Without a doubt, if we flew faster, Atlas would need guidance on where to turn, since we had just turned up.

"I'm noting that upward turn," I said aloud.

Atlas purred into my mind. "*Yes, now you see what I meant. There won't be time to stop and think. Once those elec-trify, we'll be zapped into ash.*"

Kellan hissed and huffed behind me with every change of

direction.

"I see," I muttered, focusing intently. Jaws clenched, eyelids squeezed shut, I recorded every detail, careful not to open my eyes and miss a turn or get distracted.

We slipped through the glowing, intricate structure, reminding me of the innards of a computer motherboard. It was gigantic, and I assumed it was thousands of miles thick. Although lizard-like, inside Atlas's claw, we were warmed by the rough plantar skin's heat. The air got thinner and colder the higher we climbed. I summoned all my willpower not to get distracted. I used every bit of mental energy. Innocent people might get hurt if I got it wrong.

The sick feeling in my stomach disappeared when a solid, shiny, blue wall appeared right in front of us.

"*Kellan, get the laser drill ready!*" Atlas broke the silence. "*Keep your eyes closed, Draxton.*"

"They're welded shut," I replied, feeling Kellan releasing his grip. I missed his sturdy body immediately, but kept silent, so he could do what Atlas needed him to do.

The telltale high-pitched *zing* of the laser loading behind me told me Kellan was ready to release the safety and push the button. Suddenly, we landed. Through Atlas's eyes, the hangar was dark and empty as he scanned it. Kellan scooted away, swearing disbelieving obscenities.

"*All the Zelk are on their way to the Dark Continent. We must hurry,*" Atlas urged.

An idea struck. "Why leave the laser here and shoot only at a vulnerable spot? Kellan could pull the trigger, and then we spray paint the inside with a red laser."

"Yeah," Kellan said.

"*No, we must go; we can't get trapped here. My brother and the others are dependent on our return."* Atlas was uncurling his claw, putting us down on the ice-cold steel floor. I stayed seated like a praying monk. It felt strange seeing myself, and I appreciated Kellan from another angle as he ran off like GI Joe searching for cover.

"Point the laser at that thick black box, Kellan," Atlas instructed. I watched as Kellan carefully pushed the laser into a hole and, once secure, pressed the button.

The action started. Atlas scooped me then Kellan into his claw before pivoting and launching into the air. Kellan dropped behind me, tucking his ankles under my legs and holding tight, gasping for air. Bursting through the doorway, we were airborne. It was my turn to guide us, so I focused, visualizing the maze like a map for Atlas.

Silence hung in the air as we worked in unison. The security grid flickered to life behind us, triggered by the explosions. We wove through the maze according to my mental map—down, up, left, right. We zipped through, faster than electricity itself.

This was it! We were now fully engaged in a war with the Zelk. We burst out of the grid and dove to the surface, moving so fast it felt like we were breaking the sound barrier.

CHAPTER 32

CALLISTO

HUH! HUH! HUH! HUH!
  Kill!
Huh! Huh! Huh! Huh!
Die!
We pulled our ugliest faces at our enemies and chanted the war song, working ourselves up into a killing frenzy.

My brother was quiet. His anxiety fell like a rotten fart over us as he'd landed, depositing Draxton and Kellan safely behind me. I sniffed the air, and my eye caught Atlas's, looking up at the sky as if he was half-expecting and half-wishing for a miracle.

I grimaced in question. *"What's the matter? Were you able to execute the plan?"*

"Grrrr." An uneasy low rumble came from him. He shifted his weight sideways, reminding me of when we were young and playing with a ball in the King's games and not knowing

if he should tuck his wings and run like a chicken or jump and fly like a dragon.

"*Brother, it's not time for silence,*" I grunted, mind to mind. "*I need your encouraging words. We must prepare the army to fight.*"

"*Something was happening to their shield. We activated the laser gun inside Apsu's palace,*" he whispered mentally.

I narrowed my eyes at him, sniffing the air. "*What if the whole thing comes crashing down on us?*"

"*It won't. We damaged it just enough to let Father and Ishtar through.*"

"*I think the shield is sizzling,*" he said, and everyone heard it.

"*So, it's damaged and defective?*" I asked, urging him on, so that Ouroboros's people would understand.

"*Yes!*" Atlas said excitedly, catching on. His nervousness turned hopeful as he stared up into the sky, searching for the beyond. For our fathers.

Ouro and his people finally registered the good news, and they roared louder. "*That was what I needed. They needed hope. Thanks, brother! But stop looking up at it, you don't want to alert the Zelk down here about it!*"

"*Oh, right!*" He dipped his head, his gaze sweeping down the mountainside. We were perched on a ridge, overlooking the city of clay huts Kellan and Draxton had helped built nestled to our left. Before us, our enemy approached, some already waiting at the magnetic border.

I rolled my eyes at him as he quickly started swinging his head from side to side, now sniffing the ground instead of the sky.

I caught a whiff of it—the melting electric wiring. Then I

saw it—small crackles—tiny, soundless sparks where the shield was torn open. Our eyesight and smell were better than those of the average human. For the first time in months, I caught a glimpse of twinkling stars in the night sky, bright and unobstructed, and beyond that shone a bright red moon. *"Sweet piglet fat on toast,"* I whispered in disbelief. *"Look at that bloody moon—"*

"Brother, now you are the one looking at it!" Atlas muttered.

"Yeah, you're right, sorry," I said with a wider evil grin, quickly joining him by pinning my stare on the Zelk hover-bots forming a half-moon along the coastline, just out of reach of the Dark Continent's magnetic field.

Larger hovering laser cannon ships waited behind them, each manned by two Zelk, while a long flatbed ship unloaded foot soldiers into the shallows in the distance. They didn't come through the harbor and city as we thought they would, but with our vantage point, we had a bird's-eye view of the coastline below. Thousands outnumbered us.

For me, it was just a few months ago when I last fought against the Zelk. Images of the never-ending invasion zipped through my mind, and judging by the nervous unease, I knew that was precisely what Ouroboros and my brother remembered, but for them, a hundred years had passed.

"I think you are right. Something is happening to their shield," I whispered into his mind as if someone could listen in.

Atlas's tail flicked excitedly, the scales shimmering blue, black, and purple. I'd always been jealous of the campy colors. *"It's Father finally coming to help us,"* my brother said with a hopeful tone.

I continued chanting to rally our handful of soldiers, while making our most intimidating faces and obscene gestures at the enemy. *"We're going to destroy them,"* I roared, turning my attention to Ouroboros while trying my best not to look up. I'd hoped it was the prophecy being fulfilled. It was our only hope. Our numbers were not enough. We needed a miracle.

While we decided where to look, Kellan frantically tried to calm Draxton, but Draxton was losing hope. He attempted to tally the enemy, but the count was impossibly high. He was correct; we were outnumbered by thousands to one.

The *huh-huh-huh-huh-huh*...chanting died down. Draxton walked in circles, fighting with Ouroboros and Simon, who was trying to promise him something that almost everyone was starting to think was not happening. Kellan jumped between them, pushing them apart to give Draxton space. Draxton was stirring fear and chaos, I thought. He was scared, and judging by the nervous faces of our handful of soldiers, he was not the only one.

"Atlas, we'd better take action. We should let them know about the shield opening up," I urged, not really knowing how to do it without tipping off the Zelk. Everyone who could carry a weapon was present, and as my gaze swept over the worried faces, I could see they cared about Draxton, who was holding his head in his hands.

"This is maddeningly stupid! We might as well shoot ourselves and save us the trouble of fighting," Draxton repeated over and over. But that was exactly what we all were thinking. Despite the odds, every man, woman, and child capable of wielding a weapon waited for our cue on what to do next. Atlas was supposed to be their answer, yet he was as unsure about this war now as the rest of us. He said that our father promised to return. What were we thinking?

"You are brave! We will defeat them!" Ouro roared at him and the handful of soldiers behind him. Less than a hundred people over the age of fourteen were here to fight.

"We are doomed!" Draxton yelled. "For heaven's sake, can't you count?" Draxton shouted while holding his head between the palms of his hands.

I saw the blinding flash first, and then lightning popped with a deafening crack across the sky. The strikes sounded like bomb explosions far beyond the clouds, then fine particles of cinders and ashes began to fall like rain—the shield was burning.

"The snake, the snake in the sky is returning!" Libre pointed up. "It's the snake!"

Excitedly, the youngsters jumped up and down as the time machine fell through the atmosphere. "Look at the moon!" Libre pointed, and everyone else oohed and aahed with them, forgetting about the pending attack.

Taking a deep breath of joy and relief, Ouro pointed his spear to the sky. "It's Ishtar's big golden egg. His time machine!" he yelled, and Atlas trumpeted a war cry. The air, the ground, even my fur vibrated with the promise of death to our enemies.

"*What did I say? I promised you, your end would come when the blood moon rises! Didn't I say that?*" roared my brother to our enemies while he nearly decapitated Draxton and Kellan by accident as he danced his war dance. "*When I come over to you, you are going to crackle and pop under my fire! Roaaaaaar!*" escaped from his wide, stretched jaws with spittle and sparks of fire.

On our side, the bickering about life, death, and pending doom ceased as the golden ship hovered closer and closer to the side of the mountain, then landed, sending up a storm of steam as the ice melted on the next flattened ridge below us.

The human foot soldiers siding with the Zelk scrambled to climb back onto the ship, but their backup line of Zelk blocked their paths. Some stood quivering on the shoreline, while others resembled drowning rats as their fellow soldiers used them as leverage to climb out of the water and cling to the side of the ship, begging to be helped back to safety, clearly reconsidering their decision to attack us, now that help had arrived.

I didn't feel sorry for them. They'd chosen their sides. They'd abandoned their children on the Dark Continent to live in the sun with the Zelk because they'd desired comfort. They'd called my brother and me abominations. Cian and Barkor should never have saved them from the moon. They were murderers, and finally, the day of reckoning had arrived for them.

An immense feeling of optimism coursed through me. Ouroboros and his soldiers roared with the promise of victory as they realized the battle was now even. We now had a second chance to win this war.

The line of wild animals became restless as the time machine's door swooshed open and Ishtar and my father jumped out. Their massive black boots thumped onto the ice, announcing their arrival.

Shivers, what a sight they were.

"Damn!" and "What the fuck?" and "Holy shit!" came from around me, and all I thought proudly was, That's *my* father!

"*Father!*" Atlas and I called, not taking our eyes off our enemies for too long.

They followed our gazes, looked at the front lines of our pending battlefield, and pointed to the Zelk ships. They shook their heads and shouted inaudible slurs at Apsu, who had yet to reveal himself.

Ishtar bulged his fists at the hovering ships waiting to attack us once they figured out how to breach the magnetic barrier. "Can you believe this shit? The fucking Zelk!"

"You came! Unbelievable timing. Snow, what did I tell you?" Ouroboros hollered, grinning with open arms at his small army behind him.

"Perfect timing!" Snow and Sopora bowed their heads. "My King, your return is magnificent, just as Ouro said you would be," they said while the rest of the soldiers joined him by bowing and showing their respect.

Ishtar said something to Eryn, and they parted ways.

"Hello, boys!" my father called as he sprinted over to us. Atlas raced me for the first hug like we used to do when we were little. I moved fast and excitedly, shrinking in size to meet him first. Rocks cracked, and the crowd scattered to get out of Atlas's way. His feet thumped on the ground as he thundered towards us with a big smile, revealing rows and rows of white teeth. "My sons, I missed you. I'm so happy to see you're alive. Look how big you have grown." We nuzzled our father while he patted, rubbed, kissed, and scratched us. His smell triggered feelings I thought I had forgotten. Safety, love, and protection cocooned us, and we purred like we used to when we were happy and cuddling together with our parents.

"Remind me who you are," Ishtar said to Ouro with an uncomfortable chuckle as every man, woman, and child flocked to him. Draxton and Kellan stood blinking, not moving or running, which was a good sign.

"I am Ouroboros, the leader of the last tribe of San. It's me, Ishtar. I'm older!"

Ishtar shook his head, looking stupidly perplexed. "I'm sorry, I don't remember you. But you do look familiar."

"My father's tribe has been guarding the mountain since the beginning! For you and your Kuku!"

Kellan was getting nervous. "Hey, guys, maybe look for family afterward because they're breaching the coastline."

Ishtar ignored Kellan. "Is your father by any chance maybe Gugusan?" he asked, stepping between Kellan and Ouroboros. "Where is your father now? Did he return?" he asked eagerly.

Ouro leaned to the side to pull Kellan closer. "Yes, we are his last living sons. He was our father, and no, he never came back from where you had taken him. I thought he had died in the fires, but Kellan said he went with you to another time."

Ishtar took another look at Kellan and Ouro, then threw his arms over their shoulders.

"He is dead. He died over four hundred years after you saved and left him in a cave, alone, and waiting for you," Kellan said, and he wasn't smiling.

Ishtar hugged them fiercely. "Gugusan is...um...was my best friend. He is the reason we were able to make it back here. He collected and recorded the history of Eryn. His books and research notes helped us find our way back here—to you. We are here because we knew we would defeat the Zelk and free Anzulla today. He is a hero, and you should be proud of him. I miss him very much. He was a true friend," he said excitedly. Ouro and Kellan exchanged perplexed looks, then the three embraced. Pride, relief, and fondness emanated between them and flowed through our bond to me.

"Talk to you later, boys." Our king waved and nodded affirmatively to our people. "Yes, and this better be the last time I have to kill these feelingless robotic Zelk idiots."

"We will!" Ouroboros said, shaking their hands in a hurry, then made his way to his kneeling majestic elk and mounted it.

"Boys!" my father hugged Atlas and me tighter. "I love you, my boys!" he kissed us, telling us how much he'd missed and worried about us. His voice has always been powerful, creating words loaded with meaning and carrying a promise of love. I felt what he meant to say—good job, and I'm proud of you. His emotions calmed or even excited thousands, whatever he determined his people needed, and I didn't realize how much I needed his reassurance at that moment.

"*We missed you more, Father,*" we blurted in unison, just as we did when we were young.

He rubbed his chest with his fist, and his optimistic expression faltered for a second. "*I missed you every day I was away from you. We looked at every possible outcome. Each war with Apsu ended the same. Here.*" His jaw quivered as he struggled to voice his words mentally. "*Your father jumped in front of the line of fire to save you. No matter how hard we tried, I saw his death far too many times to count. Boys, Dad died so you could live. Today. I can't bring him back or save him.*" Tears rolled down my father's cheeks as he looked up at us, speaking telepathically. King Eryn and King Ivan, our fathers, had spent all their lives saving and helping humans. All they'd wanted was for the four of us to live free and happy, knowing the humans were protected.

"*We believe you. It's how it should be,*" I said, and I truly did believe him. My father loved my dad more than anything. If he said he'd tried, then he did. This was the first time we had spoken since the war. "*For each of us, a different length of time had passed. For Atlas, it's as if he went to sleep and woke up. For me, it's been a few months. For Ouro, it's been a hundred years. How long has it been for you, Father?*"

My father hesitated to answer. He had seconds to spare, but he locked gazes with me and spoke as if he had all the time in the world for us. "It's been more or less ten years. Ten long years of outsmarting Apsu. We saved Gugusan from burning to death and took him to the future, far away from the Zelk, where he recorded everything that had happened and hid it inside one of the crates of whiskey that were stored in the mine where my brothers and I were born and grew up. The leaders of Phoenix found this information during the outbreak of the invasion, which is when and why we decided to take Phoenix City back to its origins. It also confirmed that we had to return to save Gugusan. We took him back to a safe place, close to my place of birth." My father pointed down.

Is this the place he was born, but only in another time? Is this why Draxton and Kellan fell from the sky, exactly from the same place they had taken Gugusan? I wondered.

"Yes," my father answered, listening in on my thoughts. "We initiated our mission to find every avenue Apsu had taken to reach this point. Finally, when we arrived at this time and place, we knew it was where we would return to face him in the final battle."

"*We remembered what you told us about the blood moon and the shield,*" Atlas said. "*We knew today was the day we would defeat Apsu together.*"

"*The night the red moon rises,*" I chipped in.

"The red moon?" Draxton threw his hands up. "It comes every bloody six months. How are we supposed to know which one...You know what, leave it. Just fucking leave and forget about it." He yapped over his shoulder and walked off, waving his hands over his head.

My fur shimmered blue-white as electrifying energy engulfed my being. "*Father, this is our final stand against Apsu and his Zelk,*" I chuffed, bear-barking at our enemy. Ishtar was shaking hands and introducing himself to Draxton and Kellan, who couldn't stop touching his dark blue skin as if they had never encountered a blue demon god before. *How embarrassingly racist of them.*

I gave a disgusted snort in their direction. "*Okay, no more touching and feeling our demon god's skin. Stop acting like you're not used to anything. So what, he has a blue complexion,*" I mentally reprimanded them.

Thankfully, they straightened up and backed off. "*He's so blue,*" Draxton noted.

"*Sorry, Callisto,*" Kellan apologized and took Draxton's hand. "Later, not now," I heard Kellan say.

"That's alright," Ishtar said, being friendly and coming our way after greeting Sopora and the others.

"We are still outnumbered," Draxton reminded us, but Ishtar waved it off.

Our father patted Atlas on his front leg and rubbed my belly. "No problem. We will kill them all today. They won't live. They are trapped. They thought their shield would keep us out, but they imprisoned themselves," he shouted so everyone in earshot heard him. "*But good job! Are you ready?*" He waited for us to answer.

"Of course! Let's eat Zelk until we shit wires!" I grunted and pinned the traitors with a stare that promised annihilation.

"Brother, that sounded cool! But remember to spit and not swallow, shitting wires tomorrow will not be fun." Atlas laughed, and my father agreed. I missed both my fathers, but I knew I would never see my dad again after the Zelk laser cannons vaporized him. I had made peace with it, but I always knew in the back of my mind that I would see our king again.

I turned to Draxton and Kellan. I was their guardian, after all. *"He's a badass and much more than Ishtar. Together, they are going to stop Apsu for good; they are unstoppable, and our enemies have misjudged them. I trust them. You should too,"* I told everyone connected to my mind link hurriedly, anticipating their next move.

Like my father, Ishtar removed his hooded leather jacket, discarded it to the side, pushed his sleeves up, and turned to assess the Zelk waiting to attack us. Ishtar raised his golden sickle-shaped swords, and my father lifted his spear. Then we followed, zig-zagging our way down the side of the mountain.

The golden clips Ishtar used to tame his dark, braided hair reflected the light of the torches. Their presence and our war cries announced our oncoming vengeance to cowering foot soldiers scampering from his deathly display of power and fearlessness.

As if knowing I was watching him, Ishtar looked at me and tipped his chin to me. *"Ready?"* His friendly but determined-to-win yellow-ringed eyes shone brightly.

My father's hair, a braided mullet, bounced like a pendulum, timing the Zelk's demise. Power emanated over us, stirring camaraderie, and I sensed the morale of our army increase tenfold. My father stirred in us an *I'm-here-and-every-thing-is-going-to-be-alright* wave.

His striking green-gold eyes, much like my brother's elongated ones, flickered with the promise of hope and victory. His tight-fitting black body suit with black boots made him look dangerous and untouchable as he raised his thick golden spear and then answered our roaring small army of soldiers, who raised swords, bows, and spears, with a battle cry that inspired all of us down to every cell in our bodies.

I stood on Draxton's left with Kellan on his right. "*Cover your ears,*" I said to Draxton before I pushed myself up to stand on my hind legs, roaring so loud I barely heard Ouroboros yelling as he was taking a fighting stance. "*Yes!*"

The ground beneath my feet vibrated.

"Oh, fuck, Kellan! I know nothing about war or fighting. The last time I fought, I was in primary school when Billy teased me for not having parents," Draxton yelled.

Kellan pulled him closer to his side, putting a long knife in his hand. "Stay with me! If we die today, I need you to be with me."

Far away from us, below the ridge of the rocky cliffs, our king already stood ready with his spear, pointing to the seas. He croaked low and repetitively. *Who was he calling?*

"Now!" Ishtar shouted, and my father jumped, plunging his spear into the frozen earth. Ripples of energy rolled through us. *This is new and different.*

"What's happening?" people shouted.

Fear swept through my flock of soldiers.

"It's a volcano!" someone yelled.

Draxton pointed in the direction of the town. "Look, the water is receding. It's a tsunami!"

The sea level shifted as if someone had found the plug and drained it. Seconds passed. Then suddenly, the waters swelled. The world slowed until the water blasted skyward. The ground shook. Saltwater splashing up the cliffs fell like raindrops on us.

"Bloody fucking hell! I'm glad I'm standing on a fucking waking mountain!" Draxton wheezed out with his hands in the air. Water sloshed over the harbor, toppling over Simon's ship and washing away their clay-domed town.

"Shouldn't we run?" Kellan asked Ouroboros, who, like many others, stood open-mouthed, watching as not one, but six heads rose from the depths of the ocean. Just off the shoreline, the massive, dark, lizard-like heads emerged, and then the terrifying cries followed. A claw, a snout, another claw. Green and black scales. "Much larger than Atlas."

"The beasts!" Ouroboros yelled. The elk and other land animals that agreed to help decided that was enough, and the next moment Ouro jumped, dismounting his steed while chasing them away from the flying debris and deafening noises.

"They won't hurt you; I'm talking to them. Don't panic!" my father said loudly, and we listened because there was a compulsion behind his words.

Atlas gaped, astonished. "*They came!*" he said through our mind link.

"*My Brawl brothers!*" my father's voice echoed. Loud tooting croaks, as if in agreement with my father, bellowed across the ocean, rolling in like a thunderstorm from the horizon.

"Brothers?" Draxton and Kellan asked.

"*I've called them. They are here to help us. Stay behind*

them. I will throw up a protective bubble over you. Do not exit it. The wind will blow their poison away from you and to every human not behind me," my father said, and I knew everyone heard because the panic subsided.

"Lizards walking upright, erupting from the waters. Godzillas!" Draxton shouted. "Oh my fucking stars." He closed his eyes and covered his ears. Kellan threw his arms around Draxton, holding him.

"Yeah! More than one freaking Godzilla!" Kellan shouted, agreeing with Draxton. I had no clue why they called them that, but they were thick-skinned and immune to the Zelk lasers. Plus, they were killing Zelk, and that was all that mattered now.

"Creatures of myth. Things that came from the seabed!" Draxton cried, sitting down as he looked up and up and up. Kellan dove to wrap his arms around him. Holding him.

"It's okay. They are on our side. Look, they are swatting the hoverbots like flies, following King Eryn's command. They are the army we needed to even the scales," Kellan cooed in Draxton's ear.

Draxton whispered through our mind link. *"Too much. This is too fucking much. I'm small. Very small. We are nothing. I was wrong. I was so wrong, Kellan. What else is hiding underneath us?"*

Kellan looked at me, asking for help, then spoke to Draxton again. "Not wrong. You just didn't know, like the rest of us."

"We must hide. This is no place for us!" Draxton repeated.

"They are Brawl! They are my brothers! Don't be scared," my father said over his shoulder while directing his brothers. The gigantic creatures sloshed knee-deep through the ocean.

The Zelk opened fire, their precious shield for communicating and charging their batteries disintegrating above them.

Because we were all gathered behind him and not scattered as we had been when attacked by surprise, my father threw up a translucent bubble, sheltering us.

Draxton and Kellan looked confused and panicked. They didn't know what was happening. *"He is covering us to protect us from any further attacks or poison,"* I told them.

"Really?" they asked in awe, and my heart filled with pride for them as they got up and joined everyone cheering. King Eryn lifted his spear above his head, spinning it faster and faster, creating a sound similar to buzzing insects.

"Sounds like hummingbirds!" Draxton said.

The Brawl shrieked, and my father bellowed. The sound waves rippled in the Zelk's direction, and I can only imagine the feeling of standing on the receiving end of those immensely potent frequencies.

A feeling of pure pleasure filled me as I joined them, standing on my hind legs, producing the harshest noises while pulling my most terrifying face. Drool dripped down my jaw, but I didn't stop while my brother joined us in our display of strength.

The waters only reached the Brawl's knees as they were knocking over the enemy's platform ships, sending their cargo into the tumultuous depths, while some landed just offshore and were trying to breach the magnetic line.

Ishtar and my father looked like two ants compared to the Brawl. They'd arrived just in time; they'd turned the war in our favor by making the enemy believe they had the upper hand. Apsu thought this was the final chapter, but retreating and causing the Zelk to think we were defeated slowed them down, giving my father and Ishtar the opportunity to push them into this one and only corner of our existence. I'd heard the stories about the Brawl growing up with my father inside an underground facility at the bottom of a gold mine in South Africa.

"Yeah! You should be thinking twice about attacking us!" Kellan shouted. They were smiling and starting to enjoy this as much as I was. He pointed, showing Draxton the enemy's ships where the Zelk were busy unloading their dead and dying cargo of foot soldiers.

"Okay, the battle is on!" Ishtar yelled over his shoulder.

"Yes, die, die, die!" Our army cheered as they thumped their war drums.

"The traitorous humans thought they could set foot on our continent," Ouro shouted jubilantly, his spear in the air. "The Zelk can't pass the coastline; it is magnetized!" He turned to his people. "We are saved!" He laughed, already celebrating.

Eryn pointed to where the Brawl caught and crumbled hoverbots like fireflies. "My brothers are taking care of them," he yelled as he jumped to join Ishtar.

Whrrrr-whrrrr-whrrr!

"So, it worked, after all." Ishtar laughed. "The land is magnetized, Zelk scarabs!" Ishtar shouted maniacally and began spinning a sword in each hand. He ran, using the dead humans as stepping stones, jumping, jumping, jumping, and then leaped onto a gunship, chopping off Zelk's body parts.

My brother took flight. "*Father said to melt the rock,*" Atlas bellowed. "*Like this!*" He spray-painted the Zelk-filled sky in deadly oranges and reds.

"*Really? I thought it was I who told you to do it,*" Ishtar teased. Only he has time for jokes because he is a time traveler. He disappeared behind the veil, then exited at the rear of the enemy line, working them over from behind.

I stood where my father told me to stay. Other than being useless, like the warriors, I was at least protecting Draxton and Kellan, although from inside the impenetrable membrane of slime. I was used to seeing my father creating shields around people he wanted to contain or protect. Before the Big Flood, he, my other dad, and their brother Cian created a membrane almost like this one to shelter Phoenix City from the global flood before they arrived here, in this time and place.

"Kellan, it all makes sense!" Draxton shouted as he was starting to relax.

"*Yeah, it does!*" Kellan answered via our mind link.

"*When lava rock cools, it acquires a thermoremanent magnetization from the natural planetary magnetic lines, lasting millions of years without any change,*" Draxton explained while the world outside was chaotically warring without me.

"*Atlas risked all our lives by doing it!*" Ouroboros interrupted. "*But I guess it's what saved us.*"

Ishtar cut short the empathic mind-to-mind conversation. "Right on cue, Father!" he turned and shouted through cupped hands just as the gigantic Zelk airship dropped from the sky and stopped dead midair, cutting off our view of the Brawl fighting the hoverbots and laser cannons.

Ishtar jumped back to land, swearing obscenities. "*Callisto, stay where you are. Don't move, and for fuck's sake, don't let Apsu trick you into leaving the humans unprotected.*"

"Oh, shit!" Draxton muttered. Apsu and Ishtar exchanged frightening smiles as the ship's door retracted.

CHAPTER 33
DRAXTON

COMPLETELY OVERWHELMED, I SAT DOWN, ALMOST falling over. It was all too much, I thought as I just sat there, numb, counting, calculating, feeling like a sack of uselessness. The helplessness was agonizing. My head felt like it was buzzing with a million frantic thoughts, urging me to do something, anything, but I didn't know what.

"Kellan!" I called, covering my head and ears. "Kellan! I wish I were brave enough to throw a bow and arrows over my shoulder, ride on Atlas's back, and shoot the Zelk. But I'm not. I'm unprepared and unfit to fight. I just sat and sulked for a month when I could have been training. This is real, and to be honest, I feel that this is more than just an adventure. I want to go home. I want to listen to my music," I whispered as the fiery rain of lasers and bombs began to fall. My muscles tensed and twitched. My fingers were frozen numb. The bright lights zooming across the sky were frightening, and they disoriented me. I was in the wrong place at the wrong time.

Kellan kneeled, brushing his knuckles down my cheeks. "Hey, look at me."

Breathing in deep, rushed breaths, I forced myself to look him in the eyes.

Breathtaking. Heart-stopping. Capable. Intelligent. Solid and anchoring.

I drew strength from his resolute yet kind eyes, which calmed me down. The explosions behind him looked like a firefly halo, and I smiled.

Leaning closer, I saw more hoverbots and explosions reflecting in his dark eyes, but he seemed oblivious. His gaze pierced the deafening noise inside me. "You're alright," he said calmly. "Focus on me." A smile touched his lips. How had I never noticed how *deeply* he loved me?

"Cover your eyes and ears if you need to," he murmured, pulling my head down between my knees and shielding me with his body.

I closed my eyes, rocking back and forth, nodding. "Okay. Okay. I'm okay," I repeated softly. He was leaning into me. His weight was a sturdy reminder that I wouldn't float away among the chaos. "If we die today, we will do so together," I whispered, closing my eyelids tightly shut. He was here. I was with him—the cocoon he'd created, reassuring and warm.

Minutes passed before the relentless buzzing faded away.

Kellan didn't move.

I opened one eye slowly. The lights dimmed as the noise in the sky grew quieter—less of everything, no brightness, and nothing blinding.

Slowly, I loosened my grip around my knees, and Kellan slackened his arms from around me.

I blinked, clearing the rest of my brain fog.

Deathly silence greeted us. The murmuring soldiers were clearly audible.

Taking a deep breath, I straightened up and lifted my head. "Wh-what happened?"

By a strange coincidence, the radius of about fifty feet across the clearing lay completely clear. Not one piece of debris or laser burn had fallen upon us. It was as if we were being protected by an invisible shield. Beyond that, heaps of rubble and pieces of timber surrounded the border.

Kellan, slightly flushed, rested his hands on my knees. He cleared his throat. "We are not going to die," he said. I suddenly knew I'd never forget the contours of his face, his scent, his touch. Nothing and no one would ever compare to him. I looked at him, tilting my head with a deep frown between my eyes. He kissed me, and I knew he understood and desired me. His lips were warm, plump, and soft. Sweet and worthy.

Safe.

"*Everything will be alright,*" a male voice said melodically. I was startled when an unfamiliar voice spoke to me. It was in my mind, and it was not Atlas or Callisto speaking to me.

"Who's that?"

"Shhh, don't be scared, it's their king," Kellan said, getting up and pulling me with him.

Scrambling to stand, I searched the battlefield.

"Draxton, look at me." I focused on Kellan's voice.

"We're alright?"

Nodding and kissing me all over my face, he said, "Gods, I love you! Whatever happens today, know I love you."

"You care. You understand. Never forcing me and always understanding me and never expecting me to be small, to be less than, to fit in. You care about me, like my grandfather did," I said, absentmindedly searching for the king.

"Once this battle is over, I'd like to have sex with you and show you how much I understand you." My body relaxed as I sighed and shook my head. I knew he was trying to distract me.

"Look!" Kellan exclaimed, pointing excitedly upwards. I followed his gaze, my heart racing. "What's that?"

The hairs on my arms rose. The other soldiers joined us, awestruck by the shimmering, wobbly, translucent wall that encased us like an upside-down fishbowl, pulsating with neon blue and purple sparks, like static electricity.

"*Stay inside. You are protected now. The king is protecting you. I'm going to help them!*" Atlas yelled into my mind, jumped, opened his wings, soared down the mountain over the shore, then swung upward, catching the updraft. I was so glad we got into the mountain and that his wing had healed just in time.

Up and far up, he climbed into the sky until he was just a speck of spewing fire, forcing the Zelk back to their demise as the Brawl spread out and swatted them. Mangled, broken, and burning pieces of machinery plummeted into the waters. Kellan stood next to me. I grasped his calloused hand, grounding myself. It felt like watching a movie with the volume turned down very low.

The constant zap-boom-pow of six Godzillas battling the Zelk was actually entertaining.

I bumped Kellan with an elbow. "You know what?" I shouted.

Kellan shrugged. "Tell me."

"It's comforting to think my grandpa would've loved this. I'll enjoy it for him." I smiled. The shield now covering us added an unsuspected layer of protection, so I told myself I was safe. Kellan was safe. Then I sat watching the red, blue, and orange explosions painting the sky like the Fourth of July.

They glinted and reflected in Kellan's wide eyes. "That's a good idea. I will join you, and soak it up so we can remember it." Kellan sat down behind me, wrapping his arms around me and resting his chin on my shoulder.

Bombs boomed, and laser lights zipped through the sky, making it look like a rave, but it wasn't a party. Not for the Zelk being caught, thrown, and crushed like old stale popcorn.

"There he is!" King Eryn led the attack, spear whirling. Simultaneously, Ishtar sprang into action, swiftly beheading Zelk as he charged, a demonic fury of destruction. Ouro and the others roared their approval; Kellan and I joined the cheers. It was satisfying to see my enemies fall. Their cruelty paled in comparison to the suffering Ouro and his people had endured for over a century.

"Kellan, this is crazy. It's unbelievable, isn't it? The speed, I can't believe what I'm seeing. It's not what I imagined; it's so much more. I truly thought we wouldn't have a war. This is not what I imagined when Zaidon said he would get the secret to kill them."

"He bullshitted you. But it's my fault. I should never have pushed you into his arms. I was scared to love you."

"Don't be. Never be scared of me," I said, struggling to rid myself of the guilt I felt for being naïve and not trusting my friends.

"It seems like it's all going to be over soon. The Zelk look unorganized and completely caught by surprise."

"Yeah, they are!" Ouro laughed, the lights flashing like fireworks reflecting in his big, astonished eyes.

Just as I thought the weirdness had sunk in, an enormous airship floated down through the clouds.

"Oh, shit!" I exclaimed as the door opened, just as Ishtar reached it.

"Another blue Anunnaki?" Kellan breathed.

"*Apsu!*" Ouro and Callisto whispered, and the others gasped.

His voice was deep and grating—his accent, unrecognizable.

"What's that dialect?" Kellan asked.

"Old language!" Ouro answered.

I wiped my sweaty brow. In the small clearing, in front of an enormous spaceship, Apsu stood tall, like a monster from children's nightmares. Even with a lower sound volume penetrating our shield, a sinister laugh bellowed from the strangest creature I'd ever imagined seeing.

From this distance, I could see his bulging, yellow eyes glowing. Small goat horns grew at the sides of his head, and a tassel of hair hung between those wild, monstrous eyes. He was bare-chested, with black and blue skin, wearing a leather Roman skirt. His head was covered with long, thick, dark hair that reached down to his pierced nipples. He had a long tail ending in a cow-like brush, irritably swaying from side to side as he stomped his feet and threw balls of fire from each of his hands.

"Holy shit!" I yelled as fireballs whizzed by Atlas. Now I was upset for missing most of the fight.

"That's Ishtar greeting Apsu with a dramatic bow," Ouro said. "As dramatic as one could look with golden swords longer than my arm."

"What? Nowhere to go? Nothing better to do?" Ishtar asked so loudly that we heard him clearly.

Apsu drew his sword and stepped further away from his ship. He turned, looking for an audience. "I'm your coming death, the destroyer of your world, ha-ha-ha!"

Callisto growled. Ouro laughed. "Yeah, and you are trapped like a little baby mouse," Ouro snickered.

"We've sprung the perfect trap. You've shrouded Anzulla to control us and the weather. You thought you'd insulated it, but instead, you built your own prison," Ishtar said and took a fighting stance. "I know the future. My future. My past. You know nothing. Babylon still stands. I knew you were going to take a wife, have children, and then destroy Anzulla in this time. But you can't because we're here to stop you!" Ishtar proclaimed.

Apsu laughed, bending backward. Sarcasm dripped from his words. "It can't be! Then you are stopping your birth!"

"Maybe, maybe not, and you shall never know!" Ishtar said as liquid fire rained across the ocean. Atlas changed direction, heading straight for us. King Eryn waved his spear, and the six Brawl followed him.

"Oh my God, Draxton, he's real. My father spoke about him, and I thought it was just a fantasy. Look at him. It's Apsu, Bringer of Death," Kellan said in awe.

I squinted as if that would help me remember better. "The mythical King of Babylon?"

"Yes, it's him." Kellan's face was a mixture of delight and disbelief. "Draxton, the stories were true. That's the connection. The city of Ur. King Solomon's Tomb!" He took my arm and pushed up my sleeve to look at the tattoo Simon had given me to enter Spire City buildings. "This is the connection. Look!"

I frowned. I knew it was connected, but I couldn't understand why I was so baffled, and he was excited. *It was old news by now, wasn't it?*

"Look, Draxton!" he repeated, and I turned to look. Ouro and Snow didn't give us notice; they anticipated the pending sword fight. Atlas circled above, and the approaching Brawl changed direction. Water is sloshing up the coast, the scale... was overwhelming, and my brain struggled to compute everything. But then, my eye caught the side of the airship Apsu arrived on.

"Mother-bloody-fucker! Look at the tiny lights, the shapes, the markings on the sides!"

"They were warnings!" we exclaimed together. "Sightings of Apsu!"

"Must be," Kellan said.

"*Will the two of you stop with the history lessons?*" Callisto murmured into our minds.

Suddenly, Apsu jumped, and as he came down, he threw flames at Eryn and Ishtar.

"Where did he get the fire from?" I asked, as everyone gasped.

But then something even weirder happened. Ishtar disappeared and reappeared behind Apsu. He kicked Apsu on the back. Apsu fell to his knees, and before he could lift his arms, Eryn wrapped him in sea kelp, like a silkworm pupa.

They worked as a team until nothing but a wiggling Apsu was left.

"They did say they wanted to take him away from here. That's one way to do it," Ouro said with a chuckle.

"What are they going to do now?" Snow asked.

Ouro shook his head. "Don't have a clue."

King Eryn aimed his spear at the bound Apsu, conjuring a white shell that enveloped him and the surrounding kelp. It resembled a layer of cement or a giant eggshell, which was quite bizarre, but seemingly effective, because the wiggling and protests stopped.

Ishtar picked up Apsu and carried him to his time machine, throwing Apsu inside, who landed with a metallic thud.

King Eryn then leaped, running toward another floating ship, roughly five stories high in the sky.

"There they are!" Kellan pointed to the hovering ship. "Bloody hell, it's the Malherbe brother and sister!"

"I wish I could hear what they were saying to each other," I muttered.

"*I will relay,*" Callisto said. "*My father is asking them if they can come aboard. But they laughed and said he could try to, and was welcome if he could do it.*" We watched as Eryn nonchalantly pointed his spear at the shallows. Water columns rose one by one, forming stairs for him to climb.

"Holy shit, is that even possible?" I asked Kellan.

"*If he's doing it, then yes, it's possible,*" Callisto said.

"Your mom's never going to believe this."

"*Ooh, now they are worried. Harrison told them to shoot, but Zonika is standing, palming her gaping mouth, as she watches my father walk up the stairs.*"

As if hearing us cheer, Eryn waved at us before boarding the platform of their ship.

"*Now, they are trying to thank the king for catching Apsu and trying to convince him that he had enslaved them,*" Callisto growled.

"He'd better not believe their lies," I said forebodingly.

"*I won't,*" the king told us, surprising me with the foreign voice in my head. "*Apsu couldn't resist the technology. He has Zelk inside him,*" Eryn explained to us. "*He is controlling their hive mind. They are all connected to him.*"

"*Wait for me!*" Ishtar raced up the water column stairs. As he boarded the ship, the Zelk guards surged forward, but Eryn met them with a sweeping arc of his spear, sending them dropping like crash test dummies.

"What is he saying now, Callisto?" Ouro asked.

"*I'm not sure. He is giving them something—something about the shield. That will fix their shield and disconnect the hold Apsu has on them.*"

"No!" Ouroboros exclaimed.

"*Quiet! My father knows what he is doing. They spent years figuring out how to get ahead of Apsu and his Zelk.*" Callisto chuffed.

Zonika took whatever it was, lifted it, and inspected it. Then she walked over to the side. Putting the thing onto her wrist computer, she looked over her shoulder at Eryn.

"*She's thanking him, and he's saying, 'I'm sorry. I hope your souls find peace',*" Callisto said.

"What the fuck now?" Snow exclaimed.

Ouro shouted through cupped hands. "What happened to killing everyone?"

"Yeah, I'm confused," Sopora added.

"This is boring and anticlimactic. Where is the blood, the screaming, and the dying they did to us?" Ouro agreed. Eryn and Ishtar turned and descended the pillars of water until they reached the dry ground. Eryn waved at Ishtar as he jogged and jumped into his ship. The doors closed behind him. Eryn then turned, waving to Zonika and then to us. Like fools, we waved back, still wondering what was happening.

"*Oh, look!*" Callisto said, dropping to his front paws. The few hoverbots to our far right dropped out of the sky, lights off, and splashed in the ocean below.

"What a confusing firepit war story!" Ouroboros yelled, waving his spear back and forth.

"*I told you my father and Ishtar had planned this,*" Callisto retorted just as the ship with Zaidon's siblings toppled to the side like an unbalanced helicopter. The Zelk started rolling, slipping, and falling. No one yelled in fear as they plummeted into the water, disappearing from sight.

"What did he do? What did he give to Zonika?" I asked.

Eryn's melodic voice floated through me. "*It's a virus, a computer virus.*" I knew what a virus was, but Eryn continued to explain it to us. "*I'm infecting the machines with an illness they will never be able to recover from.*"

"Yes!" Ouro and his soldiers cheered. It's making the machines not work. "Look!" Ouro pointed to foot soldiers who were walking into each other, as if drunk and ill-coordinated—falling, crawling, and seizing.

Kellan laughed. "A virus." He started clapping his hands.

I threw my head back. "Yes, a computer virus, and what about Spire City? I wonder if it will reach them."

"Oh, it will. They are all connected by the grid. Everyone knows where everyone is at all times," Snow said.

"And the traitorous humans?" Snow and Ouro asked.

"I think we should ask Lucifer." I chuckled. "He's been locked up and imprisoned for so long. He deserves to make the call."

"That's actually a very good idea," Kellan said, kissing my cheek.

Eryn's voice surprised me. *"I know the perfect place Luci can take them. I think it is unforgivable, but I agree with you. Luci should decide,"* he said, and the fishbowl popped with a snap.

The ground beneath my feet shook, and the wind nearly blew me over. A low hum turned into a loud droning noise, and as it pitched higher, I knew it was coming from Ishtar's golden egg-shaped ship. My heart nearly stopped as a loud clap-clap-clap like lightning, deafened me, while in one second, Ishtar's ship was there, and the next it was gone. Leaving only the circular imprint and steam behind. The sharp smell of fire and melting wires stung my sinuses, and I pulled a grave, unbelieving face at Kellan as I realized what had just happened.

"So Luci's taking them to Purgatory?" Kellan asked.

"But how do you know where Luci is if you just got here?" I asked, standing.

"I know where everyone is, was, and will be," Eryn said, tapping his temple. *"I'd memorized every reality, every Anzulla in every time and place."*

CHAPTER 34

KELLAN

"My feet ache too," I groaned, echoing Draxton's complaints. Our spirits were low, and though I tried to stay cheerful, I was failing. We'd been coming down from the high we'd been riding since we broke through into the Heart of Anzulla.

Everyone was exhausted. "I'm glad I didn't toss my spear, like I did with my war axe."

"Yeah, a spear's handy for lots of things—even cooking over a fire," Libre replied from ahead.

"And a walking stick," I retorted. It had saved me several times from falls that could have taken others down the mountain with me. The thing was heavy, so I had to switch hands frequently to rest my arm.

Up the steep slopes we climbed. It was warming rapidly, and most of us had shed our gloves and extra layers. I'd wrapped my long-sleeved shirt around my waist and draped my thick fur jacket over my shoulders. Though the temperature was rising, it might be needed later.

"I don't want any more fire talk nonsense; I want answers and a bed," Draxton muttered.

"Hmmm, agreed. I'm not naively believing this place will turn into the Caribbean overnight, not like my half-brother acting like Rainbow Dash. All zipidy-doo and no sore hooves," I said sarcastically.

Looking over my shoulder, I trudged onward, the fat red moon and a few stars barely visible through the thick clouds. Their dim lights barely illuminated our climb back up the mountain; snow, hail, rain, or sun—who knew what to expect? I was utterly worn down. All I wanted was Draxton in my arms, my stomach full of stew, and my bed.

The artificial ozone layer was gone, and the weather was unlike anything Ouro's people had ever experienced. A hundred years had passed for him, putting him in a completely different frame of mind than my own.

Draxton was craving the quiet darkness. "No more adventures," he'd repeated several times, clicking his tongue, clearly annoyed. But still watched where he was stepping, careful not to cause an avalanche over the trail of people following below.

Just moments before, he'd been cursing King Eryn, frustrated by the lack of answers he was getting from the Brawl king. Each slip on the debris and loose pebbles only fueled Ouro's promises of a cozy night and campfire stories. We'd both reached our limit. I waited for him to catch up, then whispered with a playful grin, "I think we just won *Weirdest Day Ever*, and I didn't even have to eat pickled pig testicles!"

Draxton ignored me. *"Ask your father about the Godzillas,"*

Draxton repeated for the third time through our mind link to Callisto. I fought back an irritated sigh.

"*I heard you the first time,*" King Eryn said from the back, his voice sounding like the wind swirling around us. "*I'd hoped you'd wait until we were settled, as Ouroboros had suggested.*"

"We all want to hear about it, not just you," Kawa added.

Draxton growled. "I heard you. I heard all of you. Did you hear me?" he boomed, pulling me closer. "Kellan, I feel something cataclysmic is going to happen. The shit just never stops hitting the fan here."

"I know, I feel it too. I'm sure once we've had a chance to sleep and eat, we'll look at everything with fresh eyes," I reassured Draxton while my eyes darted to the back of our group. King Eryn nodded subtly at me, understanding that Draxton was close to panicking.

"*King Eryn,*" I said, focusing on a mind-to-mind link with him alone, "*it took a month to bring Draxton back from the brink. Be good to him. Don't think you're just keeping him busy; I know him. He won't rest until he gets answers. You have to appease him. Please.*" I was begging, mostly for Draxton, but for myself as well.

"*I understand,*" King Eryn said, sending me soothing vibes. "*I wanted to get to know you better. Maybe if I help him calm down, we can have a small farewell. Almost everyone's leaving tomorrow, but if that's what you want, and what Draxton needs, then I won't delay.* Call me Eryn. I never liked to be called a king," he said out loud. The others waited and parted so Eryn could come closer.

His expression was weirdly knowing and friendly. Like a preschool teacher telling you it's going to be a fun day, the first day of school. His catlike eyes looked through me. I felt exposed, as if he saw me inside and out. I guess he was getting to know me anyway.

"*Oh, now you decide to say something,*" Draxton said sharply, stopping dead, turning and giving Eryn an exasperated look, threatening him. "*I swear, Eryn, if you don't start explaining, I will rip...something apart.*"

I stepped away from Draxton, letting go of his sleeve, and joked to keep the mood light. "I'm not going to tell you that you are out of line." I threw my hands up, playfully pleading innocence.

Callisto sneezed like he usually did when he thought something was funny. "*What about our Brawl uncles, Father?*" Callisto asked sarcastically, looking over his shoulder. Draxton gave him a look. Either not picking up on the playful undercurrent or ignoring it. *He wants his answers right now.*

We halted briefly, following Eryn's line of sight to where his brothers had vanished into the distant darkness. I was still in disbelief. I gave Draxton a side-eye, raising my eyebrows.

He shook his head and gave me a *shut-up, can't you see I'm busy look.* The Godzillas were on their way to the Light Continent. About an hour ago, the six specs of their black bodies had disappeared where the waters were painted with silver light cast by the moon hanging low and red in the distance.

"The sea, it's not as deep as I thought the ocean should be," Draxton remarked.

"It's because it's not the ocean. In that direction, before the war, it was all jungle," Eryn said with surprising gentleness. Draxton tipped his head to the side, muttering something to himself. Eryn smiled. I was sure he was reading his thoughts. We couldn't do that; we only spoke from mind to mind. But as powerful as the king appeared, it didn't surprise me, because Atlas and Callisto were his boys, and they already possessed some of his extraordinary gifts.

"What are you thinking?" I asked Draxton softly. He looked like someone moving to retrieve something dropped on the floor, then kneeled, squinting like he was trying to read the fine print on a cereal box.

He passed me a tremulous glance. I knew not to push. He was still thinking about whatever he was thinking. I looked up, telling Eryn to wait until Draxton was done with whatever he was doing.

Callisto rubbed his snout against my shoulder. "*My father will answer him and help him understand. Draxton's mind is unique, and he knows how to indulge him,*" he whispered to me privately.

Ouro's ecstatic, eager voice to start the fires so we could sit down and swap stories irritated me. He practically skipped down and back to the front of the line, chatting and repeating what had happened to Sopora and his soldiers.

Draxton was caught in the mystery of this reality. I knew the map, the tunnels, and the Star Cave system in the Cradle of Mankind were bothering him. Eryn's answers were coming too slowly, and I can imagine the tension building inside him. He kept close enough to hear what was said, but stopped and measured whatever he was measuring in his head when he turned his head horizontally.

I jerked back as he suddenly veered closer to Eryn and said, "Are you saying this is one big piece of land? A continent, not two continents? Not a Light and Dark Continent, and if the waters receded"—he opened his arms wide—"this is all land?"

"Yes, this continent is big. Do you recognize it?" Eryn asked with a friendly, knowing tone.

"We thought this was the Atlas Mountains, and that was Spain, and that the Heart of Anzulla ran all the way down to the tip of Africa. I thought we'd traveled back in time from 2025 about twenty thousand years, but Kellan thought it could be three hundred thousand. Which is it?"

"It's all correct."

"How can that be?"

"Well, I need a piece of paper, a pen, or sand."

"For what?"

"To draw you a picture."

And that's how Draxton and I tackled the most powerful being in five galaxies. "You motherfucker!" I swung a fist as I leaped through the air to punch Eryn. He was being disrespectful, and no one disrespects my Draxton. "How dare you?" I tried my best to pin the eight-foot giant under me. "Don't talk to Draxton as if he needs pictures to understand. He's not a toddler, you ass!"

Eryn laughed, which infuriated us even more. He was making fun of Draxton, and now he's laughing at us.

"Will the two of you stop!" Eryn laughed more. "I can explain." He laughed so hard that his eyes were closed, and he wiggled as though we were tickling him instead of hitting and kicking him.

"Don't hurt Kellan, I will fucking kill you!" Draxton shouted, pulling Eryn's mullet.

"I'm not!" He laughed and laughed and laughed. I stopped trying to punch his face because he blocked too fast. I tried punching his sides. He lifted his knees, lifting me as if playing airplane with us.

"What the fuck?" I yelled. He held me by the wrists and somehow wrapped Draxton between his legs. Okay, this was actually ridiculous, I thought, looking down into Draxton's red face.

"Stop it, you're going to kill him," I shouted.

"He will not," Ouroboros said next to my ear, sitting on his haunches, looking at Draxton below me. "He's playing with you."

"Dog pile!" Kawa shouted and landed with an oomph on my back.

"Shit pile!" Donali called, and the next moment, Eryn flipped me, Kawa, and Draxton over, covering us. Then the whole fucking tribe buried us with their bodies, while Eryn laughed and laughed and laughed. He was protecting us, I realized as stinky asses, muddy knees, and dirty hands and feet tried to mangle us. He took a deep breath, and with a loud "whooooa!" he roared, getting up and sending the whole lot of them rolling. Kawa lay laughing next to a wide-eyed Draxton and me.

"What in the ever-loving fuck was that?" I asked, short of breath, and then Draxton started laughing, sounding like a car starting as he hooped-hooped, taking breaths. It sounded awful. But they were the funniest sounds I'd heard him make. Ecstatic, overwhelming happiness bubbled up inside me. I felt like a popcorn pit, ready to burst open.

"You infected us with stupid!" I said, chuckling, pulling Draxton up to his feet.

"I did no such thing," Eryn chortled, with his nose in the air.

We reached the landing before the entrance to find the children too young to fight waiting there with one of

Ouroboros's numerous baby mothers. "We're home!" Ouro announced from the front, kneeling so all his children could hug him.

We climbed over the rubble we'd thrown down the mountain just yesterday and finally reached the entrance where the melted golden doors were.

"Thank fuck!" Draxton exclaimed. Luckily, he was in a much better mood than two hours ago.

Dragging our weapons, clothes, and weary bodies, we sauntered inside to an unclaimed fire where we collapsed, dead tired, into a pile of furs. After shifts of sleep, food, and showers, we gathered around the communal fire. Callisto, Atlas, and Eryn were already catching up and celebrating as more people joined and the circle widened.

This could have looked so much different if Eryn and Ishtar hadn't come to our rescue.

Draxton lay with his head on my lap, and together we watched the children play. Girls of various ages danced with flowers in their hair in the field of grass. The boys tried their hardest to catch their attention by seeing who could dive from the highest edge of the waterfall. Draxton was calmer, and joked and smiled, which made me happy. I cared so much about him. He had become my sole reason for existing. We'd experienced several lifetimes of adventures, and I knew many more were waiting with him by my side.

"Draxton," Eryn said as he came to sit down behind us, cross-legged. Draxton sat up, we turned as one to face him, and of course, everyone jumped up to hear what Eryn had to say. I rolled my eyes. They were so bloody inquisitive.

"I waited for you," Draxton said, picking at the hole in his pants.

Eryn smiled kindly. "I know," he said, tapping Draxton's knee with his knuckles playfully.

"You know everything, so start talking," Draxton grumbled. Strangely, everyone was quiet, as if acknowledging this was Draxton's turn for Eryn's full attention while also wanting to hear the story that would probably be told for generations to come. Eryn held a stick in his right hand and wiped the ground with his left. I scratched the back of my head.

"So when you said you needed to draw a picture, you literally meant drawing a picture; you weren't making fun of..."

"I promise you, I've never belittled anyone in my life, and I will never allow anyone to do it in my presence," he said, and I believed him.

"Draxton, my brothers are poisonous to humans. I had to hide them from the world when I was just a boy."

I gasped, snapping my fingers as realization struck. "The underground lab, the gold mine—it's near my home?" I asked, and Eryn nodded.

"A very long time ago," he pointed to Donali and Kawa, "when we were just boys turning into young men, we'd escaped those tunnels by flooding them with sludge. We thought we'd buried my brothers, but we didn't know about this place. They'd dug themselves into the Heart of Anzulla, and for many years, it never dawned on us that this place is simultaneously timeless and connected to everywhere time exists. My brothers communicated only with me; we have a bond, and they've been living underground ever since. They and many more of my brothers were responsible for accidentally killing most of the human race in 2046 A.D., and I walked around feeling guilty for most of my life."

"Oh, my god, this is so depressing. I wanted good news.

A revelation, for fuck's sake. You're sending them to the traitors on the Light Continent, we know that already," Draxton said, shaking his head, his shoulders slumping forward.

Eryn lifted a hand. "Wait, I'm talking now, please. You wanted me to talk, so I'm talking," he told Draxton in such a tone that I felt like crying.

"My brothers will return to the ground, and Atlas is the only one with magic to take them to their door. Understand that I have feelings about the matter too."

"Now I feel like shit. Okay, tell me. I promise I won't interrupt you again," Draxton said, but I saw his eyes wandering. His mind was already somewhere else.

"My sons were born after Ivan and I time-jumped with Ishtar, and we suspected..." Eryn's gaze turned sorrowful as he lifted it to Callisto and Atlas. "We suspected the time-jumping clung to us like static electricity on a cellular level. They were born with extraordinary powers. One of the powers that Atlas presented was the ability to see the fabric of time and move between realities.

"But magic is science," he continued. Draxton swallowed loudly and moved closer. I put an arm around him.

"My sons know that magic is a curse, a blessing, and a promise to keep everyone safe using it. We are all using it, just by being here in the Heart. Magic is everywhere, all around us, easily accessible."

A dull, distant rumble was coming from around us. The red crystals dimmed and brightened as a gust of wind danced across the ashy sand around the fires. The flames licked higher and higher, spiraling until the wind disappeared. Everyone had a smile on their face. Drops of water touched my face. I hugged Draxton closer. He wiped his forehead. Looking at it, he then dried his palm on his pants.

"All I do is move the ions around," Eryn said. His face shimmered with gold and blue hues, and his eyes narrowed with a smile. A flash of light flared across the cave, and the fire went out. The waterfall froze.

"That's not possible!" Draxton exclaimed.

"Sure it is," Eryn said. He waved his spear, and the water unfroze and crashed into the pond below. "All I'm doing is subjugating the molecules. Magic is everywhere; it is in the air, in water, in the earth, and in fire. Here in the Heart, which is the conjunction of the natural flow of the universe's energy, the crossing of veins of power pulsates. Since Ishtar's DNA was already in both mine and Ivan's, and of course, you saw my brothers' reptilian appearances, the dormant gene poked its head out and Atlas hatched as a little dragon."

"Do you realize that in our time in 2025, dragons and magic are myths?" I asked.

"Yes. But thanks to your father, we realized we can move around between—"

"Five galaxies!" Draxton exclaimed.

"Exactly." Eryn drew five circles on the ground. "This represents our galaxies inside,"—he drew a big circle around the five circles—"a big black hole."

"Oh my god, is it really true?" I exclaimed with my hands covering my mouth.

"Yes, your father figured it out. If it weren't for him, you probably wouldn't be sitting here today," Eryn said.

Draxton nudged my knee. "Tell us about the mine, the caves, the Heart, the twenty thousand years, and the three hundred thousand years."

Eryn connected the five circles with five more circles, then traced one as if it were a figure eight. Draxton looked closely, and I could see he found it interesting. He bit his lip. Chewed his nail. Looked at me. Looked back at the circles and then leaned closer, putting his finger right in the center. "This is the Heart of Anzulla," he whispered. I waited for it to make sense and kept quiet. It felt like I was watching a chess game as Draxton started to trace the lines with his pointer finger.

"You are correct. See." Eryn poked Draxton's finger lightly with his stick. "Let's say that's 2025, and this is Anzulla, but you are in this circle—"

Draxton looked up at me. I waited with bated breath. Even the children were silent now. Everyone waited.

"You know, you are the first person to figure it out so fast," Eryn said with awe to Draxton.

Draxton blushed. *Gods, I love him so bloody much.*

"So it depends on which of the five 2025s we came from, and that determines how far back in time we went, because we are constantly moving around the Heart of Anzulla, and Atlas can see where the lines are crossing!" he exclaimed.

"Yes, he will take my brothers to a place and time where they can roam free and not be a danger to humans. To a time so far away, like Kellan said, three hundred thousand years ago."

"How did you know they were there, beneath the water?" Draxton suddenly asked. He leaned closer to Eryn, pulling me with him.

"Before the waters covered most of the land, the opening to the Heart of Anzulla sat about where the coastline is now," he said while pointing to the west, in the direction of the village, to where the broken Obelisk stood. "Ouro and Kellan's father, Gugusan, had recorded their history, and in his diaries, he described what happened here, repeatedly, and that's how we started to figure out and learn about the history of this place—the center of the five galaxies."

Eryn continued, "For thousands of years, my brothers had been living underground, already, because Atlas will take them back in time today."

"Fuuuuuck!" Draxton exclaimed. "So that's why certain places on the African continent had access to the Heart of Anzulla."

"Yes, and these crystals are proof of what happens when realities mesh and time becomes irrelevant. They are a blessing, and they are also a side effect."

"So the crater running all the way from Algeria to the Cradle of Mankind is the exact line where all these five galaxies cut through Anzulla's crust?" I asked.

Silence followed, and then Ouroboros said, "Of course."

"But why?"

Silence.

"What? Has no one ever asked that before?"

"It was a gift from Lasitor to Ishtar."

"The AI?"

Eryn answered calmly and sincerely. "Yes, but we don't know if it has been like this all this time. We don't know if he somehow kick-started it or if Lasitor had just made us aware of it. We don't know who linked the five galaxies inside the black hole. Who knows? And it's my theory that it just happened, and it's unexplainable. No one knows."

Draxton stroked his beard. "Thank you for explaining."

I wrinkled my nose. "Tell me one thing, why did you never come to get my father?"

"We did, twice actually, but he seemed happy, and Ishtar said that the only gift he could give your father was to leave him, where he was happy."

I snarled. "He could have said hello, at least once. My father thought he'd forgotten and never cared about him."

"Right." Draxton stood. "Time to go, I'll start saying my goodbyes, and then when Atlas arrives, we are ready to go."

"What?" I asked in shock.

"Yes, it seems like time doesn't matter. We can come back, but first, let's go home. I want you to tell your mother about what we saw. Tell her about your father. It's important. He may have died ten years ago, but you can still run into him. We must go and ask her to come back with us."

"Really?"

Draxton straightened his shoulders like a soldier coming to attention. "Yes."

I shook my head. The man never stops surprising me.

Eryn stood, dusting his backside. "I agree. I've spoken to Ouroboros and most of his people. You are welcome to come back."

"Right! Then, it's sort of sorted, so what are we waiting for?" Draxton announced, and at his words, the people jumped, letting go of the breaths they'd been holding, and started yodeling. I couldn't stop myself. I fell into him, grabbing him by his shirt, kissing him.

CHAPTER 35
KELLAN

"*TAKE CARE. I'M ABOUT TO DROP YOU, SO GET READY,*" Atlas said, and Draxton pulled me into a standing position; at that moment, the claw opened slightly.

Before I could fully grasp that we were about to be free-falling, Draxton shouted, "Thank you!" then wrapped his arms tightly around my waist, pushed me forward, and dove headfirst like an Olympic diver.

"Ass-ho-le!" I shouted. Incapable of flailing, I squinted, incapacitated like a human torpedo. Blue turned to black, whooshing turned to deadly quiet, and the next second, everything was warm and musty as we plopped down on solid ground.

"Yeah!" Draxton yelled and let go of me. We've landed in the Dinaledi Chamber. The National Geographic lamp lay on its side, still on and attached to the cable running outside the cave.

"The cable prevented the light from being sucked away," I stated the obvious as Draxton picked it up and put it back onto its stand.

"Come, let's get out of here before we get sucked back!" Draxton waved hurriedly.

I pointed the way. "You lead so we can get out of here as fast as possible."

Draxton dove for the opening, and I followed, not waiting for a second invitation. We crawled through the chute, passed over the area called the dragon's back, found our harnesses, realized our fur pants were not going to fit, removed the leather shoes and trousers, then, as fast as possible, ascended up and out of the thirty-meter drop.

"Smell that!"

"Home!"

We shaded our eyes as we ran into the blinding hot South African sun. I smelled smoke and meat on a fire. The two caravans, one Draxton's and the other Tobias's, stood undisturbed, quietly baking in the sun.

"It's about fucking time; I thought you were never going to come home for dinner," Tobias said, ducking underneath the tent flaps and coming around the corner, apron on and "braai fork" in one hand.

"What in the ever...you're naked?" Tobias did a double-take. "Wait...um...Your hair, so much hair, brother. I've never seen you unshaven. You look like two bewildered scarecrows. Why are your eyes so wild, and what's up with the creepy smiles?"

We exchanged glances, and yes, his description was very accurate.

"No fucking way. Look at the two of you. I swear I never touched the ganja." Tobias grabbed the back of his neck.

We jumped, throwing our arms around him. I'd never been so happy to see my brother. We may not be brothers by blood, but he and I had always been the closest of all the children my mother had taken in from the street. It felt like decades since I last saw him. He smiled until he got a whiff of our sweaty armpits, then pulled his lip up in disgust. "Bro, what have the two of you done? You need a shower, brother."

At the first sight of the sail tent between the two caravans, we sped away. "No, you're not tripping," I called over my shoulder, and pure joy filled me as I realized what I was seeing. "Coffee!" We scrambled for cups, hands shaking as the sight of the yellow can of coffee triggered a caffeine withdrawal.

We juggled the cups and water, struggling to open the coffee container. With his eyebrows raised, Tobias scratched his head while we tried our best to hurry up and make ourselves some coffee.

"It's been months since I had a cup of coffee." I laughed as Draxton finally opened it and poured coffee granules into a cup for each of us without boiling the water first.

"Ah." I closed my eyes, savoring the taste.

"One more?" Draxton asked, already helping himself to a second cup of ice-cold coffee.

"Yes, please!"

"Fuck so good!" he said, closing his eyes, smelling the aroma.

"Yes, the best cup ever." I downed the cup and quickly made another one.

"Months? Look, what happened in that cave? I was gone

for only three hours. And why are you naked? What happened to your faces? You have hair on your head!" Tobias pointed, perplexed, glancing up and down while he walked in circles around us. "When did you get hooped ivory nipple rings?"

"We found the door, Tobias!"

Confusion turned to astonishment. "No!" Tobias said with wide, darting eyes.

"Yes!"

Tobias turned to leave the tent. "Where? I want to see?"

"No!" I shouted.

"It's gone!" Draxton yelled, waving his hands in the air.

"Unfair!" Tobias kicked the ground, sending rocks flying.

"My mother, I want to introduce you to my mother," I shouted, kissed Draxton on the cheek, and threw an arm around Tobias's neck.

"Okay, start at the beginning," Tobias said.

"Fuck, it's hot!" Draxton muttered and turned away, leaving and ignoring Tobias.

Tobias bulged his fists. He gave me a death glare. "I want to know every-fucking-thing now!

"I know," I said, standing naked in front of my brother and looking at Draxton's tight behind while Tobias looked at me as if I'd lost my mind.

"Let's go take a decent shower and shave, then come and tell my friend about our travels. After that, we go and visit your mom," Draxton hollered over his shoulder, already halfway to the bush shower.

I shrugged at Tobias. "Coming!" I lifted my hands. "Later, brother! I have tons to tell you!"

Tobias stood shocked.

Catching up with Draxton, I grabbed his hand. "You and me forever, remember!"

"Hurry up! I want to hear everything!" Tobias called through cupped hands.

"I remember," Draxton said, looking at our cocks swinging. "In case I forget, you can remind me in the shower."

"Ah, a hot-water shave. With real shaving cream. I think I forgot how to use a razor," I said and squeezed Draxton's ass cheeks. He locked his dark eyes with mine, the unspoken I love you, hanging between us before he kissed me. Water sloshed down our faces, into our mouths and noses.

"Ah, fuck, this smells good!" Draxton groaned in pleasure.

"Enough of this." I steered him into the stone wall and started trailing kisses down his jaw, slurping and sucking the wetness with reverence like a dehydrated Bushman.

"So good!" he whispered. I savored every salty drop, tasting him.

We were home, safe, and together. It felt unreal, and I planned not to let Draxton out of my sight just in case he changed his mind about me, and especially about being back. I have this feeling, a foreboding feeling that if I left him alone, he would wander off without me. He might think he just had to go and see if the door was still there and disappear without me. We needed to determine what our lives would look like. I'm taking him to meet my mother. She will love him, and he needs a mother's love.

Draxton's fingers gripped my hair and reminded me that I needed a good shave. But first things first, I nipped and bit his peck, working my way over each nipple, giving both the attention they deserved.

I'd dreamed about our first hot shower together when we spoke about going home. But ever since our warm waterfall experience, this was a moot one. The bush shower's water was heated by coiling black tubes baking in the sun. It was much hotter than we were used to; the heat was stifling compared to the cold mountain air we'd left behind.

At least now I had Draxton all to myself. We were safe and together. I couldn't imagine a day without him. I guess I've developed a codependency on him.

"Ah fuck, Professor, this is heaven."

"Hmmm, I was just thinking the same thing. I'm going to make you scream my name, and then I'm going to shave you and take you to meet my mother." I kneeled on the cement floor, knowing I was going to regret it later, but I didn't care. This here and now mattered most to me. I wanted to drink his cum right now.

"I knew you were a smart man, you've got it all planned out, don't you, Professor?" He panted like a long-distance runner.

"Oh, yes. I forewarn you, I'm about to blow your mind." I bit the flesh around his navel, licking the water collecting inside of it, knowing I was driving him mad playing with the tip of my tongue in his sensitive little belly button.

"You must hurry up. All this hot water and teasing is making me stupidly dizzy." He grunted, curling his toes. I stopped my explorations and looked up to make sure he was okay. He did sound a bit slurry.

"Are you okay?" I blinked as the water dropped in my eyes. I shook my head to clear my vision. He looked off. Expressionless. "Hey, do you want to sit down?" I jumped back to my feet, frightened by the deathly pale look on his face. "Are you alright?" Feeling his weight suddenly heavy on me, I pushed him against the wall. His eyes rolled back, and I caught him under his arms. "Fuck!" I widened my stance. He was a dead weight in my arms. I let him slide down the wall until he sat on the floor, legs splayed crookedly to the sides. He wasn't joking with me. He'd passed out. "Oh fuck, oh, fuck! Draxton?" I lowered his torso, carefully supporting his head, so it didn't hit the cement. Once I knew he was safely on the floor, I closed the taps.

I fell to my knees next to him, patting his cheeks. "Draxton?" Frantically, I searched around. Should I call for help? What should I do? The water wasn't that hot. It was probably just below 20 degrees Celsius. Perhaps it was hot because we had just come from temperatures below freezing. Yes, that was it.

Not that I'm a professional time jumper, but maybe he was jetlagged or something.

I wiped at his face while supporting his head with my other hand. "Draxton! Baby, open your eyes. Was the heat too much? Or is something else wrong with you?" Fine tremors shook me to my core. He lay like a puppet with its strings cut. I jumped to my haunches, grabbed his ankles, and pulled, straightening his body. I checked for a pulse in his neck. There it was. Fast but steady. I checked his breathing. His chest was rising and falling. His color was returning. *Now what?*

I checked for snakes and scorpions. Checked him for bite marks and found none. I fell back to my knees, placing my hand on his chest. Thank the gods he was still breathing. It wasn't my imagination. Okay, so he'd be okay.

My panic dissipated as the pink color slowly crept onto his pale white lips, and his beautiful black eyelashes fluttered. "Yes! Open your eyes, Draxton." I kissed him on his forehead, cheeks, and mouth. "That's it." His eyelids flicked open. "Hello there." I smiled. "Gods, you scared me."

His dark, stormy eyes stared up at me, filled with confusion. Dazed, he asked, "Wha-what? What just happened?"

"You passed out," I said, grimacing as I helped him roll onto his side.

"Really?" he groaned.

"Yes," I replied, rising. "Sit for a minute, get your bearings."

He rubbed his face. "Damn, that's never happened before."

"I think the heat and my kisses overwhelmed you," I said. "Let's take it easy, acclimate, before I drive you crazy again."

He looked up, frowning, legs still spread wide, his cock limp. One amused corner of his mouth lifted, and he grunted.

I grunted back in answer. "One more minute, then I'll help you up." He wasn't quite himself. "Juice or sugar water?"

He blinked, still half-smiling. "No, I'm okay."

"I thought a snake got you!" I chuckled, relieved. "Imagine, after all we've been through, dying minutes after getting home!" I offered my hand. He took it, breathed deeply, and stood. "That's enough hot showers for today. Food and drinks?"

He held my hand as we strolled outside. "Yeah, after everything, to die like that...comically tragic."

Rounding the corner of the outdoor showers, we froze, gasping. Atlas and Callisto sat on the ground, with Tobias reaching up to touch their faces.

"Bloody fucking hell, no!" Draxton exclaimed. "You ignored us!"

"We told you to wait out of sight!" I yelled.

THE END.

CHAPTER 36

BONUS

DEAR KELLAN

My boy,

My last gift to you is the wisdom of a man who has seen the edge of the cosmos from the window of Ishtar's time machine.

Among the breathtaking views I had observed in our galaxy, nestled within it, but also spinning in a clockwise direction, were four other solar systems.

Years later I had figured out that what I saw wasn't something random.

One should expect that at least one of the other four solar systems in our galaxy to spin anticlockwise. Take flipping a coin five times for example. Getting only heads five times in a row is unlikely.

I've spoken to many scientists over the years, and

I concluded that our entire galaxy was born inside a spinning black hole inside another universe. The spinning black hole twists space by rotating in one direction, and thus dragging and shaping solar systems alongside ours, causing them to spin with us in one direction. Together, the other solar systems are riding the edges of that black hole inside another universe, and do not move to the center because the encapsulating universe outside the black hole was spinning and rotating it in the opposite direction. This theory was only visually proven after simulating galaxy birth and evolution using powerful supercomputers, modelling the complex physics of how galaxies formed and changed over billions of years.

I am convinced the AI onboard Ishtar's time machine knew about this black hole, causing the solar system in our galaxy to bounce back and drift undisturbed inside another bigger universe, like space nesting dolls.

It sounds wild, but I saw on the computer screen, for the first time, the mirror image of what I had seen through the window. The simulation my cosmetologist and astrologist friends had recreated, which expanded my knowledge of Anzulla and our galaxy, is what I'm sharing with you today.

Anzulla is drifting within our solar system, within a galaxy, alongside four other versions of our solar system, each with an Anzulla like ours. In total, there are five Anzullas, each drifting inside their solar system, within our galaxy. Our galaxy drifts on the border of a black hole inside another universe.

By jumping back and forth through time, our Creators had cake-mixed streaks of light and dark, inside the black hole, which contained our galaxies. They have created something in its immeasurable depths, which fights with us to claim everything within its rim.

From the border, within and beyond.

It's something I don't have words for. It's not a void or anti-matter. Not emptiness, or nothing. The closest word I can use to describe it is "false."

It is the opposite of what we perceive, therefore it is "false." A lie, because I don't have the words for machines that consume life.

This is why I never told you, because if this consumption is coming, I'm afraid you and your children don't have much to look forward to. So, I'd decided not to tell you, so you could enjoy your life free from my kind of worries.

I apologize for not telling you this sooner.

When I met your mother and you were born, I had had enough of worrying, and I decided to live without thinking about all of that. I wanted to spend the last days of my life enjoying it with your mother and you.

That day, when *Ishtar* showed me how the sky shed its blue-purple blanket, it peeled back, the shells fell from my eyes, and I saw a starry cloak meant to bolster, to protect, cracking open, shredding the veil between our solar systems. As it was drawn away, my mind started to float past the cosmos, and my never ending worries were born because what I saw was what our *Creators* were seeing.

I was a simple man. A king of a primitive tribe, and suddenly unending questions formed and remained unanswered for most of my life.

I saw planets, moons, dying stars, and even the dust of stars that had not yet been born. I saw everything and the order of things. A rhythm to life, an elliptical dance of celestial bodies around us, and with us. All five solar systems moved as if they had been exhaled across the stillness, floating in the encapsulated bubble of the black hole that contained our galaxy. Beyond that, the cadence of untouched and unseen existences drifted.

My people, the San and the Birdmen, shared the land, but we never wondered, questioned, or waited for answers. We never wished or dreamed. Things just were—the cycle, a law of predictability—of peace.

When water flows down a stream, it doesn't know where it's going. It doesn't know it's called water. Maybe it calls itself something else, but it doesn't know if it would end up vaporized to float into the clouds to rain again on distant mountain tops. Perhaps snow, or hail, or just mist exhaled by the jungle after being suckled up by its roots, but still, water doesn't know if it will end up in the ocean or deep inside the ground, to be stored for the future. Water can go in many directions, and no one tells it where to go. It takes the path of least resistance, and that is where water flows. Constantly in the easy direction, not thinking, not choosing, it just goes, even if it never knows.

That was us. That was life on Anzulla.

But the day I saw the splendor beyond our simple consciousnesses, I became aware. I saw the predictability of things—of the moons, suns, and the five galaxies.

My boy, through the window of Ishtar's machine, I saw the darkness we filled.

I asked Ishtar, "What is that? What lies beyond all those specks of light and darkness?"

My friend answered, "Beyond that, nothingness waits. Darkness exists for us to see and appreciate light; it is the birth of life, and without it, there is only an empty void."

For centuries, I thought about his words and the original purpose, which was the balance of light and darkness versus the void.

The absence of it, the meaninglessness because of it.

I realized what my friend meant and traced its meaning back from the vastness down to the smallest ion. The energy, the center, the pit from which all of it grows to give us life. If the void can extinguish that, we stopped breathing, stopped loving, stopped reasoning —stopped everything.

What are we but the inhabitants among the four other galaxies, meant to float undisturbed and endlessly in the river of life, within the riverbanks of our black hole.

As we sprouted from that very center, the nucleus of our existence, our fathers never thought or realized what had transpired, but they rearranged it, not considering every last detail. I promise you, my Ishtar and Kuku do not have that kind of meticulousness, and I mean it lovingly; it was beneath them.

We lived primitively, as did my father and my father's father. With the Blue Demon God's arrival, we were accidentally awakened by the sown seeds of disruption. They had upset the natural laws of the primordial cosmos, its ordered and harmonious whole.

They've rearranged the galaxy, our solar systems, the light, the darkness, of all matter, of time, and scattered our souls among that. Every-bloody-fucking-thing!

Our king realized that within that scrambled mess was a connection. The streak of light and darkness caused by the zipping around of Ishtar's time machine had created an interconnection of the solar systems.

I've been stuck on this side of the door, for which I'm glad today. However, I hope somehow my work reaches the king so he can put all of us on the right path. Those two baby gods had split us from our original direction; they've warped our existence and expanded our awareness.

That day in Ishtar's passenger seat, I saw the streaks of light shining through the darkness, and beyond that, I felt the void waiting.

We are not the result of a human-enhancing experiment. The experiment was the solution to funnel us back in one direction.

You know I'm a man who ponders.

We all knew something was amiss the day we started to split, and split, and split. Our numbers shrank smaller and smaller. I would stand next to someone, one second, and the next, they would be gone. Some of us noticed, others didn't.

My knowledge of this conundrum was confirmed when even Kuku, Ishtar's mate, had asked where he came from, where he had lived, and where he was supposed to be going. I gave up explaining to them day after day and decided to live obliviously like them, but it was frustrating, hearing it repeatedly every day.

When the war came and we were attacked, I was

sure we were about to disintegrate and amalgamate with the void.

My gift to you is this knowledge. If you ever cross paths with our Creators, tell my friends that a dam needs to be built. We must contain and channel the narrowing stream of life, then return each to their rightful place in the cosmos, without disturbing the sleeping galaxies far beyond and drawing them to us. We must not awaken anomalies, neither on land nor in our oceans. We must return to life, that of the animals that graced our jungles, scorching deserts, and frigid mountains.

Tell them to leave this Anzulla and go to the other solar systems. There is no reason they should remain lifeless and silent in their emptiness. Why should our Anzulla contain all life and make us the bullseye of our enemies? Tell them to fill the five Anzullas with the opposite of the void's burgeoning hunger.

That's how they should challenge Anzulla's innumerable enemies infected by the void. Anzulla is holding her breath. She anticipates the end of the never-ending forking that would leave her floating among the dust of a disintegrating black hole.

For centuries, the San—my tribe—huddled in caves around fires, wearing animal skins for warmth. My father told me about a blue demon god who noticed them because they were playthings and food to him.

My father said the demon god thought the San were dumb, yet my people thrived in the jungle.

I don't know if the blue demon god was Ishtar himself, but this blue demon god showed them how to walk upright. They admired him and sought to resemble him. Then, after my father died, Ishtar came. We urged him to stay with us because the stories passed down from my ancestors said we must show them their mountain.

For four hundred years, I've been stuck on this Dark Continent, now called Africa. I missed my friend's yellow eyes and smooth, dark blue skin. Maybe it was him, maybe it was someone else. Maybe it was his family from afar. But when I saw him resembling the night sky from which he fell from inside his golden egg-shaped ship, as my father described him, I assumed it was him, the blue demon god, and addressed him like that. He visited us, searching for his Kuku, a lover. Although he judged us as illiterate creatures, he came to love our sweat, our bodies, our blood, and even our dirt.

He called me a human and told me I was unlike the beasts. Like him, I was ensouled with the undying spark of life, and he granted me his hidden knowledge when he thought I didn't hear, look, and see like him.

Finally, Ishtar found his Kuku; they joined us by living in their mountain, but their ignorance led to enemies rising against each other for the most foolish reasons. Brutal fights erupted due to superficial differences, such as variations in skin color, wings, even sexuality, or spoken language. You know this well—you've experienced this thing called hate. You've witnessed the horrific deaths of burned, bludgeoned, or impaled bodies.

The knowledge Ishtar gave us stirred a feeling of insufficiency, creating a hunger for more. This yearning caused great upset and chaos.

The San were awakened, but we never asked to be burdened, to be vessels for a soul. It made us see Anzulla being defiled by things that sought to fill the void.

Souls bring false superstitions about life, love, and a meaningful destiny. We prayed to the AI, the voice in the mountain. We thought it was the old gods, the father of the baby gods. We believed Ishtar brought prosperity, friendship, and blessings because he traveled with the voice of the old gods inside his time-riding machine.

We prayed, we obeyed, we wore its mark to live forever.

Then the clever ones came. They were vain, falling like rotten fruit through the door in the sky. They arrived, and the San thought it was a chance at a new life, an adventure to live among intelligent beings with shiny technology. But we realized they were trying to fill a void and tricked us.

My son, enjoy your life. Be like water, and please, take care of your mother.

Don't let anyone near that door, and stay away from the gold mine.

With all my love, your father.
Now and always.

Gu, leader of the San.

CHAPTER 37
TIMELINE

SPOILER ALERT!
Read or listen at your own risk.

25 000 B.C. Ishtar arrives at the San tribe.

25 000 B.C. Peter and Elijah jump to Anzulla.

24 970 B.C. Ishtar and Peter's crash landing.

24 970 B.C. The next day, Gugusan receives news that Ish is being held captive. Peter rescues Ishtar, thirty years after he had jumped with Elijah to Anzulla.

24 970 B.C. That night, Elijah and Peter arrive by boat at the San village. Peter gets his wings and brings the apple to the San.

24 970 B.C. Ishtar visits Anzulla, and Gugusan gives him the apple.

24 970 B.C. (Cian and his brothers arrived in Grayrak 93

A.T.) Ishtar slipped away to say goodbye to Gugusan and then met Peter for the first time.

23 000 B.C. Anzulla, Ishtar, receives a mission from the Fates.

Between 23 000 B.C. and 20 000 B.C. Draxton and Kellan's Story. *Children of Anzulla, Part One and Two: Finding Love in the World of Titans.*

3500 B.C. Hours before the war with Apsu, Ishtar and Peter bring the apple to Babylon. They rescue Elijah and seek help from Andrew in 2013 A.D.

3500 B.C. Ishtar's story begins at age 250 years. He defeats his father for the first time during their uprising. *Anzulla, According to ISH: New Beginnings Book Three.*

1968 A.D. Young André (Andrew) and Peter meet Ishtar and older Peter. (No wings yet.)

2004 A.D. Juandre and Andrew's story begins. (Just Like a Butterfly.)

2013 A.D. Ishtar, Peter, and Elijah visit Lord Andrew Whiskey Distilleries, Lexington, Kentucky.

2014 A.D. Timeline Switch. Andrew goes to Juandre, they fall in love and mate. *Just like a Butterfly: A New Beginnings Novella*

2041 A.D. to 2043 A.D. (3-5 years before Doomsday.) Eryn and his brothers are born.

2046 A.D. DOOMSDAY. Worldwide breakout of Neurotoxic biochemicals. Nuclear Winter follows.

The story of the men of Phoenix begins - *Phoenix Code: New Beginnings Prequel*

Ishtar arrives on the moon and waits for Cian, Ivan, and Eryn while guarding Barkor in Grayrak.

Then, after Ishtar meets Peter for the first time in Phoenix,

2146 A.D. (94 A.T.) he jumps back to 2046 A.D. to update Lasitor.

2051 A.D. (5 years after Doomsday.) The marriage of Mika and Connor takes place.

2052 A.D. (6 years after Doomsday.) The Big Flood (Tsunamis) happens, and, on that same day, the Romanov twins are born, marking it as the Year of the Twins: 0 A.T.

2058 A.D. (6 A.T.) The story of Eryn begins. *Eryn, King of the Brawl: New Beginnings M/M Series Part One*

2073 A.D. (21 A.T.) Mika and Brad find the apple in the Disciples of the Anunnaki's confiscated loot. Cian and Ivan's Anunnaki heritage is revealed. Eryn makes each a sword of gold by dividing the forks on his trident so that they can focus their power on wrapping Phoenix in a protective layer to save their city from a string of global volcanic eruptions that led to the almost-instantaneous melting of the polar ice caps and global storms, turning Earth on its axis.

2124 A.D. (72 A.T.) Cian's first sighting of the hydrogen mining ship of the Zelk.

2145 A.D. (93 A.T.) Cian's story begins. *Cian's Song: New Beginnings M/M Series Part Two.*

2146 A.D. (94 A.T.) After finding and losing his mate, Ishtar meets Peter for the second time. This is also Peter's second meeting, but he had already met Ishtar back in 1968 A.D.)

Ishtar returns to Grayrak with Cian after meeting his Peter, grabs his ship and jumps to Phoenix for a reboot, then returns to gather Peter to jump to 1968 A.D.

2147 A.D. (95 A.T.) Cian and his brothers evacuate Grayrak and take the last of the remaining humans with Barkor home to Phoenix. Rebirth of Earth's Timeline. Ishtar moves the Zelk to an alternate timeline to prevent them from attacking the Warship Horizon or Earth. Lots of shit goes down this year!

2147 A.D. (95 A.T.) Mika and the Leadership Team of Phoenix want answers. Ishtar gets taken into custody for questioning right after the Warship Horizon lands on Earth's watery surface. His ship and pendant are taken away from him. His inquisition starts.

2147 A.D. (95 A.T.) Three days into questioning, Ishtar and Peter escape with the apple, pendant, and ship and crash in Anzulla.

2147 A.D. (95 A.T.) Ishtar and Peter return to Phoenix to ask for help. (After Peter had rescued Ish.)

2148 A.D. (96 A.T.) Ishtar and Cian save Phoenix.

AFTERWORD

ABOUT THE AUTHOR

"I found it surprisingly beautiful. In a brutal, horribly uncomfortable sort of way." —Tyrion Lannister to Janos Slynt.

I am a Canadian speculative Male/Male Sci-Fi Fantasy and Paranormal Romance writer. I currently reside in the Rocky Mountains of beautiful British Columbia, Canada.

My writing explores who we are, where we come from, and where we are going as a human race on Earth.

I like to weave and bubblegum questions and subjects by creating new, exciting worlds and characters. My stories are unpredictable, twisted with a dash of humor, and centered on gay characters.

You will question your existence among these worlds and wish you could escape to these places filled with foul-mouthed heroes who struggle and strive to save humankind.

I hope you've discovered something that excites and intrigues you. Please share your thoughts by leaving a review or visit www.kashelchar.com to contact me or learn about my latest works.

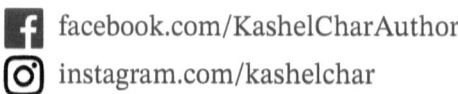 facebook.com/KashelCharAuthor

instagram.com/kashelchar

www.ingramcontent.com/pod-product-compliance
Lightning Source LLC
Chambersburg PA
CBHW020920020726
47495CB00002B/279